THE INNOCENT THIEF

A NOVEL BY

John Thomas

Copyright

Dedication

This book is dedicated to my wife, Lou. She is my sounding board, my editor-in-chief, my biggest supporter and my soul mate. I am a lucky man.

JT

John Thomas

Tuesday, August 6, 2019

ATLANTA, GEORGIA

CHAPTER 1

At 9 a.m., immediately after the doors to Providence Surety Bank were opened, Scott Burnett entered the building. He was the first customer of the bank located in the Colony Square Building Complex on Peachtree Street, in Midtown Atlanta. His hands no longer trembled. Nor did he stutter or forget what he was trying to say. Sweat didn't pour down his back or bead on his forehead. He had moved past these stages. Repetition helped as did medicine. Ativan, in particular. Anything to calm his nerves. It wasn't that he couldn't speak in public or play his piano before a gathered audience or converse with total strangers. That had never been a problem. But robbing a bank! That was different. Especially at first.

Today's heist, Scott Burnett's tenth, would be his last. He just didn't know it at the time. While he no longer considered himself an amateur, he didn't consider himself a professional either. Robbing banks was more like a hobby… like golf, but with stiffer penalties. For him, the amount of money no longer mattered. It was the adrenalin high and the thrill of the adventure that satisfied some disturbed mental behavior over which he seemed to have little or no control. Adding to his pleasure was the detailed planning required for each job so nothing was left to chance. A personality disorder to some; a way of life for Scott. In this alternative career which began in 2012, there had never been more than two robberies per year. None in the same city, calendar month, or calendar day. Being unpredictable was one of the keys to his success.

So far, the robbery had gone as planned. The weather had cooperated fully, which meant no rain. Rain seemed to turn the good-natured, southern drivers of Atlanta from Dr. Jekyll's to Mr. Hyde's. Every man for himself. Rain would have delayed or canceled the heist as Scott could not afford the traffic snarls, backups and delays that bad weather always created on Atlanta streets and interstates. Situations he didn't need during his escape.

Before entering the bank, he hesitated only slightly to mentally morph into his Henry Higgins' persona, the British English professor in *My Fair Lady*, a part he had played in a college play at the University of North Carolina. He preferred not to speak, but when he did, he would use Higgin's English accent.

Scott was familiar with the bank layout and the tellers, having visited the bank on at least two other occasions. Its layout was similar to many banks with the teller's stations a straight line from the entryway for easy customer access. Glassed offices were located to the immediate right and left of the teller stations. As Scott entered the lobby, through the double door vestibule, he noticed only one of the glass offices was occupied. Less people meant less witnesses. He headed directly to Mary Ellen Ferguson's teller line and waited until she nodded for him to approach her window. He had selected Ferguson because of her vulnerability. She was a pretty blond, married woman in her early thirties with a young daughter. Sarah Moore was his second choice. With only a husband, she was far less vulnerable. Calmly, he placed his black fire-resistant money pouch on the counter, unzipped it and retrieved ten stacks of bills bound by a blue strap indicating one hundred, $1 bills. The first and last bills were real. The rest of the 'currency' sandwiched by the two real $1 bills was plain paper, cut to the same size. He pushed the stacks of 'money' onto Mary Ellen's side of the counter along with a note and three pictures he'd pulled from his coat pocket. The type-written note simply said:

MARY ELLEN FERGUSON
1226 MASON STREET
THIS IS A ROBBERY
EMPTY YOUR TELLER DRAWER. SLOWLY
NO DYE PACKS, BAIT MONEY, ALARMS
DON'T DO ANYTHING STUPID

Mary Ellen picked up the note and read it. She was stunned at first. In her eight years as a teller, she had never been part of a robbery, witness to a robbery, or knew anyone that had. Seeing that the thief didn't appear to have a weapon, she defiantly pushed the fake money back toward Scott even though she had been trained not to do so. Her reaction surprised the thief but did not unravel him. This had happened only one other time. He calmly pointed to the three pictures and in his practiced English accent slowly said, "Your daughter is very pretty." He then shoved the fake money back to the teller.

The first picture was taken of Mary Ellen's twelve-year-old daughter as she boarded her school bus. The second was a picture of her daughter unlocking the side door to their modest house - alone. The third was a picture of Mary Ellen, in her Toyota.

Mary Ellen's defiance turned to fear and panic. The pictures had served their purpose. Without hesitation, she started grabbing the fake money packets from the teller window and replacing them with packets from her drawer. As ordered, she slowly stacked them on the counter.

"This is all I have," Mary Ellen said, stammering. "Do you want me to get more from the other tellers or the vault?"

"No. This is fine."

Scott was well aware of the maximum amount of cash that FDIC regulations allowed in each teller drawer. Usually, less than $5000. In the past when he really *needed* money, he would have had the teller pull cash from the other teller drawers. Once, he even had a teller remove cash from the vault knowing she would not sound the alarm, call the police, or say or do anything as they were trained to let the robbery take place and not be heroes. But now, all he cared about was the emotional thrill of the actual act and the escape.

As Mary Ellen placed the money packets at the teller window, Scott leisurely picked them up one at a time and examined them to make sure he had not been slipped a dye packet. Once he was satisfied with the veracity of the packets, he slipped them into his money pouch. The process was slower than most bank robberies, but it made the transaction look natural. He wasn't concerned about what the bank employees would do if they discovered a robbery taking place. Just the customers.

Once all the packets were in his pouch, he zipped it and then collected the typed written note and pictures. He shoved them into his left coat pocket and from his right coat pocket, he pulled out a pair of fire-resistant gloves and slipped them on over his clear-colored nitrile gloves. Using the same thick English accent, he politely asked the teller to hand him a dye pack. Obligingly, she handed him a bundle of $10 bills that contained the red dye incendiary device. He could still see the fear in her eyes. Scott hated that part of the job. He could never hurt anyone, but the tellers had to assume he would. That was his leverage.

As he turned to leave, Mary Ellen Ferguson, unwittingly and without regard for her safety or, for that matter, the safety of her fellow workers or customers who had just entered the bank, grabbed Scott's hand through the small opening in the Plexiglas and blurted out, "Please don't hurt my child. Please. Please."

The outburst caught the attention of two other tellers, one to Mary Ellen's right and the other to her left. Until then, they were both busily waiting on other customers, totally unaware of the robbery taking place. Almost simultaneously, they both looked over to Mary Ellen and then to the man at her window. Neither understood what was happening or what triggered the outburst. Sarah Moore, the teller to her immediate right and the mother-hen of the bank, stopped what she was doing and quickly walked over to Mary Ellen who by then had released the robber's hand and was now in tears. Before she could say anything, she saw the well-dressed man stare angrily at the frightened teller. He then pointed his finger at her, wagging it while shaking his head and in his English accent said, "Lady, you shouldn't have done that! There *will be* repercussions."

Scott had never done this before. He regretted the additional fear he had caused the poor, young teller, but no one had ever called him out before. It was totally reactionary on his part. Probably just like the teller's outcry. But he certainly couldn't stop and apologize to the woman. He had to leave. He only had seconds before everyone in the bank knew that a robbery was taking place.

He turned to the doors and walked out of the bank and onto the sidewalk. Knowing he only had about ten seconds, he immediately turned, pulled open the outer door to the bank's vestibule, tossed in the armed red-dye packet, and walked away, heading left. Once he had walked five paces, he reversed his direction and walked back by the bank's doors where he saw red smoke filling the air in the enclosed area and red paint dye splattered everywhere. Sirens could be heard in the distance.

CHAPTER 2

Scott's first robbery was in Memphis on Thursday, June 25th, 2012. At this point in his life, the heist was a necessity, not the recreational game it would later become. The amount stolen was just over $4,500, not a large amount but enough to keep his hemorrhaging financial ship afloat. He was desperate and desperate times called for desperate measures.

But his financial situation hadn't always been so dire. Only four years earlier, he and two friends/business associates, all in their early thirties, pooled their money to form a limited partnership. All three men had savings accounts, comfortable homes, nice cars, and wives with jobs that brought in enough money to maintain their current lifestyle. This allowed the three partners to focus on building their company. Their business plan had projected losses for the first two years, a break-even point during the third, and in the black by the fourth year. They had funded the company to allow for such losses. The first year went really well… better than projected. However, during the second year, they suffered some setbacks. Nothing that couldn't be overcome with hard work and an influx of money. But their planned two years of losses turned into three. Then four. By then all three partners had mortgaged every asset they owned and tapped out their line of credit to support their fledgling company. With all profits being plowed back into the company, salaries to the partners were kept to a minimum. The only benefit the company offered to the partners was its future, which still looked bright. It wasn't as though they were throwing good money after bad.

In the second year of their company's brief existence, Scott Burnett's wife, Laura, discovered a lump in her breast. The diagnosis was bad – stage 4 metastatic breast cancer. Unless the cancer went into remission, five years was pretty much all she could hope for. Even still, she continued to teach 5th grade as they needed her salary and health insurance. Plus, she dearly loved her students… her kids. She and Scott had no children of their own. But the treatment for the cancer was debilitating, so when she was no longer physically able to work, she reluctantly resigned and applied for Cobra health insurance and disability benefits.

With her salary gone and months before social security disability benefits would be approved, the Cobra insurance premiums became unaffordable. They sold their second car, 'downsized' their remaining car, moved into a studio apartment, borrowed from their parents and siblings, and enrolled in a high deductible health plan offered by the Affordable Care Act (known as Obamacare). Even so, Scott's meager salary couldn't cover their living expenses, health insurance premiums, *and* the ever-increasing medical expenses. The other two partners were sympathetic, but they, too, were strapped. They raised Scott's salary by reducing theirs, but that was not enough.

With his credit cards maxed out, no asset to sell, his wife's health spiraling downward, and the medical bills skyrocketing, Scott needed money, and fast. He offered to sell his share of the business to his two other partners. But neither had the money to buy him out. Nor could they afford to lose Scott who was the real brains of the company. Bringing in a venture capitalist was also considered. But they found no one willing to risk their capital without at least fifty-one percent of the business. So that, too, was rejected by all three partners.

With nowhere to turn, Scott began to consider alternative ways to find money.

The stock market was a possibility. Scott was very familiar with different strategies of the stock market such as selling short, buying on margins, futures and day trading. He even had a personal stockbroker early on in his career before the crash in 2008 when he was lucky enough to have moved his money out of the market and into 'seed' money for his newly formed partnership. But in the stock market, you had to have money to make money which for him was almost non-existent. And the large investment profits he needed took time of which he had very little.

Then there was gambling. It would be quick, easy and legal. With his limited experience at the tables or on the Roulette wheel, he would have to rely solely on chance or good luck which hadn't been so kind to him lately. And he was smart enough to know that in the end, the House always won and he would be even worse off.

Feeling desperate, selling or transporting drugs came to mind but only briefly. He could make lots of quick money, but he had personally seen what drugs could do to a family. His younger brother had gotten into drugs in high school and it tore the family apart almost causing his parents to divorce. Not only that, who would he contact? It wasn't like you could put out feelers, or post notices on telephone poles, or advertise on

Craigslist that your services were available. More than likely, he'd end up dead or in jail.

There was also quick money to be had in burglarizing people's homes. Knowing when people were away from their homes was easy. You looked at obituaries. They always gave out dates and times of the visitations and funerals so the grieving relatives' homes would be an easy target. And then there was Facebook. Friends and friends' friends always posted their pictures as they vacationed. So their houses were vulnerable. Piled-up newspapers on the driveway was another giveaway of a vacant home. But where would he sell the stolen goods? He knew nothing about 'fences,' or where to find them. He'd just end up with a bunch of TVs, computers, jewelry and cellphones piled up in his garage and still no money.

After careful consideration, Scott decided that banks were his best bet. Robbing banks. First of all, he was very familiar with bank operations and how their security systems worked because he had worked in the financial industry since graduating from college. He knew the average amount of money that could be stolen. He knew the typical ebb and flow of a bank's foot traffic which would help him determine the best time to pull off a robbery. The money he stole was insured by the FDIC, so neither the bank nor its customers would suffer any financial loss. But mostly, because, to quote Willie Sutton, the infamous 1920's bank robber, 'that's where the money is.'

CHAPTER 3

As Scott casually walked down 14th Street toward Piedmont Park, he could see people from the sidewalk begin to gather around the bank's vestibule curiously looking at the dying flames and red smoke coming from the detonated dye pack. No one was going in or coming out of the bank. And most importantly, no one was looking at him. Once he reached Juniper Street, he turned in front of the SCAD Theater and walked into its adjoining parking garage. Normally, he allowed ten minutes to make his getaway. But because of the teller's unexpected actions, he felt he had only seven. In his practice run, he had easily done it in eight.

He fast-walked to the emergency stairwell of the parking garage and ran up the steps, taking two at a time until he reached the top – the sixth floor which opened to the uncovered level. As of yet, no one had parked on the top level. Located behind the sixth-floor door was an open trash barrel with a plastic bag liner. Beneath the unused liner lay a large backpack and biker's helmet that he had placed earlier that morning. He reached down and pulled his hidden items out and then replaced the liner. From the bag, he pulled out six rubber door stops. He jammed one stop under the door to the sixth floor and double-timed his way back down the stairs placing a rubber stop under each of the doors as he passed until he reached the bottom floor. The rubber stops prevented anyone from entering the stairwell from the garage.

Once the stops were in place, he ran back up to the top floor, again taking two steps at a time. There, began his transformation from 'English businessman' to 'biker dude.' The metamorphous was quick. He had practiced it many times. He began by removing his fire-resistant gloves while leaving on the clear nitrile gloves. He then removed his dress coat, clip-on tie, white shirt, wingtips, dress pants, blond wig, fake eyebrows, fake teeth, fake nose, and glasses. Underneath his 'businessman's' attire, he wore a pair of skin-tight leather pants and black tee shirt with fake tattoo sleeves. From the backpack, he pulled out a pair of black leather boots, a number of large silver necklaces and a leather vest. He quickly slipped on the boots, which added two inches to his height, then the vest and necklaces. Lastly, he retrieved a jet black ponytailed wig, rider goggles, leather gloves, fake mustache and goatee which completed his 'makeover.' In less than four minutes he had transformed from a young Michael Caine look-alike to a pony-tailed Hugh Jackman impersonator.

As he set his goggles on his head, he heard the rattling of the door handle on the fifth floor along with a loud 'what the hell.' It was time to make his exit. Wasting little time, he rolled up his old clothes with all his 'accessories' inside the clothes and stuffed them in the backpack along with the money pouch. He slipped the backpack on his back, picked up the helmet and walked down the emergency stairwell to the bottom floor, kicking the door stops aside as he did. Once he reached the bottom, he exited the parking lot from the side door which had no security cameras. He made his way back to Juniper Street then fast-walked until he reached 12th street occasionally checking behind him to make sure he wasn't followed. At 12th Street, he turned left and headed toward Piedmont Park. About halfway down the street between two parked cars sat his locked 2017 Harley-Davidson FLHX Street Glide. He dumped his backpack in one of the side saddlebags, slid on his goggles and helmet, and brought his beast to life. The roar of the engine was unmistakable. Within 15 minutes, Scott was on I-85 North, heading back home to Charlotte, NC.

CHAPTER 4

The bank's door had hardly closed when Mary Ellen Ferguson began yelling and pointing at the vestibule's doors that were now splattered with red paint and filled with red smoke. "He just robbed me! He threatened Ashley!"

Sarah Moore, the teller who had earlier come to calm her, grabbed the young teller's purse under her teller station and pulled her into a nearby office cubicle.

"You need to call Ashley. Now. Make sure she's safe," she said as she handed Mary Ellen her purse.

Mary Ellen nodded and began digging through the large pocketbook until she found her cell phone. She pulled it out and dialed the school. Meanwhile, the rest of the bank erupted in chaos with customers hiding behind the teller stations or under desks in the unoccupied glassed offices or simply frozen in place.

From his glassed-in office, Dominick Garcia, the bank's branch manager, saw the bedlam that had swept across his normally serene lobby as well as the red smoke that filled the front vestibule. He knew immediately what had just taken place. Before exiting his office he hit the silent alarm. On his way to the lobby, he checked the interior of the vault but saw no one. He pulled then pushed the large door shut and turned the dial, locking it. He then headed straight to the vestibule and locked the bank's interior front doors. Afterward, he found a nearby chair, stood atop of it and began waving his hands.

"Everybody… Everybody… Please calm down and listen up." The smallish manager had a command to his voice that immediately caught everyone's attention. "I'm Dominick Garcia… branch manager." Dominick then held up his bank's ID to assure those that could see him. "We have just been robbed, but the thief has left the building. For your safety, please follow me."

With little hesitation, everyone fell into line and congregated around the tan, shaved-head, nattily dressed young man including Mary Ellen Ferguson who now had the assistant principal on her cell phone. They all followed him to the break room. Once everyone was in the room, he locked the door behind him and turned to see that almost everyone had their cell phones to their ear chattering away.

"OK. Everyone. Listen up," he said. "Everyone… Please listen up. The police are on their way. We are safe here. Before you can leave, the police will probably want to interview each of you. So please, think about what you saw and heard while it's fresh in your mind. Then I want you to write it down. Please do not share your thoughts. Now if you need pen and paper, raise your hand, and I'll bring it to you."

Only one elderly gentleman, a customer, raised his hand.

As Dominick handed the supplies to the elderly gentleman, the others began doing as they were told except the teller who was the focal point of the robbery. Instead, she approached the manager.

"Dom, I can't believe what just happened and what I did. What I said. I put *everyone* in danger."

Dominick had not seen the robbery nor had he heard Mary Ellen's shout out to the robber, so he had a bewildered look about him.

"I don't know what you mean. How did you put everyone in danger?"

"I yelled at the robber as he was leaving the bank. I was so scared for my daughter that it just came out."

"What came out?"

"I told him not to hurt Ashley. As he was leaving my station, I grabbed his hand and yelled at him. Then he pointed his finger at me. At first, I thought it was a gun. If it had been, he could have killed me or Sarah or Jennifer or our customers or all of us. I was a fool. I was stupid. I know we've been trained not to confront robbers, but I just couldn't help myself. I'm sorry." Then she began to cry.

Dom wanted to say something, but instead, he hugged her. Managers are taught not to be physical with their subordinates, but it seemed like the right thing to do. When Mary Ellen stopped crying, Dom sat her down in one of the nearby chairs and pulled another chair close to her and he, too, sat down.

"What made you think the robber would hurt Ashley?"

"He had pictures of *her* at our house and of her getting on the school bus. And a picture of me in my Toyota. He showed them to me as he handed me the note asking me for money."

"Have you checked on Ashley?"

"Yes. She's OK. I called the school and she was in first period. I'm heading over there as soon as I can."

"What about Zach? Have you called him?" Zach was Mary Ellen's husband.

"I did but he didn't answer. But I knew he wouldn't. When he's on the road, he never answers his phone. Too distracting, he says. So I left a message for him not to worry just in case he heard about the robbery on the news."

"Good idea."

Mary Ellen paused for a moment considering what she was about to say.

"Dom… Do you think *I* should be worried?"

"About the robber?"

"Yes. The robber. His note told me not to do anything stupid and I did."

"No. I don't think you need to worry," said Dom, placing his hand on Mary Ellen's. "But I would definitely tell the police what you said and what he said and what was written on the note. They'll know what to do." Then changing the subject to try and calm his young teller, he asked, "Do you know when Zach will be home?"

"He won't be home until this coming Saturday. Sometime in the morning. He's on a sixteen-day haul."

Not good, thought Dom as he looked at his watch. "The police should be here any minute. I'll also make sure they know about the threats… you know… just to emphasize your concern. Now if you're okay, I need to check on everybody else."

"I'm fine, Dom."

Dom nodded his head, stood, and started his rounds, checking on the customers and staff, making sure they had called their spouses, parents, partners, or close friends. Sarah Moore, the head teller, was the last person he saw.

"I need to let the police in. Can you lock the door behind me when I leave? And go stay with Mary Ellen. She's really shaken."

Sarah nodded. Dom then grabbed a half dozen garbage bags from the storage closet and left. He heard the lock on the door turn almost as soon as the door closed.

Within ten minutes of the silent alarm being set off, the first of four police cars arrived. By that time, the red smoke had dissipated giving the officers a clear view of the bank's lobby through the paint-splattered vestibule. They could see that garbage bags lined the floor. They also saw a young, tan, shaved-head man standing in the lobby at the door with his driver's license in one hand and his bank ID in the other.

CHAPTER 5

Dom stood back as the first two arriving police officers made their way into the bank with their weapons drawn. One of the officers immediately checked Dominick's IDs. Even though the officers were assured by the manager that the robber had left, that it was not a hostage situation and the employees and customers were safely locked in the break room, they still kept their weapons drawn and began a quick but thorough search of the building looking behind counters, under desks, in closets, and the bathrooms. The last room to be searched was the breakroom.

After three loud raps from the lead officer, an eye appeared at the peephole, and then the door quickly opened. Sarah Moore stood back as the police officers slowly and carefully entered the room checking it out as they did. Dom remained outside the breakroom as the officers had ordered. Once they were satisfied everything was clear, they motioned for Dom to enter the room. All the while, neither customer nor employee uttered a word as they curiously watched the two officers go about their job. Once the two officers holstered their guns, the chatter began again but at a more intense level. Even so, their eyes never left the senior police officer. When they saw him and his partner step into the center of the room, all chatter ceased.

"If I can get everybody's attention. My name is Sergeant Larry Nixon and this is Officer Joe Pearson. We've searched the entire building… thoroughly… and there is *no* sign of the robber. We know this isn't how you had your day planned… but neither did we. We hope to get you out of here very shortly. But before we can let you go, Officer Pearson will need to get your name, address and phone number. Then once the detectives arrive, they will need to ask you a few questions. They will be the ones to say when you're free to leave. So please, bear with us. If you need to call anyone, please feel free to do so, but *after* you've talked to Officer Pearson. Thank you for your cooperation."

Sergeant Nixon then walked over to Dom, said a few words to him and the two men left. As they walked through the lobby, Dom noticed that two other officers had now been posted at the front door. He could also see the familiar yellow crime scene tape cordoning off the bank's entrance. He and Nixon had hardly sat down in Dom's cubicle when

Detectives Sam Jacobs and Victor Marlowe from the Robbery/Homicide Unit of the Atlanta Police Department arrived, both wearing black nitrile gloves, booties and their signature APD detective's fedora… a tradition dating back to the late 1950s.

"Very creative," said Marlowe as he looked at the remains of the detonated dye pack.

"Obviously, a good understanding of the timing of dye-packs," responded Jacobs. "I can't recall anyone ever *using* the dye-packs in their escape."

"Yeah. Most of them end up wearing it."

As they made their way through the vestibule, they saw Sergeant Nixon headed their way followed by a smallish, balding man.

"Guys, this is Dominick Garcia. Bank Manager," said the sergeant. "Mr. Garcia, this is Detective Sam Jacobs and that's Detective Vic Marlowe," said Nixon pointing first to Jacobs then Marlowe. "They will be taking over the investigation from here." The officer proceeded to tell the two detectives everything he knew and then left to make his way back to the break room.

Dom invited the detectives into his office and offered them a seat at his desk across from his. Before either detective had a chance to ask the first question the young manager took the lead.

"Gentlemen, I want you to know that this bank will do whatever you ask, whatever you need to find the person who robbed my bank." The anxiety in his voice was not betrayed by the anxiety in his face. While the robbery was not a result of any oversight on his part or that of any employee at the branch, he felt it was a blight on what had so far been a stellar, unblemished career. He was only 34, very young for a branch manager. In fact, he was younger than anyone in his branch except Mary Ellen, the teller who had been robbed. Yet, his youth had not been an obstacle in his advancement in the bank. He was on the 'fast path' to becoming a senior vice president. While this incident would not deter his career ambitions, it was recognition that no branch manager wanted. "I have made sure nothing has been touched and all of the customers and employees who were in the bank are sequestered in the break room. I've asked them to think back to the robbery and write down anything that they witnessed."

"Outstanding," commented Marlowe.

Dom continued. "Unfortunately, I'm not going to be much of a witness as I never even saw the robbery taking place. I was sitting in my office going over our monthly deposit numbers when I heard an outburst from one of my tellers. When I looked up, I saw customers darting here and there and then I saw red smoke engulfing the vestibule. That was all I saw. But our security cameras would have videos of the entire encounter and from multiple angles. I'll get you a copy of the CDs before you leave. They will show everything. We're lucky… a month from now I'd have to order the CDs as they will be modernizing our security system to communicate to a remote server… probably in the cloud."

"Perfect," replied Jacobs. "Do you have any idea how much money was taken?"

"Not really. But if he only took money from just that one teller, which I think he did, then it should be no more than $5000. I don't remember her telling me if she went into the vault or not. But we can ask her. She's in the break room."

After completing their interview with the branch manager, the two detectives were taken back to the break room where they found the two police officers, five customers and three tellers, all of them anxious to leave. The detectives removed their fedora and found a free table to place their hats and satchels. While Dominick visited each of the customers thanking them for their patience and cooperation, Officer Pearson gave the detectives an update of what he'd learned from everyone in the breakroom and handed over the list of names and addresses. Afterward, he sat down at one of the vacant tables while Nixon left to join his fellow officers outside the bank.

The detectives then began their interviews, customers first, then the employees. They learned that the robber appeared to be male, six feet tall or taller, and nicely dressed in a dark suit. And he had blue or brown eyes and light brown or blond hair, depending on the witness. He wore gloves and carried a briefcase or satchel. He did not appear to have a gun. He had only approached the one teller and the teller had not gone into the vault. Almost everyone heard the robber scold the teller and agreed that he spoke with an English accent. Those that saw the thief leave agreed that he left on foot, but there was not a consensus as to which direction because of the dye pack explosion in the bank's vestibule catching everyone's attention.

Once the interviews were completed, all but one of the witnesses including employees were released to go. Everyone but Mary Ellen Ferguson.

"I'm sorry to make you stay behind," said Detective Jacobs. "But you happened to be the robber's chosen teller."

"I understand," responded Mary Ellen.

"In our earlier interview, you said he had pictures of your daughter taken in front of your house and getting on the school bus. Do you know when he could have taken them?"

"It had to be yesterday…Monday. I remember the clothes she was wearing. I always help her pick them out. She probably doesn't need any help, but I think it's her way of making me feel needed. She's so sweet."

"I understand. I have a son about her age," said Jacobs. "But he would never… never let me pick out his clothes. I do get the final decision if I think something is inappropriate. But you know how kids are these days. Anyway, getting back to the pictures, where is your daughter's bus stop, what time does she leave the house and what time is she picked up?"

"The bus stop is at the corner of Mason Street and Hillside Avenue. Almost in front of our house. We live on the corner lot where Hillside dead ends into Mason in the Oakdale subdivision. Ashley leaves the house at 8:20 and the pickup time is 8:32 a.m. The driver is very punctual and so is Ashley."

"Can you get us a list of your neighbors, left, right and across the street from you? We'll need to interview them to see if they saw anything suspicious yesterday."

The teller quickly drew a diagram of the two streets with rectangles representing the houses and names within the boxes including her own. She handed it to Jacobs who looked at it, nodded approvingly and handed it to Detective Marlowe. He reviewed it and placed it in his satchel.

"You said the robber handed you a demanding, threatening note alongside the pictures. Do you remember the wording of the note?" asked Jacobs.

Mary Ellen told the detectives everything she remembered about the note, how she'd yelled at the robber and what he said back to her.

Still needing more assurance about her and her daughter's safety, she posed the same questions to the detective as she had to Dom. "Should I be worried about me or my little girl? Do you think he'll try to teach me a lesson for what I did…said? He knows where I live and everything."

Jacobs could see the fear that gripped the teller. Hoping to assure the frightened women, he confidently responded. "In all my years in law enforcement, I have *never* known a robber to harm any bank employee or customer *following* a robbery. He's gotten his money. That's all he wants. I'm sure he's moved on."

"Yes… but… he said I shouldn't have yelled at him. I know it was stupid, but he was threatening my daughter. I hope…" Mary Ellen's voice trailed off not knowing what else to say.

Before Jacobs could respond, Dom pulled up a chair at the table where Mary Ellen and the two detectives sat. He was holding a packet of CDs that he had removed from the security closet. He pushed them over to Jacobs and then placed his hand over Mary Ellen's trembling hand trying to comfort her.

"I hope I'm not interrupting anything, but I overheard what Mary Ellen said. Just like you, I don't think anything will come of this robber's threat, but if she's *that* concerned about her and her daughter's safety, then I am, too. I know what it's like to be threatened and no matter what people say, it's hard to tell your brain to just let it go… to dismiss what can't be dismissed. Do you think it's possible to have one of your officers monitor her house for a couple of days? Until her husband gets home?"

"When will that be?" asked Jacobs.

"Sometime Saturday," answered Mary Ellen. "He drives an eighteen-wheeler for a living and sometimes he's gone for two weeks at a time."

"That long? Look, we don't want you to worry. We'll have a patrol car…" Before completing his sentence, he saw Marlowe holding a finger up and shaking his head.

"She's lives in Cobb."

"Good catch, Vic. Ms. Ferguson, you live in Cobb County. We'll have to get in touch with the Cobb Police and have them send out a patrol. If they see anything suspicious… anything out of the ordinary, they'll check in on you. We'll make absolutely sure that no harm comes to you and your daughter. That is my promise."

"Thank you," said Dom looking first at Mary Ellen who nodded in gratitude and then Jacobs. "By the way, those are the surveillance CDs starting from today and going back a month."

"Good. These should be most helpful." The detective placed them in his satchel. "That's all the questions I have for now. Vic… you have any/"

"Yes. Just one. Did the robber mention whether or not he had a partner?"

"No. Once he got the money, he left… after our uh… altercation."

"Ms. Ferguson, if you don't mind sticking around for just a little longer, we have a sketch artist coming over with our forensic team. We would like you to work with her while everything's fresh in your mind."

"What about my daughter? I told her principal that I was heading right over there to pick her up."

"I can send an officer to her school and have him pick her up, take her home and stay with her until you get there. And if you're not comfortable with that, we could pick her up and bring her to the bank."

Mary Ellen thought for a second, weighing her options.

"No. Not here. Let me call the school again. See how she's doing. Maybe if she hears my voice again that should be enough. She might even go back to class. I just want to get this done and go home."

"I think you should make the call. The FBI will be here shortly and they're gonna want to talk to you and Mr. Garcia."

Bank robberies are a federal crime and unless there was someone injured or killed in the commission of the crime, the detectives would be taking a backseat in the investigation.

Mary Ellen excused herself and headed out to the hallway for some privacy. Her daughter answered on the first ring. She was in the principal's office. Mary Ellen assured her daughter that they both were in safe hands just where they were and that she would leave just as soon as she talked to the FBI and worked with a sketch artist. She would call her once she was in her car.

"A sketch artist? Cool. Are you going to be on TV?" asked her daughter hoping for a 'yes.'

"I hadn't even thought about that, honey. I guess there will be TV crews out front when I leave. But don't get your hopes up. If you need me for any reason, call me. See you soon. Love you." Mary Ellen knew there would be no TV appearance for her. She would leave out the bank's back door.

The detectives and Dom were by the Keurig machine drinking coffee when Mary Ellen returned to the break room. She headed over to the refrigerator and pulled out a can of Coke. She then returned to the table that she'd just left, sat down and began nervously looking at Facebook on her cell phone while waiting for the sketch artist and FBI to arrive. She nearly dropped the device when it began to ring. Zach's ring. Her husband. She hardly had 'Hello' out of her mouth when he began firing off questions about the robbery. As she began to answer, she quietly made her way back to the hallway and then into a nearby conference room for privacy. She told him about the robber, the note, the dye-pack… everything including her inadvertent outburst and the robber's responding threat.

"How could you have been so stupid?" asked her husband, yelling while spitting out the words.

"I don't know. I… I…"

"Let me speak to Ashley."

"She's at school. The police…"

"What? You're still at the bank? And you left our daughter at school! Are you daft, woman? You get your ass…"

"I can't," interrupted Mary Ellen, beginning to cry. "The police won't let me go. I have to stay…"

"Put them on the phone. Right fucking now!"

When Mary Ellen opened the door to the break room, Dom and the two detectives looked up to see who was entering, half expecting it to be the FBI agent. Everyone could see that Mary Ellen was very upset. Tears were still streaming down her face. She immediately headed over to Detective Jacobs with her hand extended holding out her phone.

"My husband wants to talk to you."

Jacobs took the phone while Mary Ellen stood by and listened.

"Hello, Mr. Ferguson. I'm Detective Jacobs. Your wife…"

"Sir. I want my wife to leave *right now* and go get my daughter. I do not want her left at school unprotected. What kind of stupid idiots are you people?" snapped Zach, obviously agitated.

"Mr. Ferguson. Please calm down. We do not believe that your daughter is at risk. If so, we'd certainly be there to protect her. But just so you know, we did offer to pick her up and have an officer stay with her at your house until your wife got home. But it was decided that your daughter was just as safe at school than..."

"And who made that stupid decision?" asked Zach, interrupting the detective. "Never mind. Let me speak to my wife."

Zach's attitude did not sit well with Jacobs. He responded sternly but politely. "Mr. Ferguson, I can *assure* you that everyone is in safe hands. Your wife is doing what *we* have asked. We appreciate her cooperation. And I'd appreciate it if you'd control yourself. This is *not* your wife's fault. And I do not like the tone of your voice. ***Am I understood?***"

"Yes sir," said Zach, biting his tongue, knowing he had crossed the line… at least with the police.

Jacobs then returned the phone to his wife.

"What in the hell is wrong with you, woman? You get the police over to that school *right now.* You hear me. *Right fucking now.*"

"OK. Ok," said Mary Ellen, timidly. Before she could say anything else, he'd hung up.

Mary Ellen sat back down at one of the breakroom tables and stared at nothing in particular. She had just had one of the most traumatic and frightening days in her life and what she needed was support from her husband. Instead, he had belittled her, chastised her. Made her feel worthless. Dom saw her distress and sat down next to her, trying to console the disturbed teller whose face was streaked with tears.

"Have you ever wished you were dead?" asked Mary Ellen, looking at Dom.

CHAPTER 6

FBI Special agent Daniel Whitehead from the Atlanta Field Office arrived at the bank, around 11 a.m. Even before showing his credentials to the officer guarding the front door and signing in, every police officer who saw the man knew who he was. The dark black suit, the heavily starched white shirt and the dark red tie were a dead giveaway. It served notice that the FBI was about to take charge.

Whitehead was not a native of Atlanta. He was assigned to the Atlanta field office upon graduating from his 13 weeks FBI training class held in Quantico. Although one of the oldest trainees, he finished at the top of his class just as he had done at the Washington D.C. police academy years earlier.

Agent Whitehead was 36 when he decided to leave the D.C. Police force and join the FBI. He had been a police officer for six years and a detective for almost eight years rising to the rank of captain. The promotion was probably the underlying reason for him leaving the force. He loved being a detective, but after nearly two years of dealing with personnel issues, administrative paperwork and the politics of being a captain, it made him rue the day he left the trenches.

The agent had not changed much since his days in Washington. He was athletic, trim, and much younger looking than his 44 years. The slight graying of his otherwise dark black hair was the only sign of aging. He had yet to marry nor had any plans to do so, his work being a big factor in that decision. He had been single so long that having someone else 'invade' his space was a showstopper as far as he was concerned. He didn't want or need any distractions from him doing his job. Nothing to prevent him from taking whatever time, day or night, to work his cases. Plus, he'd known too many agents, detectives and policemen that were on their second and third marriage.

Having been in law enforcement for over twenty-two years, Daniel was well aware that robbing banks had one of the highest arrest rates of any crime in the country with less than 40% being successful. He wondered which side of the ledger this robbery would fall as he walked through the red-dye painted vestibule. The lobby was empty except for the forensic technician behind the teller station dusting for prints. The agent walked up to the counter and held up his badge.

"They're all in the break room, second door on my right, your left," said the technician, then pointed to the right.

Ignoring the unintentional slight, the agent headed to the break room where he saw a young lady sitting at a table working with the local sketch artist. Behind her, talking to a young baldheaded man, were two men that Whitehead immediately recognized – Detectives Marlowe and Jacobs. Seeing them on the case was a relief as they were two of the best investigators in the APD (Atlanta Police Department).

"Whitehead. How'd you get so lucky?" asked Marlowe upon seeing the agent.

"Everyone was on coffee break except me and the boss man. He collared me. So here I am."

"This one's pretty cut and dry," replied Marlowe. "An in and out. Less than ten minutes - max. Nobody hurt. Only one teller robbed. The guy didn't show a gun. Just a note and some pictures of the teller's kid. Got away clean."

"She the teller?" asked Whitehead, nodding his head toward the young woman next to the sketch artist.

"Good detective work. You want a job? APD's hiring," answered Marlowe, amused at his own wit.

"Overqualified. So, what's going on?" asked Whitehead.

Marlowe then proceeded to give Whitehead a detailed description of the robber including his English accent. He then told him about the note, the pictures, what the teller had blurted out, the robber's response and how he'd used the dye-packs in his escape.

"By the way, the teller that was robbed," said Marlowe in almost a whisper. "…she's pretty upset. She's afraid that the robber might come back and make good on his threat. We've all assured her that she has nothing to worry about and that seemed to calm her until her husband called… a total hot head… he made things worse. I just wanted you to know that she's on edge. So be gentle."

"Thanks for the heads up," said Whitehead.

Jacobs then handed over the bank's surveillance CDs which Whitehead immediately placed in his briefcase then sat it on the table next to the detectives' satchels and hats.

"Very clever use of the dye-pack in his escape," continued Whitehead.

"Just what we said," said Jacobs. "I can't recall a robber ever blocking the door with exploding dye-packs."

"This isn't the first time. I've read some FBI reports about other robberies in the Southeast that fit this guy's M.O. Same kind of disguise, note, pictures, dye-pack escape and English accent. If this is who I think it is, we refer to him as the 'English Bandit'."

"The English Bandit," repeated Jacobs. "Appropriate."

"Do you know how much he got?" asked Whitehead.

Dom who was standing nearby heard the question and immediately spoke up before either Jacobs or Marlowe had a chance to respond.

"I'm Dominick Garcia. I'm the branch manager." Whitehead introduced himself as they shook hands. "It's not official but we believe he got somewhere around $5000. Upper management is sending in a couple of auditors this afternoon to get an accurate count. I can let you know once they are finished."

Whitehead thank Garcia and handed him his business card. He then queried him about the robbery but heard nothing new. Once Whitehead was finished with the manager, both headed in different directions. Dom headed to his office and Whitehead walked over to look at the nearly finished rendering of the robber's face. Without question, they were drawing the English Bandit.

Once the sketch was complete, Whitehead introduced himself to the artist and the teller, found a nearby chair and sat down next to the teller. Whitehead had Mary Ellen tell him everything about the robbery which she did in detail. Having to repeat the same information about the heist did not have the numbing effect on her that oftentimes happens to many eye-witnesses. If anything, it seemed to heighten her concern about the threat made by the thief. And just as she had done with the detectives, she expressed her fears with the agent.

"I understand your concerns," said Whitehead. "For the record, scaring tellers is this particular robber's M.O. His Method of Operation. He's a serial robber and he does this with every teller. The note. The pictures. Always the same. And even though he *verbally* threatened you, I wouldn't worry. He's got his money and most likely has left the state. If you believe in statistics, last year, there were only four people killed in all U.S. bank robberies. And all four were the robbers."

Regardless of what the agent or the detectives said and how calmly they had said it, Mary Ellen still had a deep-seated fear of retaliation from the robber, possibly as a warning to future tellers and customers.

Marlowe saw Whitehead put away his notepad inside his coat pocket, stand and then shake hands with the teller who remained in her seat.

"Daniel… are you through with Ms. Ferguson?" asked Marlowe.

Whitehead nodded and stepped aside.

Marlowe took Whitehead's seat and then addressed Mary Ellen. "Ma'am, I think we've taken up enough of your time. You've been most helpful. And about your daughter… after talking to your husband and seeing your concern, we thought it best to have a patrolman pick her up from school and take her home… immediately. The officer will stay there until you arrive. And if necessary, he's been instructed to stay at the house until you feel safe."

Marlowe then stood, and as if it were a signal, the police officer who had remained in the breakroom immediately came over.

"Ma'am, this is Officer Pearson. He will be escorting you to your car and will ride back with you to your house."

"You don't have to do that. I'll be okay. I promise," replied Mary Ellen.

"It's protocol, ma'am," countered Marlowe. "You've expressed fear for your safety and we'd be derelict in our duties if we let you leave unattended knowing your concerns."

Both detectives and the FBI agent knew it wasn't 'protocol.' The courts had ruled that no government agency including the FBI and the Atlanta Police Department had any duty to protect citizens unless they were held in custody. The detective was doing this as a courtesy.

Mary Ellen couldn't get out of the building fast enough, taking the back door as she did. Unfortunately, her car did not have that same sense of urgency. Only after two failed, embarrassing attempts did the car's engine begrudgingly start and Mary Ellen drove straight home. Had she not had an officer of the law in the passenger's seat, she would have made better time. As it was, she kept the car just above the posted speed limit to the irritation of those behind her.

Back at the bank, the detectives began wrapping up their investigation of the bank premises.

"Unless you have something else you'd like us to do, we're going to grab a couple of officers and begin a search for witnesses and surveillance cameras in the area," said Jacobs. "Then after lunch, we're going to check out Ms. Ferguson's neighborhood for possible witnesses."

"Sounds good," said Whitehead, giving him the thumbs up. "One thing to note, assuming I'm right about this being the work of the English Bandit, after the robbery, we believe he changes disguises somewhere near the bank and dresses as a biker, complete with tats and a ponytail. This guy has been around a long time. No one has yet to find any clues as to who he is or where he's from. And from what I've seen and heard, it looks like we're heading down the same path to finding nothing today, I'm afraid."

"We'll call you if we do find anything," said Marlowe. Then he and Jacobs grabbed their leather satchels and fedoras and headed out of the building's front door giving a cursory wave to Garcia as they left. Whitehead left the empty breakroom and found an empty cubicle next to Garcia's. He gave the manager a heads up that he wanted to talk to him again once he'd made a couple of calls and had time to review the surveillance CD of the morning's robbery.

Garcia agreed. He wasn't leaving any time soon. He had auditors coming, he needed to call his boss and he had to call his partner.

It had been a rough morning for everyone, especially Mary Ellen Ferguson.

CHAPTER 7

Daniel Whitehead's first call was to the Special Agent in Charge, Stephen Avery, at the Atlanta FBI field office… his boss. He asked for a list of phone numbers for the agents who had worked the English Bandit case in the surrounding southeastern area. While he waited for his boss to find and email him the information, he pulled out his laptop and external CD player from his briefcase and then began reviewing the surveillance CD from this morning's robbery. Once he completed the first viewing in real-time which matched up with the eyewitnesses' accounts, he replayed the CD but at a much slower pace searching for anything that might lead to the true identity of the robber. But he saw nothing. Before long, he received an email from his boss with every agent's name, email address and the database link to every robbery connected to the English Bandit.

Daniel opened the link to the surveillance video of the English Bandit's last robbery. It was déjà vu… like he was watching today's robbery all over again only at a different bank. Everything was identical. The note, the gloves, the black money pouch, the fake money packets, the pictures, the businessman's disguise and the English accent. The English Bandit had struck again. Without question, the thief was smart. Most serial robbers were caught by the third robbery as they became cocky and less prepared. This was not the case with this robber. Everything was planned. Nothing left to chance. He was obviously very knowledgeable of the inner workings of banks. Just like the ingenious use of the dye-packs. They had not been used to stop security guards, which banks rarely used anymore. Nor were they used to prevent employees of the bank from trying to run him down, hogtie him and wait for the police to arrive. Nothing like that. The robber had used the exploding red-dye packs to stop customers from trying to be heroes. Especially in states with 'Open Carry' laws where citizens, untrained in police matters, tried to take matters into their own hands.

The note threatening loved ones was an old trick used by a lot of bank robbers. The photos just drove home the point. However, it also showed that the robber had been in the bank before, had singled out a teller and had followed him or her home. That was different. Hopefully, someone noticed a stranger taking pictures of the Ferguson's house or of her daughter getting on the school bus and remembered what the person looked like, what they were driving, and if really lucky, a license plate number or partial number. Because that was what this case was going to take to get solved. A little bit of luck.

Once he'd reviewed a few other surveillance videos from different banks at different times playing out exactly the same way, he decided to call a couple of the assigned agents. The first two calls went to voicemail. The third went to an agent who was friendly enough but offered no new information. Daniel laid his phone down on the desk and stared at his laptop of a still photo of the thief. He was getting nowhere fast.

"So, how's it going?" asked Dom, standing at the open door of Daniel's cubicle.

Whitehead looked up. "Not like I'd hope. By the way, I don't know if you overheard my conversation with the detectives, but the robber has been credited with nine other robberies over the past seven years. All in different states. He's very good. Very professional. Not your run-of-the-mill bank robber. And from what I've read, he only picks on high deposit, low foot traffic banks."

"Then I can see why we were chosen. That's a perfect picture of our bank's customer set. Look… I'm heading to Starbucks up the street for a cup of coffee. My boss says the auditors won't be here until after two. You care to join me?"

"I'm always up for a good cup of coffee."

CHAPTER 8

Starbucks was only about a five-minute walk from the bank. Both men ordered the blend of the day, no sugar or cream then took a seat at a nearby table.

"So what's the chance of catching this guy," asked Dom, then taking a swig from his hot brew.

"Truthfully? Unless we catch a break, very unlikely," replied Whitehead. "Most robbers are caught when the dye-packs explode and they're covered in red paint. It's hard to blend in when you look like Spiderman. And if it's not the dye-pack, it's usually some unexpected event like the guy getting hit by a car or getting left stranded in front of the bank by their ride. Unfortunately, none of those things happened. So, unless Jacobs and Marlowe find a surveillance video that shows a license plate of the getaway vehicle that's not fake or some other identifying evidence, we can wave goodbye to that money. On a positive note, at least no one was hurt… or worse killed or taken hostage."

"Exactly. So what about my teller, Mary Ellen. Should she be worried? I know detectives assured her that nothing would happen, but is there even a slight possibility?"

"No. The guy's long gone. Statistics are in her favor. I'll tell you like I told her. In 2018 only four people in the U.S. were killed during the commission of a robbery and all four were the robbers. So, no. She's fine. Now her mental state… that's another story. One thing that you should know… oftentimes, the teller who was the main target of the robbery, such as Ms. Ferguson, never come back to work."

"Understood. Mary Ellen was my first hire as branch manager, so she's always been special to me. And she's an excellent employee… extremely liked by everyone at the bank and our customers. But will she quit? I doubt it. I don't think her husband would let her. He's very controlling. Very tight-fisted. Cheap is a better word. She's not even allowed to eat lunch out. She always brings it to work and if she forgets, she gets by on the free Cokes and the snacks I keep in the break room. So, unless she finds a better-paying job, I don't think I have to worry about losing her. If the truth be known, she should probably be more worried about that crazy husband of hers than the robber."

"I get this feeling you don't like him," said Whitehead, then laughed. "Detective Marlowe already told me he was a hothead, so I understand what you're saying."

"No. I do not like him. Fortunately, he's out of town a lot. He drives one of those big rigs across the country. Sometimes he's gone weeks at a time. But we all know when he's back in town. And Mary Ellen doesn't have to tell us. But I didn't mean to segue into her troubles. So back to the robbery. What's next?"

Before answering, he took a swig of his now tepid coffee. "We'll do more profiling, remap all of the banks that the English Bandit has robbed trying to narrow down his base of operations, search our FBI Sentinel database for similar robberies that were not credited to the English Bandit but might actually be his earlier heists. Then we'll look at surveillance from your bank's videos and any that Jacobs and Marlowe might locate outside the bank. Hopefully, we'll find something. But we're dealing with a pro, so I'm not holding my breath."

"Is there any way I can help?" asked Dom. "The thief had pictures of Mary Ellen, so he had to have been in the bank at some earlier date. I could go over the videos for the last month or so when I get them back from you. I know a good number of our customers. They're regulars. Plus as you know, our foot traffic is very light. You never know, I might see something that y'all don't."

Whitehead considered the offer. In all his years as a policeman, then detective and now an FBI agent, he'd never had one person step up like Dom. First, he sequestered his employees and customers so the crime scene was untouched. Then he had everyone write down anything they saw regarding the robbery and now he was volunteering to spend hours looking at videos of customers that come into the bank, trying to spot one that he didn't recognize or was suspicious looking. The young man was wise beyond his years. He could see why the bank saw fit to make him a manager at such a young age.

"That just might be the break we need. When you're doing your research, don't just look for a man in the same disguise as the robber wore today. We have other videos taken in the vicinity of other similar robberies of a man driving away on a Harley in an all-black biker's outfit. His hair is in a ponytail and he has tattoos on his arms. We feel very confident that it's the same man. But that's for your ears only."

"I understand."

CHAPTER 9

Seeing the APD patrol car parked in front of her house caused Mary Ellen to wince. Not that she wasn't expecting the car. It was just a stark reminder of the earlier morning's frightful experience. How she had challenged the robber. How he had threatened her. She pulled into the driveway next to the patrol car, immediately turned off the car and hurried into the house through the kitchen door leaving the patrolman in the car to fend for himself. From the kitchen, she could see Ashley in the den, sitting on the couch, watching TV. The patrolman who was sitting at the kitchen table immediately arose but did not say anything as he watched the mother rush past him and hug her daughter like she had not seen her in ages.

As the intensity of the embrace began to ebb, so did the fear and anxiety that had consumed the mother. She was home and her daughter was safe. That's all that mattered.

"So, what happened?" asked Ashley, excitement in her voice. "Tell me everything."

Before the mother could speak, she heard the kitchen screen door open and saw the officer whom she had left in her car enter the room. Mary Ellen held up her index finger to signal for her daughter to wait a minute and quickly headed back into the kitchen. Ashley followed close behind not wanting to leave her mother's side.

"I'm sorry. I didn't mean to be so rude… leaving you in the car," said Mary Ellen addressing the first officer and then turning to the second officer. "And completely ignoring you. I apologize. I can't believe…"

"We understand," said Officer Pearson. "We're here as long as you need us."

"I'm fine now," said Mary Ellen, then turning to Ashley. "Are you okay?" Ashley nodded.

"If you're sure…," said Pearson.

"I'm sure. We're fine."

"Then we'll be on our way. Let us know if you need anything." Then Pearson and the other officer slipped on their headgear and left the house.

Mary Ellen and Ashley followed the officers out to the breezeway that connected the house to the detached garage and watched them get into the patrol car. They watched as the car began to back out of the driveway and were about to return to the house when the car abruptly stopped and pulled back up the driveway but this time, closer to the house. The officer in the passenger's seat got out and headed towards the house.

"Is something wrong? Is there a problem?" asked Mary Ellen, her previously calmed nerves now on high alert.

"Oh no. I just got a text from Detective Marlowe. He said that he heard back from the Cobb County police. They will be monitoring your house for the next couple of days. Just as a precaution."

Mary Ellen thanked the officer and watched him return to his car and then watched them drive off.

When Mary Ellen turned, she saw the look of excitement on her daughter's face had turned to worry which mirrored the angst she now felt.

"What did he mean… that policeman… about the Cobb police monitoring our house as a precaution? And why did that policeman ride home with you?"

"Let's go back into the house. We don't need to tell the whole neighborhood everything."

Mary Ellen hadn't thought about what she should tell her daughter about the robbery. She considered sugarcoating the whole ordeal. But considering the fact that two police officers had just left their house and her daughter was now aware that patrol cars would be canvassing the neighborhood, monitoring their house, whatever monitoring involved, Ashley was smart enough to see through any evasiveness or ambiguities. And there was no telling what the local TV stations and newspapers would report. So rather than having her daughter be subjected to hearsay, innuendos and gossip, Mary Ellen chose the truth. She told her young daughter everything. Once she was finished, she could see the fear in her daughter's eyes and began to question how much she should have told her. Maybe she should have left out the part about the pictures, or the note, or her outburst or the thief's response. But it was done.

"So, did the robber… like have a gun…like point it at you?"

"No, honey. No gun."

"Do you think he said he might come back to our house? Like maybe when you're at work and I'm alone?" asked the twelve-year-old.

"No, baby. I don't think so."

"Then why all the police and everything?"

"Agent Whitehead said it was protocol. Meaning…"

"Mom. I know what *protocol* means. Does daddy know about all of this?"

"I called him while I was at the bank so he knows, but I should probably call him again to let him know that you are home, safe and sound."

"When is he coming home?" Ashley asked.

"He's supposed to be home sometime this weekend. But you know how crazy his schedule is," lied Mary Ellen knowing full well when he *should* be home. His schedule was available on his trucking company's employee website and she had his ID and password. But there was no way she could tell her daughter that her daddy would rather spend his first off day with Girlfriend. Ashley adored her father and vice versa. But, Girlfriend always came first.

"Honey, why don't you go watch some TV while I call your daddy though I doubt that he'll answer. You know how he is when he's driving. No distractions. But if he happens to answer, I'll let you talk to him once I'm through. I know he'll want to make sure you're okay."

While Ashley made her way into the den from the kitchen, Mary Ellen reluctantly dialed her husband's cell number. She did not look forward to talking to him. Every call seemed to end in an argument about something. He always had a way of twisting everything, making her feel like a bad mother, an unloving, passionless, unappreciative wife and a spendthrift. Fortunately, the call went to his voicemail.

"Zach, this is Mary Ellen. Ashley and I are home. The police just left and there will be a patrol checking on us the next few nights. So don't worry. We'll be safe. Talk to you later."

Mary Ellen laid the phone on the kitchen table and sat down in one of the chairs. She could see Ashley sitting cross-legged in front of the TV. She was the best thing that had come out of her marriage to Zach. She wondered when and how she was going to tell her daughter that she was thinking about divorcing him. Would she understand? And how would she take it? Nowadays, divorce was commonplace, even among her friends. But this was her daddy, so it would be different. Surely, she had seen the mental and physical abuse Zach had inflicted on her. And it wasn't like he was home all the time. Two or three days a month was all they got. And Girlfriend got almost as much. She knew it would be tough on Ashley, but Mary Ellen was at the tipping point. She had had all she could take. The girlfriends, the abusive behavior, the battle over money, the jealousy. Zach was no longer the man she'd married. She no longer loved him.

CHAPTER 10

Within an hour after leaving Atlanta, traveling mainly on rural roads, Scott located an old, abandoned gas station. He pulled in behind it and parked between two overgrown shrubs which blocked the view of any oncoming traffic. He then quickly changed from his Hell's angel-looking biker disguise into his gentleman biker's attire, black t-shirt, blue jean vest and jeans, that he had stowed in one of the bike's two saddlebags He still wore the same non-descript boots, goggles and gloves. He also wore the same helmet but changed its look by removing the iron-cross, skull and crossbones and American Flag stickers. Also gone were the goatee, mustache, the multiple silver necklaces and the fake Georgia license plate on his bike. Not once since he began robbing banks had he altered his two disguises. That way, any eyewitness description of him would always be one of the two characters which were nothing like his own self - a 6'2" tall, young, good-looking man with short dark brown hair and brown eyes. Other than his affinity to rob banks, he was the All-American boy.

Five hours later, he rolled into the driveway of his three-story, $975,000 Myers Park townhouse in Charlotte, NC. The house was built before the 2008 U.S. financial meltdown, so its design did not mimic the current day shotgun style. On the first floor were the garage, a bedroom that had been converted into a gym, and his man-cave complete with pool table, 65" TV and leather TV chairs. The living room, kitchen, dining room and master bedroom were on the main level. And on the third floor were two guest bedrooms and a smaller bedroom that had been converted into an office. More room than he needed but not more than he could afford.

Financially, Scott's life couldn't have been better. Within two years of his wife's passing, he and his two partners had finally turned the corner on their fledgling partnership. The red ink had finally turned to black. The light at the end of the tunnel had not been a speeding debt train wreaking havoc on their dreams of success. Instead, the light was their future. Brighter than they had ever imagined. The long hours, the dedication, the determination, the sacrifices had paid off. In their company's eleven years of existence, they had grown from 6 employees to thirty-one, including fourteen Certified Bank Auditors and three CompTIA security specialists. Their revenues now exceeded fifty million per year. Scott no longer needed money. Other than the mortgage on his townhome, he had no debts. He had paid off his wife's medical debts, paid cash for his 2018 Lexus 500 LC sports convertible and 2017 Harley. He was a member of a nearby country club, the Rotary Club, the Kiwanis Club, and Myers Park United Methodist Church, serving on its Administrative Board. There was no need for him to rob banks and risk his company, his career and his freedom. Yet, he did. He understood why he had done it years earlier when his financial situation was at its lowest. But why now? Was it the thrill? Was it the fact that no bank would loan him any more money in his time of need and this was his way of getting retribution? Did he have an inner desire to get caught and possibly spend the rest of his life in jail as punishment for spending so much time away from his sick wife as he tried to build his company? Maybe a good psychologist could elicit an answer from his sub-conscience. But that was never going to happen. He planned to take this secret to his grave.

Once the garage door was closed and the Harley parked next to his Lexus, Scott removed the backpack from the side saddlebag and carried it up to his living room. There, he rolled the upright piano just far enough to the left to reveal a 16" square HVAC return. Using the screwdriver blade from the mini-Swiss Army knife attached to his bike keys, he carefully removed the grate revealing a large open cavity but no ductwork. Hidden at the bottom of the recess was a metal box.

Still wearing his leather biker gloves, he reached down the open hole, felt around until he found the box's handle and pulled it out. Inside were a pen, some blank white envelopes, nitrile gloves and one envelope filled with money from his previous robbery. Written on the outside of the money-filled envelope were the date of the robbery, the name of the bank robbed and the amount of money stolen from the bank. He set the envelope on the floor next to the metal case. After removing his leather gloves and slipping on a pair of nitriles, he pulled the money pouch from his backpack and counted the contents... $4,237. Then using the pen and one of the blank envelopes, he recorded the details of his latest robbery. He then slid the money into the envelope, sealed it, placed it in the metal box and returned the box to its hiding place. Afterward, he shoved the backpack down into the open return and threw his leather riding gloves on top. They would remain there until a new itch needed to be scratched. Once the grate was secure and the piano back to its original position, he grabbed the envelope with the money from his previous robbery and headed upstairs to his office taking two steps at a time.

Scott slid behind his desk and logged onto his computer. He entered the information written on the outside of the money envelope into a secure spreadsheet along with the name and address of the charity that the stolen money was to be given. To date, he had given away *all* of the stolen money, even the money taken in his first three heists that kept him from bankruptcy. But why? A feel-good response? A justification for his robberies? A Robin Hood complex? Another good question for a psychologist that would never be asked.

Just like the precautions he'd used in planning and executing the robberies, the same due diligence was taken in the preparation of the mailing label, the handling of the self-seal bubble mailer, the care of the 'donated' money and the location of the mail drop box. There would be no fingerprints of his left on any of those items. And no drop box was ever used twice nor was it located near his house or office.

Scott placed the mailer in his outbox and picked up his cell phone that lay next to his computer. He had intentionally not carried it to Atlanta. He couldn't risk the chance of getting a call right in the middle of the robbery. Surprisingly, he had only six missed calls. The first, at 8:30 p.m., Sunday night was from Anne Reynolds, his fiancé. She wished him a safe trip. The second and third missed calls were also from Anne. The tone of her voice had gone from sweet to miffed. She wanted to know where he was and to call her back. Scott had told her and everybody at the office that he was going on a charity motorcycle ride to Canton, Ohio and the Pro Football Hall of Fame to benefit a disabled vet. They hoped to raise enough money to buy him a handicap-enabled van. Forty-three bikers had signed up to ride. Everyone had chipped in at least $1000. Scott donated $2000 – his own money. Forty-two rode to Canton. Scott rode to Atlanta.

Besides Anne's three calls, there were three from his office. One from his secretary reminding Scott about an upcoming appointment and two others from his partners, Sid Patel and Tim Martin. Their calls were almost identical in nature. Two small banks had requested a meeting with BPM (Burnett, Martin & Patel LLC) to discuss the company's full array of financial products. One bank was in Hendersonville, North Carolina and the other one in Roswell, Georgia – a suburb of Atlanta. With Scott out of town, Tim had first dibs.

Before calling either partner, Scott mapped out in his mind what he would say. Why he never made it to Canton. It would have to be the same story he told Anne. This should have been part of his overall plan *before* he left for Atlanta. But Anne had not been part of his life during any of his previous robberies, so it totally slipped his mind. He was not good at lying but knew that if he had to lie, the story had to be believable and consistent. Once he felt he had it committed to memory, he called Tim. The call went to voicemail. He left a brief message and then called Sid who answered on the first ring. They jaw-jacked a few minutes about the potential new customers and Sid informed him that Tim had taken the Hendersonville opportunity which meant that he (Scott) had the Roswell assignment which was no surprise. He had no problems going to Atlanta, but he just didn't like going back so soon. Sid, as usual, was all business. He never once asked about the Canton motorcycle trip, so Scott never had an opportunity to practice his verbal deception before calling Anne.

After losing his first wife to cancer, Scott never thought a second marriage would ever be part of his life. He and his wife had talked about *his* future soon after she discovered she had cancer knowing there was no need to discuss *hers*. They knew her fate. Scott vowed that he would never marry again. But his wife would have none of that. She told him that it was okay to love more than one person. Just not at the same time. Scott didn't believe her and said as much, so the subject was never brought up again. But he *had* fallen in love again and with a woman that his first wife would have approved. They would have been best friends.

He waited a few minutes before calling Anne while he rehearsed in his mind how the conversation might go. He dreaded making the call. He had never lied to her. But this time, it was his only option. He could never tell her about his dark side. He hoped she wouldn't see right through his ruse. In hindsight, he wished he had called her from Atlanta on one of his burner phones. If she questioned the strange phone number he was calling from, he could have told her that he was using a fellow bike rider's phone. That would have worked really well with his story. But he hadn't.

Anne answered on the second ring.

"So, where are you? Why haven't you called me?" she asked. "I was worried sick that you might be splayed out on the highway somewhere or wrapped around a tree." She didn't want to start an argument, but she had to trust the man she was about to marry. To her, this was a one-and-done. No divorces in her family.

"I'm really sorry. I should have called, but in my haste to leave Sunday morning, I forgot my cell phone," answered Scott, knowing the less he said the better. "But I'm back here in Charlotte. I had to abort my trip. Just got here about fifteen minutes ago."

"What do you mean you had to abort your trip?"

"My Harley went out on me. Sunday night, we stayed at a campsite just outside of Beckley, West Virginia and the next morning I couldn't get my bike to start. A couple of guys tried to help me, but she was dead. I found a Harley shop about 40 miles away and had AAA tow me there. At first, they thought I would be out of there in a couple of hours and could catch up with the group that night. But then they found that they had to drive to another shop sixty miles away to get a part. To make an extremely long story short, I didn't get out of there until this morning and I'm out $1200."

"Well, that explains why no one saw you on the ride. And by no one, I mean Andy… Anderson Moss, one of my colleagues who was also on the ride. After I told him about the trip, he signed up to go. He was sending texts and photos to everyone in the office. I never saw you in any of the photos and he said that none of the riders he talked to had seen you or even knew you."

Anne's response was totally unexpected. Out of left field. What were the chances that a colleague of hers would be on the same charity ride? As far as he knew, he was the only biker in their circle of friends and among his business associates. Bikes and bike road trips were never the topic of any conversation. Maybe this Andy fellow was a newbie. Quickly he gathered his thoughts. "I'm not really surprised since I only rode Sunday. And there *were* a lot of new faces. More riders that I didn't know than I did. But I'm home now," said Scott, trying to cut short the inquisition. Then as a peace offering, he added, "But while I was there, waiting for the part to come in, waiting on the repairs, wishing I was home with you, I had a lot of time to do some soul searching, reflecting on my life… our life together. I realized that for your sake, our future family's sake, the Harley had to go. It would be selfish and irresponsible on my part to keep it. The risks outweigh the pleasure."

There was silence on Anne's end of the conversation for what seemed like an eternity to Scott. Not a good sign. Then she responded.

"If that's your form of penance or peace offering, I accept. You can't imagine how happy that makes me. I worry every time you get on that thing. Every time. So many bad things running through my mind. And I know that's because I'm not a rider and if I were, maybe I'd think differently. But I'm not and so I worry."

Scott was satisfied that he had successfully sidestepped the inquiry, as it were, and was ready to move on with their conversation. But he should have known that lawyers never seem to quit and Anne was a lawyer. A trial lawyer, at that.

"So why didn't you call me? You could have borrowed somebody else's phone?"

"That one's on me. I really don't have an excuse. And you know I'm not going to lie to you. I should have called. I should have borrowed someone's phone at the Harley shop but I didn't. You are the most important person in my life and I hope you will forgive me."

"You know I can't stay mad at you. But if you forget again…" Anne left it at that. She wasn't sure what her ultimatum would be. She didn't want to go there.

"Never again. I promise."

For most people, that would have ended the conversation. But when you date a lawyer… propose to a lawyer… that doesn't stop the lawyer from being just that… a lawyer.

"So why did it cost you $1200. I thought your bike was fairly new. Shouldn't any major repair be under warranty?"

"I thought so too, but the repair guy looked it up. Said the bike had just gone out of warranty about a month ago. I didn't want to stand there and argue with the guy. I figured I'd call Harley when I got back. After all, they do have a reputation for good customer service. Maybe I can get some or all of my money back."

"If you want, I could send them a letter on our firm's letterhead. That might help."

Anne was known as a bulldog in the courtroom and Scott was getting a taste of it right now. He had to squash this. Quickly.

"I can handle it. Plus I know your going rate." He then laughed. Quickly changing the subject. "I say we go out tonight and celebrate my conversion from a foolhardy, reckless single man to a stable, responsible nearly married man. Your choice of restaurants."

Anne accepted Scott's offer saying something legalese like quid pro quo and then laughed. For the next hour or so they talked about everything but his failed trip which suited Scott just fine.

When they finally hung up, he leaned back in his chair reviewing the day's event. The robbery had gone perfectly. No glitches other than the spat with the teller. He wished he hadn't done it, but it was done. He hoped it didn't cause any consternation on her part. And his call to Anne went as well as expected. The same with his call to Sid. All in all, it had been a very successful day.

CHAPTER 11

Colonel Robert Oliver, a 77-year-old retired Marine veteran of the Viet Nam war, and Betty, his wife of 52 years, lived directly across the street from Zach and Mary Ellen Ferguson. Colonel Oliver looked like what one would expect a 30 year Marine veteran to look like. Lean, buzzed cut white hair - what was left of it – an angular jaw and a permanent frown. His wife was the exact opposite. She had the girth twice the size of two of her Colonel's, curly white hair and a round happy face. Both the Oliver's and Ferguson's lived in similar ranch-style homes built in the '60s just outside of Atlanta. Surprisingly, given the age differences in the two families, Mary Ellen and her daughter, Ashley, had become close friends with the Oliver's. They were treated like the daughter and granddaughter the Oliver's never had. Zach… they could take or leave the "arrogant, narcissistic, self-absorbed prick" as the Colonel described him to his wife. As far as the Oliver's were concerned, the only thing Zach had going for him was his James Dean good looks.

The Colonel was in his back yard tending to his vegetable garden whose centerpiece was a statue of General Douglas McArthur when his cell phone rang.

"Hallo," snarled the Colonel. Not a 'Hello' like most normal people.

"Colonel, this is Zach. Got a favor to ask."

"Go on," mumbled the Colonel, leaning on his rake wondering what the weasel wanted.

"You hear about the robbery in downtown Atlanta?" Not waiting for an answer, Zach continued. "Well, it was Mary Ellen's bank. Some doofus robbed Mary Ellen."

"Holy shit. No. I hadn't heard. What happened? Is she OK?"

"Yeah. She's good. But the asshole threatened Mary Ellen and Ashley before he got away."

"Son-of-a-bitch. Betty and I'll go right now. Make sure…"

"No! No!" said Zach as loud as he could without screaming. "I don't think that's a good idea."

"So what favor do you want?"

"Could you watch the house for me while I'm gone? Look out for anything suspicious and call me if you see *anything*? The police are supposed to be sending out a patrol the next couple of nights, but you and I both know what that means. They'll send out a couple of rookies who'll drive by the house, slow down for a second, maybe long enough to shine a light on the house then drive off to get a doughnut. What the hell good is that? A total waste of time if you ask me. Anyway, if you could keep a lookout on the place for me, I'd owe you."

"I can do that. But if I see anything, you *don't* want me to call the police or go over there to check on things?" asked the Colonel, confused.

"No. No. Just call *me.* I don't want you getting involved with the police. Anyway, if anyone needs to call those assholes, it should be me. I'll get their ass in gear. Lazy son-of-a bitches," ranted Zach.

"Consider it done. Between me walking the dog, getting up to pee four or five times a night and being a light sleeper, nobody's gonna come near your place without me seeing it or hearing it. And if they do, I'll… I'll…"

"You'll call me. Nobody else. Understood?"

"I'm on board. Just so you know… nobody… and I mean nobody is gonna touch a hair on my two little ladies. God, I wish I'd been in that bank…"

"Me too. And please don't tell Mary Ellen that I asked you to do this. She's already freaking out and probably got Ashley all worked up. If she thinks *I'm* nervous, she'll get even more freaked out. We can't have that."

"You're right there. She won't hear *a word* about this from me."

"Thank you, Colonel."

The Colonel walked over to his fence where he could get a good view of the Ferguson's house. He wasn't doing this for Zach. He was doing this for Mary Ellen and Ashley. Everything seemed quiet. Regardless, it took all his willpower not to just throw down the rake and head right over to their house. But he had promised Zach and he was a man of his word. Now Betty… maybe just before dark, he'd get her to call them and see if they would like some of the gumbo he'd just made. She'd know if there was anything wrong or if they needed a sounding board or a comforting smile… from Betty… not the Colonel. Even when smiling, the Colonel still looked angry.

The Colonel put his phone in his pocket and went back to working his garden, but the Ferguson's were clearly on his mind.

CHAPTER 12

Zach went back inside the bar across the street from the busy truck stop where his truck was parked and sat down on the stool next to a scaggy, bleached-blond, local woman with far too much make-up. They picked up their conversation where they left off with him discussing his favorite topic. Himself. Like sailors of old, he had a 'friend' in every port or, in his case, every overnight stay along his cross-country route. The woman at the bar lived in a room at the extended-stay motel just down the street from the bar where they would spend the next few hours. Some sex but mostly sleep, at least for Zach. It was more comfortable than sleeping in the back of the truck. Add a few more beers and the old hag didn't look too bad. Zach and the whore were on first names only. No last names. A kind of an unwritten law although he suspected the old bitch had looked through his wallet while he slept. He'd been on the road since 2 a.m. He preferred driving at night as the traffic was lighter, especially through the cities, and finding a parking space at truck stops or rest areas was never a problem. Eleven hours total driving time over a fourteen-hour period was the maximum that the DOT allowed. Then he had to take ten hours off. His trucking company was very strict about their drivers adhering to the law and keeping their logbooks current. Zach had never broken that rule nor any other rule or regulation. And his logbook was always current and accurate. With only a high school education, and at the near bottom of his graduating class, he was well aware he could never make the money anywhere else as he did as a truck driver. At least nothing legal.

Zach had only been a truck driver for over eight years. And he drove the big rigs… eighteen-wheelers. He and Mary Ellen had been married over twelve having met in high school. They dated for three years. He was Senior Superlative "Most Handsome" and she was Senior Superlative "Prettiest" and "Most Likely to Succeed." They were Homecoming King and Queen. But the commonality stopped with their physical attributes. She was smart, a member of the National Honor Society and Beta Club. Whereas Zach struggled to pass. She went to church every Sunday; he slept in. Her parents were loving; his were abusive. Her father was a surgeon and her mother was a teacher; his father was a drunk and his mother worked as a waitress. Mary Ellen lived in a nice two-story brick home; Zach lived in a trailer.

Mary Ellen's parents tried not to protest too much when she first started dating Zach in the 10th grade. They figured it would pass. But it didn't pass. As their objections to their daughter's relationship with Zach became more frequent and strained, it seemed to drive the two teenagers closer.

Zach and Mary Ellen were married right after graduation from high school. It was a large church wedding with Mary Ellen wearing a stark white wedding dress and veil. Even in the tightest Spanx and with her dress pulled as snug as possible, the small rounded bump couldn't be hidden. Everyone at the wedding, and probably Augusta, Georgia knew she was pregnant.

After a honeymoon to Cancun, paid for by the bride's parents, the couple moved into a newly configured basement apartment in Mary Ellen's parent's home and began their new life as husband and wife and parents-to-be. While Mary Ellen stayed at home preparing for the birth of their daughter, named Ashley, Zach found work as a mechanic at a nearby truck stop right off the Augusta, Georgia I-20 interchange. There, he learned to work on and maneuver the large eighteen-wheelers. Working around so many long-distance drivers and hearing all of their exotic, colorful, romantic and mostly untrue tales of the road appealed to the young, married, impressionable mechanic. Slowly, he began to dream about the job, the money, the independence and the opportunity to move away from his in-laws' basement.

Then one day out of the blue, not long after Ashley was born, Zach told Mary Ellen and her parents that he wanted to get his Commercial Driver's License (CDL). He told them about the money and benefits. What he didn't tell them were the long days and weeks he'd be away from home, the dangers of hauling valuable, sometimes volatile loads or the women who preyed on lonesome and horny drivers. He also failed to tell them his plans to move his family out of the basement and to another city once he was qualified.

Mary Ellen and her parents were thrilled at Zach's ambitious plans and gladly advanced him the money to pay for his training courses. They would have gladly given him the money, but his pride driven by his poor self-worth would only let him take the money as a loan.

After passing the CDL course near the top of his class, Zach was offered a job with a trucking company just outside of Atlanta, near the Hartsfield-Jackson Airport which he gladly accepted. He moved into an extended stay motel with a fellow driver. Mary Ellen and Ashley stayed behind in Augusta. Following his six-month probationary period, he was promoted to a full-time driver with full-time benefits. He found an apartment just outside of Atlanta and moved Mary Ellen and his four-year-old daughter to Atlanta. He felt free. No longer was he under the supervision, control and scrutiny of his in-laws. Even though they were always friendly, inclusive and supportive, he never felt comfortable living under the same roof. On the other hand, Mary Ellen feared the transition from living in a small town to the big city would prove difficult. Gone were her familiar surroundings, her parent's support, her high school friends, her built-in babysitters.

The move to Atlanta was in the middle of April. Springtime. Mary Ellen drove their 2005 Toyota Camry with Zach following close behind in a small U-Haul truck containing all of their belongings. Not that planning had anything to do with the timing of their exodus, but it couldn't have been better. The city's trees and flowers were in full bloom and seemed to form an alliance with the towering buildings making Atlanta seem like more of a big town than a major metropolis. It made her think of Augusta but on a much larger scale. In Atlanta, Zach seemed to blossom as a husband and a father. He became more loving and attentive. He was proud of his newfound independence.

As a rookie truck driver, Zach's road schedule was limited to four days giving him enough time off that the three were able to explore the city, its suburbs and the nearby quaint towns such as Roswell, Marietta, Alpharetta and as far north as Dahlonega. These short excursions fueled Mary Ellen's desire to see more of the country. So she began accompanying Zach on some of his four-day hauls. Her parents were extremely willing to stay with Ashley. It was fun at first, seeing America, spending quality time together, planning for the future. But as the company's confidence in Zach grew, so did his opportunity for longer trips, in mileage and in days away from home. Over time, his four-day trips turned into seven which eventually turned into two weeks and longer. While Zach was excited about the increased time on the road, which meant more money, Mary Ellen knew her road days were over. Four days of taking showers at truck stops, microwaving every meal and sleeping in the overhead bunk were tolerable. But more than four was pushing a good thing. Furthermore, Ashley was getting older and would soon be starting kindergarten. She needed a stable home life and a full-time mother.

Within six months, Zach's time off at home was averaging only four days a month. Initially, his extended absence was difficult for him and

Mary Ellen, but over time they both accepted their new lifestyles. Mary Ellen became a 'single mom' and Zach a 'road warrior.' For some families, this type of marriage worked and it did in the beginning with the Ferguson's. Mary Ellen busied herself with her daughter, her housework, her church and a new part-time job at a nearby bank. Zach just drove, slept and drove some more. However, never a day went by that Zach didn't call Mary Ellen and vice versa. But as time passed, the calls became shorter in length and less frequent. He began to feel like he was becoming a nuisance. He felt that his calls were always interfering with something Mary Ellen and Ashley were doing or planning to do. He became envious of Mary Ellen and her life at home with Ashley as well as her freedom and her friends at church and work, especially her boss, Dominick Garcia. Zach had no home life. His truck cab was his home. And friends? He had no friends except fellow truck drivers, waitresses, bartenders and regulars at roadside grills, taverns and bars near truck stops. And as far as freedom was concerned, he was a slave to his job. He could quit. Go back to being a mechanic. But he could never make the money he did as a truck driver. So quitting was not even an option, not to mention he loved his job.

His infidelities started one night after multiple calls to Mary Ellen went unanswered. Jealous as to what *she* might be doing, he caved to the request of one of the women regulars at a roadside bar to see the interior of his truck using the 'she had never seen one before' ruse. As he eagerly explained all of the instruments on the dash, the woman began to stroke Zach's leg, her only interest being the instrument between his legs. Mentally blaming his wife, he offered no resistance to the woman's advances.

When he awoke the next morning in the upper berth, the guilt hit him square between the eyes as he saw the half-naked woman sound asleep in the bed below. No other woman had ever slept in the back of his truck except Mary Ellen. As much as he tried to rationalize his indiscretion, he couldn't shake the guilt nor could he look either his wife or daughter in the eye on his first weekend home after the adulterous affair. But then it happened again. And again. And again. And then there was no longer any guilt.

It wasn't long before Mary Ellen began to see changes in Zach. He was no longer the happy, sweet, kind, loving husband. Instead, he was moody, demanding, jealous and always critical; finding fault with her in how she looked, the way she kept house, how she parented. Everything. And he constantly berated her on her spending habits even though most of the time she stayed within budget. At first, she thought the change was due to the demand of the job and the amount of time he spent away from home. Then there was the possibility that it could be the house they'd bought two years after they'd moved to Atlanta and its constant maintenance, like the new water heater she'd just had to buy. It was only when she was washing his clothes and smelled the fragrance of another woman's perfume did she come to realize the source of the change. When she confronted Zach, he laughed it off saying it was when one of the office ladies at one of the truck terminals gave him a hug. That she was a hugger. Mary Ellen wanted to believe him, but she knew when he was lying. He had a 'tell' that always betrayed him. A noticeable tic that her dad first discovered and told her about. Zach would purse his lips if he was lying. So when she saw this, she knew. She let it go the first time. But then it happened again. Rather than confronting him, she refused to have sex with him knowing she could possibly contract an STD. That's when the sexual and physical abuse started. Knowing that Zach had an abusive childhood, she tried talking to him, pleading with him to see her preacher or to get therapy. But that only infuriated him more and made him become even more abusive. Whereas Mary Ellen once looked forward to Zach's coming home, she now looked forward to him heading back out on the road.

Her only solace came from Dom. She felt comfortable talking with him just as did the other bank employees. He was sensitive, understanding and compassionate. Being gay, Dom had experienced the same type of abusive behavior but not from his parents… only those uncomfortable with his lifestyle. He knew the type and avoided them. Mary Ellen couldn't avoid Zach. And she learned to keep Dom's name to a minimum when talking to Zach as the mere mention of his name sent him into tirades with false accusations of infidelity. Maybe she should have told Zach that Dom was gay, but she didn't nor would she ever.

CHAPTER 13

Using GPS and Mary Ellen's hand-drawn diagram, the two detectives drove directly to the Oakdale subdivision and parked in front of the young teller's house. The neighborhood was old but well kept. Like many of the older neighborhoods in Atlanta, the subdivision had gone through a youthification with the thirty-somethings moving in and the older families moving out either to smaller houses, condos or senior living.

Ashley was in the kitchen grabbing a coke when she saw the two detectives heading up their driveway.

"Mom! Mom! Two men are coming to the house!" Her voice got louder with each word.

The alarm in her daughter's voice had Mary Ellen almost running from the bedroom where she had been resting. She glanced out the front living room window and to her relief saw two familiar faces.

"Ashley. It's fine. No need to worry. They're the two detectives I met at the bank."

"But why are they coming here? What do they want?"

"I'm not sure."

Before they could ring the doorbell, Mary Ellen opened the front door and greeted the two detectives. Ashley stood close behind her mother studying the men in detail.

"Hello, Ms. Ferguson," said Jacobs, removing his fedora and showing her his badge. "Detective Marlowe and I were in the neighborhood getting ready to do our door-to-door canvas and thought we'd check on you and your daughter before we began and make sure it's okay if we park in front of your house."

"That's very thoughtful and yes, please," said Mary Ellen, seeing the diagram of the neighborhood she had drawn in one of the detective's hands. "We're okay. Still a little stressed over this morning. But we're okay. You want to come in?"

"No. We're good," said Jacobs. "But once we're finished, we'd like to stop by and chat for a minute, if you don't mind."

"That'll be fine. We're not going anywhere," Mary Ellen replied wondering why they needed a return visit. She'd already told them everything she knew.

The detectives thanked Mary Ellen, donned their hats and headed down the steps and back to the street to begin their door-to-door search looking for anyone who might have seen the person taking pictures of the teller's daughter hoping some neighbor had taken notice. The Oliver's, a neighbor across the street from the Ferguson's was their first stop.

After seeing an unknown car parked in front of the Ferguson's house, the Colonel had just started dialing Zach's cell number when he heard the doorbell ring. He canceled the call and opened the door to see two, nicely dressed men holding up their detective badges. After quick introductions, the Colonel invited the detectives in and the questioning began.

"Actually, I did see someone taking pictures of their house," said the Colonel deciding not to tell them of Zach's earlier call. "I was out walking my dog when I saw this fellow on a motorcycle stop, pull out his camera and start taking pictures. I really didn't think much of it. I thought he might be working for a realtor. That maybe the Ferguson's were selling their house." The Colonel then leaned closer to the detectives and in almost a whisper continued. "Now you didn't hear this from me, but they've been having lots of marital problems, so I thought they might finally be calling it quits. I certainly wouldn't blame Mary Ellen. I don't know *why* she's stayed married to that asshole this long. He's a real prick. A real jerk." He then returned to his natural military posture.

"Did you get a good look at his face? Did he ever take his helmet off?" asked Jacobs with Marlowe writing down the responses.

Before the Colonel could answer, he heard his wife, Betty, yell out as she and their dog entered the house from the side carport, carrying fresh vegetables from their garden.

"Who are you talking to?" she asked as she placed her gatherings in the sink. In the Oliver's household, she did all the picking and cooking and the Colonel did all the digging, plowing, planting, weeding and fertilizing.

After a quick rinse of the vegetables and still hearing the Colonel talking, she headed into the den where she expected to find the Colonel laid back in his recliner carrying on conversations with either himself, his favorite listener, or the TV news anchors with no penchant for any channel. The Colonel had his opinions and it worked out better for Betty if he espoused them to the TV news anchors rather than her since they couldn't talk back. When she didn't see him but still heard him talking, she headed to the living room where she saw two men just inside the front door, both wearing suits. She immediately thought *Jehovah's Witnesses*. The Colonel needed her help. Even though he was a tough, hard-ass Marine, he was a softy with anyone who came to the door, whether selling cookies, doughnuts or religion.

As she entered the living room, Ike, their light brown and white Maltipoo, named after Dwight David 'Ike' Eisenhower, ran ahead as interference, his shrill bark interrupting the three men's conversation.

"Shut up, dog," yelled the Colonel. The dog immediately stopped his yapping.

"He won't bite and he only barks at strangers," said the Colonel trying to assure the two detectives of the dog's intentions. Jacobs bent down and put the back of his hand in the dog's face, trying to establish a quick friendship. The dog shied away. Marlowe who was afraid of dogs just ignored the pooch.

"Honey, these two gentlemen are detectives. Detectives Jacobs and Marley," said the Colonel.

"Marlowe." Corrected the detective.

"My apologies, sir," said the Colonel, embarrassed over his mistake.

"No problem. We get that all the time. Especially at the station… and on purpose," answered Jacobs.

Relieved that they weren't trying to sell her husband anything, she smiled and said, "Robert! Where are your manners? Can we get you some coffee, Coke or a water?" Betty only called the Colonel, *Robert,* whenever he was being scolded, corrected, and/or being ill-mannered. Otherwise, she called him Bob. The Colonel never called Betty *Elizabeth.* He knew better.

"Thank you, but we're fine," said Jacobs, answering for both detectives.

"Honey, you remember hearing about that robbery in Atlanta this morning?" Without waiting for a reply, he continued. "Mary Ellen was the teller that was robbed."

"Oh my word!" said Betty, covering her mouth with her hand, shocked. "Is she okay?"

The two detectives then repeated the Cliffsnotes version of the robbery that they had previously told the Colonel.

"Honey, the detectives were just asking me a few questions about a motorcycle rider I saw yesterday. If you can think of anything, jump right in." He knew she would anyway.

Jacobs continued his line of questioning. "So, Colonel, you said *fellow*. Did he take his helmet off? Did you get a look at his face?"

"You know I said fellow because of his build. But, hell, I guess it could have been a woman for all I know, but I don't think so. Anyway, he never took off his helmet, but I did see that he had a pony tail and lots of tattoos on his arms. I can tell you we'd never put up with that kind of bullshit in the Marines. What in the hell is this world coming to? Tattoos. Nose rings. Earrings. Not like in the old days when men were men." He then saw Betty slightly shaking her head and he zipped it.

Both detectives nodded in agreement. Marlowe was glad he had worn a coat over his short-sleeve shirt covering the tat he'd gotten in Afghanistan.

"Did you see this biker take any other pictures other than the house?" asked Jacobs.

"No. But he could have. The school bus pulled up in front of the biker and stayed there for about four or five minutes. By the time the 'STOP' signal closed and the bus began to move, the biker was driving off."

"And any chance you got his license or even the state the license was from?"

"No. There was no reason. He didn't do anything that I thought was suspicious. And we do have motorcycles that come into the neighborhood from time to time. Usually, they're lost or made a wrong turn. But if I hear one of those loud numbskulls again, I guarantee (pronouncing the word *gar on tee* like the Cajun chef and humorous Justin Wilson) he won't leave without me getting their plates."

"Thank you. One last question. Did you see any cars near the Ferguson's house that you didn't recognize?"

"No. Only the biker."

"Thank you, Colonel. Ms. Betty. And thank you for your past service. It was an honor meeting both of you,"

Both detectives shook the Colonel's hand and nodded to his wife and walked out the front door. As they headed down the walkway toward the driveway, they could hear little Ike's piercing barks coming from the house. Then the constant yapping suddenly stopped. The Colonel had spoken.

"Without a doubt, the English Bandit," said Marlowe.

"No question about it" replied Jacobs immediately.

After canvasing the remaining neighbors with nothing to add, they circled back to the Ferguson's house where Mary Ellen invited them to join her in the living room. The house smelled clean and was as tidy as it smelled. There was no clutter, no frayed furniture and family pictures were tastefully placed everywhere. The young teller offered the detectives the matching chairs across from the sofa where she sat. The detectives took their seats and placed their fedoras on the coffee table in front of them.

Jacobs spoke first. Marlowe had his pen and pad out.

"Mrs. Ferguson. Since you were the focal point of today's robbery, the chosen teller as it were, we felt you should know what we've found so far. Especially, since he threatened you. First and foremost, you need not worry that any harm will come to you or your family. This appears to be the handiwork, for lack of a better word, of a serial bank robber known as the English Bandit. He is a one-man show. FBI Agent Whitehead is familiar with this robber and to his knowledge, has never harmed anyone, bank employee or customer, during or after a robbery. You appeared to be very upset at the bank, and rightfully so. But please understand, this is his M.O. His Modus Operandi. He uses fear as his weapon."

"I understand. Everybody keeps telling me that. Maybe I am overreacting, but has he ever yelled that there would be repercussions to any other teller?" asked Mary Ellen.

"Not to our knowledge, but the thief has his money and he is long gone," answered Jacobs which was neither reassuring to the young teller nor did it ease her fears. Sensing Mary Ellen's apprehension, he offered a suggestion. "One thing you might consider if you are still concerned is a home security system. Not that I think you *need* one, mind you. But it does offer your family an additional level of protection. Not only do the systems monitor any activity around your house, some systems allow you to monitor your house remotely, both inside and outside the house. Like you could check on your daughter while you are at work."

"That's not going to happen. I'm not opposed to it, but my husband would never spend the money."

What she didn't say was that if Zach did cough up the money and put one in, it would not be for the security it offered. He'd use it to spy on his family. Another layer of control.

Mary Ellen continued. "So did you have any luck finding anything… any witness?"

"Actually, yes. Your neighbor across the street, Colonel Oliver. He gave us a good description of the man… said he was driving a motorcycle which squares with what the FBI reported. What he didn't get was his license plate, which probably would have been fake."

"So why didn't he say something to me? Call the police. Anything?"

"He said he thought the guy taking the pictures might be working for a realtor."

"Good point. We get offers in the mail all the time from people wanting to buy our house. Zach calls them flippers."

Feeling they had outstayed their welcome, the two detectives wrapped up the meeting, thanked Mary Ellen and left. Unwittingly, they had also left an uneasy feeling in Mary Ellen's mind. *Why had they come by to check on us? Was there something they weren't telling me? Why the sermon on home security systems.* The front door had hardly closed when Ashley ran to her mother and hugged her. Mary Ellen wondered if she had heard everything the detectives had said or had noticed the strain on her face.

Jacobs cranked the car and did a three-point turn using the Colonel's driveway to turn the car around. As he exited the neighborhood, Marlowe sent a text to Whitehead with a summary of the interviews. The ball was now in the agent's court.

CHAPTER 14

Mary Ellen wished the two detectives had never come to her house. She understood that they were just doing their job and the visit should have comforted her. But it hadn't. In fact, it had had the opposite effect on her and Ashley. Especially Ashley. Her poor child had already been pulled from class, escorted to the principal's office, carried home by a cop, and now had the two detectives telling her that she needed a security system. It was more than a normal, insecure twelve-year-old could handle. Instead of watching TV or staying in her room, talking on the phone, playing music or video games like she would do on most school nights, she curled up on the couch next to her mom, laid her head down on her lap, and closed her eyes. Immediately, Mary Ellen began stroking her daughter's long brown hair hoping it would relieve some of the angst that they both felt. However, with every vehicle that passed in front of their house, she could feel the tension return… in both of them. She tried to think of a distraction.

"Sweetheart, what do you say we FaceTime Mimi and Poppy?"

Ashley looked up at her mom and gave her a feeble thumbs up.

"And let's not say anything about the robbery," said Mary Ellen. "I think we've both had enough of that for one day."

Mimi and Poppy were Ashley's grandparents and Mary Ellen's parents. They were as close as grandparents and grandchild could be. They were at the hospital when Ashley was born. They were at her christening. And they were there in her formative years until Zach moved the family to Atlanta. But they were never far away, keeping Ashley whenever Mary Ellen accompanied Zach on his trips out of state. Zach's parents, on the other hand, took no interest in Ashley only having seen her a couple of times while Zach and Mary Ellen lived in Augusta. Never in Atlanta.

Mary Ellen clicked FaceTime and set her iPad on the coffee table so both she and Ashley could be seen. On about the second ring, Mimi answered her iPad.

"Well, hello," she said. "I thought you had forgotten us."

"Sorry. We've been really busy," said Mary Ellen, thinking *FaceTime works both ways.*

"I understand," answered Mimi. "Hold on one second." Then she called out, "Poppy, FaceTime."

Wesley Knox quickly joined his wife, Carol in the kitchen where she had her iPad set up on the counter.

"How's my sweet Ashley?" asked Poppy while moving his glass of red wine out of view from the FaceTime's video.

"Fine," she said softly. She wanted to talk to Mimi and Poppy yet at the same time she didn't feel like talking to them. This conflicting disposition made sense to her and most teenagers.

"You seem a little down. Is everything all right at school?" asked Mimi, who seemed to have a built-in sixth sense.

Before Ashley could answer, Wesley jumped in. "I see you had some excitement up your way."

"What do you mean?" asked Mary Ellen already knowing what he meant.

"I just saw on the 5 o'clock news that one of your banks got robbed."

"Yes, daddy. It was *my* branch."

Ashley immediately got up from the sofa and headed to her bedroom. When it rained, it seemed to pour.

"*Your* branch? Good Lord. What happened? Anybody get hurt? How much did they get? They know who did it?" asked Poppy, his staccato questions firing out like a machine gun. He saw Ashley get up and leave but figured she'd gone to get a Coke or something and would be right back.

"Nobody got hurt. And they haven't caught him yet. In fact, the detectives just left here about an hour ago."

"Why were they at your house?" asked Carol.

As much as Mary Ellen dreaded going over everything that had happened, she knew her parents, especially her father, wouldn't quit probing until they knew everything. And since Ashley had left the room, she proceeded to tell them the entire story and how she and Ashley were upset and somewhat scared.

"You want us to come up there?" asked Wesley. "We can stay with you until Zach gets home?"

"Poppy!" said Mimi in a gently scolding manner. "I'm sorry, Mary Ellen, but your father has an epidural scheduled tomorrow morning at 7 a.m. We've been waiting four months for him to have this procedure. He's already canceled once before. I'm not letting him do that again. Plus I'm tired of hearing about how his back aches after he's played golf or been on one of his *skydiving* trips."

"Can't blame a man for trying," said Wesley who would have been happy to cancel again.

"Honey, why don't y'all come down here?" asked Mimi.

"No mom. I've got work and Ashley's got school. But thanks."

"Hey! Where is Ashley?" asked Wesley. "Did I run her off?"

"No, daddy. I think this robbery has gotten the best of her. She's been upset ever since the police officer picked her up from school. She probably didn't want to hear about it again. Look, I need to go check on her. Call me tomorrow… after your procedure. Things will be better here."

Both parties hung up with Wesley mad at himself for upsetting his granddaughter.

Mary Ellen closed her iPad, upset over the way she had handled the robbery fallout. She had not handled it well, primarily because she was apprehensive herself and it had affected Ashley more than she thought it would. She was about to go see her daughter when her cell phone rang. It was Dom.

"Hey. Just checking up on you two guys. How are y'all holding up?"

"I wish I could say everything's fine, but it's not. I must have underestimated the maturity level of twelve-year-olds… at least my twelve-year-old. In hindsight, I shouldn't have burdened her with *all* of today's events. Maybe I should have tempered them some. But I didn't want her to hear them on TV or from some of her friends. So that's why I told her everything. Not only that, I think she's feeding off my fears. Dom… this has been so frustrating."

"Mary Ellen… listen to me. Don't beat yourself up. Nobody can anticipate how anyone would react to something like the robbery or the threat. You do the best you can. I would have done exactly what you did."

"You're kind to say that."

"No… I mean it. That's the reason why I called. If you need me for anything… a sounding board, a friendly ear, whatever… call me. And I mean that."

"I will. I probably should go check on Ashley." They said their goodbyes and hung up. Talking to Dom had been comforting. She was glad he had called.

Mary Ellen found Ashley in her bed with the pillow over her head. Her FaceTime idea had backfired. Instead of distracting her daughter, the online session with her parents had made it worse. Usually, she could count on her dad to tell one of his long, but funny stories. How could she know that the robbery in Atlanta would be on Augusta's TV news and that her father would be watching it? In retrospect, she should have called her parents and told them about the robbery before Facetiming with Ashley.

Mary Ellen took a peek under the pillow. Only when she offered to order pizza did her little bunny come out of her rabbit hole.

CHAPTER 15

Mary Ellen lay in her bed reading her Kindle when she heard running footsteps coming from the hall. Within seconds, Ashley flung open the door and ran to her mother's bedside. She was crying and the fear in her eyes was evident.

"Oh, baby, baby. What's the matter?" asked Mary Ellen, softly, as her daughter crawled into her mother's bed and pulled the cover up to her chin.

"I thought I heard something," cried the young girl. "And when I looked out my window, I thought I saw somebody."

"Are you sure it just wasn't your imagination, maybe a bad dream or… maybe one of the shrubs?"

"I don't know. Can I sleep with you tonight? Pleeeassseeeee!"

Before Mary Ellen could answer, Ashley ducked under the covers.

"Yes, sweetie."

Mary Ellen started to lift the covers when her cell phone rang, the timing of the call making both girls jump. While Ashley pulled the pillow out from under her head and cloaked herself in more bedding, Mary Ellen picked up her phone. It was Zach.

"I couldn't sleep thinking about this robbery thing, so I thought I'd check on Ashley. She doing OK?"

Zach was only telling half the truth. He couldn't sleep because his blond bedmate had been called into work which meant time and a half for her and an early ride back to the truck stop for him.

"No. Can you call me back? I'm trying to calm her down. She thinks she saw someone outside her window. Every little noise outside the house …"

"Did you go *look*?" interrupted Zach, obviously irritated.

"No. I'm sure it's just her imagination."

"For crying out loud, woman. Use your head. Did you ever stop to think that she could be right? That maybe she did see something? Hear something? Hell. It could be a peeping tom. Some neighborhood boys looking in her window. Go outside and look. Now! And take my Glock."

Zach knew about peeping toms, having been one himself when he was in his early teens.

Mary Ellen lifted the bedding from Ashley's head.

"Honey, your daddy's on the phone. He wants me to go outside and make sure nothing's there. I'll be right back,"

"No. Please don't leave me."

"Your daddy wants me to go look. I'll only be a minute. Here. Talk to him. I promise I won't be gone but just a minute." Mary Ellen handed her daughter the phone then headed out of the bedroom before Ashley had time to protest.

"What's wrong with my little princess," asked Zach.

Ashley then proceeded to tell her dad everything that had happened to her including the police, the detectives and the robbery as she remembered it including the pictures and the note.

When Mary Ellen returned, she saw Ashley sitting up in bed with the phone to her ear. She was listening but not talking. Mary Ellen walked over to the bed and seeing she had her daughter's attention, shook her head and quietly said, "Nothing, honey. I didn't see anything. It was probably just the wind blowing the shrubs."

"Here… daddy wants to speak to you," said Ashley and handed the phone back to her mother and then slid down under the covers.

"So you had to tell our young, innocent daughter *everything* including the pictures and the note. Dammit woman, what kind of idiot are you?" he asked, yelling so loud that Mary Ellen dropped her phone. As she picked it up, she could hear Zach still yelling, almost screaming, into the phone.

"… answer me," he demanded, but Mary Ellen had not heard the entire sentence.

"I… I…"

"You have no answer because you are a complete moron. Worse than my old lady," he said, referring to his own mother. "So what about the police? Have you seen them yet? Have you told Ashley they were going to patrol the neighborhood?"

"Yes. We haven't seen them, but we haven't been looking for them either."

"Well, don't just sit on your fat ass. Get on the phone. Call them. Ask them where the hell they are. Better yet, call one of the detectives."

"I will. Soon as we hang up."

"You let me know what you find out. I need to know if *I* have to get involved. Now put Ashley back on the phone."

"Ashley, honey," said Mary Ellen, gently shaking her daughter who was still under all of her security bedding with her eyes closed and her fingers in her ears so she couldn't hear her parents arguing. "Your daddy wants to talk to you again."

Ashley's head and then arms slowly appeared and she took the phone.

"Hello, daddy."

"I'm sorry you're having a bad night, princess. I wish I was there to protect you. I would make things better."

"I don't like it when you and mommy argue."

"We weren't arguing, baby. We were just discussing things. That's what married people do."

"Bye, daddy. Here's mommy."

"Good night, princess," said Zach, but Ashley was already under the covers.

Mary Ellen put the phone to her ear just in time to hear her husband's sweet, tender goodbye meant for Ashley. It was quite a contrast from how he talked to her.

"I'm back," she said.

"Let me know if you have any problems with the police," he barked. Then he hung up. No *goodbye*, no *love you*, no *see you soon*.

Mary Ellen lifted the cover on Ashley.

"Honey, I've got to go to the kitchen for a minute. Are you going to be OK while I'm gone?"

The little girl slowly nodded her head and then pulled the covers and pillow back over her head.

Mary Ellen got up, put on her robe and bedroom slippers and walked to the kitchen. On the counter, in her purse, she found the business cards of both detectives. She picked the first one – Detective Jacobs – and dialed his number. The call was answered on the second ring.

"Detective Jacobs. This is Mary Ellen Ferguson. I hate to bother you, but my daughter and I have been having a rough night. Especially my daughter. I can't seem to get her to calm down. Right now, she's in my bed with the covers pulled over her face. She hasn't done that in years. I know it's my fault. I probably told her more than I should about the robbery. But I can't undo what's been done. You or your partner said that the police were going to be patrolling my house tonight. If you don't mind, could you have them drive up my driveway and park for a few minutes? Maybe flash their headlights so I'll know they're there? Hopefully, if Ashley sees that the police are keeping a close watch on us, she might not be so antsy. Nor would I."

"That's not a problem. I'll reach out to the Cobb Police and have them stop by your house. Better yet, why don't I come over and monitor your house. I can sit outside in my car or I can stay inside your house, whichever makes you and your daughter feel most comfortable."

Mary Ellen considered the offer. Having the detective watch the house would certainly make them feel more secure than just having a patrol car swing by the house a couple of times during the night. But she wasn't sure she wanted a stranger in the house. Then she remembered Dom's offer. Ashley knew Dom and liked him. She had spent many summer days at the bank when she couldn't stay at the Oliver's. Having him come over would be less stressful for everyone.

"That's very kind. I don't know why I didn't think of this before I called you, but I think I can get a friend to come over. Ashley would be more comfortable with someone she knows. Can I call you back if that doesn't work out?"

The detective happily agreed as did Dom. Mary Ellen then texted Zach that a detective was coming over. Not to worry. Ashley was fine. The last thing she wanted to do was to talk to Zach again.

CHAPTER 16

Dom left his condominium in midtown Atlanta within minutes after his call from Mary Ellen. He carried with him a small overnight bag with a change of clothes and his dopp kit. Before leaving, he told his partner where he was going and why. Then using the GPS in his 2016 Porsche Boxster, he made the eighteen miles trip up I-75 north in less than thirty minutes. It was fast and easy with the 265 horsepower engine in his newly acquired used sports car.

As Dom turned on to Mason Street, he down-shifted the car and coasted all the way down to Mary Ellen's house and into her driveway announcing his arrival with the sound of the car's decelerating high-performance engine. The motorcycle-like noise startled both Mary Ellen and Ashley negating all the hard work Mary Ellen had done to calm her daughter.

"Probably someone turning around, using our driveway," offered Mary Ellen, trying to keep her own emotions in check. Without waiting for a reply, she headed into the living room with Ashley close behind. From the window, she saw her bald-headed boss exiting from the driver's side of a highly polished sports car. The sight was totally unexpected. So un-Dom-like. When she had asked Dom to stay at her house, she hadn't even considered the fact that he didn't even own a car. He either walked to work or rode his bike unless it was raining. Then he took Uber.

"Dom! Yes!" said Ashley when she saw him and the bright yellow sports car in the lighted driveway…Mary Ellen couldn't keep up with her daughter as she ran out the front door.

"This is so cool," she exclaimed, quickly walking around the car, taking in all of the car's sleek design. "Is this yours?"

Dom nodded. He was all smiles.

"Can I get inside?"

Dom unlocked the door with his fob and opened it as if he were a valet, bowing as he did.

Mary Ellen took it all in. The look on both Ashley and Dom's faces was priceless. She had made the right decision in asking Dom. He was more than a boss. He was like a mother hen with a roost of baby chickens to all his employees. Always ready to listen. Always ready to give a helping hand.

"I didn't even know you had a car," said Mary Ellen. "When did you get it?"

"A couple of weeks ago. I've always wanted a Porsche and now I have one. Kind of like a mid-life crisis," said Dom who was far from mid-life.

"Well, it's beautiful and you deserve it."

Once Ashley had played with every knob, looked at every dial, and had Dom lower and then raise the convertible top a couple of times, the newness had worn off. They all went inside, found a movie on Netflix, microwaved some popcorn and all huddled on the couch until Ashley couldn't keep her eyes open. Dom picked her up and with Mary Ellen's help carried her back to her bedroom and into bed. There was no fight or fright left in the little girl.

Back in the den, Mary Ellen saw Dom reach down and grab his overnight bag.

"I probably should go. I think she's down for the night."

"Please don't go. If she wakes, it starts all over again. Plus I'm a little nervous myself."

"What about Zach? I know he doesn't like me. If he were to find out that I…"

"To be truthful, I don't care what he thinks. He's not here and I'm handling the situation the best I can. Anyway, he thinks a detective is coming over, so there's nothing for you to worry about."

"Look… I'm not worried about me. I'm worried about you." Dom had seen the results of Zach's physical abuse.

Mary Ellen couldn't help but laugh. "Isn't it ironic that we are more worried about the repercussions from my husband than the thief?"

CHAPTER 17

The loud roar of the sports car did not go unnoticed by the Oliver's. By now, the Colonel's wife, Betty, was on board as a member of the Colonel's surveillance team. Just as her husband, she was doing this for Mary Ellen and Ashley, not Zach. Being retired, other than walking the dog, going to the grocery store, tending the garden, and visiting doctors, the duo had nothing else to do to pass their time. So when Zach asked them to keep an eye on his wife and daughter, the Colonel, and then his wife, jumped at the chance.

With the first sound of the unfamiliar, loud muffled roar, the race was on to the front of the house where a pair of binoculars lay on the window's ledge. It was easily won by Betty as the Colonel struggled to get out of his recliner. As she surveyed the Ferguson's house with the binoculars, the Colonel waited patiently for his turn while looking over her shoulders. Betty's eyes were instantly drawn to the driveway where she saw Ashley running around a yellow sports car with her mother standing on the front porch, smiling and talking to a bald-headed man.

"Take a look, honey. I've never seen that man before, but he doesn't look too threatening to me."

The Colonel took the binoculars and focused them on the activity in the driveway and more especially on the bald-headed man.

"Nope. Never seen him before in my life. But you can never be too sure." Then he zoomed in on Mary Ellen's face. She did not appear to be afraid.

"Are you going to call Zach?"

"Of course. I told him I would so I am."

The Colonel pulled out his phone and hit the speed dial he'd set up for Zach's cell.

By now Zach was laying in the cab of his truck trying to get back to sleep. He had just dozed off when the phone rang. He recognized the Colonel's number and answered on the first ring.

"Zach, you asked me to call if I saw anything suspicious," said the Colonel. Betty had her ear close to the phone to hear the whole conversation as the Colonel sometimes forgot some of the details. Sometimes the most important details. "From what I've just witnessed, I wasn't sure a call was warranted, but I decided to err on the side of caution. We just saw a man over at your house that neither Betty nor I recognized. But he didn't appear to be of the threatening nature. In fact, he looked to be a friend. So that's the reason for my hesitation, but I said I would call and I have."

"Thanks for calling, Colonel. You did exactly what I asked. I mean, you can't be too careful nowadays. That man is a detective. Ashley was really scared, so Mary Ellen called the police... well... the detective and he agreed to come over and watch the house. She texted me. That's how I know. He's supposed to be staying the night so don't be alarmed if the car's still there in the morning."

"That's good. I'm glad to hear that. That'll put Betty's and my mind at ease. You know we love those two."

"Yes. I know. If you don't mind staying on guard for the next few days, I'd really appreciate it. I'll be home Saturday."

"That won't be a problem. I'm not going to let anything happen to my two little ladies. The Colonel is on duty." Betty was pointing to herself, mouthing, *me too.*

Zach felt like doing a mock salute.

"Thank you, sir. I owe you. Look... I've got to get on the road, so I'm gonna sign off. Can you text me when the detective leaves? I want to make sure he stays the night. If not, I'm gonna be pissed. I want to know that my little princess is safe. Uh... you do know how to text, don't you?"

"Son, I might be old, but I'm no idiot. Of course I know how to text," barked the Colonel.

"I'm sorry... I..."

"Forget it. I said I would keep you informed and I will."

"Thank you, sir. I do appreciate it. Goodbye."

The call ended and the Colonel looked at Betty.

"You get all that?" he asked. "He said the man..."

"Yes, dear. I got it. No need to repeat. He's a detective. That's all I need to know."

Knowing the Ferguson's were well protected, the two observers headed off to bed.

John Thomas

Zack laid back down in his tiny bed in the back of his cab. One o'clock would be here soon. Then back on the road. Driving and worrying were not a good thing, not with eleven hours and over five hundred miles to travel. But with the detective there and the Colonel keeping watch, he wasn't worried. His princess was in safe hands.

Wednesday, August 7, 2019

ATLANTA, GEORGIA

CHAPTER 18

Mary Ellen woke with a start. She had been awake, off and on, most of the night and had just finally fallen sound asleep when she heard the staccato beep of the alarm from a cell phone outside her bedroom door. It had to be Dom's. He was in the guest bedroom directly across from her bedroom. She quickly glanced at her phone which lay on her bedside table. 7:30 a.m. She pushed back the cover, put on her robe and bedroom shoes then headed to the kitchen. Twenty minutes later, Dom appeared, fully dressed.

"How'd you sleep?" he asked.

"Sleep? What's that?" she asked rhetorically. "Can I fix you some breakfast?"

"No. I'm good. I'll get something on the way to the office. I've got the auditors coming in at ten this morning. So what about Ashley? Is she going to school today?"

"I don't know. I'm thinking that she would feel safer being around her friends. I'm going to encourage her to go. But I'll leave it up to her. Let me go get her up."

As she turned from the kitchen into the den, she nearly bumped into Ashley who was already fully dressed. There would be no fretting over any decision. Ashley had already made it.

"Hey sweetheart. I didn't hear you get up. I see you're already dressed. I wasn't real sure you would want to go today."

"I can't let a little ol' bank robbery keep me away from my school work."

Mary Ellen laughed. She knew that Ashley just wanted to tell her friends everything she knew about the robbery. And her mother was like a celebrity now that she had been seen on the 5 o'clock and 11 o'clock news walking out the back door of the bank talking to a policeman.

"If it is okay with you, I'm gonna walk you to the bus stop," said Mary Ellen knowing that her daughter would rather die than be seen by any of her friends being escorted to the bus stop by her mother. Not cool. The teasing would be relentless. But Mary Ellen's maternal instincts outweighed any possible embarrassment that Ashley might endure. She had to protect her daughter at any cost.

Before Ashley could answer, Dom offered a suggestion.

"Instead of the bus, how about I drive you to school."

"Oh yes! Yes! Is that okay, mom? Pleeeasse."

"Go for it. Thank you, Dom. You're a Godsend."

Ashley hugged her mom, hugged Dominick, grabbed her book bag and headed out to the car.

Dom lifted the key fob and hit the UNLOCK button on his car. He turned to Mary Ellen and asked, "How about you? Are you going to be okay staying home alone?"

"Actually, I've got plans. I need to get someone to look at my car. I barely got it started yesterday when I left work. I certainly don't want to be left stranded."

"If it doesn't start, call me. We'll figure something out. Something that doesn't involve your husband."

"You're a good man, Dom. The world would be a better place if it had more Dominick Garcia's. Thank you,"

Never one for compliments, Dominick's face as well as his bald head turned blood red with embarrassment. He turned and left without saying a word.

CHAPTER 19

Colonel Oliver and Ike crossed the street and walked up the sidewalk toward the Ferguson's house. Ike led the way sniffing every shrub and tree within the leash's maximum length. The school bus was due shortly. He and Betty decided that he should time his morning walk to coincide with the bus arrival just in case the motorcyclist came by again. They both doubted that would happen, but if it did, he would be there to take a picture of its license plate. *Fool me once*, he thought. He heard a chirp coming from the sports car parked in the Ferguson's driveway and then he saw Ashley run out the side door and get into the passenger's seat of the car. She was smiling. The bald-headed man followed close behind as did Mary Ellen carrying a paper bag.

"Hey! You forgot your lunch." She handed the lunch to Dom's outreach hand who then passed it over to Ashley.

Dom started the engine and revved up the motor a couple of times looking at Ashley as he did. His 12-year old passenger had a big grin on her face as did the driver. Then he had Ashley lower the convertible top. As Dom slowly back out of the driveway, Ashley and Dom waved to Mary Ellen who returned the favor. She was glad to see her daughter so happy after yesterday's troubles.

As she was turning to go back into her house, she saw the Colonel and Ike walking up the sidewalk.

"Good morning, Colonel," said Mary Ellen in a cheerful voice. She, too, was in a good mood seeing the positive influence Dom had had on Ashley.

"G'morning," he responded as he walked up the Ferguson's driveway toward Mary Ellen. While he didn't look or sound pleasant, this was as good as it got from the Colonel.

"I guess you heard about what happened at the bank?" she asked and then walked over to the old man, bent down, patted Ike on the head and then stood up.

"Yes ma'am. Saw it on the news. Are you and Ashley doing okay?"

"We're doing the best we can. I'm sorry I didn't return Betty's call, but I was having a bad day and Ashley was scared to death with Zack out of town. That's why that man was here. You might have seen her leaving with him just a few minutes ago. He's a uh… detective." Then Mary Ellen remembered the two detectives, Jacobs and Marlowe, had been to the Oliver's house and they would easily remember either man. "Ashley was having anxiety issues with this robbery thing and Detective Jacobs was kind enough to get Cobb County to send out one of their detectives. I thought with him here, it would calm Ashley down and it did. He even took her to school."

"I saw her get in the car. She seemed happy enough, so that was the right thing to do. I applaud our police force. You never hear the good things they do. Just the bad."

Mary Ellen hated lying to the Colonel. He and his wife were such good friends. But Zach could never know about Dom staying over. She hated to think about what he would do to her if he did find out.

Quickly changing the subject, Mary Ellen asked, "So did you and Ike oversleep this morning? I don't usually see y'all out this late."

About that time, the school bus pulled up in front of Mary Ellen's house, waited a couple of minutes, then not seeing any riders, drove off. The Colonel looked up and down the street until the bus was out of earshot.

"I don't know if you know this or not, but Betty and I got a visit from a couple of detectives yesterday asking me all kinds of questions. I told them that I had seen a guy on a motorcycle taking pictures of your house. They think it was the same guy who robbed your bank. That's why Ike and I are out for his morning constitution so late. If that jerk comes back again, I'm gonna be here…get his license and call the police. I can't let anything happen to my girls."

Mary Ellen almost broke down in tears as she heard the concern in the Colonel's voice. If only her own husband was as concerned.

"Thank you." She then leaned over and kissed the old man on the cheek. She then turned and went back into the house.

The Colonel took little time returning to his house where he unleashed the dog, grabbed his cell phone and texted Zach.

All is well. Cobb County detective pulled an all-nighter. He also drove Ashley to school. Colonel Robert Oliver.

CHAPTER 20

After a hard workout at the gym, Agent Daniel Whitehead headed to the FBI field office on Flowers Road in Chamblee, Georgia. Knowing Marlowe and Jacobs' reputation for promptness and attention to detail, he fully expected to have a computer link to their reports, notes, interviews and any new surveillance CDs when he got to the office. He was not disappointed when he logged into his computer. Already in his inbox was an email from Jacobs and an APD link and password.

Daniel grabbed a cup of coffee, put on his glasses and began reading through all the documents and watching the videos. Other than the fact that a man by the name of Colonel Robert Oliver had actually seen the robber taking photos of the Ferguson's house, everything paralleled the information he'd retrieved from the FBI's internal information technology program called SENTINEL. The disguise, the note, the pictures, the motorcycle – all the same. Without question, the bank robbery was the work of the English Bandit. He entered the information on Colonel Robert Oliver into the system and printed a list of the cities where banks were suspected to have been robbed by the English Bandit.

Next, he printed out a map of the United States and began marking the cities of the robberies with a large ink dot. All were in the southeast. Assuming that the robber rode his motorcycle from his base of operations to and from the bank sites using no other means of transportation, more than likely the robber lived within 300 miles of each of the cities. On his map, Daniel drew a large circle around all of the cities that had dots on his map. Using the scientific eyeballing methodology, it appeared that the approximate center of the circle was Charlotte, North Carolina. It was the only major city without a visit by the English Bandit. This omission made for at least two possibilities. Either the Queen City, named after one of 'Mad King' George III's wives, was the robber's home base or it just hadn't made it to the top of the robber's hit list. His gut feel was the former.

Daniel took a swig of his lukewarm coffee and then leaned back in his chair to think about how to attack this case. So far, no other agent had made any headway. This was no ordinary robber. He was very smart and cunning. It was going to take more than good old fashion detective work to bring him to justice. It was going to take a misstep on the thief's part. Daniel wanted this one badly. He had yet to make a real mark as an FBI agent which was so unlike his stellar career as a detective with the Washington DC police. He wasn't looking for accolades, attaboys, recognitions or commendations. He just wanted to pull his own weight.

His mind turned to the getaway vehicle – the motorcycle. From the videos and documents provided by Detectives Jacobs and Marlowe and the information from SENTINEL's database, he learned that the robber initially rode a 2000 Harley-Davidson Sportster in his earlier heists but had changed in 2017 to a 2017 Harley-Davidson Street Glide. Clear images of the license plate for both bikes had been captured from several surveillance videos, but in every robbery including yesterday's heist, the bikes had used different license plates and a search of DMV records showed that the plates were either stolen or somehow counterfeited.

Since early 2015, a rumor had been circulating on the internet that all registered motorcycle owners were classified by the FBI as gang members and the agency had a database of the bikes and their owners. Not true. There was no government national database of motorcycles available that he could search. Daniel felt he had reached a standstill. With no more than the make and model of the Harley, he was heading down a long, arduous, never-ending path of trying to match the bike to an owner. He felt he needed a different approach, a different perspective. All of the other agents were out on assignments leaving him the choice between the Special Agent in Charge (his boss) and the secretary/receptionist. He chose neither. Instead, he picked up his cell and called his former D.C. homicide partner, Johnny Williams. They had worked as a team for nearly seven years until by mutual agreement, Daniel took a promotion to Captain and Williams retired. Until then, they had been the *go-to* team of the 5th District.

"Danny boy. So what do I owe the pleasure?" asked Williams who had to step off his treadmill to answer his cell. Williams was the only person to ever call Daniel Whitehead, Danny boy. It had been nearly six months since Daniel last talked to his ex-partner. Yet when they talked, it seemed just like yesterday.

"Just wanted to pass something by you. See if you can see something or think of something that I've missed… that is if your brain hasn't atrophied."

"I might be retired, but I ain't dead. I'm as good as ever. In fact, better. By the way, did you know me and the ex-wife hooked back up? After three years of living together, we retied the knot."

"Yeah. I heard. Her brain must have atrophied," said Daniel hearing Williams laugh. "So how'd that happen? I thought y'all decided to just to be friends."

"If you must know, I think I became easier to live with once I retired and wasn't living my cases. Plus, you should see me now. I'm down eighty-five pounds. I'm really taking care of myself. I'm eating healthy, exercising with hand weights and walking on the treadmill. But to be perfectly honest, I'm miserable. Just frigging miserable. Take my advice, keep working as long as you can, especially if you enjoy it. Hell, this crap about living on 80% of your salary is just a bunch of cockamamie. We're lucky if we get to eat out once a month. And travel? The only travel we do is to and from the doctors' offices."

"So you miss me?"

"Hell yes, I miss you. I even miss being called 'Wrinkles'."

Wrinkles was short for Wrinkle Butt. Everybody in the department called Johnny, *Wrinkles*. The nickname was no secret. In fact, he found it amusing and wasn't offended when people addressed him by the moniker. No one ever owned up to being the source of the nickname, but Johnny always suspected an earlier partner - a young, ambitious detective named Jason White (now a bigwig with the CIA).

"So how can I help you?"

Johnny Williams was one of D.C.'s finest detectives with a keen instinct for 'reading' a crime scene, interpreting evidence and seeing the unseen. Only his inability to handle internal politics kept him from moving up the ranks. He always said what was on his mind which wasn't always politically correct and that kept him in the doghouse with the suits. He and Daniel had worked well together as a team solving numerous high-profile cases including the Dupont Circle murders which made national headlines and earned them the Co-Investigators of the Year for the MPD (Metropolitan Police Department).

Daniel quickly brought Williams up to speed on the English Robber and his eight years of bank robberies.

"So no prints or DNA?"

"None. Like he was never there."

"And his first robbery was back in 2012?"

"Yes. At least with this English Bandit disguise."

"And never any alterations to his disguise?"

"Not that we're aware of."

"And always using the dye-packs and a motor bike… a Harley and wearing a biker's disguise?"

"Yes, at least with the dye-packs. We've only found five surveillance videos with the biker disguise, dating back to 2016, but we feel sure it's the same person."

"But always a Harley?"

"Yes. But two different ones. Early on he rode a 2000 Harley-Davidson Sportster. In 2017, he changed to a 2017 Harley-Davidson Street Glide."

"What is the total amount he's stolen over the past seven years?"

"In the neighborhood of $110,000 give or take a thou."

"How much did he take in this last robbery?"

"Around five grand. One teller. No vault."

"And the robbery before that. Same questions."

"Just over four grand, one teller and nothing from the vault."

"What was the largest amount stolen and what year?"

"$42,000 in December 2012."

"And how much is a new Harley-Davidson? Just an estimate."

"Over twenty grand."

"So what's his motive? Why is he robbing banks? It just can't be for the money. Not if he's driving a $20,000 motorcycle."

"Good question. And he certainly doesn't fit the profile of most bank robbers. You think he's doing it to get his jollies?" asked Daniel.

"I think… yes. I don't see any other reason. Maybe not early on. If he took over forty grand in 2012 he needed the money. To get that much money in one robbery, he'd have to pull from a bunch of teller drawers and the vault. And that takes time and is very risky. Now it looks like he's in and out. Takes what he can get. I think he's just satisfying an itch."

"Wrinkles, if that's his motive… satisfying an itch, it's gonna make cracking this case even that much harder. Maybe impossible."

"Yeah. Someone who's desperate is apt to make mistakes. From what you say, I don't see this dude making any kind of mistakes. He's got this thing down to a fine science."

Both men paused to think. The dead air bothered neither man.

Johnny Williams was first to speak. "Okay, let's go down a different line of thinking. In your case summary, you said that the thief had robbed banks in five states and ten different cities. Have you mapped that out?"

"Yes. And it appears that Charlotte, North Carolina seems to be the center point."

Daniel read off the names of the ten different cities where banks had been robbed by the English Bandit including Atlanta.

"So no bank in Charlotte?"

"No. Not yet."

"Charlotte makes sense. But as crafty as this thief seems to be, he could be throwing you a curve ball, leaving you open to think that he lives in or near Charlotte. Where was his first robbery?"

"Memphis. At least it's his first one in his English Bandit disguise."

"Well, that's another option. Usually, a thief robs banks in the city he's most familiar. Do you have access to DMV records?"

"We can pull driver's license photos to do facial recognition, but that's about it. I thought about requesting an Excel spreadsheet of 2016 and 2019 DMV motorcycle records and then sorting them by name looking for the same owner for those two particular bikes. But from what state? Tennessee? North Carolina? Georgia? He could have lived in multiple states. I think they're too many variables to go down that path."

"Yeah. Probably just a waste of time," answered Johnny, bummed that he hadn't come up with anything. "Maybe my brain *has* atrophied. I'm not being any help to you at all. Maybe I have been away from the trenches too long."

"I think not. So far, there have been ten different FBI agents looking into this serial robber, including me, and nothing. The guy is very clever."

"Maybe the guy isn't just clever. Maybe he knows the inner workings of a bank. Maybe he works or worked at a bank. For example, the way he used the dye-packs. He had to know how they worked… the delay and the trigger. And he obviously knows when's the best time to rob banks. And maybe he knows which banks have security guards and which ones don't."

"I think you're on to something. Bankers are not necessarily rich, even those with lofty-sounding titles. Maybe this guy got into a jam… gambling, living beyond his means, family issues… whatever and figured a bank heist would be a quick fix. And then he got hooked on the adrenalin high. Couldn't kick the habit. Being a banker or ex-banker makes sense. But it doesn't get me any closer to breaking the case."

"Any chance he robs the same bank but different branches in different cities?"

"No. I checked on that. But now that you mention it, it does appear that he robs small independent banks."

"Maybe because they have fewer customers which means fewer witnesses."

"Good point. I'll make sure that info gets distributed out to the banks."

Again there was silence as both men mulled over in their minds everything they had talked about hoping a light bulb would go off. But both came up empty.

"Daniel, I'm sorry I couldn't be of any more help. Let me sleep on it and if I come up with something else, I'll give you a ring."

"Johnny, it's been good talking to you. I do miss the good old days and I miss having you as my partner. Call me anytime. You've got my number."

"Back at you, Danny boy."

Daniel hit the red *off* button on his phone and set it on his desk. He leaned back in his chair again to rethink his and Wrinkles' conversation. It had been good talking to his old friend. But nothing had come of the conversation other than the pleasure of talking to the old detective. As far as he was concerned, this case would probably go into the unsolved case file just like the English Bandit's previous heists.

CHAPTER 21

Finding Scott Burnett, Sid Patel and Tim Martin in the company's breakroom at 6 a.m., loading up on coffee, was normal. All three men were extremely dedicated to the success of their business. Not only did they enjoy the fruits of their labor, they enjoyed the labor itself. It also gave them two hours of private time to prepare for their weekly huddle. The meeting would normally have been held on Monday, but because of Scott's absence, it was changed to Wednesday.

Scott quickly prepped himself for the meeting then scoured the online edition of *The Charlotte Observer* for any details of his robbery. Finding none, he googled 'Atlanta robbery.' He had five hits, the AJC (*The Atlanta Journal-Constitution),* WSB-TV, CBS-46, FOX5 Atlanta, and 11Alive. Each website detailed the robbery identifying the thief as the English Bandit, a known multi-state serial bank robber. The articles did not disclose the amount of money taken, but did say that the robber was not armed, no one was harmed and he escaped on foot. Scott was relieved that there had yet to be a connection linking his robber disguise with his biker disguise.

By 8 o'clock, all available auditors, security specialists and the three partners were assembled in the large conference/meeting room with the early-comers sitting around a long oblong table and the stragglers either standing or sitting in the periphery. Over coffee and doughnuts, they began a review of the previous week's financial numbers and the anticipated quarterly bonuses. Everyone who worked at BPM received a bonus based on the previous quarter's net profit. The bonus was based solely on the number of years that an employee had worked with the company and not position or salary. The partners felt this rewarded those employees who labored through the early years of the company's struggles at less than stellar pay. It also created deep loyalty. The anticipated bonus was larger than expected setting off a lot of glad-handing, high fives, slaps on the backs and a few 'hallelujahs' from those who had already spent it.

Next, each of the auditors and security specialists spent no more than five minutes discussing issues with their current projects, fixes and any additional manpower requirements. It was the opinion of the partners that meetings, especially long meetings, took away from productive worktime and so they pushed to keep the meetings to no more than an hour. It was at these meetings that future work assignments were made.

Once the company-wide meeting was over, the three partners had their own private meeting which generally lasted about thirty minutes.

"So how was your biking trek?" asked Martin, eldest of the partners.

"It was a flop. Never made it to Canton," lied Scott. He had memorized the story he had told Anne, his fiancé, so not to tell conflicting stories should he be asked. "Only got as far as the campsite at Beckley, West Virginia. The next morning, my Harley wouldn't start. Had to get AAA to tow it to a nearby dealership. Cost me over $1200 to fix the damn thing, so I'm selling it. Anne is thrilled."

"Well, we are, too," said Sid Patel, the youngest of the three partners.

"I see that I drew the short straw on the bank in Georgia," said Scott, changing the subject. As far as he was concerned, the less he lied, the less he had to remember what he had lied about.

"Well, you weren't here and you weren't answering your cell. So…," answered Martin. Then continuing, "Anyway, you're not going to believe how we got the lead in Georgia. An old Wharton buddy of mine (Wharton School of Finance, University of Pennsylvania), Rodney Pafford at the Reserve said this bank in Georgia… uh… Roswell Guardian, called him after a bank holdup in Atlanta yesterday. He said they were looking for CompTIA security references. Even though physical robberies and IT heists are not the same, he said they got spooked and wanted to audit their bank's computer systems and make sure they were not exposed to hackers, viruses or hostile computer takeover. Rodney said he would have just given him our company's name, but corporate policy required him to give out at least three. But he did say he put us at the top of the list. And that's why I took the Hendersonville bank. With me being his friend, I decided to recuse myself from that opportunity so there wouldn't be any look of impropriety… if we got the job. Otherwise, I'd loved to have gone to Atlanta."

"You did the right thing. And I don't mind going to Atlanta."

"Look. While you are there, if you have time, ask him out for dinner. I'm not sure he can accept. But it's worth a try."

"No problem. You think he'd mind if Anne tagged along? I've made tentative plans for her to come down with me Friday night assuming I can rearrange my meeting with Independent Security Trust. We'd like to try and see *CATS* at the Fox Theatre either Saturday or Sunday. That's assuming I can get some tickets from one of the ticket scalpers."

"If you got the money, the scalpers have the tickets," replied Sid.

"Don't tell our wives. We'll never hear the end of it," added Tim.

"It's kind of a peace offering. See, I forgot to call Anne on my trip," confessed Scott realizing the can of worms he'd just opened up.

"That's bad. Real bad. Why didn't you call her? Having too much fun?" asked Tim.

"No. Forgot my stupid phone. I was in such a hurry Sunday morning to get to the departure point that I completely forgot about it." Before he could segue to another subject, Sid began his mini-interrogation.

"Why didn't you use another biker's phone or one of the guys at the repair shop or buy a burner phone?"

"I don't know. Just call me stupid. I guess I was so concerned about catching up with the other bikers that my mind went blank."

"Dude. If a trip to Atlanta and a couple of tickets to *CATS* gets you out of the doghouse, then you're getting off easy," offered Sid who was very familiar with the doghouse.

"And don't worry about my friend at the Reserve," said Martin. "If it works out that you can take him out to dinner and Anne won't mind, then have at it. But take care of Anne first. She's a keeper. Plus, with her being a trial lawyer, if you ever decided to rob or kill one of our customers, she'd come in real handy." Both Martin and Sid laughed.

Scott said nothing nor was he smiling.

CHAPTER 22

Unlike this morning, the look on Mary Ellen's face as she sat in the Pep Boys customer lounge was now one of despair. She knew that Zach was going to read her the riot act when he found out that someone other than himself had worked on their car. But there was no way of covering up the bill from Pep Boys. Zach audited the credit card charges, bank checks and debits, and the emergency cash he kept at home. He was a complete control freak especially when it came to money. If there was a charge on a credit card or a check written on their joint bank account, he would know about it as soon as it hit the account as he had alerts on everything. But she couldn't risk her car dying and being stranded. Not with everything that had happened yesterday. And especially if it meant having her daughter who was frightened enough being left alone at home. Whatever it cost, it would be worth Zach's abuse.

She looked at her watch. She had been waiting for nearly an hour on the auto mechanic to diagnose her 2005 Toyota Camry. To his credit, the store manager had given her fair warning of the wait. There were two other cars ahead of her. She prayed it was just a battery. That *had* to be the reason why her car was reluctant to start. Her worries hit overdrive when her phone rang with Zach's ringtone. She waited until the fourth ring to answer hoping he'd hang up. He didn't.

"So how's my little princess?" Mary Ellen knew Zach meant Ashley. Not her. The bank robber could have tied her up, raped her, blackened both eyes and broken both hands and he wouldn't have asked how *she* was doing. Love was no longer the cornerstone of their relationship. Ashley was now the only reason they stayed married.

"Ashley's fine. She even went to school today. Her idea."

"So she wasn't afraid to take the bus?" asked Zach knowing from the Colonel's text that she had ridden to school with the detective. He just wanted to see if Mary Ellen would lie. He seemed to relish catching her in a lie. It seemed to justify *his* lies and infidelities.

"She didn't take the bus. The er… uh detective took her to school."

"The detective took her? Why'd he take her? Why didn't she take the bus? Do you think you told her too much about the robbery? Got her scared of waiting at the bus stop?"

"You've got it all wrong. Ashley wasn't afraid to take the bus. It so happens that Ashley and the detective hit it off last night and he was just being kind."

"Wait a minute. You let the detective stay *in* our house?"

"I just couldn't let the poor man stay outside all night. He was doing us a favor."

"Favor my ass. They're supposed to be on watch outside. *Outside*. Not in *my* house. So where did he sleep? You and the detective hit it off last night too?"

"That's insulting," replied Mary Ellen, looking around to see if anybody in the customer lounge was listening in to her conversation. Before continuing, she got up and walked outside. "I can't believe you, of all people, even have the nerve to ask me that question. You're the one with the girlfriend or girlfriends. But for your information, he was a perfect gentleman and he slept in the guest room."

"I bet. So what'd y'all talk about… you and this perfect gentleman? Did he have anything new to say about the asshole who took the pictures of our daughter? Or was he too busy making nice?"

Mary Ellen thought for a minute. She had to tell Zach something.

"It appears that the guy who took the pictures of Ashley was on a motorcycle. The Colonel told the detectives that during their canvass of our neighborhood looking for witnesses."

"The Colonel saw someone taking pictures of our house? Of Ashley? Why the hell didn't that old fool do something about it? Call me. Call the cops. Anybody. What an idiot."

Mary Ellen just let him rant. Challenging her husband would only feed the man's argumentative mood, which nowadays was most of the time.

"Well, he's on guard now. I saw him out this morning, walking Ike and he was ready for bear. If that biker guy comes around again, we'll all know."

"The son-of-a-bitch sure as hell *better* let us know."

"I'm sure he will."

"So are you at the bank? Are they planning on giving you any kind of… of… hazard pay… you know…a bonus for all this bank robbery shit? If not, you should demand it."

Mary Ellen decided it was best to tell Zach about the car and where she was. He'd know sooner or later. "The bank's closed today. Auditors. Just to let you know, and don't get upset, I'm at Pep Boys. The last few days, my car has been acting up. Not wanting to start. I…"

"Pep Boys!" interrupted Zach, now furious. "*Do not* let them touch my car! Do you hear me, woman? I'll be home Saturday. I can fix it."

"What if it's just the battery? What if I get stuck… and the car won't start?"

"Then call a friend. Call the Colonel. Call your bald-headed boss. But DO NOT call Uber. And don't let *anybody* touch that car. All these auto shops are nothing but a bunch of crooks."

"Actually, they've been really nice. They're not charging me anything to diagnose the problem."

"I guess you just didn't hear me. I said *do not*… and I repeat… *do not* let them touch my car."

Before Mary Ellen could respond, her husband had hung up. She had no voice in their marriage. Even though Zach was home only about four days a month, he felt he had to control everything. He was the husband and she was just a wife. An eighteenth-century marriage. Slowly she walked back into the customer's lounge and sat down. A defeated woman.

"Ma'am?" asked the Pep Boy's advisor, seeing Mary Ellen take a seat in the customer lounge.

"Huh? I'm sorry. I didn't see you. So what's the problem? Battery?"

"No. The starter. That's why your car doesn't always start on the first try. We can put in a remanufactured one and, with labor, it will be about…"

"That's okay. My husband wants to fix it himself. I'm sorry you went through all that trouble. How much do I owe you?"

"There's no charge. But I must warn you, and I'm not trying to alarm you or sell you anything, but that starter could go out on you at any moment. So, the sooner your husband fixes it, the better."

Mary Ellen left Pep Boys and headed back home. She and Zach needed to talk. She couldn't live like this anymore.

CHAPTER 23

"Hey, hon. What can I get you? The usual?" asked the waitress at the Waffle House as she poured Zach a cup of hot coffee.

"Yeah. So where's Faye. She was supposed to meet me here at ten."

"She's still at work. Wal-Mart changed her schedule. She called me when she couldn't find your number. She said to meet her at her house. She'll be home around four and she said you know where the key's hidden."

"Just great. So how am I to get there? Walk?"

"You *could* call Uber or Lyft."

"And what, pay thirty dollars. Hell, I'll just sleep in the back of the truck. If she comes by, tell her I'll see her next trip. Tell her I'll call her when I'm coming." Zach had two phones. One he called his 'truck' phone, a refillable Nokia burner phone that he'd bought six years ago. The other phone, a used iPhone 6, was his 'family' phone. Their nicknames denoted their purpose. Each phone was different in size and color and each had different ringtones and notification sounds, so he would never confuse one with the other.

The waitress yelled the order to the cook and left Zach to drink his coffee in peace.

Zach poured in the creamer and then instead of drinking his coffee, he just started stirring the spoon around in the cup, deep in concentration. His mind was on Mary Ellen. She seemed to be going rogue. Doing things she knew she wasn't supposed to do. That had to stop. After all, he was the breadwinner. Her piddling teller job hardly paid for the gas to get there and back. He only let her work there to appease her. As they say, give the old lady a bone once in a while. In reality, he wanted her to be home with his daughter.

The waitress placed the food in front of Zach and grabbed a fresh pot of coffee ready to offer a refill, but she noticed that the cup was still full. Seeing his head hung low and ignoring his food, she felt he needed to talk.

"So what's going on in that little head of yours? Everything all right? You got trouble at home or work?"

"I'm worried about my daughter."

"Something at school? She ill?"

"No. Worse. Some lunatic robbed the bank where my wife… er ex-wife works at and the dude threatened my daughter if he didn't get the money."

"When did this happen?"

"Yesterday morning."

"Oh my gosh! What about your ex?" asked the waitress, knowing full well the ex was no ex.

"What do you mean, what about my ex?"

"Is she okay? Did she or anybody get hurt?"

"Oh. Yeah. She's okay. I don't think anybody got hurt. If they did, she never said anything about it. But come to think of it, she never told me if the robber had a gun… or some kind of weapon. Just a threatening note and pictures of my little girl getting on the school bus."

"So did they catch him?"

"No. But I'd kill that son-of-a-bitch if I could get my hands on him," Zach said loudly, then banging his first on the counter.

"Okay, Zach. Rein it in," said the waitress. "Don't scare away my paying customers. At least everything's okay. Everybody's safe."

The waitress then moved over to the register to take money from a couple and then returned to Zach. She loved looking at the man. He was so handsome yet so insecure. She picked up the conversation as though she had never left.

"You know when things like this happen and it makes you stop and think. Like what if something did happen to your ex, who would take care of your daughter? I mean, you're on the road all the time."

"You're right. I've…"

"Hold that thought," said the waitress as she saw a plate of hot food ready to be served. She picked it up along with the coffee pot and hurried over to another customer. She chatted with him for a few minutes then returned to Zach.

"Okay. Where were we? Oh yeah. So, what *would* you do if your ex had been badly hurt or, even worse, killed? Does she have insurance?"

"I don't know. Maybe the bank has some on her. I think my company has some on me because of me being on the road and all that. But insurance on my ex? I don't know. I've never asked."

"Well, hon. You got a child to think about. You should know. Otherwise, who's going to take care of her if something happened to you or your ex? Her parents? Your parents?"

"There's no way I would let my parents or my ex's parents have custody of Ashley. I lived that life. My parents would ruin Ashley. And my in-laws? What a couple of snobs. Members of the country club, bridge club, supper club, garden club, wine club. Every kind of club you could imagine. Even though they tried to include me, I knew deep down, they would have been embarrassed to have me tag along. Me, with grease under his nails, the smell of gas and oil on my skin. No. I never went anywhere with them. Mary Ellen did. She was used to that kind of life. Not me. Oh… I might not have told you, but right after we got married, we lived in their basement… really, more like a dungeon. For three long years. I can't tell you how glad I was to get out from under their thumb. I'll never let my daughter go through what I did. Never."

"Wow. Aren't you the bitter soul! So why did you stay with them so long?"

"I had no money. And I didn't come from money. My folks were dirt poor. I'm sure that's why the in-laws hated me. They wanted their little darling girl to marry some rich kid and I was just a low-life mechanic. But my parents were worse. Always drunk. And my old man… he was always beating the shit out of me for no reason."

The waitress had had enough of Zach's whining. While he was so very easy on the eyes, not so on the ears. Always bitching.

"Well if you want to know what I think, I think you need to have a good talk with your wife… er... your ex and make sure you both have insurance and a plan for your daughter's future just in case something were to happen to either one of you or… or… both."

"You should go into sales. Insurance sales. You're scaring the hell out of me," said Zach, laughing on the outside, but worrying on the inside. The waitress was right.

CHAPTER 24

Mary Ellen's mind raced as she drove home from Pep Boys. When she turned onto the driveway and into the garage, she realized she had no memory of the entire trip. All she thought about was how Zach had talked to her. How he made her feel worthless and unwanted. She couldn't go on like this. She needed to talk to someone. She needed her mom. Then she remembered her dad. He was supposed to have his epidural today. Instead of leaving the car, she lowered the window, reclined her seat slightly and turned off the engine. She pulled her phone from her purse and pressed 'Mom Dad' in her *Phone Favorites*. Her mother answered almost immediately.

"Hey, sweetheart. I was just about to call *you*. With all this robbery thing, I figured you forgot all about Poppy's procedure. But he's doing fine. We won't know if it helps his back pain until next week at the earliest. But we're home and he's already wanting to get out to the golf course. But I'm not letting him do anything until Saturday at the earliest."

"I'm glad he's okay… but… but… I'm not." Then Mary Ellen began to cry.

"What's wrong, honey? Are you still worried about that robber?"

"No, mom," replied Mary Ellen, still crying.

"Is Ashley…"

"It's not Ashley," she said, interrupting her mother. She then pulled a Kleenex from her purse and wiped the tears from her eyes smearing her running eye make-up.

"It's… It's Zach."

"What's wrong with Zach?"

"I'm… I'm not sure I can live with him anymore."

"What do you mean you can't live with him anymore? What's he done? Has he hurt you or Ashley?" asked Carol, knowing Zach's quick temper.

"He's being so mean to me. He treats me like… like… I don't know. Like I'm an idiot. Like I'm his lackey. Always talking down to me. Always arguing."

"Well, we all argue. You've heard me and Poppy argue before. That's just part of being married. You have good times and bad times. Marriage…"

"Mom," said Mary Ellen, stopping her small sermon on marriage in midcourse. "You and daddy don't argue. Not like Zach and me. Has daddy ever called you *woman*, like he doesn't know your name? Has he ever called you *fool* or *idiot* or *bitch*? Has he ever thrown anything at you or slapped you?" Mary Ellen stopped talking and began to cry again.

"Oh, you poor child. I… we didn't know. How long has this been going on?"

Mary Ellen dabbed her eyes again with her tissue as the tears slowly subsided.

"I dunno. It seems like forever. But probably three or four years. Not long after he began driving the long hauls."

"Why haven't you told us? We could have helped. Have you talked to Zach about getting counseling?"

Mary Ellen couldn't help but laugh. Then she cried.

"Mom. Zach is not the same person who married me. He's not the same man who lived with me in your basement. He's not the doting husband who was by my side every minute of Ashley's birth. He's changed. More than you can ever know. Yes. I suggested counseling at my church. But I could no more get him to go to see a counselor than you could get daddy to quit golf or skydiving. Not gonna happen."

"Is he drinking? On drugs?"

"No mom. That's not the problem. He…"

Mary Ellen stopped in mid-sentence when she heard a double beep on her phone indicating an incoming call. She immediately pulled the phone away from her ear so she could see the caller's name or number. No name. Just an unfamiliar number.

Figuring it was a robocall, she hit the *Decline* icon. No sooner had she canceled the incoming call when she got a text at the top of her screen.

Mom. Come and get me.

When she picked up the phone she heard her mother still talking on the phone. "Mary Ellen? Hello? You there?"

"Mom. Let me call you back. Something's going on with Ashley at school."

Without waiting for her mother's reply, she ended the call and listened to the voice mail that had been left on her phone. It was Libby Waites, the Sedalia Park Middle School counselor, asking for a return call. In her message, she told Mary Ellen not to worry. That Ashley was not hurt or in any danger.

Regardless, Mary Ellen began to hyperventilate as she called the school.

"Ms. Waites. This is Mary Ellen Ferguson, Ashley's mother. Is she okay? Is anything wrong?"

"Ashley is fine, but she wants to go home and I agree with her. We had an unfortunate incident at school today that seems to have put her on edge… emotionally. I'm aware of the robbery at your bank yesterday and so are many of the students. One student, a good friend of Ashley and a good kid, thought it would be funny to sneak up behind her while she was getting some things out of her locker and to pretend to rob her. He told her it was a stickup and jabbed his finger into Ashley's back like it was a gun. For lack of a better word, Ashley freaked out. Began to scream and cry uncontrollably. We brought her back to my office and tried to console her hoping she might be able to go back to class, but I'm afraid she's too distraught for that to happen. She says she's worried about you and wants to see you."

"Can I talk to her?"

"Yes. Here she is." Ms. Waites motioned for Ashley to come to the phone. "It's your mother."

"Hello," said Ashley in a low, soft trembling voice.

"Baby, I'm sorry I put you through all of this. I never should have said anything. I'll be there in just a few minutes."

"Okay," said Ashley and handed the phone back to the counselor and then returned to the sofa.

"Ms. Waites, I'm on my way."

Ashley's school was only three miles from her house. On a bad day, Mary Ellen could drive there in less than ten minutes. As she returned the seat to her pre-set position, she said a little prayer as she hit the *Start* button on her Camry. This time, it started on the first try. Just like her trip home from Pep Boys, she had no remembrance of any road she traveled, any turn she made or how fast she had driven as he pulled into a 'Visitors' parking spot. Just in case the Camry chose not to behave, she left the car running. She then locked the car and headed to the school's front door where she looked into the video intercom while at the same time showing her driver's license. The door unlocked and she headed straight to the administration office where she saw two women, one was standing behind the counter that separated the visitors from the staff and the other sitting at a desk, also behind the counter.

Mary Ellen filled out the early release form on a computer terminal and then waited for the counselor to bring Ashley to the front office. The five minutes she had to wait seemed an eternity. Soon Ashley appeared and ran straight to her mother and hugged her.

"I'm sorry, mom," said Ashley, her head buried in her mother's chest.

"That's okay. I understand."

"Ms. Ferguson. If you have a minute, I'd like to talk to you. We can sit in the assistant principal's office. It's empty. Ashley, are you going to be okay waiting here?"

Ashley nodded her head and sat down in one of the nearby chairs. Mary Ellen followed Ms. Waites into the office and both found seats facing each other.

"Mrs. Ferguson, Ashley had a bad experience today. She was as frightened as I've ever seen a child. Without saying, this robbery and the potential harm you faced during the holdup was more than most twelve-year-olds can handle."

Mary Ellen was eaten up with guilt. "This is my fault. She seems so grown-up in so many ways that I thought it best if I told her what happened at the bank rather than having her hear it from someone at school or see it on TV. I see now that I should have tempered what I told her."

"Hindsight is 20/20. It's too bad there's no book we can reference regarding such issues. Every child is different and handles situations differently. You shouldn't beat yourself up over this. But as a counselor, I *am* concerned about her mental state and her fear of losing you. I think a couple of days out of school so both of you can sort things out is what I recommend. If she has any relapses or you see any significant behavioral changes, I think you might consider outside counseling."

Regardless of how understanding the counselor had been, Mary Ellen couldn't help but beat herself up mentally, wishing she could somehow retract what she had told her daughter, wishing she had never said anything to the robber, wishing she had never been robbed.

"Thank you, Ms. Waites. But I do feel guilty. She's *such* a sweet girl. So kind and loving…"

"As a mother, I understand what you are going through. But I think she'll be fine. She just needs her mother. She needs to know you are safe. This isn't about her. It's about you. Anything you can do to allay her fears is the best course of action. As far as homework, she can get her assignments online. And, one more thing. If you could call your husband and let him know that we've talked and that everything's been handled, I'd appreciate it. When we couldn't get in touch with you, we called him. But he didn't answer either, so we also left him a message."

"Zach, my husband, drives trucks for a living. When he's on the road, he won't answer his phone unless the same number calls three times in a row and within five minutes. That way, he knows it's an emergency. Otherwise, he'll just let it ring. He wants to concentrate on driving. On being safe."

"I understand. I hope you and Ashley have a better rest of the day."

That's not going to happen, thought Mary Ellen knowing that once Zach pulled off the road and heard the voicemail from the school, it was going to be another *You dumb fuck. You moron…* kind of call. He would be yelling and Mary Ellen would be crying before the day was over.

Mary Ellen and Ashley left the school and over to her Camry which, to her relief, was still running.

In the car and back on the road, Mary Ellen was the first to speak.

"Baby, I'm sorry you had a bad day. It was entirely my fault. I shouldn't have worried you like I did."

"Mom, it's okay. Like Ms. Waites said, I just freaked out. But I'm better now. I'll be okay. I think Jordan was just as freaked out as me."

"Who's Jordan?"

"He's the one who played the prank on me. When I freaked, he did too. Maybe more so than me. He kept apologizing. Saying he was sorry. He was crying as much as me. I think they are going to put him on in-school suspension for three days because of it. They say it's bullying. But Jordan wouldn't bully anyone. He's so kind. I think he did it because he likes me and that's how boys act when they're young. Stupid."

"Young lady, you're very smart for your age," replied Mary Ellen, nodding her head while thinking *better stupid than mean and abusive.* "You think if I called the school, they'd cancel the suspension?"

"I would like that. I'm not sure the school can undo what they've done. But it's at least a try."

Once they reached the house, Mary Ellen called the school and talked to the counselor. Ms. Waites said she would talk to the principal and also let Jordan know that Ashley's mom had asked. Ashley had a smile on her face. It was obvious that Ashley liked Jordan.

CHAPTER 25

While Ashley worked on her homework in her bedroom, Mary Ellen sat at the kitchen table drinking a warm diet Coke and searching the internet for the names of divorce lawyers. On a legal pad, she had written down the names of the ones who seemed to have good reviews even though she knew the reviews could be lawyer generated. She stopped at six names. Seeing their names in writing made the whole process seem real. She had been thinking about leaving Zach for almost a year but never had the nerve to move forward. She didn't really know what triggered the sudden courage. Maybe it was the robbery and her defiant behavior toward the thief. Or maybe, it had been the quiet, fun evening she and Ashley had spent with Dom showing her how a real family should live. Or maybe it had been Zach's mean-spirited, condescending tongue lashing she had endured at Pep Boys that had sent her over the edge. Regardless, she was ready. And she had taken the first step, albeit an easy one, of writing down lawyers' names. The next step was going to be the most difficult... telling Zach. And she wanted to do it today. While she had the courage and while she could do it over the phone. With the physical abuse she had endured over the last few years for small, insignificant confrontations, there was no way she wanted to do *this* face to face.

Interrupting her train of thought and her computer screen was a FaceTime call from her mother and father. It was good they had called her. She could use a good dose of parental advice.

"Is this a bad time?" asked her mother who looked relieved to see Mary Ellen's face.

"No, mom. I'm glad you called."

"How's Ashley?" asked Carol.

"She's fine. She was just having a bad day at school. This robbery thing seemed to have really upset her. After talking to the school counselor, we felt it best if Ashley came home to be with me." Mary Ellen chose not to tell them about Ashley's little friend's involvement.

"Where is she?" asked Wesley, Mary Ellen's father.

"She's in her bedroom doing her homework. You want me to go get her?"

"No. What I want is to know what's going on between you and Zach," replied Wesley.

"Things aren't going well, daddy. I don't think I can take it anymore… the abuse. I want out. I want a divorce. I…" Then she broke down in tears again.

Wesley waited until Mary Ellen's hesitant breathing had ebbed before he began speaking. "Your mom told me that you said the son-of-a-bitch *slapped* you. Why didn't you tell me?" Wesley could hardly contain his anger as he spoke.

"What could you do, daddy? You're not married to him. You're not here and even if you were, he'd deny it. He's so mean to me. I…" Mary Ellen broke down crying again.

After giving his daughter a few minutes to compose herself, Wesley asked, "What about Ashley? Has he…"

"Oh no. He would never, never hurt Ashley. She's his princess. If only he treated me like he treats her."

"Mary Ellen, you've heard me talk about my residency at Grady (referring to Grady Memorial Hospital in Atlanta, Georgia) and how I had to patch up gunshot and stabbing victims in the ER. I'm not sure I ever told you about the women who came to the ER so beat up they were almost unrecognizable. And nearly every one of them said it was an accident, a fall, whatever. But as hard as we counseled, comforted and worked with these battered women, most would recant their story. I'm sure they were scared of their husband, boyfriend, pimp… whatever." Wesley paused to see if Mary Ellen would respond. She didn't. "Have you ever had to go to the hospital because of Zach? Has he ever hit you hard enough to draw blood? Anything like that?" What Wesley didn't tell his daughter about the abused women he'd seen was that a number of them would end up back at the hospital, but in its morgue, not its Emergency Room.

"No Daddy. Not that bad. But bad enough that I couldn't go to work for a couple of days."

"Oh my God!" shrieked Carol.

"What about sexual abuse? They usually go hand in hand."

Mary Ellen hesitated for a few seconds, embarrassed. "Yes, daddy."

"Rough sex or rough and… uh… unnatural sex."

"Both. Sometimes it seemed like he was trying to punish me or prove a point. And I don't know why. I have never cheated on him. I feel like I'm a good mother to Ashley. And I don't spend a lot of money. I don't know why he's like he is. But I'm afraid of him, daddy. He's changed. Neither you nor mom has ever seen the mean, dark side of him."

"And you say no drugs or alcohol?" asked her father.

"No sir."

"Well… something's going on. Are you telling us everything?" asked Wesley.

Mary Ellen signed loud enough that both her mother and father heard her.

"He has a girlfriend here in Atlanta," said Mary Ellen, feeling like a failure. "He's been seeing her for a few years. Not too long after he started driving the long hauls. And if the truth be told, he probably has other girlfriends everywhere along his route. And get this. He's extremely jealous of *me*. And I mean extremely jealous. Like I'm the one out there fooling around."

"Honey, you don't need to live like this," said Carol. "You and Ashley can come back to Augusta and live with us. We still have your little apartment in the basement."

"Mom, I can't do that to Ashley. I can't take her away from her friends, her school or her daddy. Divorce will be hard enough on her. She and Zach are very close." Then, so not to leave the wrong impression, she added, "in a parent/child relationship."

"I think you are doing the right thing. Getting a divorce. Do you have a lawyer in mind?"

"I'm working on that right now."

"The sooner the better," said Wesley. "When do you plan on telling him?"

"I'm thinking tonight or tomorrow. While he's on the road. That will give him a few days to cool off."

"When does he get back to Atlanta?" asked Wesley.

"Sometime Saturday. He usually spends the first night with Girlfriend, but I doubt that will happen knowing I'm looking to hire a divorce lawyer."

"Then you plan on us being there Saturday," said Wesley. "No man slaps my daughter."

CHAPTER 26

"Hey, Scott," said Tim as he leaned into Scott's office. "Have you been able to change your appointment with IST (Independent Security Trust)?"

"Yes. Why?"

"And you're still heading to Atlanta Friday?"

"Yes. Why?"

"And you're meeting with the folks at Roswell Guardian State Bank on Monday?"

"Yes. Would you please get to the point?"

"I just talked to Rodney… Rodney Pafford, my friend from the Reserve." Tim then made himself comfortable in one of the two chairs facing Scott's desk. "I told him that I *thought* you were heading down to Atlanta this Friday and I asked him if he could meet you one night for dinner."

"I had *planned* to do that when I got there. So what'd he say?"

"He said the Reserve's ethics policy won't permit it, but he invited you and Anne, assuming you two are still talking, to a party he's hosting for his boss's 60th birthday. He wants it to be a huge success with lots of people. He says his boss has a big ego and a poor turnout would be disastrous for him and his boss. So he's inviting everyone. And that includes you and Anne."

"You've got to be kidding me. I don't even know your friend much less his boss. How could…"

"Scotty… We've got to make an appearance. He's my friend *and* he can be very valuable to our company. He tells me that there will be a lot of bankers at the party including the president of Roswell Guardian. It'll be a great way for you to meet him informally before your Monday presentation. Knowing him personally could go a long way in us getting their business. I've seen you and Anne at parties before. Neither one of you has ever met a stranger. And don't worry about getting a present. Rodney tells me his boss is an avid golfer, so you could bring him a couple of dozen of our company logoed Titleist."

"Okay. Enough said. I'll check with Anne. I don't think it'll be a problem. She likes parties. And getting to know a few more bankers certainly can't do our business any harm. But you owe me. Big time."

CHAPTER 27

"So how are you and Ashley doing? Everything okay?" asked Dom, calling from his office. It had been a busy day for him with the auditors checking the vault, the teller stations… everything. Providence Surety Bank had never had a robbery and upper management wanted to be extra cautious with their reports to the FDIC.

"Not good. We had a really bad day," answered Mary Ellen. "Well… not counting Ashley's ride to school in your new sports car."

"I'm sorry to hear that. What's wrong? Your car? I never heard from you, so I assumed it started with no problem."

"Well, it began with the car and it went downhill after that."

"What happened?"

"This morning, after you left, I took my car to Pep Boys. I was hoping it was just a battery. But the mechanic said it was the starter and that it could fail on me at any time. I talked to Zach and he said under no uncertain terms would Pep Boys touch the car. That he'd fix it when he got home. So I left. Now I'm worried about getting stranded."

"Does Zach know *anything* about cars? Can he actually fix them?"

"Oh yeah. Before he was a long-distance driver, he used to work as a mechanic when we lived in Augusta. And he's really good. But he's never in town. I don't know what I'm going to do if it does fail. If I get Pep Boys to fix it, he'll kill me."

"If it's money, I can help," offered Dom.

"Oh no. That'd make things worse. If he found out that you paid for it, I'd never hear the end of it. I'd rather the car break down in the middle of Peachtree than to have Zach rail at me. He can be very mean and abusive."

Dom paused for a moment to think whether he should dig deeper into what Mary Ellen had just said. But having been the victim of abuse all his life, he knew he couldn't let it pass.

"Why do you put up with his abuse? *I know* that it's not always verbal."

"Ashley. She's the reason. She loves her dad and he loves her. We stay married because of her."

"But how can you continue to live your life while fearing the man you once loved. I know I couldn't."

"No. I can't. That's why I've decided to file for divorce. I've been thinking about it for a long time. And today, I finally got up enough courage to look up some names of divorce lawyers. I just don't know how to tell Ashley. With the robbery and now the divorce, it might be too much for a little twelve-year-old to handle. But I can't keep on living like this. This whole thing has been very depressing."

"Mary Ellen… you are doing the right thing. Ashley, like most children, is very resilient. They have more inner strength than we give them credit for. And I should know because of all the kids I have."

Both she and Dom laughed at his remark knowing he and his partner were childless.

"Have you told Zach?"

"Oh noooo! Not yet. I plan to tell him today or tomorrow while he's on the road. But it won't be face to face. There's no telling what that man may say or do. I did tell my mom and dad and they're coming up here this weekend to be with me. To keep Zach at arm's length and to help comfort Ashley once I tell her."

"That's good. Divorce is never easy. By the way, I do know a really good divorce attorney if you don't like any of the ones you've found. He's very competent and I could talk him into giving you the banker's discount rate," said Dom, trying to lighten the mood.

"Thank you. I'll let you know."

"I guess I need to let you get back to checking on those lawyers before Ashley gets home from school."

"She's already home. I had to go pick her up at school around lunchtime. She was having a bad day, too."

"Why? What happened?"

Mary Ellen told Dom about the incident at school and how the counselor and she had decided it was best for Ashley to stay at home for a couple of days.

"Poor thing. How is she doing now?"

"I think she's fine. She's in her bedroom playing video games. I know you said kids are stronger than we give them credit. But I'm still worried about her. She internalizes everything… like me. I never should have told her everything about the robbery. But she acts so grown up most of the time I have to keep reminding myself that she's still only twelve."

"Things will get better. A little time…"

"I don't think so. I've got to tell Zach what happened at school and he's going to raise holy hell… at me and the school."

"Why do you have to tell him anything? Just let it slide. He doesn't have to know."

"I've got to tell him something. The school left messages for both me and Zach. When he gets off the road and reads that message, he's gonna call me and he's gonna want to know everything."

"My advice is to tell him the truth but minimalize it. Just tell him Ashley was having a bad day. That she missed you. And don't bring up that other kid. He'll probably think it's all about the robbery. So just let him. He can't hurt you over the phone. He'll just make you feel bad and incompetent. That's what bullies do. And, in my opinion, Zach's a bully," said Dom, regretting the words as soon as he'd said them. "I'm sorry. That was inappropriate. I probably shouldn't have said that."

"You needn't feel sorry. It's the truth. And I'm glad you called. You made my day better."

After ending the call with Dom, Mary Ellen called Zach. She needed to tell him about Ashley and while he was stewing over the incident at school, she would break the news that she wanted a divorce. That would really give him something to stew about.

As usual, the call went to voicemail, so she left a brief message.

"Zach. Ashley's fine. She had a problem at school, but I handled it. When you have some time, we need to talk."

When dating, *we need to talk* were the code words for *I'm miffed* or *I'm breaking up with you*. Usually the latter. In marriage, it could mean *I need some time away, so I'm going see my parents, you need a guy's trip, you've got to stop drinking, we need counseling*, or *I want a divorce*. Mary Ellen knew Zach would know what she meant.

CHAPTER 28

While Zach was having his empty trailer switched out for another load, he sat at a desk in the truck terminal's office filling out his U.S. Department of Transportation Hours of Service logbook. Zach prided himself on never having had a logbook violation or a traffic violation. He took breaks when required, never drove more hours than allowed, and was off duty the requisite amount of time. And unlike most truck drivers, he never answered the phone while driving. Too distracting. And to make sure he didn't', he had Bluetooth disabled on the truck. Today, he had had two calls on his 'family' phone that went unanswered while he was on the road.

Once he had completed his logbook and the paperwork for his next haul, he stepped outside the terminal building and listened to his voicemails. The first was from his daughter's school asking for a return call.

Why the hell are they calling me? Where's the bitch? Thought Zach, his anger directed toward Mary Ellen. He then listened to his second voicemail.

"What the bloody hell," he yelled, oblivious to the nearby employees and truckers who turned their heads towards the source of the noise to see what was happening. Most of the times when they heard this kind of yelling, it was a verbal and/or physical altercation between a couple of drivers over a woman, a parking spot, or a violation of the rules of the highway. Seeing that it was a one-man show, everyone continued with what they were doing.

"Fucking woman," Zach mumbled to himself as he briskly walked the long walk back to his truck. "She wants to talk? Well, we'll talk all right."

Once he was in his cab, had the engine started and the air conditioner running, Zach hit the speed dial button for Mary Ellen's cell. She had hardly gotten the word *Hello* out of her mouth when he lit into her.

"What the hell's going on at the school? Why did they call *me*? Is Ashley okay? "

"She's fine," said Mary Ellen, rattled and then forgetting Dom's advice, she told Zach the truth. "It was an innocent prank that someone played on Ashley that went wrong and she got upset. But everything's okay now."

"What kind of *innocent* prank would have the school counselor involved? Woman, you're not telling me everything. What the hell happened?"

Mary Ellen tried to downplay the whole situation as she told him what had happened, but Zach would have none of it.

"What's the kid's name? You have his phone number? Did they suspend that little asshole from school?"

"Zach," Mary Ellen said, firmly, trying to keep strong. "I've handled it. The school has taken appropriate actions. Drop it."

"Who the hell do you think you're talking to, woman? If I want to call that boy's fucking parents, I'll call them. That's what *you* should have done. And what's this *we need to talk* shit?"

Mary Ellen was ready. She had practiced mentally all afternoon what she was going to say and how she was going to say it. And she had to be strong.

"Zach… I want a divorce. We haven't been living like husband and wife for years and you know that. I don't love you anymore and I know you don't love me. I think you should go your way and I go my way. I've been researching divorce lawyers' names and I think you should do the same. I hope we can make this as amicable as possible. My parents are coming up Saturday and will be staying for a while. I think you should find some other place to stay while we work this out."

"JUST A FUCKING MINUTE! You *wait* until I'm on the road to *CALL ME* and tell me you want a divorce," yelled Zach, the veins in his neck and head bulging and pulsating as his anger intensified. "I'm out here working fourteen hours a day, seven days a week trying to make a decent living for our family and all I ask you to do is take care of my child. And *you've* fucked that up six ways to Sunday. Who's behind all of this divorce talk? Good ol' *Dom*?" asked Zach singsonging Dom's name. "Or maybe your highfalutin parents? Hell, they've never liked me anyway. Never thought I was *good enough* for their little princess. If you…"

Mary Ellen found the courage to interrupt Zach.

"I *am* a good mother. And my parents had nothing to do with this. They…"

"Look. I don't give a damn who's put this bug in your ear. But if it's a divorce you want. You can have it. But you know what you'll get out of it? *NOTHING. YOU'LL GET ABSOLUTELY NOTHING.* You know who owns the house? Me. You know who owns the cars… the savings account… everything? Me. Me. Me. And guess who'll get custody of Ashley? Me. So yeah. Let's get a divorce and see how you like living by yourself, back home with your parents in their basement." And then he hung up.

Mary Ellen began to cry. Things had not gone as she had planned. The stress she felt was greater than what she had felt during the bank robbery. She headed to her bedroom, closed the door and laid down across the bed sobbing uncontrollably.

Zach, on the other hand, wanted to hit someone or something. Anything. He took his anger out on the steering wheel. Once he had calmed, he shifted the truck into low gear and pulled out of the truck terminal and across the road to a truck stop. While the terminal offered overnight spaces for the truckers to park their trucks to get some sleep, most of the drivers preferred the truck stop. It had overnight spaces, showers, and a decent restaurant.

As he climbed out of the truck's cab, he heard someone call his name.

"Hey, Zach. Zachman. You wanna grab some grub with me?" asked Billy Meadows, a fellow Georgia truck driver who had pulled into the parking spot next to Zach.

"Yeah. Sure. Why not."

"Now look… if you can find a better date…"

"Shit, man. I'm sorry. I didn't mean it like that. I just got a lot on my mind."

"What you got going on that little pea brain of yours. Can't be much," said Billy, laughing at his own comment.

Zach didn't appreciate the slight even though he knew Billy was just teasing. Except for his Commercial Driver's License (CDL) training courses where he excelled, he'd always been a less than stellar student getting by mainly on his good looks.

On the way into the restaurant, Zach briefed Billy about the conversation he'd just had with Mary Ellen. They found an open booth and Zach pulled a menu from the stack leaning against the wall. As he perused the selections, his stomach ached at the prices of the entrees. He had never eaten a meal at this particular restaurant. And as it was, he normally didn't eat out but once, maybe twice a week. Wednesday was not one of his designated days. But feeling the way he did… What the hell. He put down his menu and noticed Billy hadn't taken one.

"You already know what you want?" asked Zach.

"Yeah. The meat and three daily special. You didn't see it on the board when we walked in? They got fried chicken, mashed potatoes and gravy, green beans and mac n' cheese. You get that with tea and biscuits for $8.99. And for truckers, they throw in the cherry cobbler. Can't beat it."

"Then, that's what I'm having."

The waitress came by, took their orders, left long enough to get them some sweet tea and then headed to the kitchen to place their order.

"So your old lady wants a divorce," said Billy, then took a swig of his tea.

"Yeah. I was actually just about to pull the trigger myself," lied Zach trying to save face. "She's gonna regret losing her meal ticket."

"Why's she divorcing you? You been fucking around?"

"Oh hell no," lied Zack again, pursing his lips. "She's the one with the boyfriend."

"I hope you got proof 'cause if not, she's gonna take you to the friggin' cleaners. I know that from experience."

"What the hell do you mean?"

"You still live in Georgia, don't you?"

"Yeah. Marietta. Why?"

"Well, in Georgia, she's gonna get at least half of everything."

"What do you mean half? She don't own shit. I got everything in my name. House, cars, savings accounts… everything. Half of nothing is nothing."

"That's not how it works, bubba. She's gonna get half of everything you own. At least anything that was accumulated during the marriage. That means half of the house at today's current value. Half of your savings account. Half of your cars. Anything during the marriage. But that also includes debts. "

"You've got to be kidding me. She hasn't paid for anything 'cept groceries. I've paid for everything. Every fuckin' thing."

"It gets worse. You got retirement? 401-k?"

"You're not telling me she gets half of that, too!"

"Yep. And half of your social security unless you die. Then she gets it all."

"Unfucking believable."

"Not to pour gasoline on the fire, but if you got kids, she's gonna get them and she gets child support for each one. Hell, I'm paying $800 a month for two and one's not even mine. And you gotta pay half of their medical, schooling, camps. But at least you get to see them a couple of times a month, every other Thanksgiving, Christmas…"

The ache in Zach's stomach from the price of the meal by now had been eclipsed by the ever-growing ache from what Billy was telling him.

"Now, if you can prove she's got a boyfriend, you won't be stuck with alimony for the rest of your life like I am. My advice. Lawyer up. I can give you the name of mine. Better yet. Find a good hit man. He's got to be cheaper," said Billy, laughing again at his comment then continued. "And whatever you do, do not try to hide anything… any money or whatever. My lawyer told me that. He said the judge could really fuck me if I did and they found out. And believe me, they *will* find out."

About that time, the waitress came with a tray full of hot food. She put the plates down in front of each man, walked away, then returned with her tea pitcher.

"That was sweet tea for both you good-looking men, right?" the young waitress asked, looking mainly at Zach.

Both men nodded. She topped off the tea and left.

Billy could hardly wait to dig into the daily special. Zach, on the other hand, had lost his appetite.

CHAPTER 29

Zach's 'family' cell phone rang as he and Billy were walking out of the restaurant. It was Ashley's ringtone.

"I gotta take this. My daughter," said Zach. Billy understood and headed back to this truck while Zach answered the phone and headed to his truck.

"Hey princess. What's up?" he asked. He put the phone on speaker as he climbed into the cab of the truck and started the big diesel engine, the A/C coming on automatically.

"Daddy, you got to call mom. She's in her room, crying. I don't know what's wrong and she won't tell me. I don't know what to do."

Zach could sense the apprehension in his daughter's voice. He was glad that she hadn't mentioned divorce which meant Mary Ellen hadn't told Ashley about her decision to file. His daughter had already had enough trauma with the robbery and the incident at school.

"Baby. She's just having a rough day. Probably upset over that thing with you at school."

"Daddy, I really don't think that's the problem. That was just Jordan acting stupid. You think maybe she's still worried about that robber and the mean thing he said to her?"

"I think you nailed it," lied Zach. "That's got to be her problem. Maybe you should have her call that dude that stayed with y'all last night and talk to him. Maybe he can ease her mind. What do you think?"

"Oh, daddy. That wasn't a dude. That was Dom. And that's a *great* idea… calling him. Maybe he can come over again," said Ashley enthusiastically.

Zach was so dumbstruck by Ashley's revelation that he had no reply. Instead, Ashley continued.

"And you should see his new sports car. It is *so* cool," she said, elongating the word *so*. "And guess what? He drove me to school this morning. And he played this old song *Don't Worry. Be Happy* way loud and we sang it all the way to school. Well, he mainly sang. And then at the student drop-off lane, he drove really slow so everyone could see me.

It was *awesome*. Everybody wanted to know who he was. Like he's so cute. Not handsome like you. Just cute. Daddy, I want a car like Dom's when I grow up."

The mere mention of Dom's name invoked a jealousy and hatred that was almost uncontrollable. When Mary Ellen first started working for the bank, all she could talk about was Dom. How kind and sweet he was. What a good boss he was. What a good listener he was. How all the customers loved him. And now his daughter was singing his praises. It was more than he could handle. He had long suspected his wife of having an affair with her boss and this confirmed it.

"Ashley. I hate to hang up on you, but I've got to move my truck. I'm blocking another fellow. Just so you won't worry, I'll call your mother in just a few. Love you." Zach hung up and sat in his truck staring out the front window. He was more enraged now than when Mary Ellen had asked for the divorce. "That lying bitch." Again, he took out his anger on his steering wheel, but what he really wanted to do was to hit *her*. No. He wanted to choke her senseless.

* * * * * * * * * * * * * * * * *

After talking to her daddy, Ashley headed to her mother's bedroom where she found her sitting on the side of the bed, staring out the window. She had stopped crying. Instead, she was in deep concentration. Ashley ran over, sat down and hugged her. She hated the robber for what he had done to her. Mary Ellen leaned over and kissed her daughter's forehead

"What's wrong, baby," asked Mary Ellen.

"I don't like to see you crying. Are you still scared of that ol' mean bank robber?"

"Honey, I'm fine. I just have a lot on my mind and needed some alone time. But I'm fine."

Mary Ellen's face did not show that she was fine and her daughter took notice. She instinctively hugged her again, hoping the extra hard initial clasp would squeeze the anxiety or fear or whatever worry she was feeling from her body. Her mother hugged her back with the same force needing the feel of someone who truly loved her. The embrace was ended by the ringing of Mary Ellen's cell phone.

Mary Ellen was afraid it was Zach. Ashley hoped it was him since he said he would call.

"It's Dom. I can call him back later."

Ashley saw her mother's spirits immediately lifted from the call. Obviously, her dad had reached out to Dom and had asked him to call instead. Her dad was the best.

"No! You need to answer it. It might be important."

Mary Ellen answered her cell and headed to the den. Ashley went back into her bedroom, happy. She loved her daddy.

"Hi. Can you do me a favor?" asked Dom, talking somewhat in a whisper.

"For you? Anything."

"Can you wait about five minutes and then call me back? I don't want you to say anything. Just listen. That's all."

"Why? What's going on?" asked Mary Ellen, confused by the request.

"The auditors are almost finished. They'll be heading back to Richmond tomorrow. But they want to go out tonight. I suggested *Bone's, Aria, Bacchanalia, South City Kitchen,* but they all want to go to *The Cheetah.* That is one place I *do not* want to go, so I need an out. A call from you will do it."

"Why don't you want to go to *The Cheetah*? Not your kind of food?" She then laughed knowing The Cheetah was a high-end strip club.

"As you know, not my taste and style."

"So you just want me to call you in five minutes? That's all? And you don't want me to say anything?"

"That's the plan."

"I can handle that."

Mary Ellen went into the kitchen where she had left her list of lawyers. She ripped off the page, wadded it up and threw it in the trash can. She wanted a divorce from Zach, but not at the risk of losing Ashley. She didn't care about the house, the cars, bank accounts or having to move back in with her parents. But losing Ashley was not an option. If she had to stay married to Zach to keep her daughter, then so be it. She could handle the three or four days a month that he was at home and, if necessary, the physical, sexual and verbal abuse.

The sound of Zach's ringtone caused Mary Ellen to wince. This time she chose not to answer. One browbeating a day was enough. A few minutes later, she got a text.

Pick up the phone.

She immediately deleted the text.

She had hardly put the phone on the table when she heard Zach's ringtone again. Just as before, she chose to ignore it. Soon afterward, she received another demanding text.

PICK UP THE FUCKING PHONE BITCH!!!!

She knew that for Zach, this confrontation was a battle of wills and she normally gave in. But not this time. He could call or text her a thousand times and she wasn't gonna answer. She had made up her mind. Then she saw he had left her a voicemail. She should have just deleted it. Instead, she chose to listen. Zach was so loud that it was almost as though he was on speaker phone.

I DO NOT APPRECIATE YOU BRINGING THAT MAN INTO MY HOUSE WITH MY DAUGHTER THERE. GET HIM OUT NOW YOU DIRTY LITTLE...

Mary Ellen stopped the voicemail and deleted it. How did he find out about Dom? She hoped she hadn't gotten him in trouble. When she stood up to leave the kitchen, she saw Ashley leaning on the door jamb.

"How long have you been there?" Mary Ellen asked.

"Just a minute. Was that daddy?"

"Yes. That was your father."

"He seemed really mad."

"Yes, he was. While we were talking... er... uh... some other trucker got his parking spot. He kinda went off on him."

"That's not fair."

"Life's not fair. Like I have no homework and you're supposed to be doing yours."

"No homework night. I checked. So life is fair," said Ashley, hugging her mother. "What did Dom want?"

"Oh shoot. I forgot I'm supposed to call him back." Mary Ellen quickly hit Dom's speed dial on her phone and waited for an answer.

"Dominick Garcia," answered Dom, louder than normal but very professional.

Mary Ellen didn't say anything as requested. She could hear a lot of background talking.

"Oh. Hi, Mary Ellen. How are things going?" Dom waited a few seconds and then continued. "I'm sorry to hear that." Then nuzzling his phone against his chest and projecting his voice, he said, "Hey guys, I'm on the phone." He did this more to get their attention rather than to silence them. Immediately, the background noise ebbed. Then pulling the phone back to his ear he continued. "What about the detective? Have you called him?" Then Dom paused a moment. "That's unacceptable." Then, nuzzling his phone again, he informed the group that he had a situation. "Y'all go ahead. I've got a problem I need to handle. I'll meet up with you if I can. Enjoy your evening." Then placing the phone back to his ear, he continued. "I'll see you in about fifteen minutes. I'll call you from the car." Then he hung up.

"That was really weird," said Ashley.

"That's just Dom being Dom. He never wants to offend. He's so nice." Then her phone rang again. It was Dom.

"Thank you. Thank you. Thank you. You were a lifesaver. I owe you."

"I didn't do anything. And you don't owe me anything."

"If it's okay with you, can I bring you and Ashley dinner so I won't have lied?"

"Dom, I'm glad I could help. But you're off the hook. Seriously."

"No. I insist. I'd feel guilty lying to those guys. What can I bring? OK Café? Mary Mac's? Just name it."

Mary Ellen turned to Ashley. "Dom wants to bring us dinner. What do you want?"

Ashley's little face immediately brightened up. "Chick fil a. With waffle fries." Then she ran to her room to spruce herself up.

"That's all?" asked Dom after Mary Ellen told him their choice. "What about a dessert? Or maybe a bottle of wine with the meal?"

"That sounds great, especially the wine."

"I'll be there in a few." And then he hung up.

Mary Ellen set her phone down on the table. She found herself smiling.

CHAPTER 30

Zach lay on the small twin-size bed in the back of his truck cab, gritting his teeth and clenching his fist as he visualized Dom and Mary Ellen lying in his bed with his sweet daughter somewhere nearby. If only he were there, he'd make them pay. The more he thought about it, the madder he got. There was no way he was going to get any sleep. Not with that image on his mind. He sat up, pulled off his sleep mask, turned on the overhead light, reached into one of his overhead drawers and pulled out a bottle of Tylenol PM. It was the only sleep medicine he would take while on the road. He also had a half-full prescription bottle of Ambien that a former girlfriend inadvertently left in his truck. He had never used them because of DOT restrictions against the drug but kept them just in case he needed one during his reset period, the required 34 hours of break time after a 70 hour work week.

Within fifteen minutes, the Tylenol had kicked in and he was sound asleep and in such deep slumber he never heard the ding of the incoming text.

> *Same detective's car is at your house again tonight. Will text you tomorrow if he stayed the night. Colonel Robert Oliver.*

CHAPTER 31

Mary Ellen and Dom sat in the den, each savoring a chilled glass of the Rombauer chardonnay. They had waited until Ashley had gone to bed before opening the bottle. Mary Ellen didn't think it was wise for Ashley to see her having a drink with Dom after the accusations she had endured from Zach in his earlier aborted call.

"This is a wonderful chardonnay," commented Mary Ellen. "I've never had this before. It's expensive, isn't it?"

"It is an excellent wine."

"Thank you for coming over. It's been a really frustrating day."

"So did you tell Zach?"

"About the divorce? Yes."

"And?"

"It was bad. Really bad. He screamed at me. Told me how worthless I am and said he'd be glad to give me a divorce. But he said he's gonna get Ashley, the house, the cars… Everything." Mary Ellen broke into tears as she finished.

Dom move from his chair over to the couch and sat next to Mary Ellen. He gently picked up her hand and held it tight until the tears subsided.

"Mary Ellen. I don't think that's true. Have you called any of those lawyers you found on the internet?"

"No. I don't want a divorce. Not if I'm going to lose Ashley."

"I can't see *any* circumstances in which you wouldn't get custody of Ashley. Let me call my lawyer friend and get you some free advice. Then at least you know what you're dealing with."

Mary Ellen nodded. She wiped her eyes with her hand and then took a sip of wine while Dom searched his phone contacts. He found the name of Stuart Friedman and pressed on his name to make the call.

"Stuart Friedman? This is the IRS. I have some questions regarding your last return,"

"What the…"

"Just kidding. This is Dom. How's it going?"

"I'm gonna kill you, you SOB," said Stu, then laughed. "Actually, I'm glad you called. I heard about the robbery and wanted to make sure you're okay."

Dom told him about the theft and then cut to the chase.

"Stu, I need some free legal divorce advice. Not for me but for a friend."

Mary Ellen heard Dom say *friend*. Not relative. Not acquaintance. Not bank employee. But friend. It made her feel good inside. Not worthless like Zach had made her feel.

"You know I'll do anything for you. What do you need to know?"

Before speaking, Dom pressed his index finger to his lips as a gesture for Mary Ellen to remain silent. He then placed his phone on speaker and proceeded to tell Stuart the situation as he knew it including Zach's abusive behavior. Once he was finished, Stuart wasted no time with his response.

"A couple of questions. I assume this friend lives in Georgia."

"Yes. She does."

"And isn't involved with another person, man or woman."

Mary Ellen shook her head.

"No. She's not the type. She's a wonderful, loving person." Mary Ellen turned red in embarrassment at the comment.

"With all your interest in this woman, I have to ask… have you gone over to the other side?" Stuart asked and laughed.

"If either one of us could change, this is the type of person you'd want in your life," countered Dom.

"Well, tell her, if she wants a divorce, she's got a slam dunk. As far as her child is concerned, in Georgia, unless the woman has a drug or alcohol addiction, prostitutes herself, sells drugs or has killed someone, she gets custody of the children ninety-nine percent of the time. And she'll get child support. More than likely, she'll get alimony unless she makes more than her husband. And they split all assets that have been acquired during the marriage, fifty, fifty. Tell her if she wants a lawyer, I'll gladly take the case."

Mary Ellen could hardly believe what she was hearing especially after the threats from Zach. She nodded her head enthusiastically and mouthed *Yes*.

"Are you offering a special of the week?" asked Dom.

"I am if a dinner at a restaurant of my choice is included."

"It is. I'll make reservations for this coming Saturday if you and Curtis are free."

"I'm putting it on my calendar as we speak. Have your friend call me tomorrow and we'll set up an appointment."

After some ending banter and an effusive thank you from Dom, the two men hung up.

"So there you go. You're in the driver's seat. And I'll make sure Stu gives you a good rate. But knowing him, he'll have Zach pay his fee in the settlement."

Mary Ellen was completely relaxed. Then tenseness, the anxiety, the fear… all gone. At least for now. She didn't know if it was Dom, the lawyer, the wine or the combination of all three. But she felt a complete sense of relief like she hadn't felt in a long time.

"Dom, you've been so sweet and kind, I don't know how to thank you."

"Friends do what friends have to do. Look, it's late and I've got a busy day tomorrow. I need to be going. I want you to take tomorrow off. Think long and hard about your and Ashley's future. Does it include Zach or not. If not, and if divorce is your only avenue to happiness, then call Stuart." Dom wrote down the lawyer's name and telephone number on the back of one of his bank's business cards and handed it to Mary Ellen. "And knowing Zach's abusive history, you might want to change the locks on the doors."

"My parents are coming up Saturday. And Zach is supposed to be back in town Saturday, too. But I've told him not to come home. He can stay at Girlfriend's house."

"He has a girlfriend? Here in Atlanta? What a low life." Dom realized how judgmental he sounded and immediately apologized. "I'm sorry. I shouldn't have said that. It was not my place."

"Don't apologize. You're right. Not only does he have Girlfriend here, he also has girlfriends everywhere. I live in fear that I might come down with some STD. I try to avoid having sex with him, but every now and then, he feels like he has to mark his territory. And always in a sadistic and unfeeling way."

"You *do* need to call Stu. And make sure you tell him about Girlfriend *and* the girlfriends."

Dom looked at his watch and stood up to leave. Mary Ellen immediately followed suit.

"Can you stay the night? Please. We've been drinking and if you got pulled over, I'd feel terrible. And it would have been my fault. Please stay."

Dom thought about what she had said. A DUI on top of a robbery would not look so good to upper management. His fast rise to the top could be quickly curtailed. Plus, he didn't have the heart to refuse. Mary Ellen was living in such turbulent times. Besides, what could it hurt?

John Thomas

Thursday, August 8, 2019

ATLANTA, GEORGIA

CHAPTER 32

Zach's alarm on his cell phone woke him with a start. Normally his body clock would have awakened him precisely at 2 a.m. But evidently, the Tylenol PM had unplugged it. He pulled off his sleep mask, turned off the alarm, grabbed his dopp kit and headed to the truck stop showers. Normally, the showers at this particular truck stop cost $12. But with his fill-up of over 50 gallons, his was free. And unless it were free, he wouldn't take one. Not in his budget. A free alternative was a shower at one of his many girlfriends' houses or trailer homes. He wasn't picky.

Back in his cab and before getting on the road, he thought about what Billy had told him. Surely, he was wrong. Mary Ellen wouldn't get anything. She's never paid one dime toward the house, cars, furniture or anything. The little bit of money she made at the bank was used primarily to buy groceries. *Billy's full of shit* he thought. Still, it wouldn't hurt to get some advice from a lawyer. He turned and reached behind his seat and pulled his laptop from one of the truck's many storage bins. After signing on, he did a Google search of Georgia divorce lawyers. There was obviously not a shortage with his search showing more than 10 pages of divorce attorneys. Zach had to scroll to the second page to find one that offered free consultations and specialized in father's rights. He wrote down the name and telephone number on the back of his logbook. He would call him either on his break or while at lunch.

He returned his laptop to its designated bin, slid the logbook in the side pocket and drove out of the truck stop and onto the highway. At this time of the morning, the traffic was light. He smiled. This is where he was the happiest. The bitch wasn't going to get him down and for damn sure, she wasn't going to get his money. Or Ashley.

CHAPTER 33

Ike jumped up on the Colonel's side of the bed and began licking the old man's face. As the dog had gotten older, he had started losing his continence resulting in earlier and irregular start times to the morning walks. The dog did not like having "accidents." He was a proud dog and it embarrassed him. To the Colonel and Betty's credit, they understood and never once scolded the dog. For Betty, it was her inborn kindness. For the Colonel, it was probably being a kindred spirit with the dog as he, too, was having issues with continence.

While the Colonel put on his bathrobe and headed to the bathroom, Ike ran to the kitchen and sat at the door waiting patiently, but anxiously, for the old man to arrive. With very little time left, Ike felt the need to signal his master of an impending "accident", so he gave out a couple of short yelps.

"Hold your damn horses," grumbled the old man as he entered the kitchen. He grabbed the leash off its hook and snapped it onto Ike's collar. The dog couldn't get out of the house fast enough, so he helped the Colonel open the door by pushing it with his paw and then nudging it with the top of his head. Once outside, Ike found the nearest tree just off the driveway. The Colonel looked across the street at the Ferguson's house. The detective's car was still there. It was very concerning to him. Was Mary Ellen still in fear of retribution from that robber? Was this just standard procedure by the police? Or was this simply a CYA from the police, just making sure all bases were covered? He didn't know, but once Mary Ellen got home from work, he and Betty were going to see how they could help.

While Ike continued to sniff and then mark his territory at every bush and tree within the leash's extended length, the Colonel texted Zach his morning report

> *Detective's car is still in the driveway. Another all-nighter. Will check on ME and let you know if anything is wrong. Colonel Robert Oliver.*

Zach heard the text notification ding on his 'family' cell phone but did not check the message. This was by choice. Neither of his cell phones was within arm's length. A tip he learned from a seasoned driver. That way, he wouldn't be tempted to answer calls, listen to voicemails or read texts while driving.

A short while later, he pulled into a rest area. He instinctively checked the truck's clock. He had made good time. Twenty minutes was all he allowed himself for his breaks. That way, he could have more face time behind the wheel. He drove slowly past the facilities house and parked in a spot facing out toward the expressway. Leaving the engine and air conditioner running, he swiveled the driver's seat around to the back of the cab and pulled both of his cell phones from their cubicle and set the alarm on his 'truck' phone to 7:36 a.m., his end of break. From his little built-in refrigerator, he pulled out the leftovers from yesterday's dinner. He had hardly touched it thanks to Billy's insight on divorce. But there was no way he would pay for food and not eat it. While he prepared his food in the microwave, he checked the messages on his 'family' phone. Both were from the Colonel.

> Text 1: *6:38 PM   Same detective car is at your house again tonight. Will text you know tomorrow if he stayed the night. Colonel Robert Oliver.*

> Text 2: *7:03 AM Detective's car is still in the driveway. Another all-nighter. Will check on ME and let you know if anything is wrong. Colonel Robert Oliver.*

"That son-of-a-bitch is at my house *AGAIN*," he screamed then slammed his plate of food into the side trash container as the vision of Dom and his wife lying in bed together returned. "That lying whore. That worthless piece of shit." All he could think about was all the lies she must have told him about Dom when he had confronted her about their relationship not long after Mary Ellen started working for the bank. *Oh, no. He's just my boss. Just a friend. He's not like that. Besides, he's not my type.* He wondered how long had they had been sleeping together. One year, two years, five years. The more he thought about it the madder he got. If he were home, he'd make them pay… both of them.

Zach found his cell phone on the floor where it had landed in his fit of anger. He picked it up, signed on and tapped Mary Ellen's name. The call went straight to voicemail.

"PICK UP THE PHONE, WHORE!"

He tried calling a couple more times, but the calls went to voicemail. Furiously, he texted Mary Ellen a message.

*YOU TELL THAT FUCKER THAT IF HE COMES INTO MY
HOUSE AGAIN I WILL CUT HIS BALLS OFF!!!*

Then in the heat of the moment, he threw the phone towards his bunk where it bounced to the floor. As he picked it up, his eyes were drawn to a drawer under his bed. He opened it and pulled out a small lockbox. He pressed in a security code on the lid which released the lock. Inside lay an old Smith & Wesson 38 caliber revolver and a box of shells. He had purchased the weapon in Arizona at a gun show at a private sale where no licenses were required. He bought it for his protection since he often hauled cargos of merchandise highly targeted by thieves. Pharmaceuticals, electronics and apparel. Merchandise that could be easily sold on the black market or to foreign buyers. While most freight lines forbid their drivers from carrying concealed weapons and could fire the driver for violating company policy, Zach's company turned a blind eye as long as the driver had a valid concealed weapon carry permit.

As he pulled the gun from the lockbox, he realized that his text had not been an idle threat. *Had* he been home and had been able to confront his wife's lover, he would have blown his manhood away. Maybe worse. He checked the weapon's safety. It was on. He then pointed it at his mattress imagining how it would feel to fire bullets into both their naked bodies. His psychotic thoughts were interrupted by the alarm coming from his cell phone. His twenty minutes were up. The simple sing-song clamor was like an on/off switch for his rage. For almost twenty minutes he yelled, screamed, cussed… had nefarious thoughts of killing his wife and her lover. Then, almost like a person with a bipolar personality, the cell phone's alarm caused Zach to do a one-eighty. He quickly returned the gun to the lockbox, closed the lid which automatically set the lock, closed the drawer and swiveled the driver's seat back facing the windshield. His trucking duties and responsibilities had called and he would respond. He was back to doing what he loved most… driving. However, he knew he was far from finished with his wife and her lover.

CHAPTER 34

With Dom staying over, Mary Ellen felt secure and her sleep was restful until she heard Zach's irritating ringtone… twice… followed by a ding signaling an incoming text message. She chose to ignore them until Ashley was in Dom's car and heading off to school. Having Dom around for the last two nights had been life-changing. She could see what she and Ashley were missing. A good home life. A decent and caring man. One that you could look forward to growing old with. And a life not filled with threats, insults and abusive behavior. But one filled with love, hopes and dreams. She really didn't want to read the text or listen to any message Zach might have left now that he knew she wanted a divorce. She knew it wouldn't be pleasant. But she read it anyway.

YOU TELL THAT FUCKER THAT IF HE COMES INTO MY HOUSE AGAIN I WILL CUT HIS BALLS OFF!!!

THAT FUCKER had to be Dom. The threat against him was unnerving. But how did he know that Dom had stayed the night? Did he have Girlfriend come by? Possibly take pictures so he could use them in the divorce? Maybe it was Ashley. Maybe she had called her dad. Mary Ellen wished she had told her daughter not to say anything to her father about Dom's visits. But she hadn't and now she was sorry she had asked her friend to stay the night. She checked the time on her cell phone. Not enough time had elapsed for Dom to have driven Ashley to school. She needed to talk to him and Ashley. She called her daughter first.

"Hey. Where are you?" Mary Ellen tried to keep her voice calm.

"We're at the stoplight at Powers Ferry and Delk. Why? Anything wrong? Did I forget something?"

"No. I was just worried about my daughter being in that racing car with that crazy fast driver."

"Oh mother," said Ashley, elongating her words. "Dom hasn't even done the speed limit yet. In fact, I think everybody's passing us." Dom gave her the thumbs up.

"Honey, by any chance did you tell your father that Dom had come over? That he had stayed with us last night?"

"Am I in trouble?"

Mary Ellen knew that meant yes she had.

"No, honey. But I should have told him. I just forgot."

"Mom, we're here. Gotta go." Then Ashley hung up.

Mary Ellen was glad that Girlfriend hadn't come by their house. But she needed to tell Dom and her attorney about the threat. And the sooner the better.

CHAPTER 35

Mary Ellen waited until 8:00 a.m. to call Stuart Friedman, the lawyer friend of Dom's. She expected the call to either be answered by a secretary or go to voicemail if the office hadn't opened. She was surprised when the lawyer, himself, answered the call.

"Mr. Friedman, this is Mary Ellen Ferguson. Dominick Garcia called you yesterday. Have I caught you at a bad time?" While Mary Ellen couldn't see the attorney, she envisioned him as someone Dom's age who wore a khaki suit, blue oxford shirt complete with bowtie. Later she would see that she had been right about the age and bowtie.

"I have to be in court at nine, but we're just around the corner from the courthouse, so we've got time to talk."

"I've thought about this long and hard and have definitely decided to file for divorce. What do I need to do next?"

The attorney began to pace back and forth in front of his desk as he proceeded to tell her all the steps that a divorce case entailed. As he did, she sat at the kitchen table making notes on her legal pad. Once he had given her a general idea of what she was facing, he set up a date the following Monday for her to come into the office to sign all of the preliminary documents.

"What about your fees?"

"Let's not worry about them. And anyway, from what Dom told me about your husband, we will be asking *him* to pay my fees." What he didn't tell Mary Ellen was that he was waiving his retainer fee.

"Dom is one of the reasons why I called so early today. This morning I got a text from my husband threatening him."

"Dom? Threatening Dom? Why him? Because he referred you to me?" asked Stuart.

"No. Because Zach, my husband, found out that Dom had spent the night at my house with me and Ashley. He's very envious of Dom and I'm sure that set him off."

"Why did Dom spend the night with you?"

"Because of the robbery. My daughter and I were scared and…"

"Robbery? Dom's robbery?"

"Yes. I'm the teller that he… the robber threatened."

"Dom didn't tell me that. You've got a whole lot on your plate." Stuart thought for a second. "Look. Can you come to my office… say… one o'clock? We can continue our talk then. I'll have my secretary reschedule my afternoon appointments and we can get working on your case. And whatever you do, don't delete any text, voice or email from your husband, threatening or otherwise. We might need them."

The call ended and Stuart grabbed the handle of his rolling briefcase and headed off to the courthouse while Mary Ellen scanned back through her notes. Dom was right about his friend. He seemed to be an excellent lawyer. But what did she know about lawyers? She had never needed to engage the services of one. And when they had needed one, like the closing on the house, Zach had been in control, just like he had their entire marriage. She was surprised, yet happy, that she had not gotten cold feet and had made the call before Zach got back into town and *coerced* her into changing her mind knowing full well what that meant.

CHAPTER 36

Zach looked at the mileage marker and then time on his dashboard clock. He realized that he must have been driving faster than he normally drove. His distraction had to be caused by the phone call from Mary Ellen and the texts he had gotten from the Colonel because that was all he could think about… his wife in bed with another man, the impending divorce and losing his house, his daughter… everything he'd ever worked for.

He backed off the pedal and slowed his rig down to an acceptable speed. But that didn't stop the images of his wife in bed with ol' cue ball. What could she possibly see in him? Okay. He had to acknowledge that he was a better dresser and had a better job. But the man was small, had a head that looked like a melon and probably couldn't fight his way out of a paper bag. Charlie Brown's twin. Zach had gotten older, but he was still very handsome and very good in bed.

Normally, his lunch stop was around 11:45 a.m. But with the good time he'd made, he had arrived at his planned lunch stop twenty minutes earlier than expected. The McDonald's was a popular stop-off for buses and big rigs because of its extra-large parking lot with oversized parking spaces.

Being an early arriver, all the extra-large parking spaces were open except the first which had been taken by a tour bus. He pulled his truck cab slightly ahead of the bus where he could see the vacationers as they exited the bus and headed towards the restaurant. It was a sad reminder of the times that he and Mary Ellen had traveled together in his truck, seeing America. Those had been good times. But somehow, she had changed. And now he knew why and with whom.

Zach pulled out his logbook from the side door pocket, swiveled his driver's seat around facing the back of the cab and pulled out both of his phones. He set the timer for twenty minutes on the 'truck' phone and set his 'family' phone aside while he nuked a pepperoni Hot Pockets. While it cooked, he dialed the telephone number of the lawyer that he had written on the back of his logbook. He knew free advice would not be much and wouldn't be long, but maybe it would be enough to know whether Billy Meadows was bullshitting him or not. *That bitch ain't getting half of anything.*

"Holland, Jeffords and McCabe," answered the receptionist.

"Uh… It's my understanding that you offer free divorce advice? That's what I'm looking for."

"Yes sir. Mr. Jeffords and Mr. McCabe are in today. If you want, I can see who's free."

"Yes ma'am. Free is what I want." Zach then laughed at his attempted humor. The receptionist had heard the same unfunny comment dozens of times.

"Can I get your name, sir?"

Zach gave the lady his name and waited until he heard a deep voice answer the phone.

"Mr. Ferguson, this is George McCabe. How can I help you today?"

"My wife wants a divorce and a buddy of mine tells me she's gonna get half of everything I own. Is that true?"

"Is this buddy of yours a lawyer?" asked McCabe.

"No. He's a truck driver… just like me."

"My first bit of free advice, sir, is not to take free advice about legal matters from someone who is not a lawyer."

"So what rights *do* I have in a divorce?"

"I'm sorry, sir. You've already asked your one question and I've given you your free advice. You're only entitled to one, so the next one is gonna cost you," said McCabe very seriously at first but then burst into a hearty laugh. "Just joking." He waited but heard no laughter coming from his caller, so McCabe continued. "Do you both live in Georgia?"

"Yes sir."

"And you are currently represented by any other law firm?"

"No sir."

"Has your wife already filed for divorce? Have you been served?"

"Served?"

"Has anyone handed you any divorce papers?"

"No sir. I've been on the road. She just told me yesterday."

"Good. Mr. Ferguson, divorce is never easy, especially without the proper representation. It is an intense and emotional process. Our goal at Holland, Jeffords and McCabe is to help you navigate through the legal complexities of divorce, develop a proper strategy and get you the best possible settlement in regards to asset allocation, child custody, debt obligations and alimony. Not everything is black and white in divorce cases. And the outcome of your case will depend on many factors. Our law firm is prepared to handle any issue that may arise. We *only* do family law and through our program of continuing legal education we are always current in the ever-changing intricacies of the law."

George McCabe had given the same spiel hundreds, maybe thousands of times. He needed no notes. It was committed to memory. Part of the job. Then continuing with his marketing effort, "In terms of what rights you have in a divorce, you are entitled to a fair and equitable settlement. But should you choose the wrong law firm, it could end up costing you thousands of dollars. Dollars that should have stayed in your pocket."

Zach checked his cell phone. He had about five minutes left before he had to get back on the road. His Hot Pockets were already cold and his Coke was hot and he was pissed.

"Sir, I appreciate what you are saying. I'm a long-distance truck driver and I've gotta get back on the road. Yes or No. Will my wife get half of everything I own, like the house that I bought and never paid one red dime toward the mortgage or anything?"

"Without knowing the facts of your case, I could be liable for giving out erroneous advice. But here's what I will tell you… and this information is readily available on the internet… in Georgia, any asset you acquire during a marriage, regardless of who pays what, in most cases will be subject to an even and equitable distribution among the parties, with any inheritance excluded. My suggestion is that we set up an appointment for you to come in and discuss your case in detail."

"How much are we talking about for your firm to represent me?"

"Again, that depends on a lot of factors. For example, will this divorce be contested or uncontested. Do we have to bring in expert witnesses? Do we have to hire a private investigator?"

"Can you just ballpark a normal divorce?"

"On average, our fees run around $12,000 plus a $1500 retainer fee."

"You're kidding me. I saw an ad on the web for another lawyer that said they could do the divorce for $700."

"That is an uncontested divorce where you and your wife agree on all issues of the divorce including the division of all known assets *before* you or she files. Typically, we see those types of divorces where the couple has only been married a short time with very little accumulated assets during the marriage. Do you have children?"

"Yes sir."

"We do not recommend that type of divorce when children are involved. If that's the type of representation you are looking for, we are not your firm. Do you have any other questions?" George McCabe did not wait for a reply. "If not, I've got a client waiting in our lobby. Goodbye." McCabe had been a lawyer long enough to know when he was talking to a potential client and Ferguson wasn't one.

McCabe wasn't the only one frustrated. The call had not gone like Zach had thought or wanted. He knew no more now than before the call. He had just sat through a sales pitch. He placed the Hot Pockets back in the microwave and set the timer for twenty seconds. He pulled out his 'truck' phone and found Billy Meadows' name under his *Contacts*. The microwave dinged and for the second time, he pulled out his lunch. He took a couple of bites and tossed it in the trash can. His free advice had just cost him his lunch. With his break time nearly over, he decided to give Billy a call anyway. He had a few more questions and they wouldn't cost a dime. And he knew that if Billy was anywhere near his phone, he'd pick up whether driving, eating or just sitting around.

"Zachman… what's up?" answered his friend.

"You got a second?"

"I'm getting ready to pull off for lunch in four more exits. But you got my ear until then."

"About your divorce. If you don't mind answering, how much did you have to pay your lawyer?"

"My lawyer cost me about $16,000, but we hired a private eye to see if we could catch my wife in the act. Didn't happen. So I got hit with alimony for the rest of her whole friggin' life unless the ugly bitch gets married. And the chance of that happening is somewhere between zero and zero."

"What about those $700 divorces I've seen on the internet? Why didn't you give them a try?"

"What I understand, you both have to agree to everything before going to court. And if your old lady has already lawyered up, then that ain't gonna happen. And by the way, if you lose, which most men do, you're probably going to be stuck with her lawyer's bill, too. I know I am. That was another ten grand. I'm gonna have to work until I'm a hundred to pay off all these lawyer bills. Like I said, a hitman would have been cheaper." Billy laughed, but Zach didn't.

CHAPTER 37

Mary Ellen had no trouble starting the Toyota Camry on the first try. She was still nervous that the car would fail her at a most inopportune time but not today. And now that she had gained enough confidence to divorce Zach, she also decided that she would take her Camry back to Pep Boys once her parents arrived Saturday.

Stuart Friedman's office was a white clapboard house located just off the Marietta square on Lawrence Street. While the exterior of the building was simple in design, the interior was quite the opposite with most of the furniture being antiques or replicas. When Mary Ellen entered the office, a young man who was sitting behind a large mahogany antique desk immediately arose and welcomed his guest and introduced himself.

"Are you Ms. Ferguson?"

"Yes." Mary Ellen was taken back. She did not expect to see her lawyer sitting behind what she thought was a receptionist/secretary's desk.

"Julie, our receptionist, secretary and office manager who rules with an iron fist is at lunch and we take turns filling in for her until she gets back. Today's my turn. Can I get you a Coke or some water?" asked the young man. His looks were totally different from what she had imagined other than the bowtie. Rather than a khaki suit, he was sharply dressed in grey slacks, white shirt and dark blue blazer. And unlike Dom who had nary a hair on his head, Stuart's hair was full, dark brown and slicked back in the Robert De Niro Godfather's style.

"I am so glad we were able to meet today," said the lawyer offering Mary Ellen a seat in front of the desk. He came from around the desk and sat in the other chair facing the desk and turned it to face Mary Ellen. "It's always good to be able to put a face to a voice. I must admit you don't look anything like I had imagined… and in a good way. You're much younger and prettier."

Mary Ellen blushed at the compliment. She was not used to getting any from Zach.

"So how do you know Dom?" asked Mary Ellen.

"He and I were fraternity brothers at the University of Georgia. He had hair then," said Stuart laughing and then slicking his hair back with his hand. "He and I both graduated with a business degree. He went to work for the bank and I went to law school. We've stayed in touch ever since. We go out to dinner at least once a month with some fellow bulldogs (The University of Georgia's mascot). But enough about me and Dom. Tell me about you, and I want to hear about the threat to Dom and the robbery."

Mary Ellen spent the better part of the next half hour going over her life with Zach. She told of how happy she thought they were in Augusta and at first in Atlanta when he began driving trucks. She then told how he began to change the longer he was away from the family. How he had become abusive, verbally, sexually and physically. She made certain that Stuart knew that Zach never once hurt their daughter. That she was the love of his life. That he loved their daughter more than anything in the world. Then she told Stuart about Girlfriend.

Stuart did not interrupt her until she mentioned Girlfriend.

"When Dom and I talked yesterday, he didn't say anything about your husband having a girlfriend." Stuart tried never to use the husband's name. He wanted to keep the discussion impersonal. So never Zach. Always husband. "How long has this been going on?"

"I'm guessing three or four years."

"Do you know her name and where she lives?"

"Liz Davis. Her name is Elizabeth Davis. I don't know where she lives, but it's somewhere in Atlanta."

Stuart had been writing while Mary Ellen had been talking. He circled Girlfriend's name and put a question mark on the margin next to her name. He would have her deposed and possibly called as a witness should the case go to trial.

"We'll find her. Please continue."

Mary Ellen told how Girlfriend came first. How Zach stayed with her nearly half of the time he was off the road and back in Atlanta.

"Before I forget it, I would like to see the text that your husband sent threatening Dom?"

Mary Ellen pulled out her phone and found the text and showed it to Stuart.

YOU TELL THAT FUCKER THAT IF HE COMES INTO MY HOUSE AGAIN I WILL CUT HIS BALLS OFF!!!

"And you say the threat was made because Dom had stayed over at your house?"

"Yes. A detective was supposed to stay… you know because of the robbery threat. But Dom volunteered and I thought it would be better having somebody over that Ashley knew. She likes Dom, so it would be more calming. So he came."

"And so Zach found out."

"Yes. Ashley told him."

"But why did he get so angry? Has Dom ever said or done anything to your husband to make him this angry?"

"Oh no. Never. Zach has never liked Dom. He's very jealous of him, especially when it comes to Ashley. And he thinks we are having an affair."

"He doesn't know that Dom is gay?"

"I've never told him. Zach's a homophobe and would probably make me quit working at the bank if he knew. But I will if that's what it takes to keep Zach away. I don't want anything to happen to him. You think I should tell Dom about the threat or Zach that Dom's gay?"

"You should definitely tell Dom about the threat just so he's aware of the situation. But I wouldn't worry. Even though he's on the small side, I know he can take care of himself. He came out early and his parents trained him in karate or something like that to be able to protect himself. As far as telling your husband that Dom is gay, first of all, I don't think he'd believe you. And secondly, I think we should save that as our silver bullet in case in his counterclaim he tries using adultery as his grounds thinking he can avoid paying you alimony."

"In the meantime, I'll send your husband a letter letting him know in no uncertain terms that we will have the courts issue a restraining order should he harass, intimidate, stalk or threaten Dom in any way. I can send it addressed to him at your house and his girlfriend's. This should cool him off some. But I gotta let you know that without proof, and this text is not specific enough, most judges will not issue the order. The letter is just a bluff… a warning and usually it's enough to scare off the uninformed. What I'm more concerned about, is you. Hearing how jealous, controlling and abusive your husband sounds, the sooner we file and serve him the divorce papers, the more protected you are. Once the divorce papers are filed, an MRO, Mutual Restraining Order, automatically goes into effect. This protects you financially during the divorce proceedings and prohibits your husband from taking Ashley out of state. It also keeps him from harassing you. Do you think you'll be all right until then?"

"Yes, I think so. Zach won't be back in town until Saturday and my parents are coming up that morning. Not only that, I've kicked him out of the house. Told him to stay at Girlfriend's house. And Dom told me that just to be on the safe side, I should have the locks on the doors changed."

"That's why Dom is a banker and I'm a lawyer," laughed Stuart. "If you file for divorce, you can't do what you just said. The MRO works both ways. It protects you from him and vice versa. Since your house was purchased during your marriage, your husband has as much right to live there as you. So you can't kick him out or change the locks. The best thing we can do is to get him served. Get the MRO. If he becomes abusive or harasses or threatens you, we call the police and then we can get a Temporary Restraining Order."

"So what do we do next?" asked Mary Ellen.

"You have to decide on what grounds you will be filing for divorce. There are thirteen grounds in Georgia. Most don't pertain to you. I believe your marriage is irretrievably broken and those are the grounds I would recommend. It's kind of a no-fault divorce where neither party admits guilt. You could choose to use adultery as grounds, but we would have to prove it. And getting incriminating pictures, texts, emails, et cetera would not be easy and could cost a lot. And the trial could be very embarrassing, especially to your daughter. I just wouldn't do it."

"I agree. This is going to be hard enough on Ashley as it is. Let's go with the broken marriage thing because that's what it is. I trust your opinion."

"One last thing… and this is a standard question I ask all of my clients seeking a divorce. Are you or have you ever been in an extramarital affair?"

"Oh no. Never. Zach is the only man I have ever …" Mary Ellen stopped midsentence. She had almost said *made love to*, but that was no longer what they did in bed.

Before she could find words to complete her sentence, Stuart jumped in. "Okay. So here's what we do." Stuart looked at his watch. "Julie will be back here in exactly seven minutes. She always takes an hour for lunch. Never any more and never any less. She'll get all the information she needs for us to create the necessary documents to file in court and to serve your husband. And rather than waiting on the Sheriff's office to serve your husband, we'll use a process server. Costs a little bit more, but this is the quickest way to get your husband served."

As Stuart had predicted, Julie arrived promptly at 1:45 p.m. Stuart introduced the two women and told his secretary what he wanted.

"So Julie will take over from here. She will postdate the documents with tomorrow's date just to give you a chance to make sure you want to go through with the divorce. Then if you decide to file, you can come by anytime tomorrow morning and sign the documents. Then I'll run them over to the courthouse and get the ball rolling."

Mary Ellen had made up her mind. She didn't need a day to decide, but she would do what her lawyer had asked.

CHAPTER 38

Zach pulled into a truck stop just outside of Bowling Green, Kentucky. With everything he had running through his mind, it had been a long, tough drive. While he had his truck refilled, he checked his emails and text messages on both phones. His only text was from Liz, his girlfriend, saying she was looking forward to the weekend, wanted to know when to expect him and to please call her.

Liz Davis and Zach met at the trucking company where both were employed, Zach as a truck driver and Liz as a dispatcher. She and Zach's wife were extreme opposites in regards to looks and personality. She was overweight, wore more make-up than should be legally allowed and dressed mainly in blue jeans and plaid shirts. She took no guff from any of the truckers and could tell a joke with the best of them. What attracted Zach to her was a mystery to all who worked with Liz. Behind her back, everyone referred to them as beauty and the old beast as Liz was 12 years older than Zach.

Liz had worked at the trucking company for sixteen years. She had her favorite drivers and Zach became one of them as soon as she saw him. She constantly teased him about his good looks and what she'd do to him if she ever got him in bed. Zach enjoyed her teasing and returned her taunts with similar jibes. Their sexual relationship began one night when a bunch of the truckers and office workers gathered at a local bar for a round of drinks celebrating an unexpected performance bonus. Many beers later, Zach found himself in bed with Liz at her house and stayed through the night. She did not disappoint. It was sex like he had never had before at home. Zach and Liz both figured it was a one-night stand. She got what she wanted and Zach got more than he could imagine. But the one-night rendezvous blossomed into an ongoing relationship. It became more than sex. Zach felt comfortable with Liz. They were kindred spirits, both cut from the same mold. A psychiatrist would have diagnosed Zach as having never outgrown Freud's Oedipus complex. Regardless, three years later, Zach and Liz were still lovers.

After the fill-up, Zach pulled his truck into one of the two remaining parking spots. Unlike most people, his nighttime was from 4 p.m. to 2 a.m. He had ten hours to eat and get in his eight hours of sleep. Eleven hours of driving over fourteen hours was the maximum. The hard day of driving accompanied by hours of deep thought had drained Zach to the point of exhaustion. He needed sleep, but he needed to hear Girlfriend's voice even more.

"I didn't figure I'd get a call back until tomorrow. You must be lonely," answered Liz on the first ring.

"It's been a rough day, baby. I'm glad you're home."

"What's wrong, Sweetie? Has the Ice-Woman upset you?"

"You just don't know."

"Do you want to talk about it or not?"

"Let's talk. I need to get some things off my mind."

"I'm listening."

"The bitch told me that she wants a divorce."

"You *have* had a rough day. When did this all happen?"

"Yesterday. Liz, she's gonna fuck up my life."

"You got that right. That's why I'm living in this rat hole." Liz lived barely three miles from Zach's house in a 900 square foot, wood-sided home built in the early '50s. It was located in a racially diverse neighborhood off Highway 41, near the Big Chicken, a 56-foot tall steel structure built to look like a chicken and housed a KFC restaurant.

"You were married once?" asked Zach, a fact he'd never considered.

"Yeah to a lazy, toothless, bloodsucking moron. Why I married him, I'll never understand."

"Anybody I know?"

"No. His name was Wylie Mason. When I married him, he worked as a cop. But couldn't keep his hands off the juice. Eventually, he got fired. After that, he dabbled in construction, painting and whatnot, but he kept getting laid off. So he just quit working altogether. Retired as he put it and mooched off of me. And for some unknown reason, I put up with it."

"So when did you divorce him?"

"Believe it or not, *he* divorced me. A little over eleven years ago. Didn't even see it coming. He was living the life of Riley. Me working. Him drinking. I think one of his drinking buddies got to him. Put the bug in his ear about the benefits of divorce. You know. Me still working and him still drinking but now he gets to spend *my* money any way *he* wants.

Anyway, after the divorce, I changed my name back to my maiden name. I didn't want any part of him, but he sure got a big part of me."

"How much?"

"Well, the goober got almost everything I owned. The house, my 401-k, and my savings account which had almost twenty-five grand of which he knew nothing about. And he contributed almost nothing. Nothing! I tried to hide the savings account, but somehow his lawyer caught wind of the account and I got torn a new one by the judge. And just to throw salt on the wounds, the knucklehead was asking for alimony from *me* since I was the breadwinner. If I hadn't caught him in the act *and with another man*, I feel quite certain I would have ended up paying him a monthly stipend for the rest of my life. I was so mad… and I can't believe I'm telling you this… but I actually thought about killing the bastard. But I learned my lesson. So, if you ever thought about us getting hitched, forget it, bubba. No man or woman will ever steal from me again."

As Liz told her story, Zach couldn't help but think that *everybody* who has gone through a divorce must have considered hiding money or killing off the spouse or both. It seemed to be a common thread.

"Don't worry," answered Zach. "I feel the same way. Oh. And another thing that I just found out… our sweet, little, holier-than-thou, Miss goody-two-shoes has been sleeping with her boss. I got so mad, I would have blown his bald head away if I'd been in town. You know… I don't know why I felt that way. I don't even love her nor do I like her."

"Sweetie, it's called ego. And all men have a big one when it comes to women."

"I just don't see what she sees in him. He's short, bald. Certainly not a man's man."

"So what do you see in me? I'm fat, old and certainly not a girly girl."

Zach had to stop and think. He was at a loss for words. Before he could say something to make it worse, Liz continued.

"I didn't mean to put you on the spot. But if you love someone, you see that person in a different light than the way others see them. You love me for my inner beauty," laughed Liz. "And I love you because you're fucking gorgeous." She laughed again. "If Ice-Woman is sleeping with her boss, you'd better get pictures of the two of them in bed like I did or you'll be doling out alimony every month forever. Not only that, the Ice-woman will get your kid and child support along with it. And if you can't pay for whatever reason, she can get your ass hauled off to jail."

Zach's stomach was churning and his heart pounding. Hearing Liz tell about her divorce confirmed what Billy Meadows and the free lawyer had told him. He was going to get taken to the cleaners. That was all there was to it. And he, too, had a savings account unknown to Mary Ellen or Liz where he'd been depositing his expense checks since he began driving the long hauls. He now had over $17,000 in the bank.

"Why now?" asked Liz. "What prompted her to ask for a divorce now? I know she's known about us for years. Have you done something or said something that sent her over the edge?"

"I don't know. Maybe this robbery thing has …"

"What robbery thing?" interrupted Liz.

"I thought I told you."

"How could you have told me anything? You haven't called me since Monday. So tell me about the robbery?"

Zach told her what he knew about the robbery as he knew it. The note, the pictures, the confrontation, and the threat.

"Geez. Too bad the dude didn't take her out during the heist. That would have solved all your problems."

"Yeah. I've thought about that, too."

"You said he threatened her. What *kind* of threat?"

"Hell, I can't remember exactly what the bitch told me, but it was like the dude was coming back to get her. Like payback. All I know is that she's scared shitless. I don't give two hoots about that. But what pissed me off is she told my daughter everything and frightened the ever-loving hell out of her. Got her so upset, she had to leave school early."

"Maybe you'll get lucky and the guy lives up to his word."

Zach knew he couldn't count on luck. He had to make his own luck.

CHAPTER 39

The wine glass that sat on the kitchen table was either half empty or half full of Chardonnay depending on your outlook on life. Are you an optimist or are you a pessimist? Today, Mary Ellen was an optimist. She was happy. Happier than she had been in years. The wine was not Rombauer. Just a $9 bottle she'd picked up at Kroger. But it was good enough to celebrate her difficult decision to hire a lawyer and begin the process of divorcing Zach.

While Ashley was in her bedroom Facetiming friends, Mary Ellen sent out texts to her parents and to Dom. She wanted them to know that she was moving forward.

To her parents, she texted:

> *Talked to lawyer today. Stuart Friedman. He's a friend of Dom Garcia, my boss. He's very nice and seems like a good lawyer. I will sign papers tomorrow. Are y'all still coming Saturday? I was hoping to change the locks to the house and make Zach stay at his girlfriend's, but my lawyer says I can't legally do that. I don't want to be here alone with Zach. Especially when he is served. Let me know about this weekend. He's here only a couple of days. He leaves Monday and will be gone for 2 weeks. Ashley had a good day at school. I hope she's over this robbery thing. I am. Love ME.*

To Dom, she texted:

> *Talked to Stuart today. He's very nice. I will sign papers tomorrow. BTW, Per Stuart, I can't legally change locks to house as you suggested. He said for you to stick to banking or something like that. LOL. Ashley had a good day at school thanks to you. I hope she's over this robbery thing. I am. Will see you at work tomorrow. ME.*

By the time she sent out Dom's note, she received a reply from her mother:

> *You are doing the right thing. Poppy and I are happy for you. Glad to hear Ashley's doing fine. We will definitely be there*

Saturday around noon and will stay until he leaves and you think it's safe. Do we need to Facetime? Love Mom.

Mary Ellen texted back:

No. Going to chill a bit then get to bed early. Big day tomorrow. I love you. ME.

As she typed her reply to her mother, Ashley walked into the kitchen, dressed for bed. She kissed her mother then sat down in the kitchen chair adjacent to her.

"Are you all right?" Ashley asked. "You're drinking wine. You never do that."

"Just a lot on my mind, honey. And the wine, it's just to relax me." There would never be a right time for Mary Ellen to tell her daughter about her decision to divorce Zach, but she knew that just before bedtime would probably be the worst. So she didn't. She had learned her lesson from the robbery where she told her daughter too much. One bungled decision for the week was bad enough. She didn't want to make it two.

Ashley did not push her mother for details. Instead, she wanted to firm up her plans with friends for the weekend.

"Mom… do you think it'd be okay if I spent the night over at Kelly's house tomorrow? It'd just be me, Kelly and Megan."

Mary Ellen saw the anticipation in her daughter's eyes. How could she refuse? Plus, maybe it would be good for her mental state to get away from her mother for a day.

"I think that would be wonderful. Are you sure you're okay?"

"You mean with the robbery thing? Yeah. I'm good."

"Make sure you text or call your dad and tell him your plans. That way he won't be bugging you in front of your friends." *And I won't have to talk or listen to him,* she thought.

Ashley jumped up giving her mother a thumbs up as she did. Then she kissed her and ran back to her room to FaceTime her friends with the good news. Before going to bed, she texted her dad. She did think it was weird that her mother didn't call or text him herself. But that was grownups. They're weird.

Mary Ellen picked up her phone to text the Colonel. He and Betty had come over earlier in the day just to check on them. And Betty had brought one of her famous pound cakes. Before she could start the text, she saw that she had a reply text from Dom:

Stu's a good man and lawyer. He will lead you in the right direction. Glad Ashley's OK. See you tomorrow. Dom. PS Having Varsity brought in for lunch tomorrow. This is not a bribe. LOL.

(Note: The Varsity is the world's largest fast-food drive-in restaurant taking up over two blocks in Atlanta and has served more than 25,000 customers in a single day.)

She laughed. Dom loved the Varsity food as did most of the bank employees and most of Atlanta. She could take it or leave it.

She texted him back:

Yum. Can't wait. LOL

Then she sent a text to the Colonel thanking him and Betty for coming over and sharing Betty's pound cake. She knew it was the ultimate show of love because pound cake was the Colonel's favorite and he parted ways with it rarely. Mary Ellen loved the Oliver's and could tell that they were concerned about her and Ashley. She assured them that everything was fine. She would tell them about the impending divorce once the papers were signed.

Mary Ellen pushed her iPad back on the table and reached for her glass of wine. As she peered into the light, golden liquid, it dawned on her that this was the first bottle of wine she had bought in more than eight years, the last being, ironically, an anniversary celebration for which Zach chastised her unmercifully for indulging in such a wasteful and expensive extravagance. She had never bought another bottle since then until now. But her life was changing and if she wanted to buy a bottle of wine, then she would buy a bottle of wine. She no longer feared the man she once loved. But then again, maybe it was the wine talking.

John Thomas

Friday, August 9, 2019

ATLANTA, GEORGIA

CHAPTER 40

It was 7 a.m., Friday morning, two days since Zach had gotten the news that Mary Ellen wanted a divorce. He had talked to Billy Meadows, twice, Liz Davis, once, and a lawyer whose name he'd found on the internet, once. Nothing they had said was comforting. In fact, just the opposite. He was about to lose Ashley and half of everything he'd ever worked for unless he could either talk Mary Ellen out of the divorce or talk her into going the uncontested route.

He pulled his truck off the expressway and into an open parking spot located at the rear of an already busy truck stop. He swiveled his seat around to the back of the cab and pulled his 'truck' phone from its designated bin. As always, he set his timer for twenty minutes. As he did, a calendar reminder popped up. *Call RH.*

RH stood for Ramona Hewitt, a road 'friend' he saw about once a year. Zach immediately texted her.

> *Will call you when I get to Columbia. Text me back if this doesn't work for you. Zach*

Then he tossed the 'truck' phone in its storage bin and pulled out the 'family' phone. He had heard a message ding earlier and figured it was Mary Ellen. Instead, he saw that the text was from Ashley. As he read his daughter's text, he couldn't help but smile.

> *Yo dad. Hope you're not reading this while you're driving. Fat chance. LOL. No problems at school today except the usual ones with my teachers. Ha Ha. Just wanted to let you know I'm spending the night at Kelly's... a girl. Didn't want you to worry if you called or texted and I didn't answer. We'll be busy doing girl stuff. Drive safe. I love you. Ashley.*

Zach sat back in his chair and reread the message. He then texted her back.

> *Just read your message. Stay away from those teachers and boys. Just kidding. Have fun. Will see you sometime this weekend. I love you. Dad*

Ashley was his princess. And so far, Mary Ellen hadn't poisoned her feelings. And as far as he was concerned, that would never happen. He would make *sure* that never happened.

He slid the phone into the cup holders in the arm of his chair, swiveled around and pulled a frozen sausage biscuit from the freezer section of his little fridge and popped it into the microwave. While his biscuit cooked, he pulled out his laptop from its storage bin and googled *Uncontested Divorces in Georgia.* His screen immediately filled up with law firms offering the cheap divorce. He clicked on the first ad and began reading about the pros and cons of an uncontested divorce. He liked what he saw. If the bitch was hell-bent on getting a divorce, he would agree but only to an uncontested one. He would offer her half the net value of the house and child support. There would be no court appearances, no discovery, no witnesses, no alimony and no huge lawyer's fee. He would be in control. That way he could hide his retirement money, his secret savings account and move all the divorce costs on to her. He read one more of the lawyer's ads which confirmed his thinking and closed his laptop. He slid it back into its storage bin, grabbed his cell phone from his cup holder and texted Mary Ellen his conditions for a divorce.

If you want a divorce, you can have it. It has to be uncontested. I will give you half of the current net value of the house and 350 per month in child support. I want to be able to see Ashley when I'm not on the road. I think this is fair. Text me your answer. Z

The biscuit was cold and hard by the time he pulled it from the microwave. *Just like Mary Ellen.* He ate it anyway. He was just about to swivel his chair back toward the front of the cab when he received Mary Ellen's reply.

I will let you know once I talk to my lawyer. ME

"Son of a bitch," yelled Zach knowing that most lawyers were like the one he'd talked to earlier. They were only interested in getting the big bucks. No chump change like an uncontested divorce. He needed to speak to her before she could talk to her lawyer. Make sure she told him that she wanted an uncontested divorce. He calmed himself then called her.

After a halfhearted 'Hello' from Mary Ellen, Zach immediately pounced, while trying to keep the call as friendly as he could.

"You saw my text. I think what I've offered is *extremely* fair. Better than what any lawyer's going to get you. If you want a divorce, you can have it. But I don't want those sharks taking more than what *we* get. And that's what going to happen unless we do this uncontested thing. I read on the internet that we can fill out the paperwork online and have the divorce done in about a month. What's the problem with doing that?"

"I'm sure it's fair. But divorce is a legal matter and I think I need legal advice."

"What's your lawyer's name? You just pull some bozo's name from the internet? Someone who's gonna take us *both* to the cleaners?"

Mary Ellen didn't see any harm in giving out her lawyer's name. Zach would find out soon enough.

"Stuart Friedman. He's here, in Marietta. A friend of Dom's." As soon as she said Dom, she knew she'd made a mistake.

"*Dom. Always Dom.* He fucks you and now he's trying to fuck me. I'm going to kill that son of a bitch." Zach had lost it. There was no calm in his voice. Before he continued, the 'truck' cell phone timer went off. His 20 minutes were up just like his blood pressure. "You tell that son-of-a-bitch to stay out of my life. And if you know what's good for you, you'll do what I say with this divorce thing or I'll make sure you get nothing!"

He abruptly hung up the phone and tossed it back into its bin. His heart was pounding and he could feel the pulsing sensation in his temples. Angrily, he swiveled his chair back towards the front of the cab, crammed the truck's gearshift into second gear and drove out of the truck stop and onto the expressway yelling obscenities all the way.

Mary Ellen knew she shouldn't have answered the phone. Once again Zach had threatened Dom. Sweet Dom. A man who would never harm a soul. Why had she put him at risk again?   She needed to talk to Stuart. And the sooner the better.

CHAPTER 41

The Toyota Camry struggled but still managed to crank on the third try. Mary Ellen prayed it would make it one more day. Then she would get her daddy to follow her up to Pep Boys. It was ten 'til eight when she drove into Stuart Friedman's parking lot located to the side and back of the office.

Even though the office didn't officially open until 8 a.m., Julie, the receptionist, had the front door unlocked and was sitting behind the desk where Stuart had sat the day before. Upon seeing Mary Ellen enter the room, Julie stood and offered her a chair at the desk and a hot cup of coffee. Mary Ellen refused the coffee and took her seat. Julie pulled a folder from her in-basket and sat back down. The folder contained the attorney's fee agreement, the divorce complaint and the summons. She explained what each was and asked for a credit card to pay the filing fee.

"Is Stuart in? I need to talk to him."

Julie rang the attorney and within seconds he was out of his office, down the hall and in the receptionist area.

"Good Morning," he said cheerfully. "Are we a go or no go?"

"That's what I wanted to talk to you about."

Stuart led Mary Ellen back to his office. She sat in one of the two wingback chairs facing his desk and he made himself comfortable in his leather, executive chair.

"If you want to call off the divorce, I completely understand. It happens more often than people know. There's no cost to you."

"No. That's not what I want to talk about. Two things. First, Zach says he'll give me the divorce, but he wants to do an uncontested divorce." She then told Stuart about the terms offered by her husband.

"I don't think that's a good idea in your situation. Based on what you and Dom have told me, your husband seems to be very controlling. And hearing his offer, he hasn't changed. You will be better off financially using us or any other divorce attorney than what your husband has proposed. There's no mention of alimony, health insurance, retirement funds, automobiles, and the list goes on. During discovery, if we feel he's hiding assets, we'll hire a forensic accountant who can uncover almost anything. So my advice is to reject his offer."

"I should have known that Zach was only thinking about himself. I guess then… I just need to sign the papers?"

"Yes. And the $200 filing fee to the courts. I'm sorry I can't waive the fee. It's something that our firm won't allow. But that should be all you have to pay. One other thing. If you don't want to talk to your husband, you don't have to. Once he's been served which I plan to have done tomorrow, we'll let him know that if he wants to discuss anything related to the divorce, to call us. Not you. And if he starts getting belligerent or starts harassing you, we'll get a temporary restraining order if we have to. Then we can have him kicked out of the house."

Mary Ellen signed the divorce papers and immediately felt a heavy burden lifted from her shoulders. She then gave the receptionist her credit card and she was set. Her life would be forever changed.

The following credit card alert was sent to Zach's 'family' phone: *A $200+ transaction was made at Friedman & Jones, Attys at Law on card ending in 9643.*

Mary Ellen also texted Zach the following message:

Talked to my lawyer. He advised me against the uncontested divorce.

* * * * * * * * * * * * * * * * *

It was a little before noon when Zach pulled over for lunch. That's when he saw the two texts. Instead of eating, he spent his allotted twenty minutes flooding Mary Ellen's cell phone with obscenity-laced texts and voicemails. Mary Ellen chose to ignore them and instead feasted on a Varsity chili dog, French fries and Coke.

While she enjoyed the catered lunch, Zach got heartburn.

CHAPTER 42

Mary Ellen's normal workday at the bank began at 8:30 a.m. and ended at 2 p.m. with a thirty-minute break for lunch. The early quitting time allowed her to be home when her daughter got off the school bus. As she left the bank building and headed to her car, she thought about the day's events. It had been anything but normal. When she signed the papers at the attorney's office to begin the divorce proceedings, she felt both happy and sad. Sad because it was the end of a twelve-year marriage to a man she once loved and with whom they had conceived the greatest joy in their lives. But at the same time happy because she would no longer be manipulated, controlled, bullied, abused and mentally tortured by that same man. Furthermore, the fear from the earlier week's robbery that she thought would besiege her never happened. In fact, it had been therapeutic talking to customers who were curious and concerned. During the catered lunch, she found an opportunity to talk to Dom about Zach's threats. He assumed it was because he had recommended a lawyer and Mary Ellen chose not to tell him any different. And like Stuart had said, he was not concerned and passed it off as an angry man venting.

As she sat in her old Camry, she prayed for just two more starts. One to get home today and another tomorrow to get her to Pep Boys. That didn't happen. In fact, *nothing* happened when she turned the key just as the mechanic at Pep Boys had predicted. Frustrated and upset she went back into the bank and into Dom's office, sat down in one of the two guest chairs and began to cry.

Immediately, Dom took charge. He comforted Mary Ellen telling her not to worry. Then he and his loan officer who had a pair of jumper cables headed out to the old car. Once Dom had moved his car next to the Camry, the jumper cables were attached to both cars and the loan officer slid into the driver's seat. Meanwhile, Mary Ellen stood outside the car, her arms folded, praying for a miracle. The only sound coming from the sleeping beast was a clicking noise. When the loan officer exited her car, he looked at Dom and then her, shaking his head. He didn't have to say anything. They both knew what that meant.

"I don't know what to do," she said, her voice soft and trembling.

Dom came over and put his arm around her in a fatherly manner thinking about the situation. Neither he nor his loan officer could leave the bank and take Mary Ellen home. And he needed all the tellers to stay at the bank because of the Friday afternoon rush.

"You could take Uber or Lyft," offered the loan manager.

"I don't have an account. Zach would never let me open one. Too expensive he said."

"Okay. Here's what we're going to do. You can drive my car home and bring it back to the bank tomorrow. I can either walk home or get a ride with someone."

"Drive your new car? Oh no. I could never do that."

"Yes you can. And you will. I'm your boss. And it's not a new car," said Dom, smiling, trying to make light of a difficult situation. "And it's only for a day. I insist."

With no further pushback from Mary Ellen, Dom gave her a few instructions on the car's operations and sent her on her way. It had been years since she had driven a new car, or in this case, a fairly new car, and a sports car at that. Now she fully understood how thrilled Ashley must have felt when Dom drove her to school.

* * * * * * * * * * * * * * * * *

It wasn't long after she had arrived at her house and had left the car parked in the driveway that a text appeared on Zach's 'family' phone. It was from the Colonel.

> *Betty and I just returned from the grocery store and saw the detective's car in the driveway. We talked to Mary Ellen yesterday. We thought everything was OK. Apparently not. Do you want us to go over and see what's going on? Colonel Robert Oliver*

Ignoring his own rule about never using the cell phone while driving, Zach grabbed up the phone that he had unintentionally left in his cup holder after sending out his stream of derisive texts to Mary Ellen. He hoped it was a text from her saying she had changed her mind about the uncontested divorce. That she just wanted to get it over. He was surprised to see that it was from the Colonel. Just as surprising was the message itself.

The anger that erupted within Zach was apparent by the way he drove. Whereas he should have pulled his truck off the road and calmed himself, he, instead, pressed his foot down on the gas pedal and pushed the 18 wheeler to its limits. His mind would normally have been focused on his speed, the road, the surroundings and the vehicles around him, instead, his concentration was lost on the evil thoughts that swirled in his mind - a vortex of hate, rage, jealousy and betrayal. Mary Ellen had blatantly disobeyed him and she and her lover were obviously at it again… in his house… in his bedroom. She would pay for this disobedience, disrespect and infidelity… and so would the egghead.

His inattention to his driving duties did not go unnoticed by other drivers as he became erratic, belligerent and dangerous. Multiple 911 calls were made reporting his speeding, tailgating, weaving and cutting drivers off.

Twenty miles outside of Columbia, South Carolina, the state patrol pulled the big rig over. Zach had been totally unaware that they had been following him for over three miles. The officer had Zach exit the vehicle and produce his driver's license. His anger turned to angst. Any ticket would affect his CSA score (The DOT's Compliance, Safety and Accountability record), his employment, his insurance rates, his pride.

"Sir, do you know how fast you were driving?"

"Er… uh… I thought I was doing the speed limit," answered Zach, almost trembling.

"We've had multiple reports of this truck speeding, following too close and erratic driving. Have you been drinking?"

"No sir. I'll be glad to take any test."

The officer had Zach do a couple of tests which he easily passed.

"Officer, I'm really sorry about my driving. My wife just texted me that she wants a divorce and my mind wasn't on my driving. But I'm fine now."

"Divorce. Bummer. That's going to be a lot more expensive than this ticket. I'm going to do you a favor and just write you up for doing nine miles over the speed limit."

"Officer. Before you write that up, I want you to know that I've never had a ticket before. Could you please just make it a warning? I promise this will never happen again."

"Sir. You are a professional driver. We hold you to higher standards than other drivers. Nothing and I mean nothing… divorce, death, debts, diseases… whatever… nothing should interfere with your driving responsibilities. In other words, keep your mind on your driving."

The officer handed Zach the ticket, tipped his hat, returned to his car and sped off.

Zach climbed back into the truck, threw the yellow ticket into the passenger's seat and slowly drove into Columbia, staying just over the minimum speed limit, legal but irritating to those who happened to get trapped behind him. He had been mad enough before the ticket. Having his pristine driving record ruined only intensified his anger and hatred toward his wife and *Dom*. The divorce *had* to be *his* idea. He was the one with the lawyer friend. After the divorce, Zach would be left almost penniless. He would be working the rest of his life for *her*. And the bitch would turn Ashley against him. His sweet princess might never want to see him again. He had seen what divorce had done to Liz who lived like a pauper. He had heard what it had done to Billy Meadows who said he'd be working until he was a hundred. That was *not* going to happen to him. Never.

Zach began to think of his options. Only one came to mind that did not require him paying lawyers, paying alimony, splitting all his assets and possibly losing Ashley. And the timing couldn't have been more perfect.

Once he arrived at his favorite truck stop just out of Lexington, South Carolina, he called Ramona Hewitt, a lady friend he had known for years. She was expecting his call and she left immediately to pick him up. Zach was her Georgia fuck buddy.

Zach checked the time: 4:13 p.m. Much later than normal, but considering the time spent with the state trooper and his deliberate slow speed driving into Lexington, he was still on schedule. Ramona would be there in thirty minutes or less. He grabbed his overnight bag and filled it with a change of underwear, his dopp kit, a hoodie, duct tape, both cell phones, his Smith & Wesson 38 caliber revolver, fully loaded and the box of ammo. He opened the Ambien prescription bottle and fished out one of the pills and stuck it in his front blue jean pocket. He needed it for sleep. But not him. He had other plans for the night.

CHAPTER 43

Ramona Hewitt, a woman in her early fifties, drove her 2017 red Ford Mustang into the parking lot of a small diner located across the street from the truck stop where Zach had parked his 18 wheeler. She was wearing a Gamecock ball cap and large fake designer sunglasses. The car was her midlife crisis

She easily recognized the handsome truck driver who was smiling as he held his thumb out like he was hitching a ride. It had been almost a year since they had seen each other. Zach still looked as gorgeous as she remembered. She had put on a few pounds, but she had needed to.

"Hop in, handsome," she said over the loud rumble of the Mustang's 435 horsepower engine.

"Nice," responded Zach as he quickly opened the door and hopped in. The Mustang was unexpected. The last time he saw Ramona, she was driving an old Ford Focus.

"Buckle up, big boy," said Ramona as she looked at Zach's crotch and then laughed. "You know red cars, especially loud ones like mine, attract cops. And if we get a ticket for not buckling up, it's on me. And if that happens, you get no honey from the honeypot." Then she laughed again as she pushed the gas pedal down to the floor shooting gravel out from under the tires like buckshot.

Zach buckled his belt, but his mind wasn't on the honey pot. His mind was on his plan that was now shot to hell. What were the chances that Ramona would show up in a brand new, bright red Mustang? There was no way he could put five hundred plus miles on the car and it not be noticed. On the old beater, the Ford Focus, she would have never known or cared.

"How about some Lizard's Thicket take-out for dinner?"

"That's fine," replied Zach. He didn't care what they ate or if they ate at all. He was more concerned with trying to come up with an alternate plan.

Lizard's Thicket was a short distance from Ramona's old apartment. After they got their food, she headed off in an opposite direction from her old residence.

"Hey! Where are we going?" asked Zach.

"My new apartment. It's closer to work and it is newer."

"New car. New apartment. It must be nice. Where are you getting all this money? You haven't started charging, have you?"

"Not for you, honey. I'm still at the distribution center, but I'm now a night floor manager. I tell those meatheads what to do and when."

"Good for you," said Zach all the while thinking *feminazi.*

Ramona pulled up to the entrance of the gated apartment complex and after a short wait for the gates to open, she drove to the farthest right open parking spot and pulled up next to a white 2011 Ford Focus.

"Hey! Isn't that your old car?"

"Yep. I had planned to use it as a trade. Got her all fixed up, washed, waxed and looking good. The Ford dealer wanted to give me just a little over a thousand bucks on trade for a Taurus. I told him to jam it and started to walk off the lot. But then the salesman dude jumped into action. Told me about leasing. How I could get this red beast here for less than $400 a month for 48 months with nothing down. I was foaming at the mouth. Then he told me about the mileage allowance and the additional cost I'd incur if I went over my allotted miles. That just about killed the deal until he told me that I should keep the Focus, drive it to work and save all those miles for me to drive everywhere else, like Myrtle Beach… Charleston. I kept the Focus for about six months before I realized that what I paid in taxes and insurance was way more than any excessive miles I might put on the Mustang, so I sold it… to my brother. But then his unit got deployed to Afghanistan. So, I'm keeping it here and driving it every now and then to keep it from dry rotting until he gets back."

Zach didn't give a rat's ass why she had the car. Just that she had it and he was now back to his original plan.

Once in the apartment, Ramona gave her guest a tour of the place including the master bedroom. There, Zach saw hanging on one of the walls her infamous map of the US with several different colored pins in almost every state. The pins did not represent the cities and towns that *she* had visited. Rather they represented the cities and towns of men that had 'visited' her. There were four pins stuck in different cities in Georgia. Three red and one gold. Zach was aware of the color significance and wondered who the other three visitors were. There was no doubt in his mind who had gotten the gold pin.

After the tour, they sat out on the balcony drinking sweet tea and eating their meat and three off their 'country china', as Ramona called the Styrofoam container. His chicken fried steak along with its fixin's never tasted better. Especially since he hadn't paid.

After passing the time with some small talk, Ramona made her move. She was very experienced and thus very good. Before long, Zach was ready to be another pin in the map. But not just now.

"You got anything to drink like red wine or some hard liquor?" he asked.

The question surprised Ramona. Zach hardly ever drank. Too risky and too expensive. And when he did, he only drank beer… cheap beer.

"What? Why? Am I that bad looking?"

"Oh hell no." Zach then proceeded to tell Ramona about the divorce and the speeding ticket. Ramona completely understood. Especially the part about him losing everything. Nobody had ever given her anything. Everything she had, she had earned by hard work.

"Then I say let's have a drink. Celebrate getting rid of the old ball and chain. I got all the fixin's for making Old Fashions in the kitchen. And I also have a box of cabernet in the fridge. Your choice."

"I've heard of Old Fashions before, but I've never had one. Are they any good?"

"The way I fix them they are. Come. Watch and learn, pretty boy."

In the kitchen, Ramona pulled out a bottle of maraschino cherries from the refrigerator and grabbed an orange from a fruit bowl. She peeled and pulled apart the orange and put it and the cherries into a bowl adding a dash of bitters. She then muddled the concoction using a wooden spoon.

"Some people use sugar cubes and a splash of water. I like the fruit. Adds a little something to the drink."

She then poured the contents in equal amounts into two tumblers over some ice cubes.

"I hope you've been watching because you're making the second batch."

"Yeah… I've been watching, but it sure looks like the makings of a sissy drink to me."

She then pulled out a bottle of Maker's Mark bourbon whiskey from a lower cabinet and showed Zach the bottle's unique wax seal.

"Twenty-five dollars a bottle, but it's the best. It'll put hair on your chest, big boy."

She then poured the whiskey into the two glasses filling it about an inch short of the brim, stirred it and handed one to Zach who sipped the almost straight bourbon, grimaced and then smiled.

"What do you think?" asked Ramona watching her handsome catch of the night.

"This is perfect. Just what the doctor ordered."

"Sip on that while I go put on a new doodad that I got from Victoria Secrets." She then headed off to her bedroom.

While she was gone, Zach poured out the majority of his drink into the sink leaving just enough of the bourbon for its distinct smell and refilled it with a Pepsi he'd found in the fridge

With the door to Ramona's bedroom and bathroom open, Zach could hear running water coming from the bathroom. She would be out soon. He reached into his front blue jean pocket and pulled out the Ambien pill, crushed it on the counter with the wooden spoon and swept the contents into Ramona's drink, blowing off any remains from the counter. He stirred the mixture in the glass and lifted it up in the air to make sure none of the pill residue was visible. There was none. He then carried both drinks into the den just in time to see Ramona return. She had a smile on her face. She was ready for something carnal. Ramona took her drink and they both sat down on the sofa. She took a couple of sips then guzzled the rest. Zach did likewise.

"Okay, my turn to make them Old Fashions and let the student show the teacher a trick or two."

"I like new tricks."

He then stood up, removed his T-shirt and tossed it to a nearby chair showing off his athletic body as he did. Ramona could hardly contain her excitement as he headed to the kitchen.

"Don't be long."

Zach worked as fast as he could muddling the fruit mixture with the dash of bitters. Then as before he poured a touch of Makers Mark and a lot of Pepsi into his tumbler and only the whiskey into Ramona's, filling both glasses to the brim. He left off the Ambien. He wanted her to sleep. Not die.

Back in the den, he handed Ramona her drink being careful not to spill any.

"What a nice big pour."

"Well, I knew you liked things big so…"

The two drank their second cocktail almost as fast as the first, especially Ramona. She was ready for some action.

"You want another?" asked Zach, placing his glass on a side table.

"Oh hell no. I'm already feeling it. But if you want another, go for it. Just make sure you can perform."

"That's not going to be a problem."

It was obvious that she was more interested in him making love than making another Old Fashion. She then slowly and seductively removed her skimpy negligee giving him a full view of her naked body, making him wish he was there for the night. Ramona enjoyed looking at men look at her. As she slowly moved her hands around her body touching her erotic zones, Zach hurriedly removed his jeans and at the appropriate moment pulled her into her bedroom.

The foreplay was slow and lustful followed by animalistic physical coupling that was intense and draining. Both lay naked in bed staring at the ceiling.

"That was amazing," said Ramona her words slurring as she spoke.

"So do I get a pin?" asked Zach, purposely slurring his words also.

"You damn fucking A. Another gold one."

"I don't know about you, but my head is spinning. I must have put too much whiskey in the drinks."

Ramona heard but didn't respond. Instead, she slowly crawled out of bed, looked inside the top drawer of her bedside table and pulled out a plastic container full of the gold pins. Only after a slight struggle did she manage to open the small box spilling most of the contents onto the floor.

"Shit." Holding on to one of the pins, she wobbled over to the map and jammed it in the board as close to Atlanta as she could. Then she stumbled over to her dresser and pulled out a pair of pajamas that were the complete opposite of her skimpy doodad in purpose and design. Zach could see she was having trouble getting them on but offered no assistance. Instead, he laid splayed out on the bed, face down, breathing heavy, and throwing in a couple of quick snores and snorts for good measure.

"Move over," she slurred while pushing his naked body over to one side of the bed. Zach did what she asked but in a feigned comatose response. Through his partially closed eyes, he saw the table light go off and within five minutes, his woman of the night was sound asleep.

He laid in bed wide awake going over his plan. Other than a few sporadic delicate snores and mouth air puffs from Ramona, the bedroom was deathly quiet. He thought about what needed to take place, in what order and the amount of time he thought each step of his plan would take. It was imperative that he be back before Ramona awoke. He had just started mentally reviewing his plan again when he heard a faint text message ding from his 'family' cell phone. He slowly rolled out of bed grabbing his underwear as he did and headed to the door. He could still hear Ramona breathing heavily. On the way out, he glanced up at the board and smiled. Now Georgia had two gold pins. He found his overnight bag by the doorway and his jeans and shirt in the den as he made his way to the kitchen. There he quickly dressed.

Before leaving, he checked his phones and found that he had a message along with a picture of the yellow sports car from the Colonel on the 'family' phone.

> *Detective's car is still in driveway. Betty and I are heading out for a quick bite. Do you want another report tonight or tomorrow morning? Colonel Robert Oliver*

Perfect, thought Zach. He then responded to the Colonel's text.

> *Let me know if the detective stayed the night.*

Will Do, texted back the Colonel.

> *Thanks. I will be home tomorrow around noon. Z.*

Zach laid both his phones on the counter, grabbed Ramona's keys and headed out of the apartment and down to the Ford Focus. Within minutes, he was headed down I-20.

CHAPTER 44

Being back in Atlanta so soon after his robbery was not what Scott Burnett had planned. He had a bad feeling about the whole visit. Especially staying at the Four Seasons Hotel, less than 5 minutes from his last heist. Anne Reynolds, his girlfriend and fiancé, had chosen the hotel. A concession from Scott for being AWOL while on his bike trip to Canton, Ohio. Concessions are part of any relationship. Accept it or live alone.

Anne and he had driven down Friday morning in separate cars and spent what little time they had available exploring the hotel. Before heading over to the birthday party for the unknown, as Anne had called it, they sat at the hotel's Bar Margot where they each ordered their signature cocktail, the Lady Victoria. It allowed them to relax before the party and to discuss Saturday's plans which included tickets to the evening show of *CATS* at the Fox Theatre. Scott was able to secure excellent seats to the show but at a most unreasonable price from a ticket broker.

With Anne by his side, dressed in a classic-looking black dress or "LBD" (little black dress) as she called it, they Ubered from the hotel to a house in nearby Ansley Park where the party was being hosted. Although it was only a single-level home, it took no backseat in elegance and charm to the surrounding larger two-story houses. As they awaited a response to their ringing of the doorbell, Scott questioned why he had let his partner talk him into going to a party where neither he nor Anne knew a soul. With a lot of the guests being bankers, there couldn't be a more boring group of party people with the exception of accountants and actuaries. But Anne didn't mind and had actually looked forward to the event. She could talk and listen to anyone about almost anything.

Another ring of the doorbell brought immediate results. A man of about Scott's age wearing a white golf shirt under a blue blazer, grey slacks and highly polished loafers answered the door. His dark brown hair was slicked back and the round glasses he wore gave him a professorial look. He glanced at Anne first, then Scott.

"Hi. I'm Rodney Pafford. And you must be…?"

"Scott Burnett and Anne Reynolds. Friends of Tim Martin."

"Oh yes. Welcome. Come on in," said Rodney and ushered his guests into his home that was built in 1910. "Timothy told me that you might come. I'm glad you're here. Hopefully, you'll enjoy the evening. We've got plenty of food and drinks. And don't worry about not knowing anyone. I'm giving the party and I hardly know anyone myself. So if I fail to introduce you to someone, it's because either I don't know them or have forgotten their name already."

"We'll be fine," said Anne. "Meeting new people is a passion of mine. Plus you said you had plenty to drink. My kind of party."

"Let's get y'all a drink and then I'll introduce you to the guest of honor. He's very entertaining. I think you'll like him. Just a note of warning, he's recently divorced and has a roving eye. But he's harmless except for his ego. Give him time and he'll tell you his life story."

Rodney walked them to the kitchen where a well-stocked bar had been set up complete with bartender. Both Anne and Scott selected a nice California cabernet. They were then ushered into the living room to meet the guest of honor, James B. (Jimmy) Connors, Rodney's boss who was already surrounded by several people. The slightly overweight banker with wisps of greying hair looked nothing like the famous tennis player with the same name. Nevertheless, he was meticulously dressed in an expensive, dark blue suit, heavily starched white shirt and red tie. His outward appearance was that of a confident person.

After a quick introduction and birthday greetings, Rodney let his boss take charge of the conversation.

"So you both live in Charlotte. Beautiful city. Once worked there myself in the eighties for NCNB, now Bank of America. Best years of my life. Single then like I am today." He then gave Anne a quick once over, hoping that she didn't notice. His leer was so obvious, only a blind person wouldn't have seen his inspection of the woman. But having been given the earlier warning, neither she nor Scott were offended.

The conversation did not lag as Connors took center stage with his audience, telling stories about himself while dropping names of all the famous people he'd met. It was only when Connors recognized a couple of late-arriving guests, a smallish, shaved head, well-dressed man and his smartly dressed companion, that he stopped midsentence in one of his monologs.

"Dom," said Connors, verbally stretching his name. "Good to see you. And you too, Paul." He then shook hands with both men who in return offered their birthday wishes. "I knew you two were invited but didn't know if you would make it with all that's been going on at the bank."

"Wouldn't miss it. The bank is fine. Auditors have come and gone and we're back to normal. It was Paul who made us late. He was finishing up a nose job at the hospital."

None of the guests who had congregated around Connors wanted to hear about a rhinoplasty that Paul Han had done on some old woman wanting to look young again. They were more interested in hearing about the robbery at Dominick Garcia's bank.

"So Dom, tell us what happened. I've been a banker all my life, but have never been witness to a robbery."

The young banker seemed reluctant to take the spotlight from the birthday honoree but after insistence from Connors and other guests, Dom told his account of the heist including the young teller's outburst and the thief's admonishing response. The narrative held everyone's interest, especially Anne. Scott, however, was mortified. What were the chances of a thief and his victim being at the same party!

"That poor girl," said Anne, her sympathetic feelings clearly visible to anyone who saw her. "How is she doing?"

Dom heard the question but didn't see who'd asked it. "She took it pretty badly. She *and* her daughter. The detectives and the FBI agent on the case tried to ease her concerns, but that didn't seem to help. He even offered to stay the night, but she felt uncomfortable having a stranger around the house, so I volunteered. I was no stranger and she knew that there were no ulterior motives. And I'm not implying that the detective did. Just so you know." Everybody who knew Dom and Paul laughed as did the storyteller and his partner. "She seemed better today. She came into work, very happy, so I'm happy."

Scott was glad that no one could see the shame he felt inside for scaring that poor teller. It was not his intention, but it had happened. While Dom talked, instead of listening, Scott thought about how he might be able to make amends... assure the lady that he meant no harm. Maybe a letter or a note in the teller's mailbox. Or maybe a letter to Dom apologizing for his unwarranted and hurtful response to the teller.

"You didn't tell the part about the guy being British... using an English accent," said Paul, Dom's partner who had heard him tell the same story multiple times. So much so, that he could have told it himself.

"Well. That's all there is to say," said Dom, and then speaking in an English accent. "The FBI calls him the English Bandit."

Soon, everybody who had been listening to Dom began talking in English accents, mimicking the raconteur. Everyone except Scott. Anne took notice.

"What's wrong?" she asked.

"It's very disconcerting what that robber did to that poor teller. Everyone is making light of the robbery, but all I can think about is the trauma that she and her daughter must be going through."

"Scott, you're beginning to sound like me. I'm supposed to be the teary-eyed, tender-hearted soul who wears her feelings on her sleeve. I've not seen that in you. I like it. You are a good man. Now how about a refill." Anne then held her wine glass out in front of her.

Scott left and headed to the packed bar. Meanwhile, Anne found a way to corner Dom.

"I was intrigued by your story. And that poor teller. By the way, I'm Anne Reynolds. I'm here with Scott Burnett who's at the bar getting me another glass of wine."

"Dominick Garcia. Have we met before?" asked Dom. "I don't seem to recognize your face and I'm pretty good at remembering people."

"We're party crashers," said Anne, waiting to see Dom's reaction. When there was none, she continued. "I say that because we don't know a soul at this party. We were invited by a friend of a friend of Rodney Pafford whom we just met."

"An interesting way to spend a Friday night. So you're here just for the free drinks and food?"

"I am. But, Scott, my fiancé, is hoping to meet up with the president of some bank in Roswell, Georgia before their meeting on Monday… if he's here."

"Sort of a pre-meeting ice breaker?" asked Dom.

"Exactly. Now back to your teller and this robbery. Do you mind if I ask you a few questions?"

"You sound like a lawyer," said Dom, laughing.

"I am. But not here in Georgia. Scott and I are from Charlotte. Your story kind of got to my fiancé and he's never been a softy. That's me. Any chance the teller or her daughter need any therapy after such a traumatic experience. Sometimes incidents like that can linger in a person's psyche. I know because I've represented people who had similar harrowing experiences."

"Actually, the bank offered to pay for any outside help to anyone who felt like they needed it. I personally asked Mary Ellen. That's the teller's name. But no one, including her, took us up on our offer."

Scott heard the name *Mary Ellen* as he walked up to Anne. He was holding a glass of wine in each hand. He hoped that neither she nor her new friend, Dom, could see the uneasiness he felt.

"Hi. I'm Scott Burnett… this beautiful lady's fiancé." Scott made the bride-to-be association just in case the guy was hitting on Anne. He then handed her a glass of wine.

Dom introduced himself and the two shook hands. Scott could see that the man was just being friendly and was not a threat.

"So Anne tells me you're in banking?" asked Dom.

"Actually, I'm a bank consultant. I'm down here to see the folks at Roswell Guardian State Bank. The robbery at your bank kind of spooked them and they called our firm to discuss some of our cybersecurity offerings. As you know, most robberies today are internet-based. Not onsite like at your bank. And certainly not as dangerous, but there's usually a whole lot more money involved."

"True. But like Anne and I were discussing, with onsite robberies, there is always the element of immediate danger and the emotional aftershock."

"That is something that I've… I'm sure the thieves never considered. The emotional aftershock, like with that teller of yours."

"Probably more than anyone knows. And especially because of his threat of retribution. I can tell you first hand that for the first few days after the robbery, she was very fearful for her life"

"Didn't the police or the FBI tell that poor lady that the odds of any post robbery retaliation are like zero?" asked Scott

Both Anne and Dom could see Scott's angst and both wondered why his concern. After all, he didn't know the teller, the bank or any of its employees.

Dom responded. "To answer your question. Yes. We were all concerned about Mary Ellen's mental state after the robbery. She was very fragile. The FBI, the detectives and I pretty much said what you said but maybe in a different way. And as I said earlier, I stayed at her house the first two nights after the robbery just to make sure that she and her daughter were okay. Not that I thought anything would happen. From what I can see, I really think her fear of retribution is ebbing. Probably because she's now focused on getting a divorce from her husband whom I fear is more of a threat than the robber."

Dom immediately regretted his comment.

"I apologize for that comment. Totally out of place. Mary Ellen's private life should remain just that… private."

Neither Scott nor Anne said anything, but Scott knew he needed to reel it in. He wished he'd never come to this party. It should just have been a drink/food fest with a beautiful woman on his arm. Instead, he'd found himself talking to the manager of the bank he'd robbed and discovered that the poor teller he'd berated was possibly a basket case. He needed desperately to segue from this conversation into something more in keeping with this social event. As it turned out, Anne came to the rescue.

"From the frying pan into the fire. I don't know which would be worse. A scorned husband or a reprimanded robber," said Anne. "Good luck to her." Then she turned to Scott. "Honey, I think we've monopolized enough of this good man's time. Plus if I don't get some food, you might have to carry me home." She laughed but was serious.

Scott grabbed Anne by the hand and walked over to the catered buffet table which had a variety of different finger foods, cheeses and desserts.

"I guess this is dinner," said Anne who smiled as she filled her small plate.

As other guests milled around, making small talk with whoever would listen, Dom reflected on the conversation with Anne and Scott about Mary Ellen. It made him worry that he had not done enough for her. If a complete stranger had questioned his vigilance, maybe he had not taken the threat or the emotional aftershock serious enough. Even though she said she was okay. Was she? Was she just putting on a happy face? He found an unoccupied area behind a grand piano in the living room and sent Mary Ellen a text.

> *How are you and Ashley doing? You need company tonight? If so, I can get Paul to drive me over. Dom.*

Mary Ellen immediately replied:

> *We're good. And so is your car. Thinking of cruising around the Marietta Square. How do you get the top down? LOL. Just*

kidding. Got some wine and enjoying an evening alone. Ashley's at a sleepover. Thanks anyway.

PS. Will call you once my parents get here to set up a time and place to return your car. Thank you for being a friend.

"So there you are," said Paul, Dom's live-in partner. "I go to get a glass of wine and the next thing I know, you're in deep conversation with a couple that I didn't recognize. You look upset. Is everything all right?"

"Actually, yes. I'd never met them before, but they seemed very nice. The man... Scott... he's a bank consultant. We were just talking about the robbery, but unlike everybody else who was just interested in the amount of money stolen or if the robber had a gun... whatever. He seemed more concerned about how the robbery affected the employees. I commend him for that."

"Well, don't leave me again. I got cornered by some lady who wanted my expert opinion on whether she should have her cheekbones raised. You know I hate that. I should send her a bill."

CHAPTER 45

Mary Ellen had just gotten off FaceTiming her parents when she got a text from Ashley. She half expected the text. Deep down, she felt it might be too soon for her daughter to be spending the night over at a friend's place.

> *Mom. I think I want to come home but I don't want Kelly and Megan to think I'm a wuss. I'm worried about you.*

Most likely, Ashley was more homesick and worried about herself. If Mary Ellen had to go get her, she would. But she hated using Dom's car. He had loaned it to her to get home from work, not as a shuttle bus for her daughter.

> *I'm fine. Don't come home on my account. If I get worried, I can call Dom and get him to come over. I'm sure he's worried, too... probably about his car. LOL. Just have fun tonight. And don't worry about me. Nobody's gonna get me. Love Mom.*

Just as Mary Ellen finished her text, she could see that Ashley was immediately responding. She really didn't want to get dressed and go pick up her homesick daughter, but she would.

> *OK. But all Kelley and Megan want to talk about is boys and the robbery. I'm fine talking about boys but the robbery thing is freaking me out. If I really need to come home, I'll get Kelly's dad to bring me. Is that OK? I can tell them that you need me.*

Mary Ellen laughed. It was always a fifty-fifty chance as to whether Ashley would make it through the night when she did a sleepover. Tonight was no different.

> *Yes. Whatever you decide to do is fine with me. But if you do decide to come home, don't wait too late. I'm going to bed early. It's been a rough day. Love you. Mom.*

In truth, Mary Ellen hoped Ashley would stay the night at her friend's place. Not that she was worried. She just needed some alone time to reconcile everything that had happened. It had been a rough day. And not so much about the car. It could be fixed. But her marriage. As her lawyer said, it was irretrievably broken.

CHAPTER 46

Politically speaking, the party had been a success for Scott even if they did have to leave the party early. He'd done what he'd come to do. He had made an appearance that should have made his partner, Sid, and Sid's friend, Rodney Pafford, happy. And he was able to meet the president of Roswell Guardian State Bank and they seemed to hit it off nicely. Most importantly, Anne had a great time, never once mentioning the aborted charity motorcycle trip to Canton. However, their partying was abruptly cut short when Anne felt a migraine coming on and her migraine medicine was back at the hotel. By the time they got back to their room, her head was pounding and all she needed was a dark, quiet room… alone. He blamed himself for not having dinner before the party. Anne felt too bad to dismiss his unfounded guilt. Migraines just happened. They had their own timetable. Just like headaches and cold sores.

Scott helped Anne put on her pajamas, found her sleep mask and put her to bed. Before shutting out the light, he grabbed his briefcase and headed downstairs to the bar.

Over a cabernet, he thought about the evening's discussion with the manager of the bank he'd robbed. He had no idea that he had wreaked such havoc by his reactionary outburst. But he had *never* considered the effect of a robbery on the bank personnel. Nor did he consider the amount of money taken. Just the high… the thrill it gave him. Knowing what he now knew, he couldn't let the fear in this woman go unabated… not with a possible divorce hanging over her head. That's more stress than anyone person should endure. He couldn't ease the pain of the divorce, but he could do something about the angst he had caused in this poor woman's life.

Before he'd finished his wine, he knew what he had to do.

He grabbed his briefcase, went to the night clerk and had his car brought out to the front of the hotel. He then drove over to Marietta, stopping by a CVS to purchase nitrile gloves, pen, paper and envelopes. In his car, while wearing the gloves, he wrote a note, addressed to the young teller.

I am the thief that robbed your bank. If I have caused
you fear or trauma of any kind, I sincerely apologize.

That was not my intent. My outburst was not a threat but a gut reaction to being challenged. You are a brave young lady. So that you know this note is authentic, when I came to your teller station, I showed you pictures of your daughter at your house and a second one of her getting on the bus.

Again, I apologize and hope this will ease your mind.

While the note was short and to the point, Scott hoped it conveyed his true, sincere feelings and had the desired effect. He placed it in a self-sealing envelope, placed it on the car's dash and drove over to Mason Street and Hillside Avenue pulling up to the Ferguson's mailbox and lowered the driver's side window. He checked out the house for any activity. None that he could see. Then using a nitrile glove on his left hand, he reached out to open the mailbox, but before he did, he quickly pulled back his arm and raised the window. While the note of regret would relieve his mind and hopefully the teller's, it also created an exposure that could potentially lead to his identity. Had he thought this completely through? Could he take the risk? His past robberies had never been done spontaneously. As much as he wanted to, he couldn't do it. Plus would she even believe the note was from him and not someone who wished to remove her angst? As much as he wanted to do the right thing, he couldn't. Instead, he sped off down the road and turned around.

On his way out of the neighborhood, while stopped at a red traffic light, waiting for a couple of cars to pass coming from his left, he saw a white sedan pull up to the traffic light waiting to turn into the neighborhood. The driver of the other car stared through his open window at Scott, but only momentarily and then immediately looked away as did Scott. He wasn't sure why the caution on both drivers' part since they would never meet again.

CHAPTER 47

Zach drove the 2011 Ford Focus down Mason Street past his Marietta home.   Only the kitchen light, the front porch light and the spotlight at the corner of the garage were lit. The beacon of light coming from the corner of the garage highlighted the expensive yellow Porsche parked in the driveway. It was very obvious that the bitch wanted to embarrass him by showing everyone in the neighborhood just how rich her new lover was. Adding insult to injury, by having the car parked overnight in front of the house instead of in the garage, she let it be known that the bald-headed fucker was in his house, in his bed and sleeping with her. It was confirmation as to why he was here and what he planned to do.

He drove to the end of Mason Street where he made a U-turn, turned off the car's headlights, and drove slowly back to the front of his house where he parked near the driveway but far enough away from the house spotlight that only the outline of the car was visible. The car now faced the neighborhood's front entrance giving him the most direct way out. He turned off the car's engine as well as the interior light and sat for a few seconds checking the surroundings to make sure that he saw no one and that the lights to his house stayed off.

A 10-pack of black nitrile gloves that he had bought at a Home Depot in Augusta using cash lay on the passenger's seat. He pulled out a couple and pulled them on his hands. He pulled his hoodie over his head, grabbed his overnight bag, took a deep breath, pushed open the door and stepped out of the car leaving the door slightly ajar. Then, before heading to the side door of his house, he looked one last time up and down the street for any late walkers. There were none.

Rather than use his house key, he pulled up the welcome mat where he found the spare door key. He let himself in, leaving the key in the lock, the door wide open and looked around the dimly lit kitchen. He found Mary Ellen's cell phone was where she always lay it…on the kitchen counter next to the stove, charging. He picked it up, turned it on and entered the password, 101107, Ashley's birthday. With a just few keystrokes, he deleted every text and voicemail on the phone. He then laid it back down where he found it. From his tote bag, he pulled out his revolver which had a flashlight taped to the barrel of the gun. Something he had done before leaving Ramona's. He turned on the flashlight.

Then using the lighted gun as a guide, he made his way to the back bedrooms, stopping in the living room to grab a throw pillow from the sofa. Moving down the long hallway, he stopped at the first door on the right which was Ashley's bedroom. The door was closed. He stuffed the pillow under his arm and then slowly opened it and pointed the gun/light towards her bed. It was still made up. She never left her bed unmade. An inherited trait from her mother. Had she been there, he would have aborted the operation. As it were, the kill was on. He then headed to the end of the hall where the master bedroom was on the right and the guest bedroom on the left. The door to the guest room was wide open. He pointed the gun/light at its bed. It too was empty and the bed made up as well. Everything was going as planned.

With his gun raised, the safety off and his finger on the trigger, he slowly opened the door to the master bedroom and pointed the gun/light towards the bed. He could see the shapes of two people asleep in the bed. Mary Ellen was on the left side of the bed where she always slept and Dom was sleeping on the right with the covers pulled over his bald head evidently blocking the cold air coming from the A/C vent. The image of this man in his house, in his bed and sleeping with his wife was more than Zach could stand. He raised the throw pillow to the muzzle of the gun and fired a round into the body on the right. The sound of the gun brought an immediate response from Mary Ellen who rose from the bed and looked at the figure at the foot of her bed. It was not the robber she had feared.

"Zach?"

"Bitch!"

Mary Ellen instinctively raised her hands just as Zach pulled the trigger. Her hands did not stop the 38 caliber missile but deflected the bullet enough causing it to strike her just below her left eye shattering her face bone as it entered into the brain of this once beautiful woman. The 2008 Homecoming queen of Westside High School died instantly. Zach would abuse her no more.

Seeing the fear in her eyes had given Zach great pleasure as did the bullet he had fired into Dom's head. To make sure that there were no witnesses or missteps, he fired another round into each body.

"You should have taken the uncontested divorce," Zach said spitefully. He threw down the pillow and raced back to the kitchen where he pulled the tape from around the gun's nozzle releasing the flashlight. He placed the gun in his overnight bag, grabbed the can of red spray paint that he'd bought at the Home Depot in Augusta and then raced back to the master bedroom. He pointed the flashlight at the bed sweeping the beam from left to right. There was no movement on either side. Just two dead lumps. He closed the door and then spray painted the following:

I KEEP
MY WORD

CHAPTER 48

Ike would not shut up. Betty sat on the couch, reading her iPad while at the same time watching the 10 P.M. news. The Colonel lay in his recliner, half asleep. Just resting his eyes as he would say. The dog's yapping was more than the Colonel could stand even with his hearing aids turned down to their lowest volume. No amount of harsh commands or idle threats could shut the dog up.

"Honey, I think you're going to have to take him out," said Betty looking kindly at her old mate. "I'm going to get ready for bed."

The Colonel wasn't happy but knew his wife was right. And he also knew there was no way *she* would take him out even though she was the one who wanted the dog in the first place.

"Shit," he said under his breath. Then yelling to the dog, "Hold your damn horses."

The Colonel slid his recliner to the up position, turned up the volume to his hearing aids and headed to the kitchen where he found Ike jumping at the door, ready to explore the outdoors. Even though the Colonel was still in his pajamas and wearing a bathrobe, that was not a concern. Not at this time of night. The Colonel grabbed his phone to use as a light, attached the leash to the impatient dog and headed out the side door to the carport. Once on the driveway, instead of smelling every blade of grass, shrub or tree, the small dog began tugging at the leash, pulling the Colonel down the drive towards the street. That's when the Colonel saw the silhouette of a car parked in front of the Ferguson's house.

"That's not right," said the Colonel to the dog. As quickly as his old legs would carry him, he made his way to the car following Ike's lead. He did a quick once over of the car but did not recognize it. Too old to be Mary Ellen's parents. Using the light on his cellphone, he checked the license plates. South Carolina. He then stood back, ready to take a picture of the license plate when he heard that familiar, frightening sound coming from Mary Ellen's house. Having served thirty years in the Marines with seven in Viet Nam, he immediately recognized the faint sound of gunfire.

CHAPTER 49

He'd done it. He shoved the flashlight and can of spray paint into his overnight bag and looked around to make sure he hadn't forgotten anything. His adrenaline was flowing so hard, it made it difficult to think. There were no shells because he's used a revolver. There were no fingerprints because he had on nitrile gloves. The spray paint, flashlight, duct tape, used duct tape, gun and a change of clothes were in the overnight bag. With nothing else coming to mind, he rushed from the kitchen, out the back door open, onto the driveway and right into an unexpected problem.

"What the hell's going on?" yelled the Colonel in the toughest, meanest voice this 77-year-old veteran could muster while shining his cellphone light toward the moving silhouette. Ike's bark mimicked his master's bravado, ready to attack if necessary. "Zach? Zach? Is that you? I thought I heard gunshots."

"You did, you old fool."

By the time the Colonel understood what was happening, Zach had reached into his bag, pulled out the revolver and fired toward the light coming from the Colonel's cell phone. The bullet hit the Colonel's heart, knocking him into the Porsche and then down to the ground. He didn't move. Ike immediately ran up to the fallen body and laid as close as he could. When his master failed to acknowledge his presence, he began whimpering, not understanding what was happening.

Even though Zach never saw the old man use his hands to break his fall, he was taking no chances on whether he was alive or dead. He aimed the gun at the fallen soldier and pulled the trigger, but the weapon didn't fire. The cylinder was empty. Mad at himself for failing to remember the revolver only held five bullets, he ran up to the body and kicked at the head as hard as he could, crushing in the frontal lobe. If the old man wasn't dead before, he was now.

Ike, who had crawled even closer to the Colonel's dead master's body after his fall, did not know that the old man was dead. However, he did understand the violent jolt he felt from Zach's kick to the Colonel's head. His whimpers changed to growls and he leaped at the assailant and grabbed his pants leg, latching on causing the man to start jumping around and shaking his leg and flailing away with his gun until the dog lost his hold. Ike ended up on the grass next to the driveway, a leash length away from the Colonel whose big, rough hand still held on to the handle.

Zach, who had never liked Ike and vice versa, began moving around the restrained animal as he made his way to the car. While keeping a safe distance from the dog, he couldn't help but mutter obscenities at him. About halfway around the dog, he noticed a light shining on the driveway. The Colonel's cell phone. He realized that the old man, true to his word, might have recognized that something suspicious was going on and had either taken some pictures, sent texts or both. He sat the overnight bag down on the grass and ran over to the driveway where he laid his gun down and picked up the phone. It was still in camera mode. He punched the pictures icon and saw a gallery of the last pictures taken. There were pathetic selfies of the Colonel and Betty in front of some old house. None taken of the Ford Focus or its license. Next, he checked for any texts. The last message was sent at 7:08 p.m. to Zach letting him know that the detective's car was still in the driveway. As he was about to set the phone back down on the driveway, an idea struck him. A brilliant idea. He tapped on his name in the "Message" screen and began a new text.

> *Just saw a green Honda parked in front of your house. Am checking it out. Will let you know if there's a problem. Col Oliver.*

Zach hit send and laid the phone on the driveway near the same spot he'd found it and picked up the revolver. Without warning, Ike, who had discreetly made his way back to the Colonel's side, made one more attempt at revenge. He lunged at Zach's hand but grabbed the sleeve of his hoodie, instead, causing it to tear. He immediately let go and snapped again at Zach's hand. This time the dog was more successful as he ripped through the nitrile glove and punctured the fatty pad of Zach's thumb.

"You stupid dog," muttered Zach who then took a swipe at the dog's head with the nozzle of the gun hitting him in the mouth knocking out several teeth. The dog immediately ran back to the Colonel's side and hid his bloody face in his master's already blood-soaked bathrobe. But Zach wasn't satisfied. His hand stung from the bite. The dog needed a lesson. If he had had another bullet in his revolver, he would have used it. Instead, he kicked at the dog just as he had kicked the Colonel breaking Ike's front left paw.

Zach would have enjoyed staying there, kicking the life out of the dog, but he needed to leave and the dog was no longer a threat. On his way back to the car, he grabbed up his overnight bag and shoved the gun inside. Within minutes, he was out of the neighborhood and on the expressway, heading back to South Carolina. He checked the time. 10:52 p.m. With luck, he would be back in Ramona's bed in less than three hours.

By now, Betty Oliver had given up on the Colonel. She had her earplugs in and had turned out the light on her bedside table, leaving the Colonel's light on. She wasn't worried. It was a safe neighborhood. Evidently, Ike needed more time to do his business and the Colonel never rushed him. They were two peas in a pod.

CHAPTER 50

Even though Zach had not slept in almost 24 hours, he felt exhilarated and free. The experience had not been a bad one like he feared. There was no remorse, no regret, no guilt. There was no desire to turn back the clock. He was glad his cheating wife and her hairless lover were dead. He only wished he could have taken more time to kill the bitch so that she could have felt a slow and painful death. He also regretted he didn't have enough time to take out the old man's dog. But his plan was to fulfill the bank robber's prophecy and it had to be quick and simple so no dog.

All the way back to Ramona's apartment, he worked on how he would respond when he was told of his wife's death. He would be shocked at first, of course. But how should he react when he was told that she was not alone. That there was another man in bed with her that was also killed. Should he be mad or what? He practiced different scenarios trying to get comfortable and genuine in his response. But he wasn't getting any warm and fuzzies from any of his feigned attempts. He sounded too practiced and mechanical

About eighty miles out of Atlanta, on I-20 as it crossed Lake Oconee, Zach pulled over into the emergency lane for a needed break, both mental and physical. Before leaving the car, he slipped on a couple of the nitrile gloves, wiped down the gun and flashlight and then dropped them into the lake.

By 2:35 a.m., Zach was pulling into Ramona's apartment's parking lot. Other than the confrontation with the old man and the dog, everything was going according to plan. That is, until he saw that someone had pulled into the parking space next to Ramona's red Mustang… the spot that the Ford Focus had previously occupied. A slight panic set in. Ramona would know the car had been moved. His only option was to find a reason to move the car. He pulled the Focus into an open spot two cars down from Mustang, grabbed his overnight bag and headed to the apartment. As he walked past a trashcan at the base of the apartment steps, he saw an empty fast food bag lying on the ground and an idea popped into his head.

Back in the apartment, he removed all his clothes and slowly slid into bed next to Ramona. She never moved. The Maker's Mark and Ambien had done their job. Within minutes, he, too, was dead to the world. He was too tired to think about the carnage he had left in Georgia.

About an hour later, Ramona awoke. It was 3:43 a.m. She turned over and saw Zach. He was still sound asleep. *My pretty boy just can't hold his liquor,* she thought. She then shoved him two or three times before he responded with a jerk, pulling the bedspread back, revealing his naked body.

"Oh no! What time is it?" he asked, truly concerned that he'd overslept. He wanted Ramona to see him asleep in bed, but he didn't want to be late getting his freight load into Atlanta on time.

"Almost four. Why? What time were you supposed to be on the road, big boy?" Ramona was not looking at Zach's face when she asked.

Zach breathed a sigh of relief. "Oh, thank God. No. I don't have to be in Atlanta until 10 o'clock. Just as long as I'm on the road by six, I'm good. I don't know about you, but I'm starved. Those drinks packed a punch. What do you say I run down to McDonald's and get some of their pancakes and sausage? I can use some grease in this old body."

"Best idea I've heard this morning. You go and I'll take a shower. I don't normally sleep in my makeup, but how often do I get to put a gold pin in the map?"

"I got a gold pin?"

"I cannot believe you don't remember that. Well… yes I can," answered Ramona remembering how quickly Zach had fallen asleep. "If you hurry, you might have time to try for another gold pin."

Fifty minutes later, he and Ramona sat at the kitchen table eating the breakfast he'd managed to get free of charge. Not only that, he also had an excuse for why the Focus was in another spot and why he had a wound on his left hand. All of which he told Ramona who would be his alibi.

The story he told her was fairly straightforward. While leaving the fast-food restaurant, he stumbled and fell. While trying to break his *fall,* his left hand landed on a small rock, causing an abrasion. He wasn't really hurt that bad, but his food went everywhere. The drive-thru employee happened to see the fall and immediately reported it. Zach had hardly gotten to his feet when the restaurant manager was out there with his first aid kit and cell phone. He offered to take Zach back into the restaurant to clean up his wound. But all Zach asked for were a couple of Band-Aids. The manager took pictures of the injured hand before and after bandaging it. He then wrote down what had happened along with Zach's name and address. He then took pictures of the area where Zach had taken the fall making sure there was nothing that the restaurant could have done to have prevented the accident. Zach remained calm, told the manager it wasn't the restaurant's fault and that all he needed was his food. The manager happily replaced the food and refunded him his money. Zach had his food and his excuse. And the Ford Focus had a new parking spot back at the apartment. No harm. No foul.

Not long after securing his second gold pin in as many days and while Ramona showered a second time, Zach looked at his 'family' phone and saw the text he'd sent from the Colonel's phone. It was perfect. If the police triangulated either of his cell phones, it would show that neither left Lexington, South Carolina. And Ramona could verify that he never left either. She was his alibi. To keep everything real, the 'Colonel's' text needed a response.

Sorry I didn't respond earlier. I just saw the message. Let me know if there's a problem. Z.

Saturday, August 10, 2019

ATLANTA, GEORGIA

CHAPTER 51

Betty awoke unaware of the time. She and the Colonel were early risers. Usually around five in the morning. As always, she moved her hand over to where the Colonel slept to make sure he was there. He wasn't but that wasn't unusual. He was either in the bathroom or in the den asleep in his recliner with Ike on his lap with the sound muted on the TV.

The bathroom was vacant, so she slipped on her white bathrobe and walked down the hall and into the den. But the TV was not on. Nor were her husband of 52 years and Ike, his constant companion, asleep in the recliner. When she did not find him in the kitchen, panic set in. Nothing good came to mind. She started turning on lights in every room and calling out for the Colonel and Ike. Neither responded. The last thing she remembered was that he'd taken Ike out for a walk… but that was last night. Could he have fallen? Could he have had a stroke, heart attack or anything that strikes old people? She knew that Ike would never leave his side.

She grabbed her phone off the kitchen counter and checked for missed calls, texts and emails. Nothing since yesterday afternoon. She tapped on the Colonel's phone number and listened for his phone to ring. She heard nothing in the house, so she stepped outside and tapped the Colonel's number again. She heard it ringing, although somewhat muted, like it might be coming from their car. She walked over to the car as fast as she dared and looked inside. Nothing. No phone, no Colonel, no Ike. When the call went to voicemail, she tried calling again. The sound was faint, but as she began walking down the driveway, the sound got louder and louder. Just as it ended, she looked over to the Ferguson's house. There was no need to dial his number again. She could see the shape of a man lying on the driveway near a parked yellow sports car. She could also hear a dog whimpering. Ike. Her chest began to heave, her heart began to beat faster and harder as a wave of nausea surged over her. She didn't have to actually see the man to know it was the Colonel. Maybe he'd just fallen.

"Please God," she said to herself as she crossed the street. "Please let him be safe."

When Ike stood up, using only three feet but wagging his tail non-stop, Betty could see by the light given off by the garage's spotlight and the early morning sunrise that his pristine white fur was awash with dark spots.

As she slowly made her way up the driveway and to the body that lay next to the yellow sports car, she saw the pool of blood surrounding the man's head and she began to cry. Even before she knelt down beside him, she didn't need her nursing skills to know that the only man she had ever loved, the man she had been married to for 52 years, the man that had served his country for over twenty years, the man that would give the shirt off his back and the man who was her soul mate would never kiss her, or hug her, hold her hand, or love her, again. Ever.

CHAPTER 52

The Cobb County police, EMS and a fire truck all arrived within a few minutes of each other and all within ten minutes of receiving the 911 call from Betty. The police arrived first. Two cars, four policemen. They found the shaken woman who had made the call sitting next to an old gentleman, holding his rough, old wrinkled hand with one hand and gently rubbing it with the other totally unaware that rigor mortis had set in. The white bathrobe she was wearing was covered in blood. Laying in her lap was a small dog whose fur was caked in blood. It was hard to tell who was the saddest. The woman or the dog. Both had lost their best friend.

The senior police officer looked at the fallen man and could see the damage done to his face. He immediately checked for a pulse not expecting to find one and he didn't. He then began issuing orders to the other three officers. One was ordered to string up yellow crime scene tape and then guard the entrance to the guard scene. He signaled for a second one to follow him to check out the house and the surrounding areas. The youngest and newest officer, only three weeks out of training, was directed to stay behind with the deceased man and the grieving woman.

The young officer left with the victim had never witnessed a murder scene nor had he ever seen a fatality of any sort, whether it was a victim of a crime or a traffic accident, for that matter. It was very disturbing. But the old lady, sitting in a pool of blood, reminded him of his grandmother. So he did what he would have done if it had been her. He crouched down and placed his hand on the tearful woman's hand. There was no attempt on the officer's part to lift the woman to her feet. He would let the EMTs do that after they checked her out.

"Ma'am, I'm Officer Johnson. What's your name?"

"Betty. Betty Oliver." Her voice trembled as she spoke.

"Is this your house?"

Betty shook her head. "Across the street."

"Is this your husband?"

"Ye… yes," she answered with tears flowing with every heave of her chest.

"Do you know what happened?"

"No. He's dead. That's all I know. He's dead." Then Betty looked at the officer. "What am I going to do?"

The officer didn't know what to say as there was nothing he could say. So, he didn't. He just continued to rub the poor, broken-hearted woman's clasped hands until the two EMTs arrived. Death was not new to them. As they looked at the body, they knew there was no need to check for a pulse, but protocol prevailed so they did. The young black officer saw the EMT shake her head. She then whispered something into the grief-stricken woman's ear who then nodded. The EMT pulled out her blood pressure kit and placed the cuff around Betty's arm. While the BP machine-checked her pressure, the EMT checked Betty's skin for clamminess, trying to determine if she had gone or was going into shock. Her blood pressure was slightly elevated, but her skin felt normal. If she had any shock, it wasn't medical.

"Do you live here?" asked the EMT as she removed the blood pressure cuff.

"Across the street," answered the young officer interceding on behalf of the woman,

Then looking at the officer and then the victim, she continued. "I know you don't want to leave your husband and we should probably wait for the detectives, but I think I need to take you into your house and get you into some clean clothes. The detectives will want to ask you a bunch of questions and I think your house would be better suited for their interview which they will want to do today. They want to find out who did this. Just like you."

Betty nodded. She understood.

Before moving her, they offered her a sedative, but she refused. She couldn't help her husband, but he would want her to be strong. Help find who had changed her life forever. As the two EMTs lifted the heavyset woman, she clung to Ike with both arms, never letting him leave her side. She'd already lost one loved one… her soul mate. She didn't want to lose another.

By the time the two police officers came out of the Ferguson's house, the street was filled with neighbors… onlookers, most in their pajamas and bathrobes. Each trying to understand what was happening. Rumors were cropping up faster than weeds in a sidewalk crack. Especially when they saw the blood on Betty's robe as she passed under the street light as she crossed the street on the way to her house. The slight buzz in the crowd grew even louder when they saw one of the officers stop to stretch some crime scene tape across the Ferguson's side door with everyone who saw the tape wondering what had happened inside.

Within twenty minutes of the police arriving at the crime scene, the Cobb County detectives and the forensic team drove up. Even though it was early morning, a little before six, the crowd seemed to have grown considerably with people now coming from other neighborhoods, all trying to get a view of the dead man that lay on the driveway. Once forensics set up a privacy tent, the gawking ebbed but not the chatter. Local TV stations had their crews on the scene searching for any information they could find to report on the morning news. But until the communication officer provided them with the details of the crime, they had to rely mainly on the rumors that were circulating among the crowd.

After conferring with the senior police officer, the first order of business for Al Freeman and Homer Bradley, the two Cobb detectives, was to order a search warrant. They didn't need one for a cursory search of the house and its surroundings; anything more than that legally required one. With a judge on call 24 hours a day, the detectives could expect it to be issued in less than an hour

Next, the detectives along with the two members of the forensic team and the senior police officer huddled up to assign tasks and to split up into two teams. Each team consisted of one detective and one forensic specialist. Bradley's team was assigned to the outside of the house and Freeman's team, the inside. Before starting their investigation, each member of the team slipped on booties and nitrile gloves to ensure the integrity of the investigation.

Bradley's team immediately began taking pictures of the dead man that lay on the sidewalk. They took pictures of the body from every possible angle. They also snapped pictures of the car, the cellphone that lay on the driveway near the body, the surrounding areas and the nearby spectators just in case the perpetrator had stayed around to view the fallout from his heinous act. Once the pictures were taken, the forensic specialist began dusting for fingerprints and taking samples of blood from the body and around the body while Bradley did a DMV search of the yellow sports car's plates. He found that the car was owned by Dominick Garcia with an Atlanta address. He would be contacted and questioned later.

Freeman's inside team stopped at the entry door leading into the kitchen and took pictures of the key that had been left in the knob. There was no evidence of forced entry. The forensic specialist stayed back to dust the knob and key for prints while the police officer led Freeman straight to the back bedrooms by way of the living room. The detective noted that the house was well-kept and nothing indicated any kind of disturbance. Once they had reached the back bedroom, he saw the spray-painted message left on the door. *I KEEP MY WORD.* Words by any definition meant premeditation. Inside the bedroom, using his thumb and index finger, the detective carefully lifted the bedcovers revealing two victims. The one on the left side of the bed, closest to the master bathroom was a young woman with bullet holes in her hand, face and chest area. Lying in a fetal position next to the woman was a much younger girl, maybe in her early teens and most likely the daughter. She, too, had two bullet holes in her young body. Both in the chest, either in the heart or close enough to have created havoc in her chest cavity. The little girl's old one-eyed teddy bear lay by her head having escaped any damage.

Death is hard enough when it's the end of a normal life cycle. But when manufactured like this, it's cruel and unjust. One of the victims was in the prime of her life. The other had yet to experience life and never would.

The three men did their job and tried not to think about the horrors they were witnessing, especially Freeman who had a wife and daughter about the same age. Mechanically, they took pictures and fingerprints and searched for evidence… anything that could help point them in the right direction. Once they received the warrant, they began a more detailed search. In the bedside table next to the side of the bed where the young girl lay they found a Glock 19, 9mm pistol. After forensics took pictures of the weapon and dusted it for fingerprints, the detective removed it from the drawer and inspected it. It was fully loaded and had the safety on. A quick smell test and a look in the chambers showed that the weapon had not been fired recently.

It was only during a search of a pocketbook found on the dresser that the detectives discovered the name of the deceased woman. Normally, local authorities handled local crimes, but once Freeman discovered the name of the victims and knowing that the APD already had an ongoing investigation involving the same, he thought it best to call them in. Within the hour, Detectives Marlowe and Jacobs arrived at the scene. Both immediately recognized the Colonel and had the same questions come to mind. Why had the old man been outside the Ferguson's house in the first place? Wrong place, wrong time? Had he been called? Had he seen something?

After conferring with Bradley, outside, they made their way into the house where they found the inside team in the master bedroom finishing up their work.

"You know what to make of this?" asked Freeman after greeting Jacobs and Marlowe.

"Oh, Jeez," said Marlowe as he and Jacobs looked at the door with the spray-painted message. Then they saw the two bodies on the bed – a young girl and the woman who had feared her life was in danger. "This is unbelievable."

Marlowe then told the Cobb detective and senior officer the brief history of the robbery, the dead woman and the robber's threats.

"Surely this bank robber… this English Bandit as you call him… surely he didn't do this. Usually, it's the husband or a lover," said Freeman.

"Well… the painted message on the door would certainly have you think it was our man," responded Jacobs. "If that's the case, we really dropped the ball on this one. That poor lady in there was scared to death and we pretty much dismissed her."

"So what else do you think we could have done?" asked Marlowe, looking to lessen his mental guilt. "We had their house being monitored. And you even offered to pull an all-nighter with her. I say we don't beat ourselves up over this."

Jacobs didn't say anything but knew this would weigh heavily on his mind for a while.

"Somebody needs to contact the next of kin," said Freeman. "County records show this house is owned by Zachary L. Ferguson. I'm assuming he's the victim's husband. If so, lucky he wasn't here."

"Zach Ferguson is the husband. We'll call him," responded Jacobs, remembering his confrontation with Ferguson. "He's a long-haul truck driver. A real hard ass. Got a little horsey with us over the phone while we were working the robbery case. We had to set him straight. From what I remember, he was on the road. That's why he wasn't here. Vic… do you remember when he's supposed to return home?"

Marlowe pulled his notepad and flipped a few pages. "Today."

After a brief discussion, it was decided that a split investigation would be detrimental and redundant, so Cobb ceded responsibility to the APD. All reports, pictures, DNA results, etc. would be forwarded to the

APD's online case management and all physical evidence would be hand-carried to the APD's evidence property room.

"Okay. Then, we're out of here," said Freeman speaking for the team. "Let us know if you need us for anything."

Once they were alone, Jacobs turned to Marlowe. "OK. I think we need to call Whitehead. Like it or not, he needs to be here just in case these murders *are* related to the bank robbery."

Marlowe pulled his phone out of his coat pocket, looked up the agent's number and made the call. The agent awoke immediately upon hearing the ring. The conversation was brief. Marlowe only told Whitehead that the English Bandit had struck again. That Mary Ellen Ferguson was dead. He then gave the agent Ferguson's address and told him to come as quickly as he could. Nothing more was said.

As Jacobs and Marlowe began mapping out their own investigation, they heard footsteps coming down the hallway. It was the forensic specialist, returning. He never said a word but headed straight over to the bedroom door with the spray-painted message and began removing it from its hinges.

"Hey! Uh… forensic guy," said Marlowe. "What are you *doing?*"

A burly, full-bearded man dressed in white coveralls stopped and looked over at Jacobs and then Marlowe. "You talking to me?"

"Yes. Sorry. I'm not good at remembering names."

"Wilson. Pete Wilson. Gotta take the door back to the property room."

"Make sure it's securely wrapped. I don't want that message getting out to anybody! Especially the press."

"You got it," said Wilson giving the detective the thumbs up and headed back out to his truck for a tarp.

While Wilson was gone, Marlowe and Jacobs began taking their own pictures of the crime scene and evidence. Afterward, they split up to search for anything that might have Zach Ferguson's employer's name on it. A pay stub, W-2, letter, bank statement. Before long, Marlowe yelled out from the kitchen, "Got it. Found a paystub. Cross USA Freight. It's off Fulton Industrial. Not only that, I found divorce papers and a receipt from an attorney named Stuart Friedman."

"So what's going on here," said Daniel Whitehead uneasily as he came into the kitchen from the side door. The FBI agent had made the trip from his apartment to the crime scene in less than twenty minutes. Unlike Marlowe and Jacobs who were dressed in suits, both wearing their signature fedoras, Whitehead was unshaved, wore an FBI ball cap and parka, a wrinkled pair of jeans and tennis shoes.

"Just what I said over the phone. Mary Ellen Ferguson and her daughter are both dead. Both of multiple gunshots."

"Why do you think the robber…"

Marlowe interrupted the agent. "Come with me."

He then led the agent to the back bedroom where he showed him the spray-painted message and then the two bodies.

"Oh my God!" said Whitehead. Even knowing in advance, that one of the victims was the young bank teller, the shock upon seeing the body of the pretty young woman and her little girl with blood everywhere was overwhelming. "Oh my God! This is unbelievable. What did we miss?" He then turned his eyes away from the two victims and looked first at Marlowe and then Jacobs.

"From the printed message, this was obviously payback by the robber," said Jacobs.

"Assuming it *was* the robber," added Whitehead. "Boy, the shit's going to hit the fan on this one. Who's the old man, outside?"

"Colonel Robert Oliver… a neighbor across the street. Marlowe and I interviewed him earlier in the week. He actually saw the robber taking pictures of the young girl. The ones he probably showed the teller during the robbery."

"Why was he here?"

"Good question. We were waiting on you before going to talk to her… that is, if she's up to it. The poor woman was found sitting next to her dead husband when the Cobb police got there. She was the one who made the 911 call. I'm not sure how long *she* was there, but from the looks of the body, I'd say he'd been dead at least four or five hours or more."

As the three men headed outside, they met Wilson coming back into the kitchen with a tarp. He said nothing as he passed them by. He was on a mission. Outside, they saw two men wearing white lab coats moving the dead man's body onto their gurney. They, too, were silent as they did their job. But the press wasn't. Once the three men neared the crime scene tape, they were slammed with a barrage of questions from the reporters lurking just outside the prohibited area.

No comment didn't fill newspaper columns nor two-minute TV news segments, so the reporters and their cameramen followed the three men across the street and halfway up the driveway to the late Colonel Robert Oliver's house yelling out questions before Marlowe turned and reprimanded them for trespassing.

"This is *not* public property. Please be kind enough to leave and give this poor woman her space!"

The reporters slowly disbanded and returned to the street and the three men made their way up to the house where a young Cobb police officer let them in. Marlowe and Jacobs removed their fedoras and Whitehead did likewise with his ball cap. The young officer took them into the den where they found Betty Oliver sitting on the sofa with her dog, Ike, lying next to her on a towel. While Betty had changed clothes, Ike's fur coat was still matted in blood. Both she and the dog were staring at the vacant recliner. Her eyes were puffy and still moist from intermittent crying sessions. She immediately recognized the two detectives who introduced Agent Whitehead. The three men found a seat. No one sat in the recliner. The young officer sat in a chair he'd brought from the kitchen keeping his distance from the three new guests.

"Mrs. Oliver, we're very sorry for what happened to your husband and hate to be intruding. But we want to find out who's responsible. I hope you don't mind if we ask you a few questions. We're truly sorry for the timing."

Betty Oliver said nothing but nodded her head in understanding then wiped away some tears.

"Do you know why Colonel Oliver was at the Ferguson's house?"

"No. Bob… I'm sorry. This is so hard… Bob… I called him Bob. Everybody else called him Colonel. I'm sorry if I seem addled… Anyway, Ike, our dog…" Then she patted the dog who never moved. "Ike was raising a ruckus. Wouldn't stop yapping so Bob took him out to do his business. I went to get dressed for bed. I waited about ten… fifteen minutes and when he didn't come back in, I figure Ike was going on one of his long pee treks where he smelled every shrub and tree in the yard. Bob didn't mind. I wouldn't let Ike sniff more than three. That was my limit. Anyway, I went to bed. Then around four, I woke up. At my age, I hardly ever sleep through the night anymore. I did my usual pat on his side of the bed to make sure he was there and hadn't fallen asleep in his recliner." She then looked over at the empty recliner and tears began to flow. The detectives let the poor woman feel her pain and sorrow as she tried in vain to ebb the flow of tears by dabbing her eyes with two and three tissues, but her emotions got the best of her.

"What am I going to do," she cried, shaking her head in disbelief.

No one responded. There was no good answer.

Once Betty felt that she was back in control, she continued. "Anyway, he wasn't in bed and he wasn't in his recliner. So I went looking for him. I called his cell phone and eventually heard it in Mary Ellen's driveway. Mary Ellen Ferguson... that's our friend across the street. Anyway, that's when I saw him. There was no need for CPR. I'm a retired RN. I knew he was dead. Did you see what the bastard did to his face? That son-of-a-bitch." She paused for a second, the rage turning into fear. "What am I going to do without him? He was my life." She began crying again. Ike could sense the anguish in Betty and began licking her hand. He looked up at his distraught friend. His eyes were just as pitiful as hers. He felt the need to be closer to her, to nuzzle up against her comfortable and ample stomach. But as hard as he tried to lift his small body, the pain in his front left leg caused him to fall back onto the sofa where he began furiously licking his injured paw in hopes he might somehow ease the pain and heal the injury.

Betty saw the dog's plight and obligingly lifted the dog to her lap which comforted both of them as much as the situation allowed.

Jacobs started to ask another question when Betty interrupted.

"What I don't understand is why my husband was killed with a detective staying over at Mary Ellen's house? Shouldn't he have been awake? Isn't that why he was there? I just don't understand."

"What detective are you talking about?" asked Jacobs, confused by what the woman had just said.

"The one that owns the yellow car. He's been here several times. Tuesday, Wednesday and last night. I don't understand."

"Why do you think the owner of that car is a detective?"

"Bob told me. After the robbery, Zach... that's Mary Ellen's husband... he asked us to keep an eye on Mary Ellen and Ashley, his daughter. You know... because of the robbery at Mary Ellen's bank."

The two detectives nodded their heads in acknowledgment.

"Anyway… when Bob texted him… Zach… that there was a car in the driveway that he had never seen before, Zach said it belonged to a detective. That he was staying the night. Mary Ellen told us the same thing when we went over there. Nevertheless, we… Bob and I… continued to stay on the lookout for anything unusual… like that yellow car. And he continued to text Zach with the information. I know you didn't really know Bob, but when he said he'd do something, he did it."

"For your information, the yellow car is not owned by a detective. We're not sure why it's there. But it's the only car at the house and there's nothing in the garage. We're still investigating that," said Jacobs.

"Bob wondered about that car."

"How well did you know the Ferguson's?"

"Oh, we love them. At least, Mary Ellen and Ashley, her daughter. They're sweethearts. Bob and I would do anything for them. They were always looking after us. Zach… well, Bob used to call him a narcissistic prick. We don't care too much for him. But he's never around. Gone all the time. He's a truck driver, you know."

"Yes. We do know." Jacobs paused. He wasn't ready to tell the grieving woman that her neighbors had also been murdered. Instead, he chose to wait. "Mrs. Oliver… Betty… Your husband's cell phone was found on the Ferguson's driveway. It may contain information that could be useful in solving his murder. Per protocol, we have to get a warrant to gain access to the phone *unless* you authorize our use. Would you be willing to do that and, if so, do you know his password?"

"By all means. And he doesn't have a password. He had one, but he had me take it off. He said it was a nuisance and he didn't keep anything worth stealing on it anyway."

"One last question. You said that the Colonel took your dog… Ike out because he was barking? But neither of you knew why he was raising a ruckus?"

"That's right."

"And you never heard the gunshots?"

"Gunshots? What gunshots?" said Betty, then pointing to her hearing aid.

Jacobs paused. He was at a loss for words. The poor woman had probably had the worst day of her life and what he had to tell her would only add to her misery. As he sat silent, twirling his fedora, waiting for the right words to say, Marlowe spoke up.

"Ms. Betty. Your husband was shot… then when he was on the ground, the killer kicked him. Maybe he was trying to kick your dog. We're not sure. But we have some more bad news to tell you. When the Colonel was over at the Ferguson's, he might have witnessed someone breaking into their house. That person or persons killed Mary Ellen Ferguson and her daughter. We believe that is why the Colonel was murdered."

"Oh no. No. Not Mary Ellen. Not Ashley. No. No. It can't be." The news was too much for the poor woman. She leaned forward, her head in her hands, crying uncontrollably. The young Cobb patrolman saw this and immediately ran and sat beside her. She raised up and buried her head in his shoulder. Her life, as she knew it, was forever changed.

The detectives felt they had overstayed their welcome. The Colonel had been a good man and a good neighbor. Fulfilling what he considered his responsibility… his duty…, just as he had in the service, had cost him his life.

The young patrolman stayed behind with Betty until some church friends arrived and she'd talked to her sister. Then he left. When he chose law enforcement as a career, he never knew that the job could be so hard.

CHAPTER 53

Two gold pins or not, Zach had begun to make a nuisance of himself as he constantly reminded Ramona about every ten minutes that he needed to be on the road by 6 a.m. But she wasn't going anywhere until she put on her face. She always put on her face and pretty boy who needed no cosmetic improvements wasn't going to interfere with her morning ritual.

Nonetheless, they easily made the deadline with twenty minutes to spare. On the way to his rig, and as they passed the McDonald's where Zach had fallen, he explained to Ramona why he had driven the Ford Focus to McDonald's that morning rather than her hot red Mustang. He didn't want to be responsible for anything that might happen to it. Like dings.

"Well, you should have driven it anyway. I don't care about dings. It's a lease."

"Probably so. Maybe next time," responded Zach but thought, if you think driving that little toy is exciting, you should try driving an eighteen-wheeler, especially in the rain or snow.

At the truck stop, he climbed out of the car, shut the door and waved goodbye. There was no hug, no kiss, no "I'll call you later" which didn't bother either one. She had gotten a gold pin performance from him which is all she wanted. And Zach had gotten what he wanted. An alibi.

Once he was sure she had driven away, he headed over to the truck, climbed in and slid into the back of his rig. It was when he tossed his two phones in their appropriate bin that he saw a dark stain on the toe of his right boot. It had to be blood. Either the Colonel's or the dog's. Either way, the boots as well as his pants and hoodie had to go. It had been an expensive evening but so much cheaper than a divorce.

With his big diesel engine fired up, he sat back in his plush driver's seat and thought about his new life. He was free. Free from the bitch, her parents and an impending nasty, expensive divorce. He could do as he wished, spend his money how, when, where and with whom he wished. It then hit him that he had not even thought of Ashley nor how and when was he going to break the news of her mother's death? Should he tell her that the bank robber did it? She was frightened enough as it were. But, most likely she'd see it on TV, hear it from her friends or the police. It was probably best that he tell her everything. Just like Mary Ellen had done about the robbery. But this was different. And what about Dom? Should she be told about the affair? *She's a bright girl. I'll let her figure that out on her own.*

Then there was the issue of how he was going to take care of Ashley. The Waffle House waitress in Kansas City had forewarned him earlier in the week. Yet, he was too blinded by his anger to even consider his daughter's future when he had planned his wife's demise. *So now what do I do?* He couldn't just quit his job to stay at home with her. And letting her live with either of her grandparents was totally out of the question. But Betty Oliver would work. She was now widowed. She loved Ashley. And he could offer to pay her to keep Ashley… but, of course, he'd let her bring that up.

Zach checked the dashboard clock. He needed to leave now if he was going to keep on schedule. Just as he was about to put the truck in gear, he heard a text message ping on his 'truck' cell phone. He didn't want to spend the time to look at the message. But then again, it could be important. Quickly, he swiveled back and pulled it out. It was from Ramona.

> *Hey sweetie. I really had a great time last night. Good food. Great drinks. Fantastic sex. Please call me the next time you're in Lexington.*

The text was perfect. It validated his alibi. He would keep it. Zach knew Ramona had sent it because she was afraid that she had irritated him while he waited impatiently for her to get dressed. *She's pathetic. So needy,* thought Zach. But he needed her, so he texted her back.

> *I will definitely call you.*

Ramona's text reminded him of the texts from the *'Colonel'* that were on his 'family' phone. He tossed the 'truck' phone into its bin and pulled out the 'family' phone and reviewed the *'Colonel's'* last message.

> *Just saw a green Honda parked in front of your house. Am checking it out. Will let you know if there's a problem. Col Oliver*

And then he read his response:

> *Sorry I didn't respond earlier. I just saw the message. Let me know if there's a problem. Z.*

Neither the text nor his response had been part of his plan. He had improvised. Everything impromptu. But it was so natural and a perfect diversion. It proved that he was in South Carolina at the time of the murders and the cops would be looking for a green Honda.

Zach thought a moment. Should he respond again? Yes. That would be the normal thing to do.

I haven't heard back from you. Is the detective still there? Z.

Zach checked the time on the cell phone before tossing it back into its bin. 6:17 a.m. He was late getting on the road. There would be no time for a breakfast break. Just a short stop somewhere along the way where he could dump his hoodie, pants and boots. Late or not, it had been a great day.

CHAPTER 54

The noise from the pushcart carrying their in-room breakfast woke Anne Reynolds with a start. She pushed her silk sleep mask above her eyes to see Scott handing the hotel attendant a tip.

"Smells delicious," said Anne, slowly crawling out of bed and heading over to the covered dishes placed on a table by the hotel's window. She sat down and lifted the metal cover to see eggs, bacon and a small Belgium waffle. "How am I going to be able to fit into my dress tonight if I eat all of this?"

Husbands, fiancés and boyfriends who wished not to sleep on the couch know to never answer those types of rhetorical questions. Regardless of the response, it could only get the person in trouble. So Scott answered Anne's question with a question.

"So how are you feeling?"

"Better. We can't do that again. Too much wine and too much of the wrong kind of foods is a recipe for a migraine every time. You can't let me do that again."

Scott just nodded his head in agreement but knew full well that for him to try and monitor how much or what Anne ate or drank was not going to happen. It, too, had couch or doghouse written all over it.

"What time did you come to bed? I woke up at eleven and you weren't here?"

"I wanted to make sure you had some peace and quiet, so I went down to the bar. Closed it down, matter of fact," he lied and then leaned over and kissed the top of her head just in case his eyes or mannerisms betrayed him.

While they ate, all their talk centered on their evening at the Fox Theatre and the Andrew Lloyd Webber's musical *CATS*. It was one of Anne's favorites. Their plans included dinner at Baraonda's before the play. It was an Italian restaurant a couple of blocks away from the theatre. Other than that, their day was completely open. Some options Anne suggested were the Atlanta History Center and its newly restored civil war Battle of Atlanta cyclorama, the World of Coca Cola museum, the

Atlanta Zoo or just a walk in Piedmont Park. Scott was open to anything just as long as he was with Anne.

After breakfast, Anne headed to the shower. While she took her time in the luxurious spa-like oasis, Scott checked out the morning news looking for a weather report. While he waited for the meteorologist to make his or her appearance, it gave him time to think about last night. Had he made the wrong decision not to put the note in the teller's mailbox but in a trash bin instead? Would she have been worse off knowing the robber was back in her life? Or better off, knowing that he meant no harm?

His thoughts were interrupted when he heard a news reporter say

… an unidentified elderly man died of foul play on the corner of Hillside Avenue and Mason Street. We'll have more on the story on our Fox 5 News at Noon.

He immediately recognized the names of the two streets mentioned in the short broadcast. If he had had any reservations about his decision not to leave his note, he knew he had made the right one. Otherwise, he might now be a suspect in an old man's death and foul play at that. He didn't need to add murder or manslaughter to his list of criminal offenses. Robbery was more than enough.

"You look worried," said Anne as she walked from the bathroom wearing the hotel-provided bathrobe and a towel wrapped around her hair.

The sight of his beautiful fiancé immediately lifted Scott's spirits. She was the best thing to happen to him since the death of his first wife. He wished he had never robbed that last bank or, for that matter, any of them. Why had he been so stupid? Maybe she deserved better.

"How about the Botanical Gardens?" she asked as she immodestly and purposely dropped the towel to the floor exposing the body of someone much younger than her age.

Immediately forgotten, at least for the moment, was the Fox 5 news report. Instead, he pushed the "off" button on the TV controller and reached for the extended hand of his fiancé and pulled her down to the bed.

CHAPTER 55

Agent Whitehead followed Detectives Jacobs and Marlowe to the Cross USA Freight terminal in South Atlanta. The murder of the teller as foretold by the robber's threat of repercussions and confirmed by the spray-painted message had created an alliance between the Atlanta Police Department and the FBI. While the FBI's initial mission was the apprehension of the bank robber and the APD's, the capture of the murderer of three innocent people, they now had a common goal where the success of one mission automatically completed the mission of the other.

The three men waited patiently inside the terminal building at the bay where they had been told Zach's shipment was expected. The terminal manager had been informed of the deaths of Zach's family but not the circumstance. She was also asked to leave Zach's truck cab, logbook and the contents of the trailer untouched and unmoved. That a warrant would be forthcoming. The detectives emphasized to the terminal manager that this was protocol and she should not read anything into what was considered standard procedure. She understood and generously offered the use of her office so the detective could gently break the news.

At 9:42 a.m., Zach's 18 wheeler rolled into the terminal freight yard. Early as usual. He had not sped and had only taken a short break, long enough to change into his sneakers and dump what had to be dumped. Once he had the trailer backed up to the loading dock, he jumped out of the cab and made his way up the steps to inspect his load for any damage once the trailer's back doors were open.

As Zach approached the back of his truck, out of the corner of his eye, he saw three men approaching him from inside the terminal building. It was very obvious that they were not the dockhands that were usually on-site to unload his freight. Two were wearing suits and hats and the other wearing an FBI windbreaker and FBI ball cap. The law had arrived. He had expected and was prepared for the visit but had thought it would be at his house, not at the terminal.

"Zach Ferguson?" His name seemed to echo as two different men called it out almost simultaneously. One was Jacobs and the other was a casually dressed man who came running up the terminal steps towards Zach. The three lawmen immediately thought: *reporter.*

"Are you Zach Ferguson?" asked the casually dressed man a second time.

"Yes. What's it to you?" answered Zach, not knowing what to think. It was all the confirmation the process server hired by divorce attorney Stuart Friedman needed to hear.

"Mr. Zach Ferguson. You've been served." Then he shoved the divorce papers into the unsuspecting husband's shirt pocket and quickly bounded back down the steps knowing there was always a chance of physical retaliation from the spouse. Speed was of the essence.

Jacobs, Marlowe and Whitehead were all stunned at what they had witnessed. As they approached Zach, they could hear him yelling to himself.

"That conniving bitch." Furiously, he pulled his 'family' cell phone from his pocket and hit the speed dial for Mary Ellen. Being served had been totally unexpected but was welcomed. He could act mad, irate, belligerent, like any unsuspecting husband who had just been hit with divorce papers. And the emotions were real because the bitch, even though she was dead, had the gall to follow through with the divorce filing.

Knowing that anyone in earshot could hear him, he blurted out, "Answer the phone, you fucking whore." When the phone went to voicemail he went off on his wife again. "Where the hell are you? We need to talk. Right now. I can't believe you did this after I asked you to wait." He then jammed his phone into his pants pocket. When he looked up, he saw he had three new faces staring at him.

"What?" asked Zach, looking like he could attack at any minute. "The bitch needs a whole damn army to serve me?" He made sure he used the present tense of the verb when referring to Mary Ellen.

"Mr. Ferguson. I'm Detective Jacobs and this is Detective Marlowe and FBI agent Daniel Whitehead." The detectives produced their badges as verification. Whitehead's badge was attached to his jacket. "I'm afraid there's been an incident at your house that we need to discuss... in private."

Zach put on his stunned look, the one he had practiced numerous times in front of a mirror at Ramona's while she got showered. "An incident? What kind of incident?"

"We have use of the terminal manager's office. If you don't mind, we should probably talk there."

"I don't understand." The three men didn't say anything else but led Zach to the office and closed the door. Jacobs offered Zach a chair but, instead, he chose to stand in front of the chair, arms folded, so that when told of his wife's death, he could simply drop to the chair and cover his face with his hands. That way, he could easily hide his reactions which during his practice sessions had looked forced and contrived.

"What's going on?"

"Mr. Ferguson, I'm sorry to inform you that your wife, daughter and your neighbor, Colonel Oliver were killed last night. Murdered."

Zach was not prepared to hear the word *daughter.* He was truly shocked and looked it. His body slumped and his mind became a fog leaving him unable to speak. Without warning, he began to throw up while at the same time crying vehemently.

"Oh my God. No. No."

Jacobs, Marlowe and Whitehead were all trained to watch artificial, contrived, insincere and manufactured responses. Zach's emotional response was real and unrestrained. Marlowe guided the broken man into the chair where he sat and cried. After the initial shock had subsided, he lashed out. Another response the three men had witnessed before.

"Who did this? Who would want to *murder* my family? Have y'all arrested anybody? Oh my God! Oh my God! This can't be happening!"

Marlowe offered Ferguson a bottle of water but was refused. He just sat there, almost in a trance. After being left alone to reconcile his thoughts, he slowly looked at Marlowe who was now sitting next to him.

"What happened? How did they die?"

"An intruder," said Marlowe. "Very possibly the bank robber. But right now that's just speculation. But all three, including the Colonel, were shot. My suspect is your wife and daughter were shot in their sleep. We think the Colonel was shot as he approached the intruder."

Marlowe's response seemed to satisfy the emotionally drained husband and father.

"So what do we do now?" Ferguson asked, his heart broken but his head back in the game.

CHAPTER 56

Zach rode in the back seat of Jacob and Marlowe's city-issued unmarked car as they traveled to Zone 5's precinct station. He never spoke but only stared out the window. He was told that he was being taken there to give a statement, but he'd seen enough murders on local and national news to know that the husband, ex-husband, boyfriend and ex-lover were always the prime suspects. The detectives would want to get a statement, but they would also want to interrogate him. He was prepared for that. What he wasn't prepared for was having to deal with Ashley's death. How could that have happened? Where was lover boy? Why wasn't he there? His car was in the driveway. Ashley was supposed to be at a friend's house for a sleepover. Every time he thought about his poor, young daughter, his eyes welled up with tears. His sadness did not go unnoticed by Jacobs who sat in the passenger's seat.

Once they reached Zone 5's precinct, Marlowe lead Ferguson to a small interrogation room on the first floor where the session could be videoed. Agent Whitehead, who had arrived earlier, was already behind the two-way mirror that separated the interrogation room from the observation room. Jacobs joined him. Neither man believed Ferguson was involved, not seeing how genuine his reactions were.

"Can I get you some coffee, water or a Coke?" asked Marlowe. Of the two detectives, he always played the 'good' cop role. That was his personality.

"No, I'm good."

With Zach sitting behind the table, hands folded in front of him, Marlowe paced back and forth a couple of times before sitting down on the opposite side of the table.

"I know this morning has been an extremely stressful morning for you. I apologize for having to do this interview today, but it's what we have to do. It's our job. So please bear with us."

"I understand."

Marlowe did the obligatory introduction to the video including their names, date and time and then he proceeded.

"I want you to know up front, I will be asking questions that you might think insensitive, inappropriate… maybe insulting. These questions are routine and there's no implied guilt on our part. And should you wish to have an attorney present, that is your right."

"No. I'm good."

Marlowe began by asking Zach to confirm his name, where he lived, where he worked and his relationship to the deceased.

"For the record, I need to know where you were last night between the hours of 9 p.m. and 3 a.m.?"

"I was in Lexington, South Carolina…uh… at a friend's house."

"What is the friend's name?"

"Ramona Hewitt." Zach then gave Marlowe the name of Ramona's apartment and her telephone number then he continued. "This will come out soon or later, so I want to be upfront with you. Mary Ellen and I were having problems… for a number of years. I wasn't a perfect husband by any stretch of the imagination. If it weren't for Ashley, our daughter…" Zach stopped for a moment as he said his daughter's name. The look of sadness on his face was real as were the tears that welled up in his eyes. "If it weren't for Ashley, we would have probably already been divorced by now."

"Where did you park your truck last night and was it there all night?"

"Atlas Truck Stop in Lexington, South Carolina. And yes, my rig was parked there all night."

"Do you know anyone who would have wanted to harm your wife and daughter?"

"Well, yes. And you and the other detective know who I'm talking about. That robber who threatened my wife. Isn't that why y'all had a detective staying at my house. Matter of fact, he was there last night. Where the hell was he when all of this happened?"

Betty Oliver had told the detectives pretty much the same story.

"Why did you think that a detective was staying at your house?"

"Mary Ellen told me and it was confirmed by the Colonel… oh shit. How's Betty… Mrs. Oliver holding up? I've been so consumed with my own family, I forgot that you told me about the Colonel." Zach didn't care one whit about Betty, but his 'concern' might impress the detective and the other detective and FBI agent whom he knew were watching behind the two-way mirror.

"Not so well. Just like you, her life has changed forever."

Marlowe saw the sadness once again in Zach's face.

"I'm sorry. I shouldn't have said it that way. That was thoughtless and callous. I apologize." When Ferguson said nothing, Marlowe looked down at his notes, giving him and the husband/father time to regroup. The direction of the interview was not going as planned.

"So where does the Colonel fit into all of this?" asked Marlowe.

Zach cleared his throat and wiped his eyes. Then he answered the question.

"When I found out about the robbery, I was concerned… especially since I was on the road all the time. I asked the Colonel to keep watch on our house for anything suspicious. He sent me a text anytime there was any unusual activity. That's how I knew the detective was there Tuesday, Wednesday and yesterday. Then last night he texted me… sometime around ten or eleven. This time he said there was another car in front of the house. A green one… I think. When he didn't send a follow-up text last night, I assumed everything checked out."

"Can I see your phone?"

"No problem. Just so you know, I have two phones. One I call my 'truck' phone which I use for non-family calls. The other one is my 'family' phone. That's this one. This is the one with the messages from the Colonel. You can keep it if you think it will help. The password is 3333." Zach handed the phone to Marlowe's outreached hand. He would tag it and bag it once Zach left. "I keep both phones in the truck, but I never answer any calls on either phone while I'm driving unless I receive three quick calls in a row on the 'family' phone. Then I know it's an emergency."

"I need the phone number of both phones." Zach complied.

Marlowe read the Colonel's messages as well as Zach's replies.

"So… like you said, it appears that there was a green car at your house. A green Honda."

"Yes sir. But if I may ask, where *was* the detective when my wife and child were murdered? Did the detectives just leave the car there for effect? Do you think the robber could have been stalking Mary Ellen and knew that nobody was at the house and the car was just a decoy? I don't understand." Zach needed to know why Dom wasn't at his house. Just the car.

Marlowe laid the phone down on the table in front of him.

"We're looking into it. That's all I can tell you"

Marlowe looked at his pad, then continued. "As part of our warrant, we have your wife's phone. Do you know the password?"

"Yes. 2322. Our house number. When you look at the texts and emails, especially yesterday, I sent some texts and left some voicemails that were nasty but were said in the heat of the moment… when she told me she planned on divorcing me. Obviously, now I wished I hadn't done it. But I did."

"Do you own a gun?"

"Yes sir. A Glock 19 and I'm licensed to carry. It's at home in a drawer next to my bed. The right side as you look at the bed."

"What about in your truck. Do you have one in there for protection?"

"No sir. That's a violation of company policy. They will fire you for having a gun in your cab. They do not want the liability that comes with it. And if you check, you will see that I obey all their rules and the rules of the road. I'm never late and am always on time with my freight. And I'm always current with my logbook." Zach did not mention the speeding ticket on purpose.

"Do you own a second car?"

"No sir. Usually, I hitch a ride home with another trucker or if I go over to my friend's place, she picks me up. Like I said earlier, my wife and I were having problems."

Then, as part of their interrogation strategy, Marlowe went for the jugular.

"Did *you* kill your wife and daughter?"

Zach wasn't prepared to hear the words *kill* and *daughter* in the same sentence. He thought of his beautiful daughter, her smile, her laugh, the way she called him *daddy*. It was too much and he broke out in tears again. He didn't answer but only shook his head then wiped the tears with his sleeve.

"I'm sorry I had to ask you that question, but it's standard." Marlowe and the two men on the other side of the two-way mirror could see how truly hurt he was.

"I think that's enough for today. Unfortunately, forensics will be at your house for at least a couple of days… leaving Sunday at the earliest. Do you have a place you can stay in the meantime?"

"Yes. At a friend's place in Marietta."

"We need your friend's name, address, phone number and your 'truck' phone number. Then you can leave. I'll have an officer drive you to your friend's."

Using Marlowe's pen, Zach wrote the information on the detective's notepad.

"What about the bodies? There will need to be arrangements made… oh shit… I need to call Mary Ellen's parents. They're supposed to be staying with us for the weekend. I need to get in touch with them before they get here. I don't know how I'm going to break this to them." Zach shook his head and looked down to add to the effect. As it were, he would have enjoyed nothing more than being able to tell his in-laws that the bitch… their wonderful, sweet daughter who never did anything wrong… was dead. Shot to death along with her lover. But it had been Ashley. So he really wasn't sure *how* he was going to be able to tell them.

Marlowe handed Zach's phone back to him. "I'll give you some privacy." He left Zach alone and joined Whitehead and Jacobs in the adjoining room.

The call to Mary Ellen's parents was hard for the men on the other side of the two-way mirror to watch as it was for Zach to make. He was crying nonstop and they knew the listeners on the other end of the conversation were feeling just as much pain, if not more so. When Zach was finished and had enough time to compose himself, Marlowe returned. Zach handed his phone back to the detective who in turn handed him instructions to give to the funeral home for receiving the bodies. He also gave Zach their business cards with a date and time for him to return to the precinct. With the interview completed, Marlowe called an officer who drove Zach to his friend's house.

The three lawmen went to the breakroom, got their drink of choice and convened in a conference room.

"So what do you think?" asked Marlowe.

"I think his reactions were real and he was eager to help. I know most of the time, in cases like these, it's the husband but…," said Jacobs.

"So if it's not the husband, the only other logical choice is the robber. I just don't see that happening. What's his motive? Revenge?" asked Whitehead.

"I know this is a stretch, but could there have been some collusion between the robber and the Ferguson lady?" asked Jacobs. "Or maybe between her and her boss, Dominick Garcia. His car was in her driveway. Why did she have his car?"

"Garcia did mention that the bank's auditors were supposed to be there this past Wednesday. Maybe they were skimming," added Whitehead.

"Yeah. Maybe she got scared or wanted more money. So he whacked her," answered Jacobs.

"Dom Garcia? Whack somebody? No way," said Whitehead.

"You're right. What was I thinking?" asked Jacobs. "I say we table this discussion until Monday when we have the reports back from forensics and access to the evidence. Maybe things will be clearer. In the meantime, I think we need to go see Garcia. Whitehead, you're included, too, if you want to go."

CHAPTER 57

"My poor baby," said Liz Davis, her arms open, ready to give her grief-stricken boyfriend a big bear hug. She had been waiting for him on the front porch ever since he called and told her that his wife and daughter had been killed… murdered. That's all he would say. When she saw Zach exit an APD patrol car, she understood his reluctance to talk.

Zach quickly pushed off the embrace and headed to the couch where he sat down, head hanging low and his hands clasped between his legs. He could smell the bacon and eggs, his favorite meal that Liz had cooked. But he refused to eat. His mind kept going over what he had done to his daughter. She was so innocent. The more he thought about it the madder he got at Mary Ellen and her lover. Where was he? His car was there. He was supposed to die. Not Ashley. The tears began to flow again. Liz tried to console him, rubbing his back, then his hair and then trying to hold his hands. But Zach didn't want any part of this. He just wanted to be left alone.

"Baby, you need to talk about it. You can't keep this all pent up inside of you. It'll drive you crazy. You sure you don't want something to eat?"

"Dammit, Liz. Would you just *please* shut up and let me think!"

Liz had never seen this side of Zach, but she understood and forgave him. After all, he'd just lost his wife and daughter. So she left him alone in the living room and went into the kitchen and helped herself to a late breakfast. Deep down, she was glad she no longer had to compete with Mary Ellen and Ashley… mainly Ashley.

Liz had just finished cleaning up the kitchen and had poured herself another cup of coffee when Zach came into the kitchen, kissed her on her forehead and sat down at the table next to her.

"I'm sorry I yelled at you," he said having realized that Liz was all he had now.

"Baby, I'm here for you. I understand."

"You mind pouring me a cup?" Liz jumped up, grabbed a clean mug from the cabinet and filled it and then added a little creamer. She knew exactly how he liked his brew. She set the cup down in front of him and went over to the counter where she sliced open a couple of biscuits, put a little pat of butter on them and popped them into the microwave. When they were ready, she sat them down in front of him and then sat down in the chair facing him.

"Thank you," he said picking up the cup but shoving the biscuits away.

Liz just nodded her head and took a sip of her black coffee. There was no need to rush things. He would open up when he was ready.

After Zach had finished his first cup, Liz quickly poured him another along with the creamer and sat it down in front of him.

"I can't believe my little girl is dead. She was so beautiful. So sweet." He couldn't bring himself to look at Liz. If he did, she might see the guilt in his eyes.

Again, Liz said nothing.

"It's the bitch's fault. She caused all of this," he snapped and slammed his open hand on the table, scaring Liz and causing the coffee to splatter from the cup.

"What happened?" asked Liz, thinking Zach was ready to talk.

"They were murdered. That's what happened."

"Yes. But who? And how?"

"I don't know. All I know is I was met at the terminal by two detectives and an FBI agent. They told me about Ashley and Mary Ellen. Then they took me to the station, put me into an interrogation room and asked me a bunch of questions. Asked me if I had killed them. Can you fucking believe that? They asked me if I killed them." He stopped for a moment to regain his composure. "Then they brought me here. Oh… and get this. I also got served. The bitch had me served." He then pulled the divorce papers from his shirt pocket and threw them on the table. "Guess I won't have to worry about that."

"So who do they think killed them?" she asked, carefully not to say his daughter or wife's name. "Surely not the robber. Just the other day we were talking about…"

"Liz… Stop… I know what you were about to say. You can never repeat what we were talking about the other day. You know that I am the prime suspect. That's always the case. The husband did it. End of story. Just to give you a heads up, they'll probably want to ask you questions. About me and about my relationship with Mary Ellen. If there's anything that they ask that your answer will make you feel uh… uncomfortable… you know like pointing a finger at me, just say you don't know."

"Honey, I know you couldn't have done it," countered Liz, knowing Zach's deep love for his daughter. "I don't know any question that they could ask that would throw a shadow of doubt on you. I know it *has* to be the robber."

"Who else? I'm only saying that because you know the bitch and I weren't getting along. And besides, I was in another state yesterday, staying at a… er… uh… friend's place."

"Zach, honey. I know you have *friends*. You don't think I have *friends*, too? We're both adults. You're gone most of the time. You get lonely. I get lonely. Even so, you're still my *best* friend."

"You, too," said Zach, somewhat feeling obligated to reply.

"So what do you do next?"

"I got to meet Mary Ellen's parents tomorrow at 9 o'clock at the Cracker Barrel to discuss funeral arrangements. I might need to borrow your truck."

"That's not a problem, but what's wrong with *your* car?"

"It's at my house in the garage which is now a murder scene, so I'm probably going to have to wait until they release everything. Not only that, Dom's car is probably blocking it." No sooner had the words *Dom's car* come out of his mouth did he realize he had just screwed up. He meant to say Detective's car. Fortunately, it wasn't the police.

"Why was Dom's car at your house?"

"Well, duh. He was fucking her. What do you think?"

"Was he killed, too?"

"Unfortunately, no. For whatever reason, he wasn't there."

"But why was his car there?"

"Liz… stop! You're worse than the police. I don't know. It's been there, off and on, since Tuesday."

When Liz failed to ask the obvious question, Zach offered it up.

"And how did I know it was there off and on since Tuesday? The Colonel… the old man who lived across the street from my house, told me. I had him keeping an eye on the house ever since the robbery. Mary Ellen told me the car belonged to a detective who was staying at the house as a precaution. But Ashley told me it was Dom's. So that's how I know. By the way, the old man got murdered, too. Outside my house."

"I am *so glad* you weren't there."

"Me, too," lied Zach, pursing his lips, a 'tell' that his deceased wife would have easily recognized.

CHAPTER 58

The man who answered the door looked as though he had lost a dear friend, which he had. It was easy to see that he had been crying. Dom was not ashamed to show his feelings. Agent Whitehead had made the call to Dom before leaving the precinct. Dom's initial disbelief was followed by total silence as he tried to collect himself and stifle his feelings. He readily agreed to meet with the three men.

"Please come in," said Dom, clearly unnerved. He led the three men into his living room where they found Paul, Dom's partner, pacing back and forth in front of a pair of French doors that opened onto a balcony. He was upset because Dom was upset. He knew Mary Ellen from bank functions but no more than that. When Dom entered the room, Paul looked at his depressed friend and immediately left the room and walked out onto the balcony, closing the door behind him.

The living room, decorated in light gray and off-white, had a comfortable, inviting look and feel. A lime-washed brick fireplace with bookcases on either side was the centerpiece for an original Alice William's post-impressionist street scene painting. In front of the fireplace were two off-white sofas facing each other, a coffee table in between and two neighboring gray club chairs. There were plenty of seats for everyone. Dom sat on the sofa nearest the fireplace and facing the balcony where he could check on Paul. Jacobs and Marlowe sat on the sofa across from Dom and unintentionally blocked his view of his partner. Whitehead made himself comfortable in the club chair across from Dom, giving him a good view of the man's face so he could easily evaluate his expressions and emotions.

Jacobs immediately took control of the meeting.

"Mr. Garcia, I appreciate you meeting us on such short notice. I'm sure you have a lot of questions and so do we."

Dom took this to mean he could go first, so he jumped right in before the detective could pull out his notepad.

"What, when and how did this happen? When I texted Mary Ellen last night, she seemed happy and in good spirits."

"What time did you text her?"

"Around 8:30 p.m. Paul and I were at a birthday party. I just had this feeling we needed to touch base. She had had a rough week... Oh, God... I can't believe she's dead. And poor Ashley... so young. So I ask, what, when and how did this happen?"

"They were shot while asleep in the bed." Jacobs intentionally did not say they were both shot in the same bed.

"Who did this? Zach?"

"Why would you say that?"

"He's an abusive husband. I saw what he did to Mary Ellen, both physically and emotionally and it wasn't pretty. But don't just take my word for it, ask Sarah Moore, our head teller or Stuart Friedman, Mary Ellen's lawyer. They'll tell you the same thing. He's not a good man."

"Abuse and premeditated murder are different. An abuser may get so enraged that he crosses the line and kills. But very rarely is it premeditated. Plus Zach was in South Carolina last night... So why was your car at the Ferguson's house?"

"Surely I'm not a suspect."

"Our job is to investigate the crime. Your car was at the crime scene, so we go where the evidence leads."

"Mary Ellen's car quit on her at the bank. I let her borrow mine. I don't know what time she and Ashley were killed, but I was at a party last night until about eleven. Then Paul and I came home, had another glass of wine and then went to bed."

"We're just doing our job."

"Sorry. I didn't mean to seem indignant, but I'm heartbroken over Mary Ellen."

"Did Zach know that you had loaned Mary Ellen your car?"

"I don't know. I don't think so. You'd need to ask Zach or Mary..." Dom realized what he was saying and stopped midsentence as tears began to well up in his eyes. He reached over to the coffee table, grabbed a tissue and lightly patted his eyes. It was obvious to the three visitors that Dom was just as heartbroken as the husband.

"Why was your car at the Fergusons on Tuesday and Wednesday?" asked Jacobs.

"After the robbery, I stayed over at her house a couple of nights. I think either you or Detective Marlowe or one of the Cobb County detectives had offered to come over. But Mary Ellen thought a friendly face would be better. I *do* know that she and Ashley were very concerned that the robber might actually carry out his threat. While I was there, we talked a lot. Mostly about Zach. She planned on divorcing him. Did you know that?"

"Yes."

"Do you also know that he threatened me?"

"No. Why?"

"Because I gave Mary Ellen the name of a divorce lawyer who happens to be a friend of mine. The way I see it, if Zach's the kind of person who would beat on his wife and threaten people…" Dom didn't finish his sentence. He let the implied accusation linger in the air.

"It's very obvious that you don't like Zach."

"Actually, I hardly know the man. I think I've only met him a couple of times… when Mary Ellen first started work at the bank. I believe it was at a Christmas party and a company picnic. Nice looking man. Somewhat shy. And he seemed very caring and attentive. Especially to their daughter. But Mary Ellen said he changed over the last few years. She told me that he became abusive and like I said, I saw and recognized some of his handiwork. So, no. I don't like him. I suffered abuse all my life, both verbal and physical, so I know what Mary Ellen's life was like. I have no patience for people like that."

"Understood," said Jacobs. "And until we've had a chance to check out Zach's alibi, we will certainly keep him on our radar. And if he ever threatens you again, call us or the police. We also have zero tolerance for that. Now back to our questions. Do you own a gun?"

"No sir."

"How did your bank audit turn out?"

"Meaning was there any discrepancies other than the money taken in Tuesday's robbery. No," said Dom who understood the subtle meaning behind the question. "I can give you my copy of the audit for your records. I can get another."

"So that my records match yours, exactly how much was taken:" asked Agent Whitehead.

"$4,237."

"Do you know anyone who drives a green Honda?" asked Jacobs.

"Not that I know. And I normally don't drive a car. I usually ride my bike to work. I only recently bought the yellow Porsche and it usually stays in our garage."

"Does your friend Paul own a car?"

"Yes. A Silver 2018 Tesla."

"Do you know if Mary Ellen Ferguson had a lover or ex-lover?"

"Oh no. She wasn't the type." Dom hated that he had used the past tense when referring to his late teller. "Even with the abuse that she suffered from Zach, as far as I know, she always remained faithful. And I think she would have told me if she was."

Before the detective could ask another question, Dom asked one that had been weighing on his mind.

"So what about the bank robber? After all, he did threaten Mary Ellen."

"Let's just say that he's also on our suspects' list. Probably at the top."

CHAPTER 59

The meeting with Dom had filled in some of the missing details of the case. The biggest takeaway was Zach's alleged abusive behavior toward his wife. But without a corroborating witness or police reports of the abuse, it would be one's word against the other. Once the meeting had ended, Agent Whitehead followed the two detectives back to the Midtown precinct. There, he got an electronic link to current copies of notes, videos and pictures sent to his email address which would be automatically downloaded anytime the files were updated. A follow-up meeting was set for Monday at 8:30 a.m. By then Zach's alibi would have been corroborated and any warrants, subpoenas, court orders and official requests would have been granted giving them access to phone records, phone location data, financial data and truck logs.

On his way back to his apartment near the Atlanta Braves stadium, his Bluetooth-connected phone rang in his car. Without taking his eyes off the road, he pushed the TALK button thinking it was either Jacobs, Marlowe or his boss.

"Hello, Danny boy."

"Wrinkles… What the hell. I thought one call every six months was adequate. What's the occasion?"

"The wife's gone to Oregon for a couple of weeks to visit her sister and her husband. You know I can't stand his pompous ass. A friggin' know-it-all. Anyway, I was hoping to come to Atlanta… you know… to catch a Braves game… maybe stay with you for a few days."

"Wrinkles, when did you start watching baseball? You never watched the Nationals while we were partners. You always said it was a waste of time, like golf. I bet you couldn't name a single Brave."

"Tom Glavine."

"He hasn't pitched for the Braves in over ten years."

"Well, you just asked me if I knew a Brave. You didn't say which year."

"So you just want to get out of the house. Can't stand it being all alone?"

"That and you got my detective juices salivating when we talked the other day about that English Bandit. Thought maybe I could come down and help."

"And not be alone?"

"Yeah. And not be alone. I've kinda gotten used to someone always underfoot. I didn't think it'd be so bad with me having a few days to myself. But doing nothing with somebody is better than doing something alone. You'll see. You'll be there one day."

"I gotta have a somebody before that ever happens. Look. I could use the company and I could use your detective brain again."

"Surely he hasn't struck again so soon. If so, I'd say copycat."

"No. Worse. I don't remember if I told you this or not, but during this last robbery, the thief and the teller got into a little confrontation. He threatened the teller saying there would be retributions. No…he said repercussions. Anyway, last night, the teller was murdered along with her daughter and a neighbor."

"No way."

"I wish it weren't true. But, sadly, it is."

"Don't go anywhere. I'm leaving in ten minutes. I should be there around 8:30."

"Not gonna happen. That's a nine-hour trip without stops."

"8:30 or earlier or dinner's on me."

CHAPTER 60

Only one Cobb County police car and a Cobb Crime Scene Unit SUV remained parked in front of the Ferguson's house as Zach and Liz slowly rode by the scene of the triple homicide. Even though he was the architect of the chaos, it still bothered him to see the yellow crime scene tape surrounding his house knowing its meaning. When a police officer walked out the side door, Zach immediately sped up. He had seen what he had come to see. Dom's yellow sports car had indeed blocked the side of the garage where Mary Ellen normally parked the Toyota. But, both garage doors were open and the car wasn't there, in either space. When he reached the end of the street, he turned around and drove past the house on his way out of the neighborhood but at a normal speed offering Liz only a brief view of the house.

"Well, the car's not there," said Zach as he drove out of the neighborhood. "I hope to hell the bitch didn't take it to Pep Boys."

"I'm totally confused," said Liz. "Was something wrong with her car?"

"Yeah, the battery or the starter. I was supposed to fix it this weekend."

"So you think maybe her boss loaned her his Porsche?"

"If he did, he's a fool. But that's the only thing that makes sense."

"Nice boss."

"Nice boss, my ass. I'm telling you, the bitch was banging the asshole. Plain and simple."

"Zach. Listen to yourself. You're still mad at the woman and she's dead. You need to reign it in or the police will stop looking for the real killer and pin this whole thing on you. You're easy pickings."

"You got a point."

A trip to the nearest Pep Boys proved fruitless. The sales technician at the counter could only find in their computer system an estimate for replacing the car's starter, but the work had never been done.

"So what's next?" asked Liz. "I don't know about you, but I don't want to spend my whole weekend looking all over Atlanta for your car."

"Understood." Before pulling out of the repair shop's parking lot, Zach pulled his 'truck' phone out of his pocket along with one of the detective's business cards and punched in the cell number he found on the card.

"Zone 5, Detective Jacobs speaking."

"Detective Jacobs, this is Zach Ferguson. I hope I'm not interrupting anything, but do you happen to know where my car is? I drove by my house and saw the garage open but no car. At least, not my car. The detective's car was still there in the driveway. So, is my car part of the investigation? Have y'all hauled it somewhere to be inspected or something? You know… like for prints?"

"No. Your car is not part of the investigation. I think it's still at the bank. I believe Dom Garcia said it broke down there. You should call him first to make sure he didn't have it hauled off somewhere. Do you have his number?"

That son-of-a-bitch had better not had my car hauled off, thought Zach, trying to control his anger.

"No sir."

Jacobs gave out the number and the call ended. Jacobs tried not to read anything into Zach's switch from grieving spouse to unemotional, matter-of-fact, "where is my car" kind of guy. Everybody dealt with grief differently. A case in point, in one of his first murder cases, Jacobs found the innocent husband of a murdered family out cutting his grass. But it was his way of dealing with his loss. While he found it strange, he learned to understand the erratic behavior of those who were grieving. Had he been in a similar situation, he had no idea how he would react.

Zach immediately typed Dom's name and cell phone number into his 'truck' phone's 'Contact' list on his phone. He then tapped on Dom's name and the phone rang.

After three or four rings, Dom answered.

"Dom… this is Zach Ferguson. Could you tell me where my car is?"

Dom was taken aback. He had never expected a call from Zach.

"Uh… Zach… I am so sorry for your loss. I am heartbroken over the deaths of Mary Ellen and Ashley. They were such kind and wonderful people. If there's…"

"Do you know where my damn car is or don't you? I've got things to do and I need my car."

"Yes. It's in the employee's parking lot, just off 13th Street. Mary Ellen couldn't get it..."

"Is the lot open? I need my car and I've got a funeral to plan."

"I understand. No. It's Saturday so the lot is closed, but I can open it up for you if that would help."

"I think that's the least you could do. I will be there in thirty minutes. You think you can make that happen?"

"I will."

* * * * * * * * * * * * * * * *

Dom was standing at the open gate of the bank's parking lot when a silver Ford F150 truck slowly turned into the open lot. He immediately recognized Zach as the driver. He then looked at the passenger side of the vehicle. The seat was occupied by an older, heavy-set woman. *Surely this isn't Girlfriend.* Zach chose not to acknowledge Dom, but instead, gunned the truck as he drove past him and directly over to the lone car in the lot. Neither man cared for each other, so the snub wasn't unexpected.

Zach parked Liz's truck next to the Toyota and exited the vehicle, leaving its engine running. By the time Dom reached the car, Zach already had the vehicle unlocked and was sitting in the driver's seat trying unsuccessfully to start the engine. It was just as dead as his wife.

Dom leaned into the open-door driver's side and asked, "Anything I can do to help? You want me to call AAA?"

"If I need your help, I'll ask. Now get out of my way."

Dom stepped back and Zach got out of the car. Anybody who looked at Zach could see the mad on his face as he raised the car's hood. Using a pair of booster cables found in a large toolbox in the back of Liz's truck, he tried to jump-start the car. Nothing happened. A bad starter, just as diagnosed by the Pep Boy's technician.

"I've got to go get my tools and buy a starter. Any way you can leave the parking lot open for a couple of hours?" asked Zach humbly since he was now at the mercy of his antagonist.

"No problem. Anything to help. If you don't mind calling me when you've finished your work, then I can come back and lock it up."

"Thank you," mumbled Zach, the words killing him.

Once Zach and Liz had left, Dom closed the gate without locking it, jumped on his bike and rode back to his condo. He felt sorry for Zach. He had lost his wife and daughter. But he also felt sorry for himself. He had lost two friends. He silently prayed that God would give comfort to Zach's soul and that proper justice be rendered to the person responsible for this unforgivable act of violence.

CHAPTER 61

It had been almost three hours and Dom had yet to hear from Zach. He figured that the man was under so much stress that he had forgotten to call him back. Even though the parking lot would be empty, he had unlocked the gate, so he was responsible for locking it back. Figuring he'd waited long enough, Dom hopped on his bike and rode over to the parking lot. He fully expected the lot to be empty and the gate still open. Instead, he saw the hood of the Toyota up and a man leaning in. Liz's silver truck was parked alongside the old beige car and it, too, had its hood raised. He pedaled on up to the car. The noise of the bike's tires on the gravel caused Zach to pull up from under the hood.

"How's it going?" asked Dom.

"*I told you* I would call you. But I'm just about done," answered Zach, irritated that he might now be on the clock. He'd overstayed his welcome. "I just need about five more minutes to get the battery connected and try her out if that's all right with you."

"I'm good. No rush."

Zach nodded and stuck his head back under the hood to continue with his repair.

Liz Davis was sitting in her truck, texting with friends when she saw Dom. Zach had not introduced her the first time she saw him. She wasn't going to let that happen again. She got out of her truck and went over to the man on the bike.

"Hi. I'm Liz Davis," She then extended her hand.

Dom laid down his bike, took off his helmet and shook the hand of the woman that Mary Ellen called Girlfriend and introduced himself.

"How's Zach holding up?"

Liz looked at her boyfriend and then back at Dom wondering how much she should say to Zach's deceased wife's lover.

"Not well at all. Ashley was the love of his life. She kept that marriage alive. But *you* probably know that."

Dom understood the subtle slight as a slam on his involvement in Mary Ellen's divorce, meaning his approval of the divorce and his lawyer friend, Stu Friedman. But Liz meant it to be Dom's love relationship with Zach's now-deceased wife.

Dom did not want to have his emotions go unchecked, so he kept the conversation formal.

"I'm sorry to hear that. Mary Ellen and Ashley were lovely people. I know Ashley was very popular at school and a very good student. And Mary Ellen… everyone liked her… her friends at the bank, her customers… me. I am going to really, really miss her. Do you know when and where they'll be holding the funeral service and the name of the funeral home?"

"Zach's meeting with Mary Ellen's parents tomorrow. That's all I know."

"Do you know if there's anything I can do for him? I know he's not fond of me and not sure the reason. But I'm available for whatever he needs. He has my…"

Before he could complete his sentence, he and Liz heard the Toyota's engine start and they saw Zach jump out of the car, leaving the engine running. He walked briskly over to Liz and Dom, never taking his eyes off of Dom.

"You do know that you and the bank are responsible for this," Zach said loudly, emphatically, not happy that Liz seemed to be befriending Dom.

Dom did not want to confront the man, especially when his feelings were on edge.

"Zach… I'm very sorry about what happened. Mary Ellen and Ashley were the sweetest, kindest, most…"

"Shut up. Do not mention my daughter's name ever again. She's the innocent one here. If the bank had done what they should have done when Mary Ellen was threatened, this would never have happened. They both would have been alive. You would have been happy and I would have been happy."

"Zach, I'm terribly sorry for your loss." Dom then leaned over and picked up his bike. He faced it towards the gate and rode out of the parking lot without saying another word. There could be no winner in this argument. He had considered telling Zach that he had gotten the bank to agree to pay for all funeral costs. But the bank's policy was to avoid publicity, good or bad, resulting from a tragedy, so the funeral home would be the one to convey that news to the family. And as far as the gate to the parking lot was concerned, he and Paul could return later and make sure it was locked.

"Honey, I know you are upset and don't really like Dom, but don't you think you went a little overboard? He seems like a nice guy."

"Whose side are you on? The fucking bank should have made damn sure nothing happened to my family. They are the ones responsible for all of this."

Liz understood the hostility and the lashing out that her boyfriend was doing. He had lost his daughter forever and there was nobody to blame, so he blamed everybody and even himself. She needed to somehow focus his anger on some*thing* and not some*one*.

"Look, if you feel that way and I agree, why don't you sue the bank? Make them pay. I know a guy at work who got run over by one of our trucks. Probably his fault, not the driver. But he got a lawyer and the company settled for over a half mil. Tax free."

"Shit! It would serve them right."

"If you want me to, I can get you the name of that guy's lawyer. The bank's got plenty of money," Liz joked.

"Yeah. I should have thought of that myself. I like that… a lot. I want to make that bald-headed fucker pay… big time. He's the one who should be dead. Not my little girl." Zach did not hide the rage in his voice and it was not directed towards some*thing* like the bank as Liz had hoped. It was directed towards some*one*… Dom.

CHAPTER 62

The weather had been accommodating allowing Scott and Anne to walk to South City Kitchen for lunch and then to the Botanical Gardens on Piedmont Drive. Scott enjoyed the walk through the different gardens. Anne, even more so. She seemed to stop at almost every plant, shrub, tree… anywhere there was a sign to read and she did. It seemed like she wanted to know *everything* about every planting. The country of origin, its species, its Latin name. Everything. All Scott cared to do was to look at the plant and move on.

Once Anne recognized Scott had had enough of nature, they walked back to the hotel where they each ordered a glass of wine at Margot's. This time, Anne drank Chardonnay. Fool her once… She wanted no part of a migraine on her *CATS* night.

* * * * * * * * * * * * * * * * *

The television at the bar at Baraonda's was showing the 3rd round of the Northern Trust golf tournament at the Liberty National Golf Club in Jersey City, New Jersey when two stools, next to each other, opened up. Scott immediately pounced on them. There was no sound on the TV. Just closed captions. After ordering a Margherita pizza to share and a glass of Classico Riserva Chianti for Scott and a Jordan Chardonnay for Anne, the couple began watching Patrick Reed vault to the lead in the tournament with a birdie of the 17th hole. Anne loved golf. Golf is what brought them together when they were paired in a Mixed Four-Ball Tournament at the country club where they both belonged. One round of golf led to dinner which led to more golf, then to dates and then a marriage proposal.

Once the tournament on the TV ended, Anne took a sip of her wine and then excused herself to go to the 'lady's room.' Scott continued to watch the TV monitor as the CBS station switched to local news. The lead story centered on the triple gunshot homicide in a quiet Cobb County neighborhood earlier that morning. A reporter was standing in front of the ranch-style house surrounded by yellow crime scene tape as three body bags were being loaded onto the coroner's truck. As the reporter mouthed the names of the victims, the closed caption displayed them on the screen. Scott couldn't take his eyes off the words on the screen especially when he saw the following caption:

> *We have a reliable source that says there is evidence linking the midtown robbery at Providence Surety Bank to the murders. That one of the murder victims, Mary Ellen Ferguson, a teller at the bank, had been threatened by the robber. Evidently, he carried out his threat.*

Without thinking, Scott blurted out, "That's not true!"

Everyone around him looked at the man including Anne who had just returned from the bathroom.

"What's not true? Are you okay?"

"I meant to say *that can't be true.*"

"About what?" asked Anne who had not seen the news report.

"You know, last night, we were talking to that guy whose bank had been robbed earlier in the week? Well, I just saw on the TV that the teller he was talking about at the party… the one who was threatened by the robber. Well, she was murdered last night. The reporter says they have evidence linking the murders to the robbery. That's just so unbelievable."

"Are you sure it's the same woman?"

"Yes."

"You're right. That is unbelievable. It's too bad the police weren't as concerned about that woman's safety as you were last night?"

"But I was talking about the woman's mental state… not her safety. The fact that she might be in jeopardy never crossed my mind. In all my years in the banking business, I have *never* heard of a robber coming back *after* a robbery to do harm to anyone. It just doesn't happen. But what the manager said about that woman's fear, paranoia, anxiety did bother me. I don't think the banks really worry about the mental trauma that a robbery might inflict on the people whether it be teller, customer, employee. Well, except maybe that Dom fellow we met last night. He seemed to really care. I bet this whole murder, robbery thing has really hit him hard."

This conversation was not your usual small talk over a glass of wine and Anne's lawyer antennae went up.

"You make a valid point about the mental issues. But obviously the bank… the police … somebody dropped the ball. Especially after the robber threatened that poor woman. *Somebody* should have listened to her and her fear for her safety. If I were that family's lawyer, and believe me, there *will* be a lawyer involved, I could easily ask for twenty million and settle for twelve… maybe fifteen. Even the worst of lawyers could win this case… in their sleep."

Scott listened to his fiancé but didn't hear her. His concern was what evidence the police might have that linked *him* to these murders. He then saw Anne looking at her watch.

"Honey? It's time to go. The show starts in fifteen minutes."

The show was wonderful, the cast was great and Anne cried when they sang *Memory* in Act II. Scott wouldn't know. While his face seemed to be enjoying the evening, his mind wandered back to Friday evening when he had driven over to the teller's house. Could someone have seen him stop at the mailbox and have remembered all or part of his license plate? And what about that guy in the white car who saw him drive out of the neighborhood? Would he remember his face or his car?

But the bigger question was who did kill those people? And why? One thing was for sure. Scott knew it wasn't him.

John Thomas

Sunday, August 11, 2019

ATLANTA, GEORGIA

CHAPTER 63

It was 7:10 a.m., past time for the hotel's complimentary newspaper to have arrived. Scott had already checked three times outside his room's door to no avail. He had just opened the door, ready to head down to the lobby in his bathrobe when he saw an attendant rushing down the hallway dropping off papers as he went. Scott waited at the door and took the paper from the attendant's hand and gave him a five-dollar tip. The attendant never looked at the amount. He just stuffed it in his pocket, mumbled "thank you" and rushed on to the next room.

Once inside his room, with a freshly made cup of coffee from the hotel's in-room coffee maker, he sat down by the window and opened up the front page, setting the other sections on the floor. He didn't have to look hard to find the story about the three murders. The major headline read: Bank Robber Murders Three in Cobb County. The paper only carried a picture of the Colonel, in his younger days, in full military dress.

Scott's heart was pounding as he read the gruesome details of the three killings. The story told how two bodies were found shot in bed and a third, a retired Marine colonel, was found shot outside on the driveway. The article stated that the detectives and FBI agent were only willing to say *No Comment* to all of their questions. However, an unnamed source disclosed that the murders appeared to be the work of a serial robber known as the English Bandit because of his English accent. The same thief that had robbed Providence Surety Bank in midtown Atlanta on Tuesday, August 6. The source stated that the police had evidence linking the two crimes but would not disclose that information. Further down in the story was a list of previous robberies thought to have been committed by the English Bandit. It then gave a description of the thief.

By the time Anne awoke, Scott had read the article three times. Regardless of how many times he read the story, other than the possibility of someone seeing and remembering his license plate when he stopped at the Ferguson's mailbox, there was nothing that came to mind linking him to the murders.

"You're up mighty early," said Anne as she sat up in bed. "So what does a woman have to do to get a cup of coffee around here?"

"They're bringing breakfast at 7:45, but I can make you a cup of the room coffee. They've got a variety of K-pods."

"I can wait for breakfast, but I *need* coffee… now. Whatever they have is fine if you don't mind making it. And you know what I like."

While Scott brewed her a cup of coffee and made himself a new one, Anne went over and picked up the front section of the Atlanta paper and sat in the chair facing the one where Scott had been sitting.

"Oh my God! This *is* awful," said Anne as she read through the article. "This is horrible. What kind of person could do such a thing?"

Scott carried both coffees over to the window table handing Anne's cup to her outreached hand. She immediately took a small sip and continued.

"It says here that the robber, the one they call the English Bandit, is thought to be responsible. That it must have been the revenge he threatened."

"I don't want to disagree with an unnamed source, but I, personally, find it highly unlikely that the robber waited three days and then went back to kill that teller. That just doesn't happen. It doesn't make sense. The police need to be looking elsewhere."

"You mean like the husband, boyfriend or … fiancé?" Anne laughed. Then her best 'cop' impression, "So… where were *you* on the night of the murders?" Then she laughed again.

Scott didn't. In retrospect, he should have just dropped the subject, but he didn't.

"Seriously. In all the years that I've worked in the banking industry, I do not think that has ever happened. I'm telling you, they've got that all wrong. They need to be looking elsewhere."

"Surely you're not defending this monster. He robs a bank. Threatens a teller. Then makes good on his threat. I see that as being very believable. And there's always a first time for everything. And just to let you know where I stand, when they catch this guy, I hope they cut his balls off before they slap the needle in his arm."

"Ouch. He better hope you're not on the jury." Scott laughed. Anne didn't.

"I haven't had enough coffee yet to get into an argument over this. I think we need to drop this before you really get into serious trouble."

Scott didn't say anything but thought, *I think I already am.*

CHAPTER 64

Zach sat across from Mary Ellen's parents at a table, next to a window at a Cracker Barrel restaurant, just off I-75 and Delk Road. No one wanted to be there. It was a command performance for all three.

"Do you know when they will release the bodies?" asked Wesley, Mary Ellen's father.

"The detective called last night and said the bodies were available. They also said that by noon I could get back into my house. But I'm not sure I'm up to that right now," said Zach who stopped eating long enough to answer his father-in-law's question. The Knox's could hardly eat, much less watch the man across from them tear through the food as though nothing had happened. Their hearts were broken. Eating was the last thing on their mind.

"Have you selected a funeral home?" asked Wesley.

"I really haven't had a chance. I spent all day yesterday fixing my car. It broke down in the bank's parking lot where Mary Ellen worked. Plus, I'm not sure how I'm gonna pay for..."

Wesley had already expected as much. Before Zach could finish his sentence and feel embarrassed, Wesley jumped in.

"Let's not worry about the costs. Let's just get it planned. Carol and I know that you have a lot on your plate, so earlier we did some research and found a name of a funeral home that's close to your house. They seem to have a good reputation. I hope we haven't overstepped our bounds."

"No. I'm good."

"Then if it's okay with you, we'll call them and let them know they can pick up the bodies. They deserve the best and that's what they're going to get."

"What about the pastor. Do you know his name?" asked Carol.

"No. Not really. But I do know where the church is located. I went to Ashley's..." Then he stopped in mid-sentence and stared out the nearby window trying not to show the tears that had welled up in his eyes. Seeing emotions breaking forth in Mary Ellen's husband was comforting to the Knox's knowing there was love and feelings in the man's heart, at least for their granddaughter.

"… her commencement… no… her…"

"Her confirmation," said Carol, trying to help out her son-in-law.

"Yes. Her confirmation. But y'all were there. It's the same church. I can't recall the preacher's name."

"We'll find out," said Carol. "If you would like, I could meet with him… the preacher and plan the service. If that's okay with you."

"Yes, please."

"Then that's settled. Now we'll need to know the name of some of Mary Ellen's co-workers, friends, etcetera. Same for Ashley."

She then produced a yellow pad and the three of them worked out as much of the details as they could. Carol and the preacher would do the rest.

"Have you thought about what you are going to wear at the funeral?" asked Carol.

"No. Not really. I only have one suit and I don't know if it fits me anymore. It was pretty tight the last time I wore it at Ash…" Zach stopped midsentence to compose himself again.

"Look. This has been tough on all of us. And the next few days are going to be even tougher. We just all have to somehow get through it. I think Ashley would want her dad to be all dressed up nicely, so if it's okay with you, we'd like to pay for you to get a new suit. I think Macy's has a nice selection," said Carol who then reached into her pocketbook, pulled out her wallet and handed Zach three one hundred dollar bills.

Zach reluctantly took the money. He was embarrassed, but not so embarrassed that he would spend his own money. After all, how he looked was more for them than for him or Ashley. They just didn't want to be embarrassed in front of all of their country club friends. But he would do it …for Ashley.

Zach waited until the Knox's were about to leave and then he brought up the elephant in the room.

"I know that everyone thinks I did it. It's always the husband. Always. But I didn't do it. I didn't kill Mary Ellen and Ashley. I know I wasn't a very good husband. And you probably know that Mary Ellen was planning on divorcing me. In fact, I was served the papers just seconds before the police told me what happened. Just so you know, I had already sent her a text consenting to the divorce. But kill my family. No way. You know I loved my daughter more than anything in the world. I would never knowingly do any harm to her… or Mary Ellen."

"Do the police have any idea who did it or why?" asked Carol as Wesley looked at his son-in-law with contempt.

"They told me they have evidence that points to the robber. Maybe it was a form of payback for Mary Ellen standing up to the jerk. If I had been there, this would never have happened. I have a Glock. I… I…"

"I think we should go," said Wesley seeing the look on his son-in-law's face and the rage in his eyes. He imagined it was the same rage that his daughter had long endured.

CHAPTER 65

Daniel put his empty coffee cup in the dishwasher and headed back to the guest bedroom where he found Johnny still fast asleep. Obviously, this was a new habit acquired from his years of retirement. As far as Daniel was concerned, Wrinkles had had enough sleep for one day. If they were going over to look at the crime scene, they had until noon. That's when the crime scene tape went down and the officers left.

Last night had been fun for the two ex-Washington DC detectives as they talked about old times, old cases and Wrinkle's doctor appointments. When their past stories ran dry, they began looking over documents and videos from the murders and the robbery staying up until 2 a.m. Daniel gave him the lowdown on Zach, Dom and their obvious dislike for each other. Johnny had pretty much said nothing, taking it all in. But that was his technique. Look, listen and learn.

"Wrinkles, you've got twenty minutes to get your lazy ass out of bed, showered, shave and dressed. We don't have much time. I'm only doing this for you." He could no longer say *fat ass*. His partner was in better shape now than at any time when he was on the force. Regardless of what Johnny had said, retirement had been good to him.

"Can't a fellow even get a hot cup of coffee around here? What kind of host are you?"

"I'll bring you one to the shower. And I promise I won't look." Daniel knew how his partner liked his coffee. He always said, *Black, like me.*

The trip over to the crime scene was at Johnny's request. Looking at pictures was not the same as looking at the actual crime scene. On the way over to Mason Street and Hillside Avenue, the two men grabbed a Chick-fil-a chicken biscuit and another cup of coffee. Johnny's wife limited her husband's fast food intake while at home, but he had been given a kitchen pass and he was making the most of it.

While Daniel drove, Johnny munched and reviewed his notes, the photos they'd printed off from the APD computer link and the list of the evidence he wanted to see firsthand. Unfortunately, he wouldn't get to see what he considered the most interesting piece of evidence, the bedroom door with the ominous message.

For the better part of two hours, Daniel and Johnny examined the entire crime scene starting with the outside and the location of the Colonel's body and then moving to the master bedroom where Mary Ellen and Ashley Ferguson were fatally shot. For Daniel, it was déjà vu from his Saturday investigation. For Johnny, it was a nostalgic reminder of his past life as a well-respected detective.

Daniel kept his thoughts and opinions to himself as his old partner quietly but methodically checked out the crime scene. Once Johnny had seen enough, the two old friends walked outside and over to Daniel's car.

"Well… what do you think?" asked Daniel. When they were partners, he always looked to his older partner for his insights, thoughts and possibilities.

"Reason would have us believe that the robber and the murderer were not the same person. That just doesn't happen… at least not that I know. But let me ask you a couple of questions. First… has this robber, the English Bandit, ever used a gun during any of his suspected robberies?"

"No. Not from any FBI reports of his previous robberies, the videos I've reviewed or from any eyewitness's statements."

"How did the intruder get a key? I saw no forcible entry."

"We're not sure. That's a question for Zach Ferguson at his next follow-up session, Monday."

This Dominick Garcia. The owner of the yellow sports car. You never mentioned his relationship with the Ferguson woman. Were they lovers?

"He's the victim's boss and friend. No romantic relationship. In fact, he's gay. He loaned the victim his car when her car failed to start as she left from work."

"I don't remember if you told me whether Garcia had an alibi for the night of the murders."

"He did."

Johnny then looked at some of the photos that Daniel had given him. Then he looked back at Daniel.

"Based on what I've seen inside and outside the house, plus all the photos including the spray-painted message, and the fact that both the robber and the murderer were approximately the same height and both right-handed, it is very possible… considering the threat to the teller, that they are indeed one and the same. Yet, I'm not convinced. This act of retaliation against a teller by a robber after the heist just doesn't happen. And to wait three days? What does he stand to gain? Revenge? Notoriety? Make good his promise? I don't think so. It's always the husband, ex-lover, disgruntled worker, neighbor… whatever."

Daniel would not challenge Johnny. From the years they had spent together as partners, he knew Johnny had always had a 6th sense… his gut feeling, as he would say, about how he viewed crimes. But he had been retired for a while. Could he have lost some of that innate skill because *everything* seemed to point to the robber.

Johnny slid the pictures in his briefcase. "I think I've seen enough here. You sure it's okay to go see the Colonel's widow?" asked Johnny.

"Yes. I called Mrs. Oliver while you were showering. She wanted to help and said to come over anytime."

Betty Oliver must have seen Daniel's SUV parked in front of the Ferguson's house because she immediately opened the door after Daniel's push of the doorbell. Betty and Ike, who now had his left leg in a small cast and wearing a plastic cone collar, greeted the two men at the front door. Surprisingly, with all that had gone on the day of the shooting, she remembered Agent Whitehead. Ike did not and began barking and hopping around on his three good legs until Betty shushed the animal. He meekly slid behind Betty's legs and got as close to her as the cone allowed. Once inside, Daniel introduced Johnny as an outside crime consultant. He politely shook Betty's hand. She then led them to the living room where the two men found seats opposite the sofa where she and Ike sat.

Whitehead had Betty review what happened on the night of the murder. As hard as she tried, she could not hold back the tears. Johnny had to look away a couple of times himself. Once she had told what she knew, Johnny asked if she minded answering a few questions.

"Ask me anything. I want to help."

"Just to confirm, earlier, you said that Zach Ferguson had asked your husband to watch his house for any suspicious activity?"

"Yes. That is correct. In fact, we both were. Bob… that's the Colonel… he and I would race to see who got to the binoculars first whenever we thought we heard something."

"Did you ever see anything out of the ordinary at the Ferguson's house?"

"The yellow car. We saw it Tuesday, Wednesday and Friday. That was all. But that was the detective's car."

"Who told you it was a detective's car?" asked Johnny.

"Both Mary Ellen and Zach told Bob," said Betty, stroking her small, helpless companion.

"On Friday night, when the Colonel took your dog out to do his… er… whatever, he texted Zach that there was a green Honda parked in front of the house. Did you happen to see the car or know whose it is?"

"No. I didn't. If there was another car outside, I didn't hear it or see it. But my hearing isn't what it used to be and I never looked outside. But are you sure that *Bob* sent that text to Zach?"

"Yes. Why? You seem hesitant."

"That just doesn't sound like Bob."

"What do you mean?"

"Bob wouldn't know a Honda from a Chevrolet. Not only that, he was colorblind. He couldn't tell brown from green. And mix in reds… oh my gosh. Plus it was at night. If he had to identify something as green or brown, he'd usually say it was a dark color. But then again, maybe he saw the car's logo and guessed the color. Maybe he was just in a hurry." She then teared up just thinking about her lost mate.

Johnny gave the grieved woman a few minutes to compose herself. When he felt she could continue, he proceeded to his next question.

"How well did you know the Ferguson's?"

"Mary Ellen and Ashley… extremely well. We loved them dearly. Mary Ellen was the daughter and Ashley was the granddaughter we never had. When our power went out a couple of years back, they had us stay at their house. She had a fire in their fireplace and that's where she cooked our meals. They were always looking after us. That's why when Zach asked Bob to keep an eye on their house this past week, he gladly accepted. We'd do anything for them."

"What about Zach? You didn't mention him. Were you aware that Mary Ellen had filed for divorce?"

"No. But I wouldn't doubt it. He was *never* home, but when he was, to quote the Colonel, he was "an arrogant, narcissistic, self-absorbed prick." No one liked him. And I'm not a hundred percent sure, but I think he has a girlfriend."

"I don't like asking this question, but it's part of the job. Did Mary Ellen Ferguson have a boyfriend? Did she have a regular visitor, if you will?"

"Oh no. Bob and I would know if she did. But she wasn't that type. She was a very moral, Christian lady."

"Mrs. Oliver, you've been most helpful and we are very sorry for your loss. The Colonel sounds like he was a fine man and an asset to our country's military. If we have further questions, is it all right if we call you?" asked Daniel as he and then Johnny rose from their seats.

"Absolutely. Thank you for coming by. I hope you catch that bastard."

Daniel headed to the front door while Johnny gave Betty a hug. Not something he would have done had he still been on the force. The two men then went back to Daniel's SUV where they sat and mulled over what they had seen and heard.

"So what do you think? You still have your doubts about the robber and the murderer being the same guy?"

"I'm keeping my options open. What concerns me the most is the text message that the Colonel sent to Zach. Not so much that he named the make of the car, but he identified a specific color. I'm colorblind, so I can relate. The difference is Mrs. Oliver said the Colonel chooses to say dark colors rather than guess. I just guess which annoys my wife to no end."

"I don't see the text as an issue. The text was to Zach… not Betty."

"Good point. Any chance I could get a copy of all the texts on Zach's phone?"

"I'll make that happen Monday."

"And have they checked out his alibi with the woman in South Carolina?"

"My understanding is that they were supposed to reach out to her yesterday. I'll find out Monday. We meet at 8:30 a.m. Zach comes in at ten."

"Any chance you could bring your *crime consultant* to the meeting?" asked Johnny.

"And what do you think, Mr. Crime Consultant?"

"I think I need to make other plans."

CHAPTER 66

"Thank you for calling. I'm sorry I couldn't get here sooner," said Ed Jernigan, a lawyer from the Harrison, Chapman and Jernigan law firm. If the way one looked or dressed could speak words, Jernigan's screamed lawyer. The ruddy complexioned, pudgy man with wisps of gray hair and round-rimmed glasses, was dressed in a pair of white linen pants, a light blue oxford, button-down collared shirt with coordinating suspenders and bowtie. He spoke with a slow southern drawl. Coming from Pennsylvania, it had been an acquired accent requiring years of practice. It was now second nature. Zach immediately liked him even without knowing his win/loss success rate. All he knew was he'd gotten a half-million dollars for a man whose toe had been run over by a tractor-trailer truck. He salivated over what he could get as a man who had lost his wife and daughter due to sheer negligence.

"I'm sorry we couldn't meet at my house," said Zach, somewhat embarrassed by Liz's tiny, but neat old clapboard house. "I just couldn't bring myself to go back there… not just yet."

"Completely understandable," said Jernigan. "When Ms. Davis called, she gave me a quick rundown of what happened. It really piqued my interest. Do you mind going over the details again? I'd like to hear it from you. You're the victim here."

The story wasn't completely new to Jernigan. He'd heard it on the news and seen reports on TV. When he got the call from the answering service, he was laying out by his pool. Normally, they wouldn't have bothered him. They were supposed to tell the caller that a lawyer would contact them on Monday or Tuesday. But fortunately for Jernigan, the answering service recognized Zach Ferguson's name and was aware of his horrible tragedy. Their suspicions were confirmed by Liz Davis who had initiated the call. She was immediately connected to Jernigan.

After hearing Liz's brief description and before coming to meet Zach, he'd read everything he could about the robbery and the recent murders. The media attention it was getting was only a step away from being national news. Jernigan would have taken on the case for free just for the publicity. But the case had the potential of paying off his mortgage, funding his grandkid's college, buying a new BMW and shortening his time before retirement, so he'd try for a fifty/fifty split but would settle for thirty/seventy with Zach picking up the expenses.

Over a cup of coffee, Jernigan listened to Zach tell the story of how the detectives met him at the truck terminal and told him the news of his family's deaths and how they were killed. Then they took him back to the station house and grilled him… like he was the one who murdered his family. He told Jernigan he had an airtight alibi. He was dead drunk asleep in Ramona Hewitt's bed in her apartment in South Carolina. They had spent the early part of the evening drinking his first-ever, Old Fashions made with Maker's Mark. He then told Jernigan about the robbery, the threat and then the murders. Every time he mentioned his daughter's name, he teared up. The lawyer wished he could bottle up that emotion and summon it on demand. A broken-hearted father and husband could easily add an extra million to the award if the case ever went before a jury.

"If it's okay with you, I'd like to put a face to a name so it becomes personal to me. Do you have a picture of your wife and daughter?"

Zach reached for his wallet in his back pocket. He had a six-year-old photo of Mary Ellen and last year's school picture of Ashley.

Jernigan took the picture, looked at the beautiful woman and her pretty daughter. With Zach's Hollywood good looks and his beautiful family, a jury would have no trouble finding fault and placing blame on the bank. He couldn't have mentally salivated any more over the potential payday from this case than if he'd been a hound dog in a meat market. He then handed them back to Zach who took a long look at Ashley's picture before returning them both to his wallet.

"So the detectives told you that they definitely have evidence pointing the finger at the bank robber… a guy the FBI calls the English Bandit. A known serial robber?"

"Yes."

"Do you know if this English Bandit has ever killed anybody else before?"

"I don't know much about him other than he threatened my wife during the robbery. The police or FBI should know." Zach then gave the lawyer both of the detective's business cards. He wrote down the information and Zach returned the cards to his wallet.

"I would assume the bank has a video of the threat as well as the robbery. We'll need to get a copy of that. I want to see everything."

Liz, who had stayed in the kitchen, peeked her head into the room. Zach motioned her to come in.

Jernigan had only talked to Liz and her voice was prettier and slimmer than the woman that entered the room. Certainly not even in the same league as Mary Ellen. Maybe in her younger, slimmer days.

"How long were you and Mary Ellen married?"

"Twelve years."

"A good marriage?"

"To be honest, not the last few years. We discussed divorce, but neither wanted to do it because of Ashley. At least until recently."

"Um… not good."

"Look. I already know I wasn't that great of a husband. But she was fucking around too. With her boss. And just so you are aware, I got served divorce papers moments before the detectives told me about their murders."

Jernigan shook his head. This wasn't good. The jury wouldn't see a grieving husband. Only one taking advantage of a bad situation. "Do you know when she hired her lawyer and his name… or her name," he added, looking at Liz then Zach.

"Just a couple of days ago." He then gave Jernigan the divorce papers which showed Stewart Friedman as the lawyer.

"I know Stu. Good man. Excellent lawyer." Jernigan was silent for a minute while he thought. He needed to turn this divorce into something positive for Zach. Then suddenly, it came to him.

"Did your wife ever fear for her life?"

What first came to Zach's mind was the look on Mary Ellen's face when she saw him standing at the foot of the bed with gun in hand. Without question, the woman feared for her life.

"Yes, she did. To the point that a detective spent the night at her house this past Tuesday and Wednesday. She and Ashley were afraid that something might happen. Not only did someone stay at her house, I also had the neighbor across the street keep an eye on the house, texting me if he saw anything suspicious. It cost him his life."

"The old man found on the driveway… Is he the one you're talking about?"

"Yes. The Colonel. Good man," said Zach, mimicking Jernigan's earlier reply. "He and his wife, Betty, live directly across the street from me."

"Do you have her telephone number?" Jernigan could see the possibility of a second case.

"Yes. In my phone but I gave it to the police. But it's the only Robert Oliver on Mason Street." Jernigan wrote down the name and address.

"Okay. Here's what I see. I see a woman who is frightened for her life. Enough so, that she has to have a detective stay with her for two days. Detectives don't ordinarily do this. *You* were worried enough that *you* had a neighbor checking in on her. I think she had to be going through something equivalent to PTSD. Her decisions are not rational. That's why the sudden decision to file for divorce so soon after the robbery. The bank should have been able to see the change in her personality. They should have provided her with the appropriate security as well as emotional support. I think we have a winning case."

Zach sat for a minute or two as he watched the lawyer look at him, then at Liz. Finally, he stood from his seat and went over to the lawyer. He extended his hand.

"Sir. As my lawyer, I think we have a winning case, too. What do we need to do next?"

"Number one. Do not talk to any reporters. We'll do that at the appropriate times when I feel we can make the greatest impact. And number two, you'll have to sign a Contingent Fee contract. And all that means is you agree to let Harrison, Chapman and Jernigan law firm represent you and that you pay nothing unless we win. Then we split the settlement. As a wrongful death, your share would be non-taxable. Our firm normally gets fifty percent. Are you good with that arrangement?"

"I was thinking more along the line of sixty/forty, my share being sixty. I think that's what the dude that you represented at Cross Freight got. Is that okay?"

"I believe that's what we worked out with that client, but he paid the expenses out of his share. Will that work?"

"What kind of settlement are we talking about? Like a million or so?"

"Oh no. I think we ask for eight and settle for four if we don't have to go to trial."

"Four million?" asked Zach his mouth dropping as he mentally calculated his portion.

Jernigan was way ahead of his client. He'd figured his share after paying ten percent of the gross award to the firm would net him about a million and a quarter, at worst.

"Where do I sign?" asked Zach.

The lawyer pulled out the Contingent Fee contract which had already been filled out except the settlement distribution, the expense obligation and the signatures. Jernigan looked at Zach as he eagerly signed the document without reading the first line. With his family's good looks, their jobs as hard-working average, middle-class people, the youth and innocence of their pretty daughter, the national publicity of a serial bank robber and the graphics of the horrific murder, the case could be won by a first-year law student. He just prayed the son-of-a-bitch wasn't guilty. He would never ask nor did he want to know.

Monday, August 12, 2019

ATLANTA, GEORGIA

CHAPTER 67

Scott's weekend had not gone the way he had planned. What were the odds that he would meet and have a conversation with the manager of the bank he'd just robbed? Then, have the teller that he'd robbed and threatened be murdered. And finally, have his first argument with his fiancé over the murder suspect. Fortunately, the rocky start with Anne on Sunday morning was interrupted by the hotel attendant bringing their breakfast. After breakfast, they spent the rest of the day at the Atlanta History Center. True to her nature and just as she had done at the Botanical Gardens, Anne seemed to read every label, descriptive note and tag and watched every video in the museum. Nothing was said again about the murder, the teller, or the murderer which was perfectly fine with Scott. When she left later that day, heading back to Charlotte, they were back on happy terms. The marriage was still on.

Scott sat with a cup of coffee and read the morning AJC (Atlanta Journal and Constitution) newspaper that he had retrieved from the lobby. He was no longer at the Four Seasons. His company would only pay for moderate accommodations, so he had moved to a hotel off Holcomb Road, close to his Monday appointment at Roswell Guardian State Bank.

The triple homicide still commanded the front page of the paper but as a secondary story. Unless there were newer developments, it would find itself shoved to the rear of the paper as the week wore on. From what he read, the husband was not a person of interest. His alibi had checked out and the article stated he wasn't even in the state at the time of the murders.

So if not the husband, who, thought Scott. He leaned back in his chair and considered who else would benefit from the teller's death. Could she somehow have been involved in some embezzlement scheme at the bank and got whacked because she got greedy? Could she have had a lover who used the robber's threat to silence her because she was planning on making their affair public? Then again, what about a contract killing by her husband? Or could it simply have been a random act of violence? All possibilities. But the paper said an unnamed source said there was evidence linking the murders to the bank robber. Him. Scott Burnett.

But that wasn't true. He was no murderer. He was a robber. A thief. An innocent thief.

CHAPTER 68

Everybody who was invited to the Ferguson murder case update at Zone 5's precinct station arrived early. The stark meeting room with its whiteboard, old long, rectangular table and a smorgasbord of chairs brought back memories to Daniel of the times he and Johnny were in Washington. Sitting around the table were Jacobs, Marlowe, Daniel, the Cobb County detectives, Freeman and Bradley and Pete Wilson, the forensic technician, also from Cobb County. Each man had an open laptop and a cup of coffee in front of them except Wilson who had a diet Coke. Someone had brought doughnuts, probably Marlowe since he was leading the session.

He began the meeting with a brief summary of the three murders, the evidence taken at the scene, the cause of death and the verified identity of the three victims. He then had everyone open the Ferguson Case Management Folder from the APD's Records Management System. All information from the Cobb Police Department including the physical evidence taken from the crime scene had been moved over to the APD's data system and Evidence Property room.

"Let's start first with Pete Wilson, get forensics out of the way, then he can leave if he wants."

Pete had everybody open their computerized folder to the forensic section. He slowly and methodically discussed the evidence: fingerprints, ballistics, blood samples, partial shoeprints and the spray-painted message on the bedroom door. There was nothing unexpected and the takeaway from Pete's session was that the person who spray-painted the message was about six feet, one-inch tall and right-handed; the weapon used in the killings appeared to come from a Smith & Wesson 38 Special; DNA results from the blood samples were pending; no traces of skin residue found under the nails of the victims; and the partial shoeprints were from a boot of an undeterminable size.

Once Wilson finished, he looked up to see if there were any questions and if everybody was still awake

"Questions? Observations?"

Nothing else was said. When everybody started getting up for more coffee or reaching over to grab one of the few remaining doughnuts, Wilson closed his laptop and found a seat next to Al Freeman, the Cobb detective who leaned over and said, "Good job."

Marlowe waited until everyone was seated and he had their full attention. He then played the interview he had done with Ramona Hewitt. A transcript of the interview was included in the Ferguson Case folder. She vouched for the whereabouts of Zach Ferguson on the night of the murder. She said she had known him for years but only as her Georgia fuck buddy. And that's all. She had no reason to provide him with an alibi. She said that they ate dinner, had some drinks, went to bed around 7 p.m. and stayed there all night until about 3 a.m. the next morning. She said that they had strange sleeping hours because she was a night shift manager and Zach drove at night. A review of Zach's truck log verified the mileage driven, the time on and off the road. And she drove a 2017 red Ford Mustang.

No one challenged the veracity of Hewitt's alibi for Ferguson. Her phone records confirmed their occasional relationship. And her financial records showed that she had not benefited from providing Ferguson with an alibi. It was apparent she was not hiding anything. She slept with him only when he happened to be in town. Nothing more, nothing less.

Marlowe continued. "Included in the folder are the results of our warrants. As far as the Ferguson's financial records are concerned, he is in better shape than most families. No large amounts of cash have been recently withdrawn from any account, no small regular amounts withdrawn over time, no large checks, no bitcoin purchases, no vehicle leases, nothing out of the normal. Also no outstanding debts, credit cards or otherwise, except the mortgage which was easily manageable on Zach's salary. They were very thrifty. Zach had a savings account with over $17,000 found in a bank in Alabama. It was not a joint account. My speculation is the wife didn't know about the money. Any questions?"

There were none.

"Okay. Ferguson's truck cabin was very orderly. No weapons, shells, drugs, spray paint cans, boots or bloody clothing. Nothing that would tie him directly to the murders. As far as his cellphone records from the providers, they are pending. Ferguson has two phones and he readily gave us permission to look at either. There were texts on his 'family' phone, as he calls it, from Colonel Robert Oliver, the victim found outside by the yellow Porsche. Oliver, at Ferguson's request and verified by Oliver's wife, was keeping an eye on his house and texting him if anything looked suspicious. Ferguson asked Oliver to do this *after* the robbery. He said he was concerned for his wife's safety. We looked at both Ferguson and Oliver's phones and there are texts to confirm Oliver's involvement. The last text from Oliver to Ferguson says he, Oliver, had seen a green Honda parked in front of the Ferguson's house. So far, we have no leads on that car."

"Besides the texts from the Colonel, IT found numerous texts and emails on Zach's phone, some deleted, some not, which showed his relationship with his wife was anything but rosy. He seemed to be verbally abusive, jealous and controlling. We did a geo-tracking on both of Ferguson's phones and neither left the Lexington, South Carolina area. But you don't have to have your phone with you to kill someone. Still, we all witnessed his shock, his disbelief, his raw emotions when we told him of the deaths and pretty much every time we discussed his family's deaths. Either he's one hell of an actor and can cry on demand or he's a heartbroken father and husband. I tend to think the latter. Anybody see it any differently?"

No one said anything. The way the facts were playing out, everyone in the meeting seemed to believe that the robber and the murderer were one and the same.

"As we look at the victims, I think we all can agree that Colonel Oliver was an innocent victim. We think he was just out walking his dog and maybe saw the car or heard the shots and got killed trying to be a good neighbor. And just like the Colonel, we think the daughter was an innocent victim. Mary Ellen Ferguson was the killer's main target. Now we do know she was planning to divorce her husband. We saw that first hand when Zach Ferguson was served at the freight terminal. It appears that she had just started the proceedings this past Friday. As in most divorces, *irretrievably broken* were the grounds. Not adultery. Not cruel treatment. From her phone records, there does not appear to be a spurned lover who might want to harm her. Now there *are* also several calls from her boss, Dominick Garcia, and vice versa and we know he stayed over at her house a couple of days last week, but I think we all know that he was only a friend trying to help her out. And his bank's audit verifies there were no internal issues, like embezzlement, within the bank. He was just a friend. Even loaned her his expensive Porsche."

Marlowe paused then reached over and picked up the last doughnut.

"So that's all I have. Does anybody have anything else to add?"

Neither of the Cobb detectives said anything. It wasn't their case anymore. They were ready to leave, so they did.

With the meeting over, the next order of business was the second interview with Zach Ferguson. Both Jacobs and Marlowe excused themselves and headed to the bathroom leaving Daniel Whitehead alone.

As he read through his notes, he saw where he had written down and circled boots. Next to it, he had also written *bikers wear boots*. Then thinking of what Johnny would have written if he were in the meeting, he wrote down *truck drivers wear boots.*

CHAPTER 69

Zach was sitting in one of the uncomfortable hardened plastic chairs near the front desk of the Atlanta Police Department, Zone 5 when he saw Sam Jacobs open the door directly across from his seat. He stood and the detective came over to greet him.   The two men shook hands and Zach followed Jacobs down the hall to Room 1-2. While not the same room where he had been interviewed on Saturday, it was definitely its twin with its one seat on the back wall side of the room with a small metal table separating it from the two chairs on the door side of the room and a two-way mirror on the side wall. Zach knew which side to sit on.

No sooner had the two men taken a seat when Marlowe stuck his head in the door.

"Anybody want any coffee, Coke or a water?"

Both men declined, so Marlowe came in and took the seat next to Jacobs. Zach wondered if this was a good cop / bad cop interview, if there was such a thing. And if so, which detective was taking which role.

"We appreciate you coming in so early. You have any trouble getting someone to cover for you at work?" asked Jacobs.

"No sir. I talked to management right after I left here Saturday. They were very understanding. Very sympathetic. They got somebody driving my routes."

"That's good. I don't think this will take long. We just want to go over a few things and tie up some loose ends. We'll start with a review of your last interview."

Zach was prepared for the 'review.' That meant that they weren't sure of his innocence. That they would compare his answers from both sessions, checking to see if there were any discrepancies. He nodded his head and Jacobs began. It didn't surprise Zach that Jacobs was doing the second interview since Marlowe had conducted the first.

"We know you are a truck driver… on the road most of the time. And you have two phones, one for your truck friends and one for family. Is that correct?"

"Yes sir."

"And we have the 'family' phone. Is that correct?"

"Yes sir."

"Do you have your 'truck' phone with you? If so, we would like to exchange that phone with the one we have." Jacobs chose not to tell Zach that he had no choice. That they already had a warrant for both phones. He wanted to see how cooperative the man was.

"That's not a problem." Zach then reached into his pocket and produced his 'truck' phone and exchanged it with the detective. He wrote down the password on a blank page in Marlowe's small notebook.

"Thank you. Now… why did you think you needed to have the Colonel watch your house after the robbery?"

"The man… robber threatened my family? I have… had a twelve-year-old daughter who oftentimes stayed by herself. So I called the Colonel and he agreed to keep an eye on my house."

"Do you own a gun?" asked Jacobs.

"Yes sir. A Glock 19. It's in my bedside table. That's the table on the right of the bed as you walk into the room."

"Do you own any other gun? Maybe one you keep in the truck?"

That they would ask those same questions again concerned Zach. Was there something he'd forgotten? He thought for a second but couldn't think of anything.

Whitehead who was observing the interview through a two-way mirror took notice of the hesitation.

"No sir. Against company policy. You get fired if you get caught. I like my job too much to chance something like that."

Marlowe had checked with Zach's company and was told pretty much the same thing except they said they knew some of their drivers carried. Since Ferguson had answered the questions the same as before no red flags were raised.

"What type of boots do you wear when you're on the road?"

Trick question, thought Zach. He had thrown away his boots that had blood on the toe. He was now wearing his sneakers. And until the case was finalized, that's all he would wear.

"No boots. Just these sneakers. When you're on the road as much as I am, you have to be comfortable."

"Besides yourself, who has keys to your house?"

"Besides me? Mary Ellen, Ashley and her parents. Maybe the Oliver's. We also keep one under the mat just in case we lose the key or lock ourselves out of the house. We started doing that after Ashley left her key in the house a couple of times and had to stay at the Oliver's house until Mary Ellen got home from work."

The detectives could see the sad look on Zach's face as he spoke of his family. It was all real. Nothing fake about his feelings.

"When Colonel Oliver texted you that there was a green car in front of your house, late Friday night, why didn't you call your wife or the police. Especially when the Colonel didn't respond with a follow-up text?"

"The Colonel was supposed to text me back if he thought there was a problem. He didn't and so I thought everything was okay. Not only that, there was some detective staying at the house."

"And you say that because of the yellow car parked in your driveway?"

"Yes. The Colonel texted me a picture of it."

"Did it not concern you that the detective was at your house again? For the third time?" asked Jacobs.

"Yes, but not for the reason you think. I figured he was there because they were having an affair, she and that *Cobb* detective. But if his car was there, *where was he*? Why wasn't he murdered instead of my daughter?"

"The car belongs to Dominick Garcia. He loaned your wife his car when hers failed to start at the bank."

"No. That can't be true. Garcia doesn't even own a car. The little prick rides a bike everywhere." Zach hesitated for a second, but only for effect. "So no detective was ever there. Just Garcia?"

"Just Garcia."

Zach shook his head. "I should have known it was *him*. I've suspected this affair has been going on for years… just not at *my house*. But now that he has a car…"

Jacobs looked at Marlowe, confused. Did Zach not know that Dom was gay? Regardless, neither Jacobs nor Marlowe nor anyone in the APD would disclose Dom's sexual orientation as it would be a violation of his personal privacy.

"Is that why you threatened Garcia? The affair?"

"I have never threatened him."

"Mr. Ferguson, you're not being completely honest with us, are you?"

"Yes. I am. I don't know what you are talking about."

"Our IT department reviewed your cell phone records as well as your wife's. I'll read you one of your texts that were deleted from both phones."

"You tell that fucker that if he comes into my house again I will cut his balls off."

Zach knew that the police would somehow find that text and he was prepared for that question.

"Look. I didn't know that it was Garcia staying at my house. The Colonel was the one who told me it was a detective from Cobb County. Look back at my texts from him if you don't believe me. I sent that text when I found out he had stayed in the house overnight and not in his car like I thought most detectives would do when doing surveillance work, I figured she was sleeping with him, too. That text was meant for him… the detective. That's why I asked the Colonel to take a picture of his car this past Friday. I needed some sort of proof that she wasn't being faithful because of the divorce case."

"Have you ever abused your wife, physically or sexually?"

"Never. Why would you ask that question? I'm not the murderer. My wife and I had issues but so do a lot of married couples. And a lot of couples get divorced. Not murdered."

"This friend you have. Liz Davis. The one you're staying with, is she just a friend or is it more than that?"

"We're more than friends, but what does that have to do with any of this?"

"Do y'all plan on getting married anytime in the near future?"

"Me? Liz? Have you seen her? I love being with her but us getting married? Not in a million years. And she wants no part of marriage either. She's already been burned once. She says never again."

Jacobs had heard that before. A lot of 'friends' will say that so as not to scare off a possibility.

"Are you going back to her house after the interview?"

"No. I'm going back to my house. I've gotta do it sooner or later."

"How much insurance do you have on Mary Ellen and Ashley?"

"Unless the bank has some on Mary Ellen, there was none on either. Now, my company has some on me, I think about a hundred thou. But all of Cross's truck drivers have that."

"Other than the robber, do you know of anyone that would have wanted to murder your wife and daughter?"

"No. No one." Again, tears began to well in Zach's eyes as he thought about his daughter.

"Did *you* kill your wife and daughter?"

Zach slammed his hand on the table and then jumped out of his chair. The tears in his eyes had been replaced with rage.

"This fucking interview is over," he yelled. "My daughter was my life. Nobody… and I mean *nobody* accuses me of harming my daughter. Not you, not him, not anybody in that room," said Zach, pointing at each of the detectives and then to the two-way mirror. "What's wrong with you people?"

Jacobs stood up as did Marlowe. The rage in Zach was real. Before Zach could round the table, Marlowe blocked his path by standing in front of the door.

"Mr. Ferguson, please sit down."

Zach, instead, tried to push the man away from the door. Jacobs slid in beside Marlowe to reinforce his partner, but neither man touched Ferguson.

"Sir, you need to calm down and take a seat. We are just doing our job," said Jacobs, emphatically.

Zach first looked at Jacobs and then Marlowe knowing he had made his point. He then returned to his seat. Once the two detectives were certain that all was calm, they did the same.

"We're sorry we've upset you, but our job is to find the person *or* persons who murdered your wife, daughter, and Colonel Oliver. That is our mission. We hope you understand."

Zach had time to calm down. He realized that the detectives were trying to get him to react to the question rather than answering it with caution and forethought. A cavalier answer or reaction could put him in prison. He had done good.

"I should be the one apologizing. I know you are just doing your job, but it just hit me the wrong way. These last few days have been very trying. I'm sorry I lost it."

"No apology needed. I think we should call it a day. If we need you for anything else, we'll call you. By the way, you said you were going back to your house today. Just be aware that we've taken a bedroom door, your sheets, bedding and some swatches from your mattress as evidence. The mattress is ruined and the police will not replace it, the bedding or the door."

"I appreciate the heads up," said Zach as both Marlowe and Jacobs stood up and opened the door.

"And your Glock is in the Property room. You're free to take it with you. I'll be glad to walk to the room."

"Yes sir, please. I don't want to spend a night alone in my house without it. If that asshole decides to come by again, he'll wish he hadn't. That's all I'm gonna say."

At the property room, Zach signed the release form and picked up the envelope that contained his gun and the ejected magazine. He left the building feeling confident he had passed their test. And there had been no good cop / bad cop routine during the interview. Was that on purpose? Was there no need? Or was that just something they did on TV detective series?

CHAPTER 70

Detective Jacobs saw Ferguson out the door and met Marlowe and Whitehead in one of the open conference rooms. They had already begun discussing the interview.

"You have any thoughts?" asked Marlowe, his question directed to Whitehead.

"For the most part, he answered the questions and reacted like I think a grieving husband and father would react to the murder of his wife and daughter. But especially his daughter. Like when he went into his little tirade right there at the end of the interview yelling that no one should accuse him of harming his child. He never once mentioned his wife."

"Yeah. I caught that too," said Jacobs. "But you got to give him a little slack. After all, he just got served divorce papers, so there's probably not a lot of love lost between the two."

"Point taken," said Whitehead.

"One other thing. I did notice that he was hesitant before answering my question about owning another gun."

"Yeah, I think we all noticed the hesitation," said Marlowe. "But a hesitation is not always an indication one is … uh … uh … uh … lying." Marlowe laughed at his poor attempt at humor. Nobody else did. He should have learned from the forensic guy that this was a tough crowd.

"So I told Ferguson that stuff about the door, his sheets and mattress exactly as you asked. What was all that about?" asked Jacobs, his question directed to Whitehead.

"I wanted to hear his response." Whitehead's guest and crime consultant had asked him to offer that information to Ferguson and to write down his response.

"Well? Did it tell you anything?"

"Not really."

"I think we need to wrap it up for today," said Jacobs. "While you do your FBI stuff, we're going to make a call on Ferguson's girlfriend and hit her up with a few questions. Then we'll call the bank and ask about life insurance. But right now I really don't see any red flags. I think we all know who's responsible."

CHAPTER 71

Zach couldn't get out of the police station fast enough. He hoped it would be his last visit. All had gone about as well as expected. He had just passed the Windy Hill exit on I-75 North when his 'family' phone rang. But he didn't answer. His rules of the road were the same whether he was driving an 18-wheeler or a car. Plus, unless it was a hands-free device, it was against the law in Georgia. He waited until he exited onto Delk Road and pulled into a gas station. It was a voicemail from his 'truck' phone, the one he had left with the detectives.

> *Mr. Ferguson. This is Detective Marlowe. You received two texts on your phone after you left. I will read them to you. The first is from Ed Jernigan.* **It says: Call me ASAP.** *The second message is from Wesley Knox. It says:* **It's Wesley. Call us. We need to get together to go over the church service.** *Those are the only two text messages. You need to let your friends, family and co-workers know that this phone is unavailable. I will not be forwarding any more messages. Thank you.*

Of the two calls, Ed's was the most important. He answered on the first ring.

"Zach, where are you?"

"I'm heading home. Why?"

"Good. We have a short window of time to get this lawsuit made public. We have to do it before your wife and daughter's funeral, so I've scheduled a news conference today at three o'clock in front of your house. I hope you don't mind, but we have to strike while the iron is hot."

"You're the lawyer. I trust your judgment."

"Good man. Do not dress in a suit. If you have a blue, long sleeve shirt and a pair of jeans, that's what I want you to wear. I want you to look like a working man… not a banker. That's who we're suing."

"Yes sir," responded Zach. "I don't even own a suit. At least, not one that fits."

"Also, no girlfriend. That complicates matters. I do not want you two in public together until this lawsuit is settled."

"Yes sir. I will call her right after we hang up. So I guess this means you've already filed?"

"This morning. I filled out all the paperwork yesterday and was at the clerk's office at 8 a.m. this morning. There is a filing fee that I paid out of my personal account. Normally, you're responsible, but I'm waiving that since you didn't shop your case around. I appreciate that."

"Who all are we suing?"

"Just the bank your wife worked for, Providence Surety Bank Holding Company."

"What about the police. Shouldn't we include them in the lawsuit?"

"That's too difficult and might take longer. I think if we play our cards right and don't get too greedy, we can settle out of court in a month or so. If we go to trial, it could take a year or more."

"I like the first option. I want this thing over."

"Okay. Here's the plan. I will meet you at your house at 2:15 p.m. We can go over a few things of what to say and what not to say if asked. There's a chance the press will come knocking at the house before I get there. Don't answer. Please. Please. Let me do the talking. The press has a way of screwing things up and we want to orchestrate this press conference and the lawsuit on our terms. You good with that?"

"Yes sir. See you at 2:15." While he talked to his lawyer, he couldn't help but smile. All he ever cared about was not having to give the bitch half of everything he'd ever worked for. And now, he was about to become a millionaire. And he wouldn't be giving her anything. Nada. Nothing. He was pumped.

CHAPTER 72

Liz Davis was in her office at Cross USA Freight when her cell phone rang. It wasn't a familiar number and she let it ring out. Within seconds, she saw that the caller had left a voice mail. Detective Marlowe of the Atlanta Police Department wanted a call back at her convenience. The message did not sound alarming, but she decided to call immediately. Just in case.

Marlowe answered the return call on the second ring. Liz identified herself, the detective informed her that the call would be taped and the mini-interview began with Marlowe's phone on speaker so Jacobs could also hear.

"I understand that you are a friend of Zach Ferguson. Is that correct?"

"Yes. I've known Zach for over six years."

"And your relationship is more than just friends?"

"Yes." There was no need to lie. They would find out anyway.

"Did you know that Zach's wife was planning on divorcing him?"

"Yes."

"How did he take the news?"

"Exactly how you would expect someone to react who's been married for twelve years and who has a daughter he worshiped. He was pissed."

"Pissed enough that he would want to kill her?"

"Look… Zach's a lot of things, but he's not a killer. Plus he would never, ever harm his daughter. She was really all he had."

"Has he ever physically or sexually abused you?"

"Not and lived to tell about it," Liz said, laughing at her response.

"Now that Zach is no longer married, what are your plans?"

"If you mean, did Zach or I kill his wife and daughter so we could get married… that's a bullshit question. I've been married once. Not going down that road again. Not even for someone as good looking as

Zach. He's great for my ego. People at work, behind my back, call us *Beauty and the Old Beast.* I am not the beauty."

"Do you own a gun?"

"You damn straight. A Sig Sauer P365 9 millimeter and I am licensed to carry. I keep it in a drawer by my bed. Fully loaded. Safety off."

"When was the last time it was fired?"

"I'm guessing four or five months ago when Zach and I went to a range."

"We may need to see the gun. Is that a problem?"

"Not at all. I check to make sure it's there every night before I go to bed. It's my security system. Like setting the alarm. I don't live in that safe of a neighborhood, so I have to be prepared."

"Where were you this past Friday night between the hours of 11 p.m. and 3 a.m.?"

"Pulling a second shift at work. I'm a dispatcher for Cross USA Freight and the second shift dude called in sick… Probably drunk. Anyway, I was there from 3 p.m. Friday until 7 a.m. Saturday. You can check with my boss." Liz then gave Marlowe her boss's name and telephone number and extension.

"What kind of car do you drive?"

"Truck. I drive a truck. A 2018 Silver Ford F150." While Marlowe talked, Jacobs verified the truck and gave a thumbs up.

"Do you know anybody who drives a green Honda?"

"Not right off hand. Most of the people who work at Cross drive trucks."

"Do you know a Ramona Hewitt?"

"No."

"Do you know what kind of boots Zach wears?"

"He either wears sneakers or loafers when he comes to my house."

"Don't you usually pick him up at the freight terminal?"

"Only when my schedule allows. If I can't pick him up, he gets a ride to my house from another trucker buddy."

"Does he change clothes before he comes to your house?"

"Yes. Our company provides showers, lockers, washers and dryers, and lockers. Before he leaves the terminal, Zach *always* showers and changes clothes."

"And shoes?"

"That's possible, but the men's locker room is inside the terminal. My office is inside the main building, so I wouldn't know. I've never had a reason to know what clothes or shoes he wears while he's driving. I do know that he always looks and smells nice when he's at my house."

"You've been most helpful, Ms. Davis. Thank you for your time." Marlowe then gave the woman his cellphone number and the phone call ended.

"I think she was straightforward with us, but we need to swing by and check out his locker," said Marlowe.

"I'll get the warrant," responded Jacobs.

The next call was to Dominick Garcia. Jacobs made that call.

The bank manager was at his desk reviewing resumes for the open teller position when his phone rang.

"Mr. Garcia, we would like to ask you just a couple of more questions if you don't mind."

"You've got my undivided attention." Dom then closed the online resumes. His heart wasn't in the search for Mary Ellen's replacement anyway.

"How much insurance, if any, does Mary Ellen Ferguson have with the bank?"

Dominick clicked on the bank's personnel file and brought up Mary Ellen Ferguson's records. He told Jacobs that all hourly employees had a $25,000 life insurance policy paid for by the bank and that the primary beneficiary of Mary Ellen's policy was her daughter Ashley and the secondary beneficiary was her mother, Carol Knox.

The call ended with a request by Dom for Jacobs to get a warrant for the information he'd already given to protect the bank and himself. The detective readily agreed.

The detective then uploaded the two interviews to the Ferguson folder and sent a link to Agent Whitehead's email.

Nothing in either interview had changed their mind. As far as they both were concerned, the prime suspect was still the English Bandit.

CHAPTER 73

Johnny Williams eyed every woman that came into Rush's Restaurant looking for one wearing a South Carolina Gamecock hat. Ramona Hewitt had suggested the place as it was somewhat in between work and home. After waiting twenty minutes, he began to get the feeling that she was a no-show. Just as he was about to get up and order take-out, a woman wearing a garnet ball cap came in the side door and nervously looked around. Johnny waved to her and slid out of the booth and stood to greet her. She recognized him by the Atlanta Braves baseball hat he said he would be wearing. One that he had borrowed from Daniel.

"Thank you for meeting with me," said Johnny, offering her a seat at the booth across from where he had sat.

"I'm still not sure I know who you are or why we're meeting. I've already talked to a detective in Atlanta."

"I'm a crime consultant for Daniel Whitehead, an FBI agent out of the Atlanta office. He was in a meeting this morning and asked me to come in his place." He then produced his old Washington D.C. Metropolitan Police detective's badge, did a quick show and returned it to his coat pocket. He was beginning to like being called a *crime consultant.*

"Would you like to eat first?" asked Johnny smelling the hamburgers, hotdogs and French fries as they were being cooked.

"Good idea."

"So what do you recommend?"

"I like the hotdogs and the fried chicken sandwich. Or just the fried chicken platter. It's all good."

A few minutes later, the two were talking and eating. The good-tasting food was also a reminder of how he'd gotten so overweight. He liked eating fast food.

"So tell me about Zach Ferguson. How do you know him?"

"Hell, I'm not sure I remember where or when I met him. I just know about once a year or twice if I get lucky I get a call from him and we meet up."

"You know he's married… or was?" asked Johnny then finished his chilidog. He wanted another one, but his new self-denial kicked in.

"I'm not married, so it doesn't matter to me. That would be his problem. I am sorry to hear about his wife and child. That's got to be really hard on him."

"Yeah. Hard on everybody. My understanding from Detective Jacobs… he's the one that called you… Zach was here with you from about 5 p.m. Friday until about 6 a.m. Saturday?"

"Yes. He never left my apartment other than to run out to McDonald's around 4 a.m., Saturday, to get us some pancakes."

"I like their pancakes," said Johnny, again thinking about all the fast food he'd given up. "Do you own a green Honda?"

"No. A 2017 red Ford mustang."

"Any extra miles put on your car that you can't account for?"

"You mean did Zach use my car to drive down to Atlanta and kill his family. No. The man fell asleep before me and woke up after me. He never left the bed. And I'm a real light sleeper."

"But no extra miles?"

"No. It's a leased car. I keep tabs on what I drive each week and it hardly varies. I would certainly know if someone put an extra five or six hundred miles on my car."

"Do you remember what you ate and drank that night?"

"You're a detailed son-of-a-bitch, aren't you," said Ramona and then laughed. "I like that. I'm the same way. We ate Lizard's Thicket and had a couple of Old Fashions. We talked and then we went to bed. That was it until the pancakes the next morning."

"Lizard's Thicket?"

"Local chain. Southern food. Great fried chicken. You need to take some back with you."

"You make the drinks or did Zach?"

"I made the first. I had to teach Zach how to make one. He's usually a beer drinker. But if you think Zach put a Mickey in my drink, I think I would have known. The only time that has ever happened, I woke up the next day wishing I hadn't. I felt like shit. I had no such feeling with Zach. So don't go there."

"Did he talk about his wife?"

"Only about the fact that she was divorcing him and she would take him to the cleaners. Not his words. But that's the impression I got."

"Was he angry… like he would never let that happen?"

"You mean, do you think he was angry enough to kill his wife? If that's what you're asking. Absolutely not. He was mad, but not any more than what you would expect from someone who's about to lose everything he's ever worked for. Now if that'd been me, she'd wish that she'd never fucked with me. But Zach? No. A big no."

"Do you know if he owns a gun?"

"If he does, he's never brought it to my place. I don't allow guns. My apartment. My rules."

"Did he ever mention that he owned one?"

"No."

"Your apartment. Does it have security cameras at the entrances?"

"Only one entrance and I don't know about the cameras."

"Are you heading to your apartment from here?"

"Yes,"

"Do you mind if I follow you to your apartment and stop off at the office?"

"Be my guest."

"Did Zach ever mention that his wife worked at a bank? And that bank had just been robbed that week?"

"No. Never. We never got that personal."

"Do you know a Liz Davis?"

Ramona thought for a second but nothing came to mind. "No."

"Okay. One last question," said Johnny, knowing that he was reaching. "Zach ever talk to you using a British accent? You know, just playing around, acting the fool?"

"You're kidding. First of all, Zach doesn't play around. He's a very serious man. There's very little fun in that man. And second, the only accent he knows is Southern."

"Ramona, thank you very much. You've been very helpful. I appreciate your patience."

"No problem. I hope you understand that it wasn't Zach who killed his family."

Johnny slid out of the booth and waited for Ramona to exit her side. Once they were both out, he gave her Daniel's card with his cell number on the back. They shook hands and she headed out the side door with him close behind. After she reached her car, a red Ford Mustang, he waved to her and headed over to his car. Ramona drove out of the parking lot and headed to her apartment with Johnny close behind. Once at the apartment complex, Ramona badged herself through the security gates and into the parking lot. Johnny pulled into a parking spot just outside the gates at the front office. When he got out of his car, he did not see any cameras. Not a good sign. The office manager confirmed his suspicions and there was no log of who entered or left the complex.

He felt Ramona had told the truth as she knew it, but his gut feel told him that something just wasn't quite right. But then again, it could have been the chilidog.

CHAPTER 74

Before opening his front door, Zach peered out the front window of his living room to see who was knocking. Jernigan had told him, no press, and he was going to make damn sure there wasn't any. Once he saw his plumpish, balding lawyer, he quickly opened the door and let the man in. Jernigan was dressed in a light blue seersucker suit, a la *Matlock*, a heavy starched white dress shirt, suspenders and matching bowtie. His shoes were wingtips, highly polished. The clear round-rimmed glasses he had worn earlier had been replaced by similar-looking sunglasses. Zach liked the look. The last thing he wanted was a slicked-back, black-haired New York-looking lawyer. It made him look too greedy. Nor did he want any part of a lawyer with long grey hair pulled back in a ponytail… a look he, and the whole world, associated with guilty people. He wanted Ed.

Zach had dressed just as Ed had asked and got a thumbs up as the lawyer entered the house. Once the two were seated, Ed mapped out the entire news conference. What he was going to say, not say. What Zach could say and not say. Jernigan asked if there was anything special in Ashley's life, like a doll, stuffed animal, snow globe, anything that he could cradle during the interview. The mere mention of Ashley's name caused Zach to tear up as he nodded and softly said, "A teddy bear." His mind visualized his daughter, lying in his bed, under the covers, holding her little teddy bear as she always did, right before he ended her life. It was supposed to be Dom. Fucker.

Jernigan immediately recognized the Pavlovian response in Zach almost every time his daughter's name was mentioned. He saw it the first time when they had met at Liz's house. And just now, his suspicions had just been confirmed. He would use Ashley's name in the news conference when he felt Zach's tears would have the greatest impact. Anyone watching the news conference could tell his emotions were real.

Once Jernigan had finished his briefing with Zach, he asked for a tour of the house. He wanted to understand the pain that his client must have felt when he first walked into his now vacant house where his wife and daughter had been ruthlessly murdered. He wanted to see where they were killed. The more he knew, the better the news conference, ergo, the better the lawsuit.

As they walked through the house, Jernigan could sense Zach's nervousness, especially when he opened the door to his daughter's room and then as they entered the doorless master bedroom.

"I didn't realize that they both were killed in the same bed," said Jernigan upon seeing the two bloodstain marks on the mattress trying to avoid using the word *daughter*. He was saving that for the news conference. "You think the killer thought that was *you* in bed?"

"I don't know what he thought. But now I wished it had been me," said Zach.

"I completely understand. So where's the door," asked Jernigan as they headed out of the master bedroom.

"The police took it. The killer had written a message on it."

"What kind of message? I didn't see anything about a message in the newspapers."

Zach realized he'd screwed up. There had been nothing, not by the newspapers, not by the police, that had mentioned anything about a message. But the damage had been done. He had to contain it.

"And you won't. I only learned it from the police when I was giving my statement. I wasn't supposed to say anything about it. We can't disclose that or I'm in deep shit."

Jernigan heard his client's flimsy excuse and chose not to dig any deeper. He didn't want to know what lay behind the handsome face he was representing. He just prayed that he wasn't representing the killer.

"Gotcha. Nobody will hear it from me."

Before the clock struck three, reporters from the local TV stations and newspapers were gathered in front of Zach's house along with curious neighbors. Betty Oliver viewed the gathering from the front porch of her house. She left Ike in the house. She didn't want his constant barking to be an irritant.

At precisely three o'clock, the front door of the Ferguson's house opened. Jernigan came out first, followed by Zach. Their somber appearance set the tone for the news conference.

"Thank you for coming on such short notice," said the lawyer, speaking into the bouquet of microphones. "My name is Ed Jernigan. I'm senior partner in the law firm of Harrison, Chapman and Jernigan, located in Marietta, Georgia. This morning, I filed a wrongful death lawsuit on behalf of my client, Zach Ferguson, against Providence Surety

Bank Holding Company. This is the bank that Zach's wife, Mary Ellen Ferguson, worked. It is our contention that the bank knowingly and willingly failed in its duty to provide the proper security for Mrs. Ferguson after she was threatened during the commission of a robbery at said bank on August 6, 2019. You may ask, why the rush to file? Imagine you are a long-distance truck driver. That you have been on the road for over two weeks. Two weeks without seeing your family and you are met at the freight company's loading dock by two Atlanta Police Detectives and an FBI agent. They tell you that Mary Ellen, your wife of thirteen years, and Ashley, your twelve-year-old daughter, have been shot in bed. Not just once but twice. Both dead. The mother murdered… murdered in the prime of her life and his beautiful daughter, Ashley, with her entire life ahead of her. Murdered. This should have never happened. But why the rush? Big Banks such as Providence Surety tend to forget the pain and suffering as time goes by. But Zach will never forget and we don't want *them* to forget. I can assure you had Mary Ellen been *an officer* of the bank, her request… no… her plea for security would not have been taken so lightly. We want the bank to know that all employees are important regardless of position. This lawsuit will make sure they do."

Jernigan took out a handkerchief from his coat pocket and then removed his sunglasses. He wiped them and then his forehead. Zach had responded just as Jernigan had thought he would. The first mention of Ashley's name caused tears to well up in his eyes and then spill down his face. He wiped them with the rolled-up sleeve of his light blue long sleeve shirt. The press took notice with the video cameras moving from the lawyer to the distraught widower.

"I'll be glad to take any questions."

"Do you know of any robbery where a teller has ever been killed by the thief after the robbery?" asked one of the journalists, holding his cellphone close to the attorney.

"No. But that doesn't excuse the bank from providing adequate security for an employee who was singled out and threatened with retribution."

"What about Mr. Ferguson's responsibility as a homeowner. Shouldn't he have had a security system installed?" asked another reporter, he, too, holding his cellphone close to Jernigan for an answer.

"This has always been a safe neighborhood and safe area. Crime is almost non-existent. And this is a working-class neighborhood. Most people who live here don't have the extra income to install a security system much less pay the monthly monitoring fee."

Zach moved up to the mike surprising Jernigan.

"I *do* have a security system *now*," he yelled into the bank of microphones. "I've got my Glock in my bedside table and I invite that son-of-a-bitch who killed my wife and daughter…" Zach couldn't finish the sentence. Instead, he shook his head as tears began to well up in his eyes. Jernigan put his arm around Zach.

"Before you is a broken man. This should have never happened and we will make sure that it never happens again at Providence Surety. This news conference is over."

Jernigan led Zach back into the house and into the kitchen where Zach found a seat at the table. Jernigan went to the refrigerator and found a couple of Cokes. He brought them back to the table, sat down and pushed one of the sodas over to his client and opened the other for himself.

"I think it went well," said the ruddy-complected lawyer. "Your outburst took me by surprise, but it really worked to our advantage. They saw your hurt. They felt your pain. It was perfect."

"Well, I meant it. I wish that son-of-a-bitch was here, *right now*," said Zach, not thinking of the robber but Dom.

"You've made your point. But I don't want to see any kind of anger in you again, especially at any public events. A little bit goes a long way. I don't want *anyone* thinking you have a dark side. Okay?"

"Yeah. I'm cool with that."

Jernigan and Zach sat down in the kitchen and the lawyer started going over the interrogatories, subpoenas and depositions they would need to request when he heard the sound of a text ding on his phone. He looked at the lawyer for approval to go get his phone which had been left on the kitchen counter.

"Yes. Yes. It could be important."

Zach's phone had three missed texts and one missed voicemail. All four were from his in-laws. *Shit* was his only response as he listened to the voicemail.

> *Zach. This is Wesley again. You never returned our texts so we went ahead and finalized the church service with the pastor and made all the funeral arrangements. The visitation will be tomorrow night at Parks Funeral from 6 to 9. We need to be there*

around 5:30. And the funeral itself will be on Wednesday at 11 am. We will meet at the funeral home at one and they will drive us to the church. We hope that's all right with you. I know you were worried about the cost of the funeral and we were willing to pay but Mary Ellen's bank has already paid the bill. The only thing we are responsible for is the cemetery plots and if it is okay with you, we would like to have Mary Ellen and Ashley buried in Augusta. We have enough open plots for all of us, including you, if you so choose. Just let me know.

"Hell no," yelled out Zach, taking Jernigan off guard.

"What's the matter?"

"My ga'dang in-laws want to bury Ashley in Augusta. That's not going to happen."

"What about your wife?"

"Yeah. Her, too."

"That's not their decision to make. Do you want me to get involved? I could call them on your behalf and tell them that *you* will decide where your family is buried. But what I don't want is any family infighting. Nothing that might hurt our case. Plus do you even own any plots?"

"No. But they can't cost too much. I've seen the size of them. What? Three by six?"

"I've got four plots. They set me back about $4000 each. That was ten years ago. So you're probably looking at about six to ten thousand… each."

"Unfucking believable. I guess they'll be buried in Augusta."

"That'll make your in-laws happy and make you look like a good guy. What about the funeral costs? Where are you getting the money for that? I could include that in our settlement. That's got to be at least twenty or thirty thousand."

"The bank is paying the funeral cost. Is that going to mess things up? Make them look like they're the good guy?"

"Oh no. This is fantastic. Better than fantastic. This has *guilt* written all over it. Maybe it's just a generous gesture on their part, but I will make it look like they are trying to buy us."

Jernigan began thinking that maybe this case was worth more than he thought. Maybe he was shortchanging himself. A settlement of four million might be an insult. Six million sounded better.

"Okay, I'm outta here. Make sure you text your in-laws back. And text me the funeral arrangements. I want to be there with you so I'll drive."

He left with a smile on his face thinking maybe eight million. It was such a nice round number.

Zach hated the idea of having Ashley buried in Augusta, but the cost and the goodwill outweighed his feelings. He picked up his phone and texted a reply back to his father-in-law giving him the okay on everything.

As he laid his phone down, he heard another text ding. It was Liz.

Just a heads up. The police called me. We need to talk. Can you call me back?

"Okay. What the hell's going on?" asked Zach as soon as Liz answered the phone, his impatient tone of voice most noticeable.

"You need to get off your high horse, buster. I'm not the enemy here. The police called and I got the feeling that they were looking at you as the prime suspect and maybe me as an accomplice. I don't like that one damn bit."

"I'm sorry, baby. There's nothing to worry about. They did the same thing with me. They asked where I was the night of the shootings, my relationship with Mary Ellen and with you. Did I have insurance on Mary Ellen? Why did I get the Colonel involved? Did I kill Mary Ellen and Ashley? They asked me that twice. But that's their job. They're just going through the motions. They know who murdered my family and they have the evidence. It's that bank robber. So don't worry."

"Easy for you to say."

"I'm telling you, there's nothing to worry about. By the way, the news conference went great. Ed is really good. I appreciate you getting me in touch with him. I'll make sure you get a finder's fee when we get paid." Then he laughed. Liz knew that Zach's idea of a finder's fee lay between his legs.

"So when is the funeral?" she asked.

"Wednesday at two. And I don't have to pay a damn thing. The bank says they are going to pay all the funeral expenses. Ed says that's like an admission of guilt or that they're trying to buy us off. And I don't have to buy any burial plots because we're going to use some plots the Knox's own."

"Do you want me to go to the funeral? You know… for support?"

"Not going to happen. Ed doesn't want you anywhere near that church. Too risky. He thinks it would look bad. Not only that, he doesn't want us seen together. Not until this thing is settled. Hopefully out of court. It'll cost me money to settle, but a jury trial would take at least a year. I don't want to wait that long."

"It's all about the money with you, isn't it?" asked Liz and then hung up before Zach could answer.

CHAPTER 75

Throughout his meeting with the folks at the Roswell bank, Scott found himself constantly having to push the deaths of the teller, her daughter and neighbor out of his mind. And for the most part, he had been successful. The meeting had gone extremely well. They liked Scott and his company's offerings. It hadn't hurt that he had met the president of the bank at the Friday night party, so a lot of the 'feeling out' small talk was already out of the way. At their meeting, he did discover that the president and Dominick Garcia were friends, both having worked at the Bank of America before moving on to different banks. When he left, he had a good feeling about this one. But he'd had those good feelings when they didn't win the business. The bank had two more consultants to see and would make a decision Tuesday.

Once he was back in the hotel, he sent a text to both partners telling them that he was going to stay in Atlanta in case there were some follow-up questions. Scott didn't need their approval and vice versa. The text was merely a courtesy. He also found that he had three emails from people wanting to buy his motorcycle. He would decide later. All he cared about was getting the bike out of North Carolina and making Anne happy.

Tired from the preparation for the meeting and the meeting itself, Scott lay down on the bed. But his mind wasn't on the meeting, its success or failure. All he could think about were the words from the paper:

> *An unnamed source disclosed that the murders appeared to be the work of a serial robber known as the English Bandit. That the police had evidence linking the two crimes.*

What evidence? thought Scott. There was no evidence because he had not committed the crime. Not that crime anyway. Just the bank robbery and that had gone off without a hitch except for the unfortunate confrontation between him and Mary Ellen Ferguson. Somehow, he needed to let the authorities know that it wasn't him. He picked up the newspaper and found the names of Detective Victor Marlowe, Detective Sam Jacobs and FBI Agent Daniel Whitehead as the persons in charge of the investigation. For no particular reason, he decided on Whitehead.

Within the hour, he was sitting in the privacy of his car in the free-of-charge Cell-Phone Parking Lot at the Hartsfield-Jackson International Airport. Wearing nitrile gloves and using a burner phone that had been purchased on his way to the airport, he dialed the Atlanta FBI field office and asked the duty agent to speak to Agent Daniel Whitehead.

Shortly, he got Whitehead's voicemail. Using his English accent, he left the following voicemail:

I am the English bandit. I did not commit those murders. I am innocent.

He then hung up and drove out of the parking lot, dropping the phone out the passenger's window as he did, making sure his rear tires destroyed the phone. Hopefully, the message set everything straight.

On the way back to the hotel, he thought about the voicemail and considered what he had said:

I am the English bandit. I did not commit those murders. I am innocent.

What the hell was he thinking? How could he be so daft? Anybody could have left that message. He wondered how many quacks had already left similar or more convincing messages. He needed to redo his message and leave the agent with some information that only the robber would know to convince the agent that he was the real deal. But there was no way he was going back to the airport to redo the message. Too risky. And he needed some time to think about a more believable message. One that left no doubt as to its authenticity.

Scott headed back to the hotel, grabbing some fast food on the way. In the room, he sat down at the small desk, ripped open the sack that held his dinner and flipped on the TV. He flipped the stations until he found a local news channel, WSB-TV. The five o'clock news had already started. He was hoping to hear an update on the murders. Maybe they had caught the real killer. Only after about thirty minutes of other killings, accidents, weather reports and commercials did he see a preview of an upcoming news segment that caught his attention. The news teaser showed two men, standing in front of the teller's house and the newscaster reporting, *the husband of the slain bank teller sues bank.* Scott had time to finish his burger and fries before the bank lawsuit story was aired. The onsite reporter gave some background details of the robbery and the lawsuit and then played a portion of the video of a news conference where the lawyer is responding to a question posed by one of the reporters. The video then shows the husband of the slain teller rushing over to the assembled microphones completely surprising the lawyer and yelling: *I do have a security system **now**. I've got my Glock in my bedside table and I invite that <bleeped> who killed my wife and daughter…*

Before the news segment had concluded, Scott was standing in front of the TV staring at the two men on the video, looking mostly at Zach. He instantly recognized the man's face and knew exactly when and where he had seen it.

"It was you!" he yelled even though he was the only one in the room.

He then began pacing back and forth, shaking his head, trying to think.

"*You* killed your wife and daughter and now you blame it on *me*? That's not going to happen." His voice was so loud that it even surprised himself. He sat down on the bed and thought about what he needed to do next. They… the police… the FBI… whoever… they needed to know that the husband was the murderer. And the husband needed to know that he knew.

CHAPTER 76

It took Johnny almost four hours to make the drive from Lexington, South Carolina back to Daniel's apartment, mainly because of Atlanta's five o'clock traffic. Since retiring, he didn't do traffic anymore. Today's trip reminded him why.

"No wonder you left the force. Looks like you got banker's hours now," said Johnny who found his former police partner digging around in the refrigerator.

"I was getting a beer. You want one?"

The two men sat down outside on the deck and took in the surroundings. Daniel's apartment was on the third floor, overlooking the pool which made Johnny feel as though he was at a resort rather than an apartment.

"So how was your trip?" asked Daniel.

"You mean did Ferguson's alibi stand up?"

"Yeah. Something like that."

"I don't see any holes. But he still could have done it."

"You're not going to let it go, are you?"

"Not yet. Did you tell Ferguson about the door, sheets and mattress?"

"I didn't, but Detective Marlowe did and exactly as you asked."

"What was his response?"

"He thanked us for the heads up. Kinda what you'd expect."

"And he never asked why the police took the door? Or which door? Or why only his sheets were taken for evidence and not his daughter's?"

"No."

"The way I see it, he didn't have to ask. He already knew."

"Johnny, I think you're grasping at straws. You're trying to make a case where there isn't one. The man had gone through an hour of interrogation. He was just glad to get the hell out of there. He's not thinking like a cop."

"I guess."

Daniel could see the disappointment in his friend's face.

"You might be interested to know that I received a voicemail today from a guy with a British accent. He said that he didn't commit the murders. So maybe it is the husband after all."

"You think he's a nutjob, don't you?" asked Johnny.

"Yeah. Most of them are."

"But most of these screwball callers *admit* to the crime. They don't usually push the blame elsewhere."

"Okay. Let's say it was the English Bandit. He could just be playing with us… trying to confuse the issue."

"Or he could be telling the truth," said Johnny as he finished his beer and headed into the kitchen for a bottle of water.

"So what's with the water? You always told me you were allergic to it."

"The old lady has me drinking one bottle after every real drink. So it's become a habit. I actually sleep better when I do, but don't tell her. Next thing I'll know, she'll want me to give up my only pleasure left in life."

"She won't hear it from me."

Daniel threw down his beer and headed to the kitchen for another. He didn't have anyone monitoring his intake and the way his dating life was going, he might never.

"So if you think the husband did it, how? Why?"

"The way I see it, the husband has enough time to drive from South Carolina to Atlanta, murder his family, and get back to South Carolina without the woman he's sleeping with knowing that he was gone. I made the trip there in a little over three hours and I had some traffic. At night, he can make even better time. And all he had to do was to make sure she stayed asleep. And we know there are legal drugs that can make that happen. He just needed a car and that's where I have a problem. She said that there were no extra miles on her car. She keeps track of the mileage because it's a lease."

"So why don't you just accept the hard cold facts. The man has an alibi and you saw the first interview. He was heartbroken. You of all people know when someone is acting. He wasn't."

"I know but… Has anybody checked the insurance angle?"

"Yes. Mary Ellen has a $25,000 policy. It's on all hourly employees. But her husband is not the beneficiary. Her daughter is primary and her mother is secondary."

"What about the girlfriend. Could she be involved? Or maybe a hired gun?"

"No and no. She has an alibi, air-tight. We checked her finances just like we did with Ferguson. Nothing, and I mean nothing out of the ordinary."

"You think I've made up my mind as to who's responsible and am now only looking for evidence to justify my conclusion? Rookie mistake?"

"You're no rookie and I will never discount your instinct. And as far as I'm concerned, Zach Ferguson is high on my list… just under the English Bandit."

CHAPTER 77

Zach turned the mattress so that the dried bloodstains were closer to the foot of the bed. He then removed the mattress pad, trashed it and replaced it with a pair of old fitted sheets. Hopefully, the idiom, *out of sight, out of mind*, would prevail. Being at home, alone, had been tougher than he had expected. There were no sounds of his daughter's happy voice coming from her room as she talked to her friends on the phone or on FaceTime. Nor was there music or the sounds of video games. Those days were gone forever. If the bitch had just agreed to the uncontested divorce.

When he had arrived home earlier that day for the first time since the killings and before the news conference, he didn't have time to think about how the quietness would trouble him. He barely had time to shower and dress before Jernigan arrived. But now that he was alone, he could hear every creak in the house. He knew when the A/C turned on and off and when the ice-maker dropped newly formed ice into its reservoir. He heard barking dogs that he'd never heard before. He flipped on the television hoping that the background noise might help, but in the end, he knew he was alone. And that wasn't going to change…ever. He wanted… no… he needed to get back on the road.

With bedtime approaching, he wished he could have stayed at Liz's. But Ed would have none of that. Nor would Zach if it meant jeopardizing the lawsuit. Maybe he should have kept a few of the Ambien pills, but that could be equally risky, jeopardizing both the lawsuit and his freedom. As an alternative, he headed to the kitchen to warm up some milk and eat a couple of cookies, staple items for Ashley. In the refrigerator, he saw the carton of milk, but he also saw a half bottle of white wine. He never allowed Mary Ellen to buy wine… too expensive. But tonight he was glad she had bought it *and* had not drunk it all.

He grabbed the bottle by its neck, headed over to the far cabinets and reached up to the top shelf and pulled out the only clean wine glass left. The glasses had been a wedding present from some of the Knox's rich friends. They were only used when his in-laws were in town and brought their own wine. He set the glass down, pulled the cork and filled the glass almost to the brim. Then mocking his **ex**-mother-in-law, he sniffed the wine, held the glass up looking through the golden liquid and then took a sip. It wasn't bad. It had a nice taste. He took another sip, holding his pinkie out, again mocking his **ex**-mother-in-law. Not bad. Not like the cheap wine that he and a bunch of high school mates had experimented with after football games. Since he was going to be very rich, very soon, then maybe he should learn what wines the rich drank. He was going to be one of *them*... soon.

After topping off his glass, he headed back into the den and set his new liquid friend on the table next to his recliner. He collapsed into the chair, picked up the TV remote, pressed the MUTE button and set the controller on the armrest. He then pulled his phone out of his jeans and dialed Liz's phone number, adding it to his 'family' phone's contact list. Ed had said he couldn't see her, but he didn't say anything about talking to her.

"What'cha doing?" asked Zach as he pulled the lever back causing the chair to recline.

"I hope the hell you're in a better mood. If you really want to know, I'm getting ready for bed."

"I bet you wish I was there?"

"Not really. You know I gotta lay low if I'm gonna get my finder's fee." Liz laughed when she said it. Zach understood.

"No. I meant what I said. You put me in touch with Jernigan. And I'm a man of my word."

Liz knew Zach well enough not to go on a spending spree. He was all talk except in bed.

"By the way, I saw you on TV. You are *one* handsome devil. And, let me tell you... that bullshit about television adding ten pounds to your weight... well, it's just bullshit. And I loved it when you went off on that reporter about your new security system, I thought I'd die. You put his ass in his place real quick."

"Well, I meant it. I've got my Glock locked and loaded in a table next to my bed and I'll use it if I have to."

"I completely agree. You know I never liked the Ice Woman mainly because you never liked her, but nobody... and I mean nobody has the right to play God. And poor Ashley. Her whole life in front of her..."

"Let's not talk about Ashley," said Zach, tears welling up as he mentally pictured his sweet daughter's pretty face.

"I understand. I know you miss her. You just have to be strong."

"I didn't realize it would be so lonely around here without her. Hell… without Mary Ellen. As much as we fought, I still miss her."

"Time will heal, baby. I know when I lost my mother, I was devastated. I didn't think I could make it to the next day. But over time, you don't forget them. You just sorta get numb. One word of advice. Don't try and drink it away. I tried that and almost lost my job and my liver."

"You know me well enough to know that's not gonna happen. I've seen what it's done to a couple of drivers. They're not drivers anymore. And just so you know, I am having a glass of char-do-nay I found in the fridge. Courtesy of either my wife or Dom," said Zach elongating the man's name. "But I felt I needed something to help me sleep tonight."

"My poor baby. Why don't you sneak over here tonight? Nobody would *ever* know."

"No can do. I can't do anything that will risk my big settlement. You wouldn't either."

"What was I thinking? If you don't get paid, I don't get paid."

"Okay. Cut it out. You'll get some money. I promise."

"So where are you sleeping tonight? I hope not in the same room where Mary Ellen was shot."

"Same room. Same mattress."

"Unbelievable. I can't believe you didn't buy a new mattress. You're a cheap son-of-a-bitch, aren't you?"

"Look. I didn't call to get into an argument. That's what the bitch and I used to do. I gotta go. Big day tomorrow. I'll call you when it's over."

Zach pushed the red *off* button on his cell phone and chugged down the rest of his wine. There was no real buzz. Not like the Maker's Mark. But he did feel relaxed. He headed back to the kitchen for a refill then back to his recliner. As he slowly consumed his second glass, he thought about the conversation he's just had with Liz. Just like he used to have with Mary Ellen. He wondered how much longer he wanted her in his life.

Tuesday, August 13, 2019

ATLANTA, GEORGIA

CHAPTER 78

As a retiree, 8 a.m. was the new 6 a.m. for Johnny. He slowly managed to get out of bed, used the bathroom and walked to the kitchen. He didn't see Daniel. Using his highly trained detective skills, he concluded that Daniel was at work. The Keurig had just completed his brew when he heard the door to the balcony open and his friend walk in holding his cell phone and a cup of coffee. *Maybe I need a refresher course in detecting*, he thought.

"I thought you'd be at work," said Johnny as he threw the used k-pod in the nearby trash can.

"I *am* at work. In fact, while you were asleep, I was on a conference call with the APD guys."

"Why didn't you wake me?"

"You were sleeping so soundly, I didn't have the heart. Plus you really didn't miss much," said Daniel as he brewed this third cup of the day.

"What is *much?* Fill me in."

The two friends moved to the balcony, both with coffee in hand.

"They got the DNA test results back and they'll be in the crime folder the next time we log in. But other than some DNA from an animal, the rest is from the victims. I figured the animal DNA was Ike's since we saw him with his paw in a cast and a cone around his head."

"Go on."

"The cell phone records for everybody involved are in the folder. Nothing that we haven't already discussed. Nothing that points a finger directly at Zach. No smoking gun. He's just a bad dude. I wouldn't treat a dog like he did his wife. But that doesn't make him a killer."

"Any record of physical abuse?"

"No. None. Marlowe said they checked for reports in Cobb and Fulton counties. Nothing."

"Yeah, but you and I know how often abuse is reported. Almost never. But it doesn't mean that it didn't happen," responded Johnny. "How about work? Anything there?"

"The guy's spotless. His manager says he's one of their best drivers. Reliable, always on time, always current with his logbook, and until recently, never a speeding ticket. Marlowe also checked out his locker at the truck terminal. Nothing of interest… like boots."

"The speeding ticket… when did that happen?"

"Sometime Friday around 4 p.m."

"Bummer. What did they say about your caller?"

"I wasn't the only one getting calls. They've gotten at least three. All crackpots. All wanting to take credit but none offering any other real information except what they've heard on TV or read in the papers. They're just getting their jollies."

"You tell them *your* caller had an English accent and that he claimed that he *didn't* commit the murders?"

"They thought he was just a different kind of weirdo. And I have to agree."

"Did they say if Ferguson ever called about his missing bedroom door?"

"No… nor did they expect to hear from him. Per your request, they'd already forewarned him about the missing door."

"I'm telling you, something's not right here."

"Well… as far as the APD is concerned, there is only *one* suspect. The bank robber. They're pulling up stakes and moving on. It's on me, now."

"So what's next?" asked Johnny.

"Do you mind calling Mrs. Oliver and asking what happened to the dog? That way, I can check in at the office and let them know I'm gonna be working from home. Then I'd like for us to go back over everything in the Ferguson Case Management folder in detail to make sure we haven't overlooked anything… if you're up to it. Kinda like the old days but with no whiteboard."

"Like the old days," said Johnny, happier now than at any time during his retirement.

CHAPTER 79

"If he calls again, patch him through to me or make sure he has my cell number," said Daniel, his voice raised, excited.

He ended the call and then went outside onto the porch where he found Johnny sitting in one of the wrought iron patio chairs and talking on his phone to Betty Oliver. Daniel sat down and motioned to Johnny to put the phone on speaker so he could hear both sides of the conversation.

"So what did the vet say?" asked Johnny and he pushed the phone's speaker button.

"His poor little leg was broken and he had a couple of teeth missing," said Betty. "Dr. Parker said he thought that Ike had been kicked… maybe more than once."

"And you say that this happened between the time that the Colonel took Ike out for a walk and when you found your husband lying on the driveway?"

"Yes. I'm just thankful poor Ike wasn't killed by that monster."

"Do you think there was any chance that Ike could have bitten the killer and that's why he… Ike was kicked?"

"I have no doubts. He was very protective of Bob. If he could, he would have latched on and never let go."

"Would it be all right if we came by to pick up his old leash? We can bring a new one to replace it."

"I'm sorry. It was so nasty with all of the bloodstains on it that I couldn't bear to look at it so I threw it away."

And possibly the killer's DNA, thought Johnny. Daniel knew what Johnny was thinking.

"Any chance the trash is still there?"

"No. It was picked up on Monday. I'm sorry."

The call ended and Betty Oliver went back for another cup of coffee with Ike as close to her side as his plastic cone collar allowed. She would never know and no one would ever tell her that the DNA on Ike's leash might have been the single most important piece of lost evidence.

"Bummer," muttered Johnny.

"Yeah. Well, one of my voicemails might pique your interest. Listen to this," said Daniel as he put his phone on speaker and laid it down on the patio table. The caller had an English accent.

> *I am the English Bandit. I called once before. As proof of who I say I am, the amount of money taken from Providence Surety Bank was $4,237. I DID NOT murder those people. But I did see Zach Ferguson entering the neighborhood the night of the murders around 11 p.m. I'm a thief. Not a murderer.*

"Play it again," said Johnny who got closer to the phone so he could hear better.

Once it finished playing, neither detective said anything for a few seconds.

"Well, the caller was definitely the robber," responded Daniel. "He knew exactly how much was stolen. But that still doesn't change my mind. I think he's playing us. Like why would he admit to being in Ferguson's neighborhood around the time of the murders without offering an explanation? And then indirectly accuse the husband of the murders by saying he saw him entering the neighborhood? Maybe he's gotten bored with robberies and has progressed to a darker area of crime. It's most confusing to me. So, what's your take on this Mr. Crime Consultant?"

"I don't know about you, but I believe this guy," said Johnny. "To me, this is a game-changer. Now I have to admit, it is odd. I think we should start from the beginning again. Go over all the notes, evidence, videos… whatever and when we are finished, log anything that seems suspicious or needs further investigation. Let the evidence find the killer. Just like the old days. That's what I'd do."

"Then that's what we'll do. While I still think it's the robber, the fact that you don't makes me question my conclusion. The last thing we want is a flawed investigation."

For the next couple of hours, the two men sat silent, in separate rooms, going over every detail of the case and making notes and observations. After a brief break for lunch, the two men sat down in the kitchen with notepads and computers in front of them ready to compare notes.

"Okay. You're the guest. Fire away," said Daniel.

"Thanks a lot. Let me start with the English Bandit as the primary suspect. The video of the robbery shows that the teller did grab the robber's hand and *he did* threaten her. *There will be repercussions.* And then the teller, her daughter and an innocent bystander are murdered. To make our job easier, the killer leaves a confession on the bedroom door, *I keep my word.* That way, we don't have to guess who was responsible. But then, to confuse us… muddy the waters, he leaves a voicemail saying that he did *not* commit the murders. That Zach Ferguson, the husband, must have been the killer because he saw him entering the neighborhood on the night of the murder. In all of my years as a detective and now my three days as a crime consultant, I can't recall any murder case, mine or otherwise, where a bank robber waits three days then goes back at night and then kills the teller simply because she begged him *not* to hurt her child. He then leaves a spray-painted message saying *he* did it and then tries to pin it on the husband with a voicemail. I have seen and heard of some strange murder cases, but this one takes the cake. As for a motive, the only one that makes sense is that the robber wanted to fulfill his threat. *There will be repercussions.* But why would he admit to being at the Ferguson's house on the night of the murders? What would be his reason? And why blame the husband? If he really did see Ferguson, what make and color of car was he driving that night?"

"I'd also like to know the answers to those questions myself. Continue."

Johnny got up, popped another K-pod into the Keurig and waited for the last dribble of coffee to fall into his cup. When the machine signaled it had finished, he grabbed the cup and sat back down across from Daniel.

"Now. Zach Ferguson… the husband. Historically, we know husbands, lovers, ex-lovers… they're always considered the suspect until they're not. But Zach has an alibi. He was asleep with his girlfriend, Ramona Davis, in Lexington, South Carolina. Having made that roundtrip myself, Ferguson had enough time to drive to Atlanta, commit the murders, and drive back and jump into bed with his South Carolina girlfriend without her knowing. But the girlfriend insists that there were no excess miles on her car. So, unless he used some other car, like a green Honda, his alibi seems firm. From the ballistics report, the weapon used in the murders could have been a 9mm, 38 caliber or 357 magnum. Ferguson and his girlfriend, Liz, both have Glocks, but neither weapon has been fired in quite some time, so that rules them out as the murder weapon. But as a long-distance truck driver, Ferguson had plenty of opportunities to buy guns at a gun show from a private seller. One that doesn't require registration. So we can't ignore that possibility. Now, we come to motive. Financially, the Fergusons were not in any trouble. The only debt they had was their mortgage and with both him and his wife working, they could easily manage the monthly payment. The insurance policy on Mary Ellen Ferguson was small and Zach was neither the primary nor secondary beneficiary. So that rules that out. That leaves either the pending divorce or jealousy. After reviewing the notes from the interviews and transcribed texts taken from everybody's cell phones, it was quite apparent that Zach was quite jealous, especially of Dominick Garcia. And based on everything I've read, Zach was not aware that Dom was gay. But I don't think there is enough evidence to think that jealousy alone would have been his motive. Not to kill his wife *and* daughter. The same with the impending divorce and all of its financial and personal ramifications. Not individually. But collectively, they could have pushed him over the edge."

Johnny stopped and took a swig of his now cold coffee. He saw that Daniel had taken extensive notes of what he had said. It made him feel needed again. Something that he had lost in retirement. He then continued.

"So here is what I think happened. Because of the threat to Mary Ellen Ferguson by the robber, she asked for someone to stay at her house. We know the APD detective volunteered but was turned down. Instead, Dominick Garcia stayed… for two nights. Somehow Zach found out igniting his jealousy. I base that on the threatening text Zach sent to his wife on Thursday morning. While Zach said it was intended for the detective that he thought had stayed the night, I think he knew it was Dom. When the Colonel texted Zach on Friday that the detective had shown up again, I think that set Ferguson's plan in motion. Based on texts from Zach's daughter, she was supposed to be staying with a friend. But then texts from the daughter to her mother later that night showed she got scared or nervous and wanted to come home. Zach didn't know that his wife had borrowed Garcia's car. He thought it was his wife and Garcia in bed when he shot them. Killing his daughter was never part of his plan. And the green Honda, I think Zach texted that message from the Colonel's phone after he shot him just to throw us off. I base that on the previous texts sent by the Colonel compared to that last text he was supposed to have sent. He always signed his messages, *Colonel Robert Oliver.* The last message was signed *Col Oliver.*"

Johnny paused a moment to see Daniel's reaction, if any, to the inconsistency in the Colonel's text signature. He saw him drawing a couple of stars next to his last note.

Johnny continued. "Of course, this is all hypothetical. There are questions that need to be answered to prove or disprove my theory. Like, how did Zach get to Atlanta and back to South Carolina if he didn't use Ramona Hewitt's car? And he had to have a 2nd gun. So where did he get it? Why didn't he call the APD about the missing door? And, most importantly, in his initial interview video, he had a Band-Aid on his left hand. Could it be hiding a dog bite? That's all I have. What do you think?"

"Wrinkles, your insight on this case is remarkable, especially for an old retired codger. I especially like how you honed in on the different signatures of the Colonel's texts and the Band-Aid on Zach's hand. But let me play the devil's advocate. The Colonel was monitoring Zach's house at his request. Why would he have the Colonel do that if he was planning on murdering his wife? We do know the Colonel was out walking his dog the night of the murders. Maybe he did see a green Honda and was in a hurry to text Zach. Thus, the shortened version of his signature. And the Band-Aid on Zach's hand, that could have been there for days and the fact that Betty Oliver thinks that her dog could have bitten the killer is purely speculative on her part. But as a follow-up, I do think we need to call Zach and ask about the bandage just like I think we should call Dom to dig deeper into his allegations that Zach was abusive to his wife. So let's assume he was abusive and the texts and interviews certainly show that side of his personality. Most murders from abusive spouses are during a fit of anger… spontaneous. The murder of this teller was premeditated. Planning was involved just like the robberies. So until we know more… until we find that proverbial smoking gun, I don't think there is a case against Zach. No DA in his right mind would take this to court. Too circumstantial and speculative. And from what I've witnessed of Zach's emotional behavior, it is real. No jury would ever find otherwise. And finally, everyone… well, almost everyone including Jacobs, Marlowe and me, believes the robber committed the murders. 'Now… have I offended you?"

"If you didn't, I'd think you'd gone soft."

CHAPTER 80

Back at the apartment after a leisurely lunch at Paces & Vine, Johnny headed straight to the guestroom for a quick nap. A refresher as he called it. Daniel headed to the kitchen where he looked over the notes he'd made from Johnny's analysis comparing the two prime suspects and their motives.

Premeditated murderers always had a motive. For the bank robber, the only one that made sense was revenge... fulfilling his threat. But why? Was he that angry at the teller for yelling at him and grabbing his hand? Did humiliation play a role? After reviewing the video a number of times, he found it inconclusive. And after years in law enforcement, he was well aware that the criminal mind had different trigger points and possibly the teller inadvertently pulled the wrong one.

With Zach, his motive was easy. As Johnny had so expertly put it, neither the pending divorce with all of its financial and personal ramifications nor his extreme jealousy was sufficient evidence, individually, to be motive enough to kill his wife and daughter. But, collectively, they could have pushed him over the edge.

Daniel had just reached for his phone when Johnny appeared at the kitchen door, all perky.

"You get any more calls from your man, EB?"

"EB? Like in ebb and flow?"

"EB. Like in the English Bandit."

"No. No calls from EB. But I was just getting ready to call Dom. Then Ferguson. I've been reading my notes on your dissertation this morning and I want to make sure there are no loose ends."

Johnny didn't wait for an invite. He pulled up a chair across from Daniel, all ears.

Dom answered the call immediately. Daniel identified himself, explained that the conversation was being recorded and put the phone on speaker so he could make notes and Johnny could listen.

"Dom, the other day when we talked to you at your apartment, you mentioned that Zach was an abusive husband. Can you expand on that?"

"I didn't think that Zach was a suspect. That he had an alibi? Has something changed?"

"Nothing has changed.   However, we must be thorough in our investigation. Until it is completed, Ferguson, along with others, will remain on our suspect list. Now, can you tell us more about Zach's abusive behavior and what proof you have? For the record, there have been no incidents of any kind filed in Cobb or Fulton County."

"I don't doubt there would be. That would have been embarrassing to her and her daughter. She would have never let that happen. As far as proof, we talked. She told me. But as far as any real proof, it would be my word against his."

"You're right. And that won't hold up."

"I do know that Sarah Moore, our head teller, once found her in the restroom, trying to apply extra makeup while at the same time crying. She begged Mary Ellen to call the authorities, but she said it was her fault. We all knew when Zach was in town. We could see it in her eyes and hear it in her voice. And just so you're aware, after her death, I called her divorce lawyer, Stuart Friedman… a friend of mine… to let him know about her death. He immediately thought that Zach had killed her just like I had. He said they discussed getting a restraining order. That she feared him more so than the robber. She told me the same thing when I stayed over at her house those two nights."

"Does Zach know you are gay?"

"I don't know, but why does that matter?"

"Just looking at the jealousy angle. One last question. The security videos. You told me that you planned to review them to see if you saw anyone suspicious coming into the bank prior to the robbery. How is that coming?"

"It's taking longer than I expected. I'm only through the last four days and nothing so far. But I'm not giving up."

Daniel thanked Dom and ended the call. He looked up at Johnny.

"Well?"

"No help. Nothing we didn't already know."

"Okay, let's call Zach."

Only after six rings did Zach pick up the phone. Daniel identified himself and, as in the previous call, said he would be putting the call on speaker so he could take notes. That the call was not being recorded.

"So how can I help you? I thought Detectives Marlowe and Jacobs were handling the case."

"The FBI is now handling both the robbery and the murders. We're trying to tie up a few loose ends and have a couple of questions."

"If you can make it fast. I've gotta get dressed for the funeral reception." Zach had plenty of time, but the more he talked to the police or FBI, the more chances of a slip-up.

"We were reviewing the tapes and noticed you had a Band-Aid on your left hand. When, where and how did your hand get injured?"

"I'm not sure what this has to do with my wife and daughter's murder, but if you must know, I slipped down at a McDonald's and scraped it while trying to break my fall. This happened while I was in Lexington, South Carolina this past Saturday. If you want to check for yourself, you can call the manager at that McDonald's. They saw me fall. They took pictures, documented it and I signed some documents saying I wouldn't sue. But why should I sue? It was my fault and I got my food for free," said Zach, then laughed. Neither Daniel nor Johnny thought it was funny. He then gave Daniel the name and telephone number of the McDonald's manager.

Daniel ended the call while looking at Johnny who just rolled his eyes.

"What? The man's been very open... very cooperative. I don't see how you still think he's our man."

"Too cooperative if you ask me."

The next call was to the McDonald's in Lexington. The manager who answered the call was not the one who had been at work the day that Zach had claimed to have fallen. But he was aware of the incident. The owner of the franchise had come immediately to the restaurant after the fall. He was relieved to see the manager on duty had taken pictures and had gotten the injured party to sign a *Waiver of Liability* form. He used the incident as a teaching lesson to all the other managers in an online group meeting.

Daniel asked if the manager could send him a copy of the *Waiver* along with the pictures.

"I don't have that authority. Plus it's at our headquarters. We are a franchise and the main office is in Columbia, South Carolina. I can put in a request if you'd like or you can call HQ and ask them yourself."

Daniel got the number and called immediately. After several transfers, he got to the legal department. The lawyer for the franchise agreed to overnight a copy of everything related to the incident but requested a follow-up warrant to which Daniel agreed.

While he had made the calls, he saw Johnny standing on the balcony looking down at the apartment's swimming pool. His mind was not on the swimmers or sunbathers. It was on Zach. His alibi, his total cooperation, his real emotions. Exactly what you would want from someone who had nothing to hide. Someone who was innocent. Yet, it bothered him. Why couldn't he just let it go?

CHAPTER 81

Ed Jernigan honked the horn on his shiny black Mercedes. He strummed his finger on the steering wheel as he waited impatiently outside of Zach's home for his client to appear. He wanted to talk to him before tonight's visitation at the funeral home. There would be a lot of people from the bank attending. He knew Zach was a hothead and he wanted to make sure that Zach kept his cool, especially around Dominick Garcia.

Zach walked out the side door carrying Ashley's favorite teddy bear. He was dressed in a new black pin-striped suit, white shirt and red and green striped tie, all courtesy of his in-laws. He could have easily passed for a lawyer, banker or businessman. Certainly not a truck driver. His Hollywood good looks made Jernigan briefly consider taking the lawsuit to trial. But only briefly. There was no way he would put Zach up on the stand facing a good defense attorney.

"So what do you think of the suit?" asked Zach as he sat down in the car's passenger seat. He looked around at the beauty of the interior of the car and felt the luxuriousness of the leather seats. He would be driving something like this shortly.

"Nice," responded Jernigan who was dressed in the same white linen pants and light blue oxford, button-down collared shirt that he'd worn when he first met Zach. Only the suspenders and coordinating bowtie were different. He had a navy blue blazer on a coat hanger in the back seat of the car. "Before we go, I want to go over a few things with you."

Zach nodded as he adjusted the tightness of his tie. His father-in-law had worn one every day of the week and Sunday, at least until he retired. Zach never understood the old man. Ties were not in *his* future. Just Bermuda shorts and t-shirts. That's all he would wear once he had his money and had moved to the beach and as far away from his in-laws as possible.

"Regarding the lawsuit, the bank was served this morning and I've already gotten a call from their lawyers. They want to see me this Friday. You don't need to come. I'm thinking they're going to make us a low ball offer to see if I jump… to see if we're desperate. As your lawyer, it is my obligation to inform you of any offer. My recommendation is that we wait them out. We have a really strong case and hopefully, they will want to settle sooner rather than later. If they choose to stand their ground, especially if *they* think the offer is fair, I'm prepared to go all the way. *We* should be the judge of what's fair. Do you have a problem with that?"

"No. I'm good. As long as I can keep driving my truck around the country, I can wait forever. I just want them to pay. Especially *Dom*. I want his ass fired. Can you make that part of the settlement? I'd give up fifty grand to make that happen."

"Not gonna happen. This lawsuit isn't about making Dom pay. It's about making the bank pay for the loss of your family. For ignoring your wife's pleas for safety and security. They failed her. Dom didn't fail her. And that's the other thing I want to talk to you about. *Dom*. You *cannot* get into a confrontation with him whatsoever. I don't care if he fucked your wife, your daughter, your…"

Before Jernigan could finish his sentence, Zach turned to him, grabbed his suspenders and pulled him over to him. He looked him straight in the eyes and yelled, "Do not ever talk about my daughter that way again or I will kill you." He then shoved his lawyer back over to the driver's side of the car.

The rage in Zach's eyes scared the lawyer. He knew it was inappropriate to have said anything about the man's wife or daughter, but he was trying to make a point. Without question, he would never ask the man if he was innocent or guilty. He didn't want to know. This case was a gold mine, his retirement nest egg, his golden parachute.

"Zach… this is exactly what I'm talking about. See how quickly you turned? How angry… how violently mad you got? And I'm your lawyer. I'm on your side. You cannot ever fly off the handle like you just did. People will see you in a different light. They might think *you* killed your family. I don't care what you think about Dom, what he says or what he does. You *have* to keep your cool. Ignore him. Leave him alone. Stay away from him if possible."

"I understand. You just touched one of my hot buttons, but that won't happen again. Too much at stake for me to be acting like such an idiot." Zach understood the huge financial loss his uncontrolled temper could incur. He would not let that happen again.

"You damn right. For me, too. And FYI, the bank's lawyers might be there. And the police. Not out of respect. Just to observe you. So, do I need to tell you how nice you have to be to everybody?"

"I got you the first time."

On the way over to the funeral home, Jernigan baited him, trying to push his buttons. But Zach seemed to understand his role. Needless to say, he did not ask Zach if he killed his wife and daughter.

At the appointed time, Jernigan dropped Zach off at the front door of the funeral home and left to go find a parking space. His plan was to stay in the car until about 6:30 p.m. before going inside. Visitations were bad enough. Being the first person to show was the worst. Like a captured audience.

Zach met his in-laws in the lobby. The preacher was standing just outside the parlor where the two caskets sat, side by side.

"Zach," said Carol, the mother-in-law. "You look *so* handsome… *so* distinguished. I love that suit. Mary Ellen would be proud." Seeing Zach holding Ashley's little bear was almost more than she could withstand. It took all she could do to keep from crying.

Wesley shook Zach's hand out of courtesy, but neither said anything.

"Would you like to go see Ashley? She's so pretty. They really did a good job." This time Carol did break down. As uncomfortable as Zach had always been around his mother-in-law, he hugged her and she hugged him back with tears flowing from both parties.

Afterward, Carol led Zach into the parlor where he saw two caskets. One open and one closed. She stopped in front of the closed casket.

"I'll give you some time with Ashley. They couldn't do anything with Mary Ellen. The damage was too great. Oh God, my poor baby girl."

She turned away from Zach, tears flowing down her face. Wesley immediately came to her rescue and the two found a nearby chair.

Zach had never attended a funeral. So when he walked over and looked down and saw his beautiful daughter lying motionless, her smiles, her laughter, her hugs… gone forever, his knees buckled and he collapsed to the floor dropping the stuffed animal as he did. The pain was unbearable. The funeral director who was standing nearby rushed over and helped the grieving man to his feet and over to a chair next to his in-laws where he sat, tears flowing and his head shaking in disbelief.

It was her fault. Hers and Dom's, thought Zach. *He was supposed to be in that bed. Not Ashley. Oh God! What have I done?*

The preacher who had witnessed the whole scene, rushed over and kneeled down in front of the broken-hearted family and began quoting

Bible passages meant to console the bereaved. Zach heard nothing and wished that the man would leave. Carol and Wesley appreciated the reassuring words and thanked the preacher.

Throughout the whole ordeal, the funeral director continued to check the clock on the wall over the closed double doors. When he saw that the visitation hour was near, he leaned over between Carol and Wesley and reminded them of the time and asked if they wanted to delay the start. Both shook their heads. The funeral director then had everybody stand and then moved them just in front of the two caskets. The order of the receiving line was Wesley, Carol then Zach followed by the preacher who stood just past the two caskets for anyone needing spiritual support.

When the doors to the parlor were opened, there were only a few visitors in the hall leading into the room with hardly anybody in attendance fifteen minutes after the visitation started. This suited Zach just fine. But by six-thirty, the parlor was full of friends and relatives of Mary Ellen, Ashley and the Knox's. The only people Zach recognized were his lawyer, his manager at Cross Freight and Betty Oliver.

Jernigan dutifully paid his respects to the bereaved and moved over to the farthest corner of the room but in a position where he could watch his client. When Dom arrived and moved to the back of the visitor's line, he could see Zach tense up. Jernigan became especially concerned as Dom neared the receiving line. But Zach made it through the charade with flying colors. Jernigan's next challenge was to get Zach to maintain his composure through the funeral and it would be clear sailing from there on out.

As the line of visitors bogged down at the Knox's, the funeral director took the opportunity to walk over to Zach and hand him a note.

"A friend of your wife, a red-headed man with a red beard, asked me to give you this. He said to tell you he was sorry that he couldn't come inside, but ever since losing his own wife, he couldn't bear to look at caskets. We see it all the time. It's called Death Anxiety." The director handed Zach the note and walked away. Zach stepped back from the line and turned to give himself some privacy. He opened the envelope and read the hand-written note. It was not what he had expected.

**Truth will come to light,
murder cannot be hid long,
…. In the end, truth will out** [1]
Zach Ferguson – MURDERER

Zach immediately crushed the note, stuck it into his coat side pocket and looked around to find the funeral director all the while trying to control his anger. He saw him exiting the parlor. Without saying anything to his in-laws, he left the receiving line and caught up with the man in the lobby.

"Excuse me," said Zach, tapping the director on the shoulder. "Did you happen to get the name of the man who gave you that note?"

"No. Why? Didn't he sign it?"

"No. No, he didn't. It was… uh… so uh… nice, I just wanted to thank him. Did you happen to see what kind of car he was driving?"

"No. He came into the lobby gave me the note and left. You know, the Death Anxiety phobia. But if it helps any, I think he was British or something because he spoke with an English accent."

* * * * * * * * * * * * * * * * *

That night, before going to bed, Zach opened the drawer to his bedside table to make sure his Glock was still there. He pulled it out and checked to make sure that the magazine was full and a round was chambered. It was. His security system was set. He laid the gun on the table and turned off the table lamp. Like the previous night, sleep did not come easy. Not in the same bed, the same house where Ashley had died. The note just added to his insomnia. After thirty or so minutes of tossing and turning, he turned on the bedside light and headed to the kitchen where he poured himself a double shot of whiskey from a bottle he'd bought on the way home from the funeral home. It wasn't Maker's Mark. It was some cheap brand that he's never heard of. But as long as it calmed him, made him sleepy, that's all that mattered. He carried the bottle over to the kitchen table and sat down. The liquor seemed to be helping. So as soon as he emptied his first glass he poured himself a second. Were it

---

[1] **Shakespeare** *The Merchant of Venice* (2.2.76-79)

not for an early funeral tomorrow, he considered getting shit-faced. It had been a hell of a day for him. Not only did he have to suffer the horrors of having to look at his young daughter's dead body, but then he had to endure two hours of sheer torture of thanking nameless and faceless people that he didn't know and didn't care to know. That was only made worse by being forced to put on a friendly face and shake the hand of Dominick Garcia.

And then there was the note and the red-headed man with a British accent. Who was he? His mind swirled with all the possibilities. Surely it wasn't the robber. It had to be some weirdo just getting their jollies at his expense. Then again, if it was the bank robber, why the note? Did he want some of his settlement money? Or was it a trick by the police? Did they want to see how he reacted? Were they expecting him to give them the note? After a half-finished third drink, he decided it was too risky to report it to the police. If they challenged him, he could always say he forgot. He had too much on his mind with the reception, the funeral and the lawsuit.

Using the table for support, he pushed himself up and stumbled down the hall to the doorless master bedroom. Without turning out the light, he laid down on the bed and was asleep almost as soon as his head hit the pillow. While the sleep came easy, so did the nightmares. He dreamed that he was driving around his daughter's open coffin in a new, expensive car. A yellow Porsche. He waved at his daughter, but she never returned the wave. Her eyes never opened. Then he saw Mary Ellen. She only had one eye open as the other was nothing but a hole with blood seeping out of it. She was pointing her finger at him, yelling at him in an English accent: *MURDERER!*

Wednesday, August 14, 2019

ATLANTA, GEORGIA

CHAPTER 82

At 8:30 a.m., Scott's cellphone alarm began to beep followed shortly by the automated wake-up ring on the phone in the hotel room. He slowly rolled out of bed while the alarm and the phone continued their nagging, persistent attack until he shut them both up. It had been a rough twenty-four hours and the next twenty-four were not going to be any easier. He felt sleep deprived having slept less than four hours. He had spent most of the night traveling to Charlotte, exchanging his Lexus for his Harley and returning back to Atlanta. Yet, he was amped.

Aside from his trip and a few hours in preparation for his presentation at the Roswell bank, Scott spent most of his time that morning reading or watching anything that had to do with the three murders in Cobb County. He seemed obsessed. So far, the only person the police had mentioned as the prime suspect was the bank robber. The English Bandit. Him. Scott.

Initially, his only response to the allegations had been to leave a lame voicemail with the FBI saying that he hadn't done it. It was only when he saw the husband on TV and recognized him as the man he'd seen driving into the neighborhood on the night of the murders that he knew he had to do more.

The handwritten note that he'd asked the funeral director to give to Ferguson had been a good start. In his second call to the FBI, he'd positively identified himself as the bank robber by disclosing the exact amount stolen. He'd also let them know that he had seen Zach Ferguson entering the neighborhood at about the time of the murders. Yet, he needed to do more. But what?

CHAPTER 83

"Let not your heart be troubled[2]," said the senior pastor of the small, filled to capacity, East Cobb United Methodist Church as he stood at the altar behind the two closed caskets, one draped in roses, the other in yellow and white daisies with a small one-eyed teddy bear sitting on top. "Ye believe in God, believe also in me. In my Father's house are many mansions: if it were not so, I would have told you. I go to prepare a place for you."

Zach couldn't bear to look at the caskets, especially Ashley's. Nor could he look at the preacher as he read the New Testament scriptures from the book of John.

The funeral service had been written by Mary Ellen's parents, Wesley and Carol Knox, with the help of Mary Ellen's local pastor. The music selections included "In Paradisum" from the seventh movement of Fauré *Requiem*, "Amazing Grace", Billy Joel's "Goodnight My Angel" and Mary Ellen and Ashley's favorite, "Lord of the Dance."

When the soloist, a friend of Dom's and a member of Atlanta Symphony Orchestra Chorus, sang Joel's sweet lullaby, a song chosen specifically for Ashley, there was not a dry eye in the church, including the soloist who had a hard time getting through the song. Zach cried off and on throughout the service which included eulogies by Betty Oliver, whose husband would be buried the next day with full military honors, one of Ashley's teachers, Ashley's friend Jordan and Dom. Dom was the last and would not have been included if Zach had had any hand in writing the service. But he didn't.

Once Jordan had finished his short, but heartfelt tribute, he stepped away from the pulpit and made his way back to his seat. His head hung low with tears streaming down his face. As Dom passed him in the aisle, he whispered to the young boy, "That was beautiful" and made his way up to the pulpit. After adjusting the microphone and pulling out his folded-up notes, he began.

"My name is Dominick Garcia. I am a friend of Mary Ellen and Ashley. About six years ago, Mary Ellen came to work for the bank. I

---

[2] All verses of the Bible reference in the book are from the King James Version.

was fortunate enough to be her boss and she was my first hire. Right from the start, I knew she was a keeper. She was friendly, reliable, punctual and amazingly accurate. Everybody at the bank as well as her customers loved her. She always had a smile on her face. If I or anybody in the bank was having a bad day, she knew how to cheer us up. To her, work was fun. She loved us and we loved her. The bank will never be the same without her. She cannot be replaced."

"Now, I'm not a storyteller, but I want to tell you this one about Mary Ellen. I promise to keep it short. One day, she brought a book to work. One she'd gotten as a birthday present. A self-improvement book. One that helps you learn a new word every day. Unfortunately, her first word was *anonymity*." Dom struggled with the correct pronunciation himself, taking three times to get it correct. "Obviously, not a good first word. Every time she tried to use it in a sentence, it came out with a different pronunciation or even a different word like animosity, anomaly… whatever. Needless to say, she didn't bring the book to work the next day."

The story was a needed diversion that had everyone in the church smiling except Zach.

Dom continued. "But speaking of anonymity, just before the service began, I received a text from a peer at one of our other branches, and I'll read what it says." He then pulled out his cell phone from his coat pocket.

"Just had a gentleman… a redheaded man stop by the bank, handed me an envelope and left. The envelope contained $5,000 and a note that read: **In Memory of Mary Ellen and Ashley Ferguson. Please donate to a worthy cause. I will never forget.**" Dom then looked directly at Zach, who never once looked up, and said, "And Mary Ellen… Ashley… we will never forget either."

Dom paused a second to wipe his eyes and then continued.

"As I look around, I see a lot of people from the bank. We all remember Ashley from the time she was six years old… mainly during the summers when she would come and "work" at the bank." Dom air quoted *work*. "She helped us out where needed, but mainly as a greeter… directing customers to the teller line. When not handling the customers, she would raid the refrigerator bringing cokes and snacks to everyone, including herself. Mary Ellen and Ashley were the sweetest, kindest people that God ever put on this earth. I am especially grateful that I was able to spend a few days with them this past week after Mary Ellen was threatened during the robbery at our bank. Mary Ellen and I shared stories, dreams and sorrows along with a nice bottle of Chardonnay. And without a doubt, the best time I ever had driving my little sports car was when I took Ashley to school. We had the top down and the wind blowing our hair everywhere… well, her hair. But she didn't care. We were in our element. We sang *Don't Worry, Be Happy* all the way there. Today, I don't worry about Ashley being happy. I don't worry about Mary Ellen being happy. They are with the Lord. They are in a happier and holier place. The world would be a better place if we had more people like Mary Ellen and Ashley. I know I'm a better person for having known them."

Zach never once looked directly at Dom while he eulogized his wife and daughter, yet he still cried as he visualized his young, beautiful daughter riding to school with the wind blowing through her hair. At the same time, he was jealous that his wife's lover was up in front of the entire church assembly speaking so fondly of his daughter. She was *his* daughter, not Dom's. If he had his Glock, he would have finished the job.

Dom left the altar and walked slowly back to his pew. He sat down between Stuart Friedman and Paul Han, his partner, who reached for his right hand and gently squeezed it. It was a show of love and compassion. One row in front of them were Wesley and Carol Knox who sat on either side of Zach as a show of support. While the authorities said that Zach wasn't a suspect, it did not alter Dom's feelings that her abusive husband was somehow directly or indirectly responsible.

Seated in the far back of the church were Agent Whitehead and Johnny Williams. They were there to pay their respects, observe Zach and look for any suspicious mourners. In the past, there had been cases where the murderer actually attended the funeral services as an act of defiance. No one piqued their interest including Zach. There was no question that his emotions were real just as they had been at the police interviews, especially when anyone talked about his daughter.

After having the congregation sing "Lord of the Dance", the senior pastor ended the sermon with a prayer and paraphrasing selected verses from 1st Corinthians Chapter 15.

"Let me reveal to you a wonderful secret. For those who have died, they will be raised to live *forever*."

The pastor paused for a second, looked at Wesley, Carol and Zach and then continued.

"Then, when our dying bodies have been transformed into bodies that will never die, this Scripture will be fulfilled: Death is swallowed up in victory. O death, where is your victory? O death… *where* is your sting? Amen."

* * * * * * * * * * * * * * * * * *

Once the service had ended, Zach and Mary Ellen's parents were ushered over to the church's banquet hall. The two lawmen felt they had seen enough and chose not to attend the reception. They left immediately following the benediction.

The banquet hall was filled with tables of food, bowls of a red-colored punch and a large assortment of pictures of Mary Ellen, Zach and Ashley during happier times. As the line of friends and acquaintances formed along the windowed wall, Zach and the Knoxes positioned themselves just inside the hall's entry door with Zach first in the receiving line. Not where he wanted to be but where Carol placed him.

Unlike the visitation where the receiving line started small and steadily grew, the line of mourners at the funeral seemed to go on forever with no end in sight. Zach never looked up at any of the mourners as they expressed their sorrow for his losses. Ed Jernigan and Betty Oliver were the only exceptions until a red-headed man, with a red beard and wearing sunglasses, shook Zach's hand, hugged him and whispered in his ear using an English accent, *"There will be repercussions."* The man immediately turned away and headed out the nearest exit. The encounter took Zach completely off guard causing him to stumble backward. After composing himself with Wesley's help, he opened the hand that the red-haired mourner had shaken and realized he was holding another note. Before anyone could see it, he quickly stuffed it into his coat pocket. He didn't need to read it. He knew what it said.

CHAPTER 84

Once the reception was over, those who were going to the burial service in Augusta headed to their cars and waited to fall in line behind the long, black hearse, Ed Jernigan who was driving Zach and then the Knoxes. As the procession slowly turned out onto the street in front of the church where the traffic from both directions had been stopped, Zach heard the loud rumble of a nearby motorcycle whose engine was being throttled up and down. When he looked out the right passenger window, he saw the red-headed man sitting on the motorcycle mouthing, *Murderer.*

You son-of-a-bitch, Zach mouthed back at the motorcyclist.

Jernigan never saw the exchange.

Zach continued to stare down his antagonist as the man put on his black helmet and then drove off in the opposite direction.

Once the procession was out on the expressway, Zach loosened his tie and thought about the red-headed man. Who was he? The robber? An imposter? Why was he doing this? Revenge? Intimidation? Harassment? And what did he hope to achieve by all of this? If he were the robber, he certainly couldn't go to the police. If he were an imposter, what did he have to gain from this charade? His thoughts were interrupted by Jernigan.

"You're mighty quiet over there. I know these funerals are…"

"Excruciating," said Zach, finishing Jernigan's sentence. "Especially having to listen to *Dom.*"

"Funerals are never fun. But you did really good. I must say it was a beautiful service. I loved the music. And as much as I know you dislike Dom, he did an excellent job. Can you believe that someone gave an anonymous gift of $5000? I wouldn't have done that. I would want a receipt to write it off on my taxes. But some people have more money than brains."

"Yeah. I wonder," answered Zach.

"By the way, the bank's lawyers called today. They made an offer of $150,000. Kinda like throwing a dog a bone when what he really wants is the meat house. They said they would have the papers ready to sign at the Friday meeting. I told them if that was the purpose of the meeting, then we weren't wasting our time. That we'd already discussed a minimum settlement and they were nowhere close. And if that was the best they could do, we would see them in court."

"But that would mean waiting at least a year. Isn't that what you said?" With the red-headed stranger getting bolder and more visible, Zach had no intentions of waiting that long. He wanted his money and wanted to leave Marietta, leave Georgia, and maybe leave the USA.

"Yes. But we can wait them out. I doubt they want this to go to court. The meeting is still on for Friday and that's when I'm gonna hit them up for what it will take for us to settle. It will probably take a few meetings, but I think we can wrap this thing up in a couple of months at worst."

"Well, don't push them too hard. I don't want to wait for a jury trial."

"I hear you. I'm ready to cash in, too. I've been a lawyer way too long. I want to spend a few years doing what I want to do. Spend time with my wife, children and grandchildren." Jernigan immediately regretted his insensitive response. Zach had no family. No wife, no daughter. Just a girlfriend. "I'm sorry. I shouldn't have said that. Jeez, we just left the funeral."

"Forget it." Zach hesitated for a moment. "Actually… I *don't* want you to forget it. And I want you to make sure that fucking bank doesn't forget it either. They're the reason I don't have a family. They're the reason Ashley is dead." Tears began to roll down his face as he thought about his daughter. Did she know it was her own father who had shot her? Did she hear her mother call out his name? Would these questions haunt him for the rest of his days? "I want you to sue the shit out of them. Take no prisoners… especially *Dom*."

Jernigan had already had his say about Dom. But the man was grieving, so he let it lie. "Don't worry. We've got them by the short hairs. Did you see how many people were at the funeral? And all the TV news trucks in the parking lot videotaping the procession? No bank wants bad publicity. They'll settle and they'll settle big."

"Just don't screw it up. And don't get too greedy. I don't want to go to court. I don't want this thing to drag on and on. If they offer two or three million, take it. I'm ready to get off the road. Unlike you, I'm one nod, one distraction or one swerving car from hitting a bridge, an embankment, a guardrail or a tree and putting my ass in the grave."

CHAPTER 85

Even the newly signed $1.75 million contracts from Roswell Guardian State Bank couldn't lift Scott's spirits. During the four-hour meeting with the bank, he had faked his smile and his attitude, but the funeral of Mary Ellen and Ashley Ferguson weighed heavily on his mind.

Once he returned to the hotel, he sat on the side of the bed, thinking of his next move. Any more phone contact with the FBI seemed too risky. He'd already left them two voicemails. He'd told them everything he knew, pointing the finger at Zach. Most likely they were now prepared to track the location of a third call. It was a chance he couldn't take. He'd have to find another way, like mail. And after two notes, Zach would be on the lookout for a third. Scott knew the man had a Glock and had threatened to use it. Killing the English Bandit… the man accused by the police of killing his family would make him a hero in the public eye. Regardless, he had to do more. There was no way he could let Zach get away with killing three innocent people, blame Scott and then cash in on their deaths. But what?

As he mulled over his next move, his cell phone rang. It was Sid Patel, the eldest of his two partners.

"Well, I've waited long enough. Did we or didn't we?"

"What do you think happens when you send in your star quarterback?"

"Yes!"

"One point seven five mil. But who's counting."

"When are you coming back so I can get the team together for a celebration?"

"Glad you asked. I've been so busy, I haven't had a chance to call Anne. This is my second strike and I don't know if I'm gonna get a third. So if she's willing, I'm taking her to Charleston for a long weekend if she's not tied up."

"You don't have to ask my permission. I'll not keep you from your next call and I'll tell Tim."

Anne picked up the call on the fourth ring… just to make Scott nervous.

"I was beginning to wonder if you'd forgotten my number."

Scott laughed nervously. "Uh…what are you doing this weekend?"

"Oh, the usual. Nothing. Waiting on my fiancé to find his way back home unless he's taken up permanent residence in Georgia."

Scott chose to stay away from any possible confrontation. Instead, he used a lawyer technique he'd learned from Anne, he answered a question with a question.

"How about another mini-vacation? A long weekend?"

"Is this another peace offering? Two in the same week? Not a good sign."

"You can call it a peace offering. I call it a red-letter day. We got the contract at Roswell Guardian. Almost two million. Then, the coup de grace, I think I sold my bike. I'll know later today."

"A red-letter day for sure." Anne was more excited about the bike sale than the contract or the long weekend trip. "So where are we going?"

"Charleston."

"You pick the hotel and I'll meet you there tomorrow afternoon."

"That will work and will get you off the hook… this time."

"You're a sweetheart. Look, I've got to run. Work to do. I'll see you there. Love you."

"Whoa. Hang on there, buster. What's with the 'wham, bam, thank you mam' phone call? You got something better to do than talk to me? Is there something going on that I should know about? You've been acting really strange ever since that party Friday night. Actually since your aborted road trip to Canton."

This was Anne, the trial lawyer. He wanted so badly to spill his guts. Tell her everything. Keep no secrets from her. But that was never going to happen.

"Honey, there is nothing going on. Sometimes I get so involved with my work, I lose track of time. For so long, I haven't had *anybody* who worried about where I was, when I was coming home or even if I was alive. Having someone who actually cares about me is still somewhat foreign. But I'm learning. I'm sorry I didn't call earlier. It won't happen again. I promise. Just so you won't worry, I'm supposed to meet the president of Roswell Guardian at six for a few drinks. That's all."

"You're a good man, Scott Burnett. I love you. And I do trust you. You take care of what you've got to do on your end and I'll take care of the reservations. Call me when you're on the road."

Scott hung up feeling guilty that he had lied to Anne again. He only wished that nothing was going on.

CHAPTER 86

"Well, you did say you were coming down to Atlanta to see a Braves game. They're playing the Mets tonight. I say we go. You got to see their new stadium. It's phenomenal. And there are great places to eat in and around the stadium. And I'm buying."

"Why didn't you say that right up front? Of course, I'd love to go. Is this like a date or something?"

"I'm not that desperate."

"What about the case?"

"What about it? I think we've done about all we can do."

"You wouldn't rather stay here and…"

"And what, review the same old reports, interviews, evidence… whatever? I'm not wasting my time. I want to go to the game."

Johnny had worked with Daniel long enough to know when he was frustrated. The case was going nowhere. The ballgame was just a diversion. Something to take his mind off work. Every detective or in this case, FBI agent, needed one from time to time. With Daniel's apartment being so close to the stadium, they walked to the stadium… something Johnny couldn't have done in his obese years as a detective.

The Braves were beating the Mets, 1 to 0 when Daniel got a text from his office's duty agent.

That Fed-ex envelope you were expecting just arrived from our offsite security facility. I put it on your desk.

Daniel shoved his phone back into his pocket and looked over at Johnny who had the look on his face of a typical male at a ballet performance.

"Just got a text from my office."

"Yeah," said Johnny, his face lighting up a bit.

"Would you rather stay here and finish out the game or go back to my office and see what's in the Fed-ex letter I just got from that McDonald's franchise in South Carolina?"

"Really? You have to ask?"

In less than thirty minutes, the two men pulled into the parking lot of the Atlanta FBI Field Office. Daniel badged in and signed Johnny in as a guest. Johnny had never seen Daniel's office. As he stood at the office door, he gave the place a once over. It reminded him of the cubicle they'd shared in Washington, D.C. Daniel's University of Maryland diploma hung on the wall closest to his desk. Surrounding it were the numerous awards, citations and pictures of him and his partners. One of the pictures was an early photo of Johnny Williams, decked out in his newly issued D.C. police uniform and standing next to his highly polished squad car. When Johnny retired from the force, he gave a copy of the picture to Daniel as a reminder of their days together. Another picture hanging alone and very prominently displayed was the two of them receiving the Investigators of the year award in 2007 for solving the Dupont Circle murders. The case made local and national news.

"Let's do this in the conference room. More space," said Daniel, holding the fed-ex envelope in his hand.

Sitting across from each other at a large rectangular, wooden table, Daniel dumped the contents of the previously opened large envelope out onto the table. FBI's protocol did not allow any mail or packages to come directly to the field office. All mail and deliveries went first to an offsite location where they would be checked for explosives, poison, radioactive material… anything that might harm the agent or the office. Daniel's package passed inspection and was sent out on the last delivery of the day. It contained four photos, an incident report and a liability waiver.

Daniel read the incident report and passed it on to Johnny to read. The report stated that the customer, Zach Ferguson, had stumbled and fallen down as he approached his car while carrying the food he had just purchased inside the McDonald's store. The drive-thru attendant had seen the whole thing and the fall did not look intentional. To break the fall, it appeared that the customer extended his left hand as he fell to the ground. His hand, primarily below the thumb, suffered only slight cuts and minor abrasions. A picture was made of the injury. There were no other injuries reported. The customer willingly signed the liability waiver with the understanding that the waiver relieved the McDonald's franchise of any future liability.

"The injury was quite convenient, but knowing the man's penchant for money, you'd thought he would have jumped at a small lawsuit unless…" Johnny stopped his sentence midstream.

"Yeah. Unless what?" asked Daniel. "What this proves is that the bandage on Zach's hand could have come from the fall. Nothing more. Nothing less." As far as he was concerned, everything still pointed to the bank robber.

Frustrated, he picked up a picture, scanned it and was about to slide it over to Johnny for his review but then he didn't. Something he saw wasn't right. He looked at the picture again without focusing on the hand-wound.

"Wait a minute. I think our boy Zach might have been lying to us." He then tossed the photo over to Johnny who looked at the picture of Zach's wounds. Then he smiled. "Partner, I think we might have ourselves the old proverbial smoking gun."

The photo in question was one taken by the McDonald's manager of Zach's injured hand. It wasn't the image of the injury that fueled Johnny's *smoking gun* claim. It's what else the two men saw in the picture. Shown below Zach's injured hand were the toes to a pair of boots with dark splatter marks on them.

"Not so fast," responded Daniel. "Here's what I see. I see a picture of an injured hand and the toes of a pair of boots. There is definitely a dark stain on the right boot. But it could have come from a wound or coffee. Maybe oil… cooking oil. Without the boots, we are only speculating that it's blood. Without the boots, we have no DNA. Not only that, we can't be sure they are Zach's. We don't know the angle at which the photo was taken, so the toes of the boots in the picture could have been the manager or another employee. No DA's gonna ride that horse."

Daniel continued. "Something else I've been thinking about. And this is really reaching. But these voicemails… what if the caller was Dominick Garcia?"

"The bank guy who gave the eulogy at the funeral."

"Yes. The same guy. The one who had you all teary-eyed."

"That was just sweat. But that little fellow pretending to be EB? No way."

"I told you it's a stretch. But hear me out. From all the conversations I've had with Dom, he despises Ferguson. As far as I know, other than EB and law enforcement people, he's the only other person who knew exactly how much money was stolen. That was to make us think *he* was the robber." Daniel air-quoted *robber.* "And the British accent? Dom has the video of the robbery, so he could easily have perfected it to the point of fooling us. And lastly, to say that he saw Ferguson coming into the neighborhood just as he was going out. That is so farfetched. I think with all the grief that Dom has felt, his obvious dislike of Ferguson, and the fact that there's now been a wrongful death lawsuit filed against his bank, I don't think we can turn a blind eye."

"I say never discount the obvious *or* the dubious."

"You ready to call it a night?" asked Daniel as he pulled the pictures and the documents over to his side of the table and began straightening them up.

"You mind if we go over this stuff just once more? I got this gut feeling that we're overlooking something. Like I've read something or I've seen something in one of these pictures, but I just can't put my finger on it."

"Then let's do it." Daniel never questioned Johnny's 'gut' feeling. It was an intuition that couldn't be taught. He grabbed the report for himself and shoved the pictures over to Johnny.

"Well, what do we have here?" Johnny was holding up one of the pictures.

"What? What? Tell me."

"Remember that report from the McDonald's manager where he said that Zach stumbled and fell down as he approached his car while carrying his food? Well, this is one of the pictures taken of the area where Ferguson fell and it shows the left rear side of a car and its wheels. The food sack, pancakes and plastic containers are on the pavement next to the car. It's a white car with Ford hubcaps. Take a look." Johnny then slid the photo over to Daniel.

"I'm not following you."

"The white car. The Hewitt lady drives a red Ford Mustang. Not a white Ford. Something's not right."

"Yeah… it's you. Did you ever stop to consider that Ferguson could have been walking to the passenger's side of the Red Mustang car when he fell? That the white car you see in the picture is parked to the right of Hewitt's car."

"I can tell you that I never walk to the right side of my car when I'm carrying food. I get in the driver's side and set the food on the passenger's seat. One of us is right and I'm gonna find out." Without waiting for a response from Daniel, he picked up his cell phone, did a quick search of recent calls and hit the green dial symbol.

After seven or so rings, the phone automatically disconnected. Johnny hit the number again. After three rings, a testy voice on the other end answered. Johnny immediately put the phone on speaker.

"I don't know who the hell you're trying to reach, but if you're not the fucking police…"

"Ms. Hewitt," said Johnny interrupting Ramona from her fury. "This is Johnny Williams, crime consultant working with the FBI. We met this past Monday at Rush's."

"Oh shit. I'm sorry. I…"

Not waiting for her to finish, Johnny continued. "I hate to bother you, but I need to ask you a couple of questions. As I recall, you own a red Ford Mustang. Do you by any chance own a white car… a Ford?"

"No sir," replied Ramona wondering what her red Mustang had to do with the murders at Zach's house.

Daniel saw Johnny's whole body slump when he heard the answer and then perk back up as he heard her follow-up reply.

"But my brother Andy does. A white Ford Focus. He's in Afghanistan, so I'm keeping it at my apartment and driving it to work about every other day so it doesn't die."

"Do you keep track of the mileage on the car?"

"On that old clunker? No. But if you are thinking that Zach drove *that* car to Atlanta and killed his wife and kid, you are way out in left field. He was with me all night. Not only that, the car probably wouldn't make it that far."

"One last thing. Was Zach wearing boots the day he visited you?"

"I really don't know. Feet are not something that grabs my attention if you know what I mean." Then she laughed and the call ended.

Before Johnny could speak, Daniel spoke up. "Okay. So now we know that Ramona Hewitt has a white Ford and Ferguson drove it over to the McDonald's in Lexington, South Carolina. But she's adamant that he never left the bed and there was no way her old car could make it to Atlanta. Not only that, where does the green Honda fit into this whole picture. I don't think it's time for us to be high-fiving… not on a bunch of circumstantial evidence. I'm gonna update APD's folder, then I say we go home, get some sleep and give ol' Zach a visit tomorrow morning."

Johnny knew Daniel was right. Every piece of evidence *was* circumstantial. Even an old retired cop like himself knew that. It was just wishful thinking on his part that he might help his old partner solve the murder crime before returning to Washington. It would have made for a great finish to his vacation.

CHAPTER 87

Ed Jernigan thought that six hours in the car together would have been enough for Zach. Three hours to Augusta and three hours back. But the man was lonely and, after all, he was his golden goose.

"Yeah. I'll have a nightcap with you. But just *one*," said the portly lawyer who had worked enough DUI cases to know the seemingly never-ending consequences of overindulging.

Before exiting Jernigan's plush Mercedes, Zach felt the smooth leather seats one more time and sucked in a deep breath of the luxury that he would soon be able to afford. After sliding out of the car, he felt embarrassed to see his old Toyota sitting in the driveway next to the lawyer's stately car. He should have parked it in the garage.

As they headed to the house, both he and Ed saw it almost simultaneously. Illuminated by the light at the back door was a vase filled with beautiful, dark red, almost black roses.

"Who are they from?" asked Ed.

"I don't see a note," answered Zach as he culled through the bouquet, thinking that he didn't need any more notes.

"Obviously, the person who bought them must not have known that black flowers mean death," said Ed. "I know because I grow roses and I know roses. These are called Black Pearl."

Zach didn't need a note to know who they were from. He handed the vase to Ed and was opening the back door when they heard the distinct loud engine noise coming from the street. Both he and Ed turned to see a rider dressed in black and wearing a black helmet on a black Harley stopped in front of his house. He revved the engine three or four more times and then squealed out of the neighborhood.

"What the hell was that all about?" asked Jernigan.

"How should I know? It was probably road rage. You know. One of those nut jobs that got stuck behind you as you drove five miles under the speed limit. Like an old lady," offered Zach as a distraction while knowing exactly who the biker was.

The two men headed into the house where Ed placed the flowers on the kitchen counter and took a seat at a nearby table.

Zach walked over to the cabinet nearest the refrigerator but seemed to forget why he was there as he eyed the black flowers and thought about the biker dressed in all black.

"Are we having a drink or not?" asked Ed, ready to end his time with Zach for the night.

"Oh yeah." Zach then found a couple of juice glasses, grabbed the rotgut liquor off the counter and sat everything on the table in front of the lawyer.

"Jeez, is that all you got?" asked Jernigan, spying the brand of liquor he hadn't drunk since his fraternity days.

"It's not bad. You just have to get used to it."

"Not this boy. I'll be right back."

Jernigan jumped up, headed out the kitchen's side door. That gave Zach time to contemplate the recent actions of whom he assumed was the English Bandit. If two notes, some flowers and some loud motorcycle noise were his ideas of repercussions... *Bring 'em on*, he thought.

Jernigan made short time of his trip and when he returned, he was holding the gold drawstrings of a purple bag containing a bottle of Crown Royal Canadian whiskey. He set it on the table in front of Zach.

"What's this?" asked Zach.

"God's gift to man. I keep it in the trunk for special occasions and when I play golf."

Zach opened the pouch and pulled out the uniquely designed bottle.

"Well, just don't look at it. Pour us a shot."

Since it wasn't Zach's whiskey, he was very liberal with his shot pours.

"To the good life," said Jernigan as he raised his glass.

"To the good life," echoed Zach.

Zach emptied his glass in a couple of swallows. Jernigan sipped his.

"You mind?" asked Zach with the bottle in hand, ready to pour again.

"Go for it. Pretty damn soon, you'll be able to afford any kind of whiskey you want."

"You damn right. When I get all that money, I'm gonna buy my own truck and be an independent. Drive the hell where and when I want. I won't even care if they pay me. And I'm gonna quit eating all that microwave shit."

"You won't have to drive trucks if you don't want to."

"But that's all I got left. I don't have a family no more. And Liz… she…" Zach chose not to finish the sentence, but instead poured himself a double shot of the Crown shot and slugged it down.

"Zach, my boy. Crown Royal is sipping whiskey. You might want to go a little easy on it or you'll get drunker than a coot. And I'm telling you, I ain't putting you to bed. I don't care how pretty you are." Then Jernigan laughed and took another sip.

"You should be so lucky," slurred Zach who was now pouring another shot, ignoring Jernigan's advice on moderation. "You know, other than last night, I can't remember the last time I tied one on. Too risky for a truck driver. You have to be on your toes every time you're behind the wheel. So if I drink, I usually stick to a couple of beers. No more. Not like now. But just so you know, I do plan on getting shitfaced tonight. I've had *way too much* in-laws and *Dom* the last two days. Not to mention the horrors and nightmares of having to sleep in this house and in that bed."

Jernigan wasn't as concerned about the amount of liquor that Zach drank as he was about the man's airtight alibi. How could he forget that long and detailed story of how he and one of his out-of-state bimbos got hammered on some Old Fashions made with Makers Mark? Did he really forget or did he just tell a bald-faced lie. Regardless, Jernigan wasn't going there. Better to not know. His self-funded pension, his early retirement, his golden years made golden, depended on Zach.

"If you think my bottle of Crown Royal will help you sleep better tonight, you can keep it. But I gotta go. I need to be sharp in court tomorrow morning. I can let myself out."

"Can't you stay just a little bit longer? Please. You don't know how quiet and lonely it gets."

"I can loan you my wife if you want. Quiet is not part of her makeup. She's always talking. Yap. Yap. Yap. Give me a dog any day. Hey. Maybe that's what you should get. A dog."

"Yeah? So you gonna come feed it and take it out to shit while I'm on the road? No thank you. You know what I want? I want my daughter back. She was so sweet. So loving. God, I miss her." Almost like clockwork, tears welled up in Zach's eyes.

"From what I saw of her pictures and heard at the funeral, she must have been a very special girl. What kind of lowlife, son-of-a-bitch, would kill…"

"Look at her last text to me," interrupted Zach and then pulled out his phone from his coat and handed it to Jernigan.

> *Yo dad. Hope you're not reading this while you're driving. Fat chance. LOL. No problems at school today except the usual ones with my teachers. Ha Ha. Just wanted to let you know I'm spending the night at Kelly's… a girl. Didn't want you to worry if you called or texted and I didn't answer. We'll be busy doing girl stuff. Drive safe. I love you. Ashley.*

While Jernigan read the message, Zach reached in his pants pocket, pulled out his wallet and found Ashley's school picture. When Jernigan returned the phone, Zach handed him the picture.

"She was beautiful. And you can see by the message she left me she loved me with all her heart. How could she be dead? She wasn't even supposed to be home that night. She shouldn't have been killed. Oh God, I loved her so much." Then doing a one-eighty. "But if Mary Ellen had had her way with the divorce and all, the bitch would have turned my little princess against me. I know it. I'm absolutely sure of it. I'm glad she's dead. And you know what else? She was sleeping with that little baldheaded fucker right here in my house… in *my* bed. I hate that son-of-a-bitch."

"Whoa. Hold on a second. Do not ever say that again… to nobody. That kind of talk could have serious ramifications with our lawsuit and the amount of money we're gonna get from the bank."

"Well, it's true. She was gonna take me to the cleaners. Take my child. Take everything. The bitch deserved to die." Then Zach realized how he was sounding. "But that's just between you and me. I won't say that to anybody else." Then with his right hand, he feigned zipping his lips and then laughed.

Jernigan stood up and handed Zach his picture back. He was witnessing his client move from the euphoric stage of drunkenness to one of depression, sadness and anger. It was time for him to leave. He wanted to take the bottle of the Crown Royal so Zach wouldn't drink anymore. But he'd already given it to him.

"Zach. I gotta go. I want you to get some sleep. And remember… it's sipping whiskey. And one other thing… do not get on the phone with anybody… please."

Zach saluted his lawyer as he headed out the back door. "Yes sir. You buy yourself another bottle and charge it to my account." Zach laughed, but Jernigan had already mentally added that to his bill along with the billable time he'd spent with the knucklehead the last few days.

Zach pushed himself away from the table, picked up his phone and wallet then slid them into his coat pocket. Then he grabbed his juice glass, the bottle of Crown Royal and headed into the den where he collapsed into the La-Z-Boy recliner. The chair had been given to him by his in-laws as a housewarming gift. At first, Zach was embarrassed at the oversized, overstuffed chair thinking they were meant for old people. But it didn't take long for him to grow to love it. He never told Mary Ellen or her parents.

He poured himself another shot, sat the bottle on the side table next to his recliner and eased the chair back. Unlike his other shots, he sipped this one just like Jernigan had asked. As he did, he looked at the picture of Ashley. Tears welled up in his eyes and he took another sip. A bigger sip. Yet the liquor did not dispel the all-consuming quietness of the house. Nor did it lessen the ever-present heartache. Finding it hard to look at his daughter's face, he carefully placed the picture on the side table next to the liquor bottle.

He needed to talk to someone. Anybody. But Liz was the only person he had left. Ignoring his lawyer's request to stay off the phone, he reached into his pocket for his cell. There he found it along with the notes the red-headed man had given him at the visitation and funeral reception. He sat the phone on the left armrest and opened the note.

Woe, destruction, ruin, and decay;
the worst is death
and death will have his day. [3]

Zach Ferguson - MURDERER

---

[3] **Shakespeare** *Richard II* (3.2.102-103)

Zach looked at the note for a couple of seconds then crumbled it up and shoved it back into his coat pocket along with the other opened note.

Pompous Asshole.

Zach was pissed but not scared. Yet… *Maybe I should go get my Glock… just in case.*

He pulled the chair's lever, and the recliner eased forward into an upright position. Then after a couple of unsuccessful attempts, he managed to extract himself and stumbled back to his bedroom using the walls in the hallway like bumpers in a pinball machine. As he entered the bedroom, he tried not to look at the bed where his daughter had died. He tried not to think of what he had done… how he'd killed her thinking it was *Dom.* Yet images of her dead body kept flashing through his mind. He hurriedly pulled his Glock from the bedside table and rambled back into the den where he plopped back down in the recliner. There he managed to eject the Glock's magazine, checked its capacity, and shoved it back into the gun's handle. Automatically, he turned off the safety and placed it on the recliner's right armrest… *just in case.* He then drained his glass and poured himself another shot. As he sat there staring through the amber liquid in the glass, trying to decide whether he should call Liz or not, his phone rang. It was Liz. He answered immediately.

"Hey baby. How you holding up?" asked Liz.

"All is well. Everything's fine. Just hunky-dory. What the hell do you think?" asked Zach, his words slurring to the point of almost being unrecognizable.

"Are you drunk?"

"Maybe yes. Maybe no. But getting there."

"The funeral that bad?"

"And the burial. Liz… this house is soooo quiet, Soooo lonely. I hate this. I miss my little girl. She was all I had."

Liz wanted to say, *So what am I? Chump change?* But, instead, she tried to console her drunken friend.

"Zach, honey. It'll get better. You know what they say… time heals. But you will never forget them. You just sorta get…"

"I know. You just get numb. Liz, you're repeating yourself like a ga'dang old woman. But for your information…" Zach took a large sip. "I'm already feeling pretty damn numb right now. Any chance you could come over and let's take care of business?"

"What about what you said earlier that I should stay away until the lawsuit was over?"

"Oh yeah. Ed would be pissed if he found out, but I won't tell. I promise. On scouts honor," slurred Zach.

"I think I should stay *right* here. Plus, in your condition, I'm not sure you *could* take care of business."

"Ga'dang woman. You're starting to sound like the bitch." Zach's hateful, slurring words were more than Liz could stand. That was not why she'd called. She had only called to give Zach some comfort. Not to be berated, rebuked and belittled. She didn't need that nor would she take that from anyone.

"I gotta go. It's my bedtime. You need to get some sleep yourself."

"Do not tell me what I need to do. Nobody tells me…" Liz hung up before he could finish.

"Fucking women."

Once again, the house was eerily quiet. Needing the noise, Zach reached over to the nearby table, grabbed the remote and turned on the TV. He had no idea what was on nor did he care. Nor did the liquor numb the memory of his daughter and how she died. Tears began to roll down his face. He wiped them with the sleeve of his jacket which he had yet to remove and poured himself another shot.

"I'm sorry, baby," cried out Zach as he downed the pour. "I am so sorry."

He then lowered the recliner into the horizontal position and within minutes was sound asleep. Dead to the world.

CHAPTER 88

Since the killings, the dreams, or nightmares as it were, had been a nightly event only this one seemed so real. Zach was now in the fourth stage of sleep, the REM cycle where there is rapid eye movement, quick breathing and the body relaxes and becomes immobilized. He could see, even feel himself being strapped down onto a gurney and being rolled into the execution chamber where he would be injected with a lethal dose of some kind of deadly drug. He fought the straps, but they were secure. Then he saw the bright light. Was he dead? Was he going to hell or was he already there? He wanted to wake up. Remove himself from this horror. Yet as hard as he tried, he couldn't open his eyes. The overindulgence of the fine Canadian whiskey had taken its toll, acting like an anesthetic. As the night terror wore on, he thought he heard his name being called out in an English accent. Was it the robber? If so, why was he here? Had he come to kill him? Was this his punishment... his repercussions? Would the dream ever end?

The man standing at the foot of Zach's recliner, dressed in all black, was not a dream.

Thursday, August 15, 2019

ATLANTA, GEORGIA

CHAPTER 89

After Ed Jernigan's five phone calls to Zach Ferguson had all gone to voicemail, he had his secretary cancel his court appearances and he stormed out of his office. *Why isn't he answering?* he thought as he walked to his assigned parking spot and hopped in his big, black Mercedes. Leaving his prized bottle of whiskey with an amateur drinker had obviously been a big mistake. He needed to see Zach and now. The bank's lawyers had called this morning and had made a very substantial offer. They were ready to cut their losses. The fact that the bank had caved so fast concerned him. Had they asked for too little? Should they reject the offer? With any other client, he would be prepared to stand their ground. Wait for the bigger settlement. But Zach wasn't a normal client. He was a hothead. It was probably best for all concerned to take the offer and run.

As he rounded the corner of Mason Street and Hillside Avenue, he had a sinking feeling in his stomach – an intuition acquired over his thirty-two years of practicing law. What seemed too good to be true... He pulled into the Ferguson's driveway and parked next to Zach's Toyota. He grabbed his leather briefcase and cellphone, hopped out of the car and fast-stepped, as quick as his portly body would allow, to the back door pressing Zach's speed dial number as he did. As he approached the back door, he could hear the faint ringing of a cell phone inside the house.

"Pick up the phone you nitwit," he mumbled under his breath.

When his call went to voicemail and the ringing simultaneously stopped inside the house, it was a clear indication it was his call. Next, he rang the doorbell a couple of times and then knocked as hard as he could. But just like all his phone calls, there was no response. When he didn't see any movement in the house through the glass pane back door, he turned the doorknob and found there was no locked resistance. So he let himself in.

"Zach. It's me, Ed. I got some good news. Zach, did you hear me? Where are you?"

With no answer, Ed dialed the phone again and followed the ringing sound into the den. There he saw his client slumped over to the far side of the recliner. On a side table to the left of the recliner was his Crown Royal bottle, nearly empty.

"Zach. We got places to go, people to meet, things … Oh no! No! No! No! No! No! No!" he screamed and dropped his briefcase to the floor upon seeing dried blood on the recliner and the left side of Zach's head. His client's dark blue eyes were staring vacuously into space. As he quickly inspected the scene, he spotted a gun lying on the floor not far from Zach's outstretched hand. In the back of his mind, he could see his golden goose flying away; his golden parachute streaming to the ground; his early retirement put on permanent hold.

He wanted no part of this. He slowly backed away from the recliner, grabbed his briefcase and headed out the back door. As he quick-stepped to his car, he saw a black Jeep Cherokee SUV turn into the driveway and park. He immediately did a pirouette and headed back into the house where he called 911 from the kitchen. While he was on the phone, Daniel Whitehead with Johnny Williams by his side came to the open back door, knocked and then presented his FBI badge. Jernigan who was pacing back and forth motioned them in with his hand and then stuck up a 'wait just a minute' finger as he continued to give the 911 operator all information that was requested and then hung up his phone.

"I'm sorry. I'm Ed Jernigan. Zach's lawyer. There's been an accident here and I just called 911 to report it."

"What kind of accident?" asked Daniel.

"Zach. He's dead. I think suicide." Then Jernigan placed his finger in the shape of a gun to his head to indicate the form of suicide.

"Where is he?" demanded Daniel, perturbed at the lawyer's cavalier attitude.

"The den." Jernigan then pointed out the location.

"Have you disturbed anything in any way?"

"No, Agent… er."

"Whitehead. Daniel Whitehead."

"No sir. Actually, that was why I was heading to my car… to call 911," lied Jernigan.

"Do not leave. I want you to stay right here until the police come and we've had a chance to talk." Jernigan nodded and sat down at the kitchen table where he and Zach had shared drinks the night before staring and the prophetic vase of black roses.

Daniel pulled out a couple of pairs of nitrile gloves from his back pocket and gave a pair to Johnny. Once both men were gloved, they rushed into the den where they saw Zach. While Johnny flipped on the overhead fan/light, Daniel hurried over to Zach and checked his pulse, not that he expected to find one. He and Johnny looked at the deceased. A wallet size picture of Ashley was lying face up, on his chest. A handgun lay on the floor near his hand. Upon close inspection of the entry wound, Daniel saw evidence of blackening, burning and singeing of hairs as well as a gun grease collar. All as a result of the blowback phenomenon indicating the gun was pressed firmly against the head. Normally, a sure sign of suicide.

Within minutes of the arrival of the firetruck, EMS and the Cobb County police, the streets were filled with curious neighbors and onlookers just like the Saturday before with each wondering what else could have happened at the Ferguson's house. Since Johnny was not officially part of the investigative team, he left the house and found a spot in the crowd just outside the crime scene tape. Even though the death appeared to be suicide, the fact that it was the result of a gunshot wound meant the police had to treat it as though it were a crime… just in case. Thus, the crime scene tape.

While the EMS and Cobb police checked out the body, Daniel went into the kitchen to call Jacobs and Marlowe. He then sat down across from Jernigan who was nervously checking his watch and his cellphone.

"I hope you don't have any place to be," said Daniel. "The detectives are going to want to talk to you… get a statement."

"Not really. I canceled my court appearance this morning before I came over to see Zach. I couldn't reach him by phone and we have… well…had an offer from the bank that I wanted to pass by him. I don't understand this at all. He would have been rich. He'd never have to work another day in his life. Why would he do this?"

Daniel could hear the hurt in Jernigan's voice. Not over Zach's suicide. But over his own financial loss.

"When did you get here?"

"Around nine. Probably ten minutes before you. Like I said, when I couldn't reach him by phone, I drove over here. Last night, we had a few drinks… well, I'd say he had a lot of drinks and I thought he might be sleeping it off. The bank wanted an answer to their offer by ten this morning, so I came over to rouse him. That's when I saw him slumped over in his chair and blood on the recliner and on the side of his head. I was heading out to my car to call 911 when I saw you drive up."

"How did you get into the house? Do you have a key?"

"No. The door was unlocked. I left it that way last night when I left. I guess he never locked it."

"Was there any indications last night that he might take his life?"

"Zach was all over the place last night, emotionally. He was happy, angry, sad, depressed. But mostly sad and depressed. He really missed his daughter. But those emotions are not unusual for someone drinking heavily, which he was. I do know that when *I left*, the bottle of liquor was half full. This morning, when I went into the den, I saw that the liquor bottle was nearly empty. So he didn't stop drinking after I left. And *I did* ask him to stop. But having drunk that much alcohol, he must have become even more depressed to the point that he felt life without his daughter was not worth living, regardless of the amount of money he was going to get from the lawsuit. I just wished I had stayed with him or he'd have called me or I'd have taken the liquor away. But I didn't know he was so fragile… mentally."

"Was he worried about the investigation into the death of his wife and daughter?"

"No. That was never mentioned."

"You said he was angry. Angry at whom or what?"

Jernigan did not want to cast any doubt about his client's culpability regardless of what he thought or heard, so he lawyered his answer. "I'm sorry, but that is client/attorney confidential information."

"What about Dominick Garcia? Any anger issue about him and Mary Ellen Ferguson?"

"Again… client/attorney confidential information."

"What time did you leave Zach last night?"

"Close to eight… eight-fifteen. Like I said, he…"

Before he finished his answer, there was a knock on the door and then Pete Wilson, one of Cobb County's forensic specialists, opened the door and entered the kitchen.

"Agent Whitehead. I'm Pete Wilson. I was here before."

"Yes. I remember. Forensics. Correct?"

"Yes. So where's Jacobs and Marley? Have you called them?"

"Marlowe. Jacobs and Marlowe. Yes. I've called them. They should be here soon."

"So we have a possible suicide here?" asked Wilson.

"Yes." Daniel then pointed towards the den.

"Man… I wouldn't want to live here. This place has got to be cursed." Then he left.

"Why did he say possible suicide?" asked Jernigan.

"Until we know for sure and have notified next of kin, we keep that information confidential. Do you know Zach's parents' name and address?"

"Now that I don't know. He has… had a friend, Liz Davis. She might know. I can give you her phone number."

"Thank you, but we already have that on file."

* * * * * * * * * * * * * * * * * *

"Agent Williams. What are you doing out here? What's going on?" asked Betty Oliver as she struggled to hold Ike against her chest before finally giving in and gingerly setting him on the ground attached to his new leash. The cone was gone.

"Hi, Mrs. Oliver. How are you doing?" Johnny asked, avoiding her questions.

"Still struggling. I pray a lot and I talk to my sister and myself a lot. But obviously doing better than the Ferguson's. What's going on over there?"

"Follow me." He then led the Oliver woman over to an area not packed with onlookers.

"I'm telling you this in confidence because you were involved with the first incident. It appears that there was a suicide at the Ferguson's house."

"Zach?"

Johnny nodded.

"Oh my God. I guess losing his family was too much to bear. I can understand. I've had those thoughts myself. You know… suicide. But I could never bring myself to do such a thing. My faith is too strong and Bob would be furious at me. So why are you out here and not inside?"

"Just in case it wasn't a suicide and the killer is lurking among the crowd checking out his workmanship. We do this all the time."

"Oh my! You think it could be the robber? You know… maybe he came back to finish the job? Last night… about 7 o'clock, I heard a loud motorcycle stop out front of my house and the Ferguson's. You think it could have been him?"

"While I highly doubt it, we'll check it out. But most likely… a suicide."

"Thank you, Agent Williams, for indulging me. I'm not really a busybody. I'll keep this to myself and let you get back to your duties." Then she turned and ambled back towards her neighbors with Ike limping along beside her, trying to keep up.

Johnny immediately texted Daniel.

> *Just saw Betty Oliver outside the Ferguson's. She said she heard a loud motorcycle stop in front of the Ferguson's house around 7 o'clock last night. You think EB?*

Daniel replied almost immediately.

> *Who else?*

* * * * * * * * * * * * * * * * * *

Once Jacobs, Marlowe and the two Cobb County detectives, Freeman and Bradley, arrived and checked out the possible crime scene, the four of them and Whitehead assembled in the kitchen to discuss the situation. Jernigan was asked to step outside but not to leave.

"Wilson thinks it's suicide," said Freeman. "While he's not an ME (Medical Examiner), he's seen enough of these kinds of wounds to know a suicide when he sees one. And based on what he saw, he said that the gun's muzzle was either pressed against his head or was very, very close. The angle of the entry and exit holes also validates his findings. They found a Glock 19 near the victim's hand. It had been fired recently and only one bullet was missing from the magazine. They also found the bullet casing approximately 10 feet away, near the entrance to the hall and the bullet embedded in the sheetrock where the bullet would have exited Ferguson's head. Everything pointing to suicide. I don't know about you but unless the ME finds something different, I think we should call it a day."

"I'm sure he's right, but knowing that Ferguson had been drinking heavily the night before, he could have been passed out and somebody else whacked him. I just got a text from an associate who says that Betty Oliver, who lives across the street, heard the roar of a motorcycle last night around seven. We have surveillance videos of the English Bandit making his robbery getaways on a Harley. What the Oliver lady heard could be coincidental, but I'd feel better once the ME issues his report," said Whitehead.

"Speaking of Wilson," said Jacobs who saw the burly, full-bearded man dressed in white coveralls entering the kitchen.

"Thought you might want to see these. I found them in the victim's coat pocket." Wilson then laid the two notes on the kitchen table for everyone to see. Both notes were in clear baggies for their protection. "They appear to be printed on the same type of paper using the same font and font size. Very possibly left in the black flower arrangement I found on the kitchen table. But I didn't see any envelope and not sure why *two* notes."

Freeman picked up the first baggie, read the note and passed it to his left. Then he looked at the second note and passed it to the right. After everyone had a chance to look at the two notes, Bradley spoke up. "Is this some kind of old English poetry?"

"It certainly reads like it," said Jacobs.

"It's Shakespeare," said Whitehead, looking at his phone where he had looked up the quotes. "These notes… they could change everything."

"You don't really think this was suicide, do you?" asked Marlowe.

Whitehead continued. "With the two voicemails I got from someone who spoke with a British accent, the motorcycle and now the two notes quoting Shakespeare who was also English, I'm thinking the English Bandit was going out of his way to place the blame for all the murders on Zach Ferguson and take the spotlight off of him. Yet there is very little real evidence that points to Ferguson as the murderer. My opinion for what it's worth… I still think the evidence points to the English Bandit, so for that reason, I think he also staged Zack Ferguson's *suicide*." Daniel air quoted *suicide*.

"I say we wait for the report," said Jacob, frustrated. "If there's *any* hint of foul play, then we set up a meeting to review the situation."

No one objected and the informal meeting was adjourned. The four detectives set about completing their investigation which included questioning Jernigan. Like Betty Oliver, he, too, had heard the roar of the motorcycle. Other than that, he offered nothing of value. Meanwhile, Whitehead stayed in the background, observing the detectives and talking to Wilson. It reminded him of his days as a detective on the D.C. police force with Johnny. It also reminded him that he had sent his former partner out among the curious neighbors and bystanders.

"Where are you?" asked Daniel, heading out the door and looking beyond the crime scene tape for his old partner.

"Out here with all the scumbag reporters, neighbors and anybody who has a cell phone. But I got to tell you… it's been interesting being a casual observer and listening to all the gossip among the gawkers. So many conspiracy stories going around you'd think that Qnon was headquartered in the neighborhood. You got to come and get me. Are you almost through? Anything I should know as a Crime Consultant?"

On the way back to Daniel's apartment, he told him about everything they had found and that the forensic specialist thought it was suicide. Then he told him about the two notes.

"That reeks of EB. Maybe it pushed Ferguson over the edge. But, do I think he faked this whole suicide thing? No. But I'm guessing you do."

"Yes. I think it was staged. But I say we wait for the forensic report. We are supposed to get the initial report this afternoon being that this is a high-priority case."

Both men had their opinion and there would be no arm twisting for either to change their minds. That is how they had worked as partners in Washington and they were one of the best teams at the time. So the two friends rode silently back to Daniel's apartment to wait for Wilson's report.

CHAPTER 90

Dom was in his office when his cell phone rang. It was Paul.

"Have you heard the news?" Paul asked. The excitement in his voice was evident.

"What news?"

"Zach Ferguson. He's dead. They say he killed himself. They being WSB-TV."

"Best thing he's ever done for Mary Ellen and Ashley. Too bad he didn't do it sooner."

"You don't seem surprised."

"It's not that. Zach Ferguson doesn't deserve any more of my time. He was a mean person. If anyone deserved to die, it was him."

"You still think he killed his family, don't you?"

"What I think doesn't matter. What matters is this world has one less wife abuser. And yes I'm glad he's dead."

"Ouch. Aren't we a little irritable today. Guess you didn't get enough sleep last night."

"No... I didn't. Mary Ellen's funeral really upset me. After I went to bed, all I did was toss and turn. I got tired of just lying there in bed, so I got up, read some and then reviewed more of the security footage. I hope I didn't wake you?"

"Only when you got up. But I never heard you come back to bed. Did you stay up all night?"

"Uh... yes."

"Poor thing. You must be exhausted."

"Actually... no. Maybe it will hit me later. But right now, I feel fine. Actually, better than fine."

CHAPTER 91

"I decided not to wait this time for you to call me," said Anne Reynolds as she turned on to I-77. "Where are you?"

"At the airport, waiting for my flight."

"The airport? What happened to your car?"

"I drove it home late Tuesday and drove my Harley back to Atlanta."

"What! That's crazy. Why'd you do that?"

"You remember I told you that I thought I had sold my Harley? Well, guess who bought it?"

"I'm not playing guessing games. I'm *really* upset that you came back here and didn't even tell me. You had to have been on the road at least eight hours."

"Something like that. I thought you'd be happy that I sold it."

"I am. But I can't believe that you didn't call me and let me know you were coming. What if you'd gotten killed?"

"Oh boy. Back in the doghouse. By the way, I have my cell phone in my hand and was just about to call you. So see, I am learning."

"Yes, you are. So who'd you sell it to?"

"The president of Roswell Guardian. We completed the deal last night over dinner and drinks. I'm sorry I didn't call you, but we stayed out really late," lied Scott. "He's a talker and we jaw jacked until almost nine. By the time I drove the bike over to his house and he drove me back to the hotel, I didn't get back to my room until eleven or so. I figured it was too late to text or call. Oh… he paid cash for the bike," added Scott, trying to change the subject.

"Cash is good. By the way, I don't know if you've had time to see or read the news, but do you remember that bank teller that got murdered… the one you were so concerned about at the party last Friday? Well… her husband committed suicide this morning. I just heard it on the radio."

"Unbelievable… but not surprising. Uh… did they say if he left a note?"

"If he did, they didn't say," said Anne.

"If you want to know my opinion, I think *he* killed his family, not that bank robber guy. At least that's what happens most of the time. You know, it's *always* the husband."

"Should I be scared?" asked Anne, then laughed.

"I'm not your husband, yet. Anyway, I'm more into robbing banks than murders."

Anne laughed at the absurdity of the comment.

CHAPTER 92

"You up for a video conference call with the forensic guy handling the Ferguson case?" asked Daniel. "I'd like you on it if you have time."

"Let me check my schedule."

"You'll have to be behind the scene if you know what I mean."

"Say no more. But what's it all about? You think they found a suicide note or something?"

"He didn't say. I thought he was going to email his GSR report and the preliminary autopsy, so I don't know what's changed, but he has me, the APD and Cobb detectives as attendees to this video thing."

Less than twenty minutes later, Pete Wilson was joined by all five attendees with Johnny Williams sitting silently at an angle that he could see Wilson but he, himself, not seen.

"Thank you all for jumping on this conference call on such short notice. I think you will find it worth your time. I promised you the results of the gunshot residue (GSR) tests and I will get to that shortly. The deceased, Zachary Lamar Ferguson, was found dead of a gunshot wound Thursday, August 15, 2019. He was pronounced dead by the Medical Examiner at 10:19 a.m., but his actual time of death is estimated to be between 11 p.m. and 1 a.m. His blood alcohol concentration... his BAC at the estimated time of death would have been in the range of .19 to .21."

Wilson turned the page of his notebook and continued.

"Now for the results of the GSR tests. They show unquestionably that the victim pulled the trigger on the Glock that was found nearby. The gun was registered to Zach L. Ferguson. His fingerprints were on the weapon and there was GSR on his trigger finger and on nearly every sample we took of the victim's right hand as well as his coat sleeve. We also verified that the victim *was* right-handed. I have emailed everyone on this call the preliminary reports and autopsy results. You will receive the final report in four to six weeks."

Wilson paused. "Now... for the real purpose of the conference call." He paused again.

"After all of you left and while we were moving the body, one of the EMTs noticed a cell phone stuck between the armrest and victim's body. It was a burner phone with no password. The phone had not been used to make calls or send messages. It only contained a video which I think you will find very interesting. So, without further ado."

The first image to appear was Zach's face spotlighted by a very bright light. He was sound asleep. Snoring hard. As the video zoomed out, it showed him strapped to the recliner in his den where his body had been found.

"Zach. Wake up." The words were spoken with a British accent as the intruder shook Zach's face. *"Wha... what the hell's going on? Who are you? Wha... what do you want?"* Zach's words were slurred and the video showed Zach struggling to free himself from the straps. Both Daniel and Johnny recognized the suit that Zach was wearing as the same one he had worn to the funeral.

"That's not important."

"It's... it's you!" Zach then shook his head as if trying to clear his thought.

"I thought it was time to set things straight."

"Are... are you going to kill me?" There was a slight tremor in Zach's slurred voice.

There was a long period of silence.

Then, **"I was at the funeral today. It was a beautiful service... the sermon, the music and the eulogies. Especially the one given by Dominick Garcia. Mary Ellen and Ashley were very much loved. They didn't deserve to die."**

"No... not Ashley. She... she was beautiful. B...best thing in my life." The video showed tears beginning to well up in Zach's eyes. *"It was the bitch's fault. You didn't know her. You never had to live with her and her constant yapping on about how wonderful Dom was."* The sentence was drawn out as Zach tried to complete the sentence. Then his voice took on a different tone. One of hatred and anger. *"Well... did you know that Little Miss Goody Two Shoes was fucking him... here... right in my own house... my own bed. She and that little baldheaded prick should have been the ones killed. Not my Ashley."*

"Surely you must know that Dominick Garcia is gay?"

"You're fucking shitting me. Mr. Potato Head is queer? Makes me hate the bastard even more."

"So why did you kill Mary Ellen? Couldn't you have just divorced her? Was it the money?"

"Oh… so that's what this is all about. The money. The money. Is this your idea of uh… of uh..repercus… Oh shit. You know… getting your share? How much you want."

"After killing Mary Ellen, why did you murder Ashley? Did she see you kill her mother?"

"Oh my baby, Ashley. Tears streamed down Zach's face. *She wasn't supposed to be here at all. Not at all."*

"Collateral damage."

"Don't you call my daughter collateral damage. She was beautiful. Not supposed to be here." Zach's emotions vacillated from being angry to melancholy. *"She… she…"*

"That must have been really hard to stomach listening to Dom talk at the funeral about the fun he and Ashley had driving to school in his sports car. Singing. Enjoying life. At least what was left of it?"

The video showed Zach's face turned blood red with anger.

"I said to leave my daughter out of this. She loved me. Me! Me! Not Dom. Her death was an accident. She wasn't supposed to be at home. Dom and the bitch were the ones who were supposed to die. Not my beautiful princess. It was an accident…I never even saw her. She had the covers pulled over her head. Oh God! What have I done? What have I done?"

The video showed Zach shaking his head then he looked at the intruder with tears streaming down his face. Then the video stopped.

Jacobs was the first to speak up.

"That certainly looked like a confession to me. But he appeared to be drunk. You think it was the alcohol talking?" Jacob's question was offered to the group.

"In vino veritas," answered Daniel. "In wine, there is truth. So, yes, I think he let his guard down. And the intruder, whoever he was, certainly knew how to push his hot buttons."

"From the video, it appears that Zach seemed to think it was the robber," answered Marlowe.

"I'm not so sure," responded Daniel. "His voice and accent weren't exactly the same as I heard on the surveillance videos." Johnny gave him the thumbs up. "But if it *wasn't* the English Bandit. Then who was it?"

No one spoke for a moment. Meanwhile, Johnny wrote a quick note to Daniel and slid it over to him.

Check the gloves at the start of the video. They're blue ... not clear. Surgical???

Daniel thought about it a second and gave Johnny a nod.

"Pete, can you restart the video from the beginning and halt it when the intruder first shakes Zack."

Wilson did as requested.

"You see those gloves. In every video I have reviewed of past robberies by the English Bandit, he has always worn clear gloves over his hands. These are blue and might even be surgical. Our robber is a creature of habit. Everything, including his clothes, disguise, shoes, money pouch... they're always the same. He does not vary from his normal routine. So I doubt he would change anything for this intrusion into Ferguson's house."

"So maybe the English Bandit is a doctor," said Marlowe. "Maybe he ran out of clear gloves."

"Or maybe he has a friend who's a doctor. Like Dominick Garcia. His partner, Paul Han, is a surgeon," countered Daniel. He then wrote himself a note to call Garcia.

"Really? We've all met Garcia. There is no way..." Jacobs stopped midsentence. Then, "Pete... how sure are you that this was a suicide?"

"One hundred percent, sir."

"So regardless of who the intruder was, he did a better job than we did in getting Zack to admit to killing his family. And he was never threatening. There was nothing forced. So, unless the final ME report shows otherwise, I say that this murder case is closed. We have our killer and justice has been served. Do we all agree?" asked Jacobs.

There was no disagreement and the meeting was adjourned.

Daniel looked over at Johnny who was all smiles, then said, "Best damn vacation ever!"

CHAPTER 93

"Zach did it. He killed them. Mary Ellen, Ashley and the Colonel. He admitted it. I've got it on video if you'd like to see it. I kept a copy and the police should have found their copy by now. I know I should have told you what I was planning. But you would have tried to stop me. And I had made up my mind. There was no turning back. Their deaths couldn't go unpunished. I couldn't let that happen. They didn't deserve to die. I knew Zach was lying from the start. It made me sick to my stomach to see him crying like he really cared when all he cared about was the money. You know… I'm glad he's dead. But before you ask… yes, it *was* suicide. All I wanted was the video of him admitting to the murders. It was his choice to kill himself. I had no part in it. It would be against my Hippocratic oath," lied Wesley Knox to his wife Carol.

CHAPTER 94

While waiting at the gate to board his plane to Charleston, Scott watched a nearby TV monitor that was turned to CNN. He wasn't interested in the political commentary coming from the two talking heads. Instead, he read, multiple times, the news that scrolled at the bottom of the screen.

> *Zach Ferguson, husband of murdered bank teller, Mary Ellen Ferguson, was found dead this morning in his Marietta, Georgia home of an apparent suicide. Evidence was found linking the husband to the death of his wife, daughter and neighbor.*

Scott thought about the notes and warnings he'd given to Zach as well as the black roses and the motorcycle drive-by. Had they somehow encouraged him to take his own life? If it did, he did not feel guilty nor did he feel sorry for the man. After all, Zach was the murderer, not *him* as the public had been led to believe.

As he reread the scrolling message, he couldn't help but wonder what evidence the police had found linking Ferguson to the deaths when only days earlier, the same police had found evidence linking *him* to the murders. Regardless, he knew his bank-robbing days were over. He would send a letter to the FBI that this chapter in his life was now officially closed.

Scott's mind turned to Anne. Marriages were built on trust. Yet, he had a dark past that he had always planned to carry to his grave. Was this fair to her? Shouldn't she know the truth before committing her life to him?

Scott continued to weigh his decision the entire flight to Charleston, the cab trip to the Market Pavilion Hotel and his walk down the hallway to the room where Anne waited for him. As he swiped his key-card in the door, he asked himself, can I live with this woman and keep my secret past stowed away forever?

When he saw Anne's smiling, beautiful face, felt her warm embrace and her gentle kiss on his lips, he knew his answer.

Yes... Yes I can.

CHAPTER 95

"Are you pulling another all-nighter?" asked Paul as he watch Dom pour through the first of five surveillance tapes he'd brought home from the office.

"This is it. When I finish with these, I'm done."

"But why five more? Why anymore? The thief… er… robber was innocent. Zach was the killer. He was the guilty one."

"Yeah… maybe of murder. But he *robbed my bank.* Had that man never stepped a foot into my bank, Mary Ellen, Ashley and the Colonel would be alive today. That I cannot forget or forgive nor should he get off scot-free."

"Can I bring you a glass of wine? That might ease the pain," said Paul feeling his partner's angst.

"That would be nice."

Within a few minutes, Paul was back with a glass of Chardonnay in each hand. He carefully placed one next to Dom's computer, kissed him on his shiny, tanned bald head and headed into the living room. While Dom continued to cull through the videos, Paul sat at the piano and his surgically skilled hands softly played Chopin's Nocturne in E-flat Major, Dom's favorite.

Dom was only ten minutes into the surveillance video when he recognized a man walking into the bank. He was not a customer.

EPILOGUE

As **Scott Burnett** and **Anne Reynolds** pulled into the driveway of Scott's townhome, returning from their long weekend trip in Charleston, S.C., a black Jeep Cherokee SUV and two Black GMC Yukon Denali SUVs pulled in immediately behind Anne's Audi. Scott said nothing to his fiancé as he exited the car with both hands raised. Anne's parting words to a man she thought she once knew were, *get a good lawyer.* He was sentenced to fifteen years of prison time.

Wesley Knox was a moral man. So murdering Zach weighed heavily on his mind. He had never planned to kill him. He just wanted him to confess. At first, like everybody else, Wesley thought the **bank robber** had been responsible for his daughter and granddaughter's deaths. It was only when he, Carol and Zach met at the Cracker Barrel to discuss the funeral plans that he became aware that his son-in-law was the true killer. Zach had a tell, an unconscious facial expression, that he oftentimes exhibited when he was lying. Wesley discovered the tell when Zach and Mary Ellen first started dating. So over breakfast at the Cracker Barrel when Zach brazenly said that he had nothing to do with Mary Ellen and Ashley's death, that he didn't kill them and then pursed his lips... his tell, Wesley knew. He wanted to reach over and stab the man in his heart with his fork, but, instead, he began to make plans... plans that Carol would know nothing about. Mary Ellen and Ashley's deaths would not go unpunished.

All had gone well at Zach's that night... at least initially. Zach, in his drunken state, had mistakenly assumed that the intruder was the bank robber. That the visit was his form of repercussions. By pushing Zach's hot buttons, Wesley had gotten Zach to confess to the murders. Everything was videoed on his Go-Pro camera that was attached to his black skydiving helmet that he wore over a ski mask.

However, everything went sideways as he returned from the kitchen where he had made copies of the video onto two burner phones – one for him and one for the police. Zach called out his name. He had recognized Wesley by the cologne he always wore. Zach's attitude immediately changed from being remorseful and guilt-ridden to arrogant, unashamed... even boastful. He began to taunt his father-in-law and berate Mary Ellen. He bragged about how frightened she looked when she saw the gun in his hand and how easy it had been to kill her. That he was glad she was dead. That she deserved to die.

Zach continued to harass Wesley to the point that his father-in-law had had enough, his temper getting the best of him. With Zach securely strapped to the recliner, incapacitated, Wesley rushed up to the smirking man and pressed down on his carotid arteries. He expected to see fear or panic in his face along with some sort of resistance. Instead, he saw acceptance and resignation. The still and quiet of the moment did nothing to extinguish the intense hatred that Wesley felt for the man that now lay passed out before him. He had made up his mind and there was no turning back. He began by removing the restraining straps. Next, he grabbed the Glock that lay on the side table, wrapped Zach's hand around the weapon and placed the unconscious man's index finger on the trigger. Then he pressed the muzzle against the temple of the man that had killed his daughter and granddaughter, wrapped the gold string from the Crown Royal bag around the trigger and pulled the string. Zach died instantly.

Wesley took no pleasure in what he'd just done. It would not bring back his daughter or granddaughter. He had taken it upon himself to be judge, jury and executioner. He was never sure if Zach had forced his hand and had baited him into an assisted suicide, cowardly afraid to take his own life or if, subconsciously, he had planned to kill him all along. Regardless, he would have to live with the knowledge that he was now no better than the man he had just killed.

On the one-year anniversary of Mary Ellen and Ashley's death, and Wesley Knox's 67th skydive, his main chute and his backup chute failed to open and he plunged to his death. Neither ripcord had been pulled. He left no note. Wesley Knox was a decent man, a Christian man and he no longer could endure the never-ending guilt he felt for having murdered Zach Ferguson. His wife, **Carol Knox,** now lives alone with only her memories.

THE END

Afterword

WARNING SIGNS OF DOMESTIC ABUSE:[4]

Unexplainable injuries.
She has very little to say about her life.
She becomes timid when her husband or boyfriend is around.
She distances herself from people and acts withdrawn.
Her social relationships have narrowed.
He makes all the rules.
He puts her down in public.
She is afraid.

National Domestic Violence Hotline 800-799-7233

---

[4] Copied from the Internet

Acknowledgements

My sincere thanks to my "Editor-in-Chief", **Lou Thomas**, also my wife and best friend. She pours over my books for hours looking for errors, omissions and giving her suggestions.

To **David Paul Burnett**, my friend since the third grade, and his wife, **Cyndi,** thank you for your continued support. They have now edited both of my books with never a complaint.

A big thank you to **Deb Shapiro** for all the work she did in helping me get my book edited and published, as well as her kind words of encouragement.

To the **FBI Media Relations** and the **Atlanta Police Department,** many thanks for fielding my numerous calls and emails. I know I was a pest but you never made me feel that way.